THE
LORDS
OF
HAVENSTONE

DHRESDEN'S RISE

MATTHEW STOREY

ISBN 978-1-64114-858-0 (paperback)
ISBN 978-1-64114-859-7 (digital)

Christian Faith Publishing, Inc.
832 Park Avenue
Meadville, PA 16335
www.christianfaithpublishing.com

Printed in the United States of America

To Kedron & our Children;
For Whom I War,
And For Whom I Labor

"Blessed be the LORD my Rock, Who trains my
hands for war, And my fingers for battle—"
—Psalm 144:1

CHAPTER 1

A crisp fall sun dawned on a small group of mourners passing deep into the heart of the Forgotten Wood. At the head of the column strode a man whose presence commanded the respect of any who knew his name and all who met his gaze. Almost invisible beneath a green cloak, his deep brown, nearly black eyes peered out watchfully from within the folds of his hood. In times past, such vigilance had proven needful, but today he surveyed his surroundings out of habit rather than necessity. There would be no fear of peril or ambush this day in the hearts of these pilgrims from Havenstone as they traveled within the Wood. The Kelvren who lived within the shadow of the ancient trees were the enemy only of those who held the Elder ways in disdain. They were not warriors by nature, but had waged wars victoriously out of necessity. They were most skilled with the bow, though not limited to such. By them, nature was looked upon as a resource, but a resource of which they considered themselves stewards. The Kelvren moved about as well in the trees as upon the ground, and could remain hidden easily, largely due to their complexion. Their skin appeared as it were deeply tanned, but did not fade in winter. Another aspect contributing to their ability to conceal themselves was that a full-grown male Kelvren stood a head and a half shorter than a man of the same age. It was not known abroad the origin of these diminutive people, but it was generally believed that they were the descendants of a tribe of elves that had mingled blood with the Montsho, dark men who had traveled far inland, traversing from sea to sea. The Kelvren of the Forgotten Wood, though short in stature, were looked down upon by none. As scholars of the Elder ways, they were held in high regard by royalty and commoner alike and usually given a wide berth by brigands and other such evil men.

The travelers passed swiftly into the wood, seemingly unencumbered by their baggage and burdens. At a glance, the man leading carried naught but a shoulder pack, but beneath his cloak was sheathed a small arsenal at the ready. While his heart bore the weight of thoughts and memories that threatened to preoccupy him, his mind was ever alert. Following behind him, the two young men that had been nicknamed as the twins shared the burden of an ornately carved memorial case but walked on in silence. Shrouded in gray, the woman mounted upon the brown steed looked often upon the coffin before her. Slight age showed about her eyes, but she was not old by the measure of those days. Occasionally a sad smile would play at the corners of her mouth, at other times silent tears flowed freely down her somber face. A younger reflection of herself rode beside the lady, her gray mount keeping pace and allowing her the opportunity to attend the elder woman should she need or allow it. At the rear walked a man clad in black chainmail whose stealth and ease belied his towering stature and vast weaponry. A double-bit battle-axe was sheathed upon his back, at his belt he bore a flail pouch, upon each thigh he wore a wicked looking dagger, while in the crook of one arm he carried a short spear.

On they walked in silence, passing through the forest upon a path known to few outside the Wood. It was about midday when they came to a small natural clearing beside a quaint, free-flowing stream.

"We shall rest here a bit. Let the horses roam free while we eat, but do not kindle a fire. We have not been given leave to take from this land and presumptuous guests are not well accepted. Here, let me help you please, my lady," the dark eyed man spoke with authority, but his tone and eyes softened as he spoke this last. Taking the woman's hands in his, he quite gently lifted her from her saddle and set her upon her feet in the soft green grass.

"Thank you, Dhresden. I know that I must eat, but it is not a thing I any longer enjoy," her sorrow shrouded her as completely as did her cloak.

"Yes, I know, lady," Dhresden replied, "but I also know that given enough time, joy will return to your heart. Meanwhile, please humor us all. Mallory will attend you there beside the stream."

The younger woman had already spread a blanket upon the ground and was busy producing bread, smoked meat, and other victuals from the saddlebags of her horse. Though her gaze seldom met Dhresden's, she often watched him, wondering many things and longing to one day wonder no more. The lady walked over to the picnic area and reclined upon the blanket, allowing Mallory to serve her, though she ate little.

The giant man came and spoke to Dhresden in hushed tones. "I fear that we are being followed in the wood. I have caught wind of movement about us several times, and it is not that of beast or bird. I cannot tell whether we are followed to good or ill, but I am unsettled nonetheless."

Looking up into the other man's eyes, Dhresden smiled knowingly. "Three of the Kelvren are about us and have been since we entered this forest. They have been sent to guide us should we need it, well knowing there will not be a need. They are a curious people and eager to acquaint themselves with those of us they have not yet met. Rest easy, Orrick, they are no threat. I shall walk ahead a bit, when I return, we shall press forward."

Orrick watched him disappear into the wood then looked about at the trees curiously. Accepting the word of his guide he strode to the edge of the clearing near to the stream and, sitting comfortably with his back to a tree, partook of his own stores.

The twins had set the case down in the shade of one of the great trees and busied themselves refilling the company's waterskins from the nearby stream. No words passed but it seemed as though there was no lack of understanding between them. They both wore long hooded tunics of brown; embroidered in black upon the chest of each was the symbol of a tree, its branches sweeping to the right as if blown by a strong wind. They bore no weapons except for a wooden quarterstaff, but beneath their tunics, covering their forearms from elbow to the tip of their longest finger was a strange material that no ordinary blade could cut. Little else was known of this fabric, only that the Makani referred to it as terephthala. The waterskins full again, they redistributed them among the group and sat upon the ground a little apart from the others and ate.

These three groups—the women, the twins, and the giant strongman, Orrick—sat apart resting and eating. Obviously their origins were not the same. The women were well dressed but not extravagantly so, though their beauty would not have been diminished had they worn burlap sacks. Each bore braided auburn locks and was neither heavy nor light. Their loveliness was displayed most vividly in their bearing, eyes, and smiles; the last of which had become rare as of late. They wore their privilege lightly and looked not down upon those with whom they traveled. The twins were somewhat mysterious, hailing from the desert region in the west. The insignia upon their tunics indicated that they were members of the Makani, a legendary order of wise men who forsook anything but the basest comforts and dedicated themselves to the development of mind and spirit. Orrick was a kind unto his own. He stood fully a foot taller and broader than most men, but his movements were as swift and fluid as a bird in flight. His mind was sharp and quick, much like the arsenal he carried, and his senses of smell and hearing surpassed that of an ordinary man. Little was known of his past by the others, save that which could be read in his steel blue eyes or in the several scars upon his body. Whatever his past, it was clear that the present of this wheat-haired giant was united with these others through his friendship with Dhresden, the scout and guardian of the lady, and her daughter.

The space of almost an hour had passed when Dhresden spoke from the edge of the clearing. He had pushed back his hood, but in the shadows of the wood his brown skin and dark curly hair had kept him hidden from his companions as he surveyed their readiness.

"Lady Jovanna, Miss Mallory, it is time we were on our way. We have much ground to cover before sundown. Khalid and Khaldun shall assist you in packing and mounting the horses."

Within moments the six were again passing through the shadowed wood, and the small clearing was soon left far behind. Several hours later, as the sun began descending, they came to a section of forest that seemed even more aged than that through which they had already passed. The trees before them had grown so large and gnarled that their trunks actually touched each other, allowing not even sunlight to pass between them. Dhresden stopped and, looking upward, called out in a tongue unknown to the others.

"*Asan nelli' mih'tem!*"

Immediately a wooden platform was lowered from far above, coming to rest upon the ground a few paces away. Upon it stood three short men; the one at the forefront greeted them.

"Welcome to Kelvar. Please, come aboard the lift and we shall take you into the city. The night hastens, and sleep beckons. We have stables and fodder for your horses and rooms and food for the rest of you. Tomorrow, Phaelen, our chieftain, shall breakfast with you."

At Dhresden's assent, the company, including the horses, boarded the lift. It rose quickly but gently into the air, coming to rest beside a wide wooden parapet nestled within the branches of the trees. They were led onto the parapet and then down a long ramp to the ground within the sanctuary of the impenetrable trees. An expansive village, well protected by the surrounding forest and teeming with activity greeted their eyes. They followed the three Kelvren to a large thatched house, simple but sprawling. It contained six rooms with beds and baths, and a great room furnished with a roaring fire and a banquet table laden with much food and drink.

"You will find all that you need here," the man spoke to Dhresden, "I shall take your horses to the stable, and these two shall relieve you of the burial case."

At this, both Lady Jovanna and Mallory opened their mouths to protest, but were silenced by Dhresden's words. "Thank you, Wyeth; you have performed more than that which I had requested. I wholly entrust you with these tasks without remorse. *Akarreb,* and goodnight."

After Wyeth and the other Kelvren left, the six pilgrims found their rooms, bathed and then ate together in the great room. They spoke little, each left to their own thoughts. One by one they retired, until only Dhresden and the lady remained before the hearth. The fire crackled alone in the silence until it was broken by the sad melody of Jovanna's voice.

"I do miss him deeply, Dhresden. I fear I shall always possess an emptiness that only he could fill. I know that you also are suffering this loss. I hope that one day you will allow me to be a part of your life, not to take the place of your mother, but to help you to better know your father. He was a noble man, and I love him still."

Dhresden was silent a while, staring into the flames of the hearth. When he spoke, his words came softly, slowly. "There was a time in my youth when I would have called a thousand plagues against you for father returning to you and leaving my mother and I. Long years have passed and I remain convinced that no child should ever mature without the constant nurture of both of his parents. But here among the Kelvren I have learned that a man's responsibilities require him to make hard choices. I know that he loved mother and I, it is clear in his provision for us even in his absence; but I am equally sure that his love for you and Mallory is what urged that he return to you both. Though I should have enjoyed the company of my father as I grew, it would have been more wrong for him to desert you and your daughter for the love of another. In choosing the lesser of two evils, he returned to his first love. Mother passed a few years ago, as you know, and tomorrow we bury my father. I shall long covet that you would look upon me as a son one day, that I may at some point adopt you and Mallory as my family and care for you as such."

The Lady Jovanna smiled her first true smile in many days. "You truly are a noble and just man, so much like your father. You will need to be, if you are to carry on his legacy. I see in you much strength, that of both your father and your mother. Ciana was a beautiful woman, intelligent and wise. Yes, I knew her, knew her well. I like to think that we became friends before she died. They both loved you deeply, and I have come to love you in much the same way. Mallory still has many questions, as I am sure you do, but that is for another time. Sleep well, son of Ciana, son of Dhane; tomorrow comes quickly." With that she turned to go. Dhresden still sat before the fire, but his eyes were upon Jovanna as she disappeared up the stairs.

"Goodnight," he whispered softly, "sleep well, my lady, my mother."

CHAPTER 2

Orrick awoke early, shortly before the rising of the sun. He lay there a moment, listening to the deep breathing of his sleeping companions. Shortly he rose, dressed, and donned his arms. Stepping from his room into the hallway, he saw that all doors save Dhresden's remained closed. Walking to the open door and peering in, Orrick observed that the bed was undisturbed. He walked down the stairs to the great room, finding no one. The fire blazed as with fresh logs and the clutter of their evening meal had been tended to, but by whom or when he could not say. He had slept more deeply and awoke more rested than he had for many seasons. The big man stooped and walked out the doorway into the main street of the village. The street was empty except for a handful of the little residents scurrying off to unknown tasks. He stood there a while, enjoying the slowly brightening day, a light breeze bringing the aroma of fresh cooked breakfast to his nostrils. Mingled with them, Orrick caught a familiar scent. Turning to face the wind, his keen eyes searched the street until he spotted Dhresden walking toward him. The small Kelvren, Wyeth, walked at his side; the two were conversing quietly.

"Hail the dawn, Orrick. Does it find you refreshed?" Dhresden asked. Wyeth bowed low in greeting but did not speak. He carried the air of an attendant, deferring all authority in the conversation to Dhresden, but willing to enter into the conversation at their bidding.

"It does indeed; though it would seem that you should be tired, as you did not make use of your room. Tell me, what have you been about, *Ne'res-aerem?*" Wyeth seemed both surprised and pleased to hear this barbarian-looking man speaking Kelvren words.

"Pardon me, Orrick of the Wanderlands, but though it gladdens my heart to hear you speak so of the son of Dhane, I wonder: why do you speak of him as both a chief leader and also a close friend? Rarely do the two titles combine in the eyes and mouths of common folk."

"It is due first to our friendship. Much has passed between us that I can never forget nor repay. He is the son of royalty, and I believe much more will come to light about him in time to come beyond that which any can foreknow. And you would be remiss, Wyeth of Kelvar, to think me common." Orrick's answer brought a chuckle of delight to the small dark man. Dhresden stepped forward and wordlessly gripped his large friend's shoulder, holding his gaze a moment. Releasing him, Dhresden asked, "Shall we let them slumber 'til noon, or shall we rouse them?"

Looking toward the house and listening a moment, Orrick shook his head. "They are stirring, I hear the ladies' feet moving about in their rooms, and the twins in their morning routine of mandara."

The three of them entered the house and seated themselves around the fire to await the rest of their companions. Shortly the twins arrived, clad again in brown, but without their quarterstaffs.

"Have you a cloak, Orrick?" Dhresden inquired. "Banquets, weddings, and funerals among the Kelvren are sacred events at which weapons are not permitted in view. I know that you are loath to leave your blades behind, but if you have not a cloak with which to conceal them I am afraid you have no recourse."

Orrick stood without a word, bowed to those about him, and climbed the staircase. He returned shortly cloaked in black, his weapons nowhere in sight. Behind him came Lady Jovanna, adorned in an unassuming refined gown as gray as predawn. With her, Mallory was similarly clothed. The pair was strikingly beautiful, though serene with sorrow.

All had risen respectfully at the arrival of the women, but now Wyeth approached and knelt before them. "My ladies fair, your arrival is as the caress of mist upon a lush wheat field. Phaelen chieftain has had many delicacies prepared on your behalf and awaits your company. Would you honor me as your escort? Please, this way!"

12

Exiting the house, they went down the wide road, Wyeth leading and pointing out items of interest. The women at his sides showed polite interest, the men following also took in the sights and sounds of the village Kelvar. After many strides, they entered a grand hall by means of another lift. The structure was called in the native tongue *hTeme Elua'*, which in the trade tongue was "Truth Hall," and was both the open court and formal hall of the Kelvren chieftain. It rested within the upper canopy of an expansive oak tree and was not arrayed in fine metals and gems as were other courts of the lands. Its adornment was that of wood, intricate carvings of nature and history upon the walls as well as the natural beauty of the wizened oak branches arching along the ceiling. Upon a gnarled and carved throne sat a white haired man, himself rather gnarled and timeworn. This small, wispy man bore a simple wooden crown, though his kingly bearing confuted his humble attire. He looked on them with kind, knowing eyes.

"Welcome, outlanders. I, Phaelen, greet you as friends and bid you join me in banquet. Please, eat and drink your fill. Come, come!"

His vibrant, booming voice belied his aged appearance and he moved quickly to the table and stood behind his chair awaiting his guests. Following his lead, the six traveling companions walked to the table and stood behind their own chairs. Phaelen looked upon his guests, greeting each by name and inviting them to be seated. The tables in the banquet hall of *hTeme Elua'* were large and round, the center of each had been cut out to allow servants to tend the guests from the inside. There was a narrow stairwell in the serving area of each table that led down through the floor into the kitchen, allowing the attendants to come and go as needed with ease. This morning, the only table in use was the one at which the travelers sat with Phaelen. As the chieftain engaged his guests in conversation, two servers came and went, providing a seemingly endless supply of food and beverages unique to the culture of the Kelvren.

"Is there something that would be more to your liking, Lady Jovanna?" Phaelen had noticed that the lady, seated at his left, had scarcely any interest in the food before her.

"I mean no offense, Phaelen Chieftain," Jovanna apologized. "The food truly entices, but I fear that I am too full already of grief to indulge in such fine cuisine."

The old man beckoned to one of the servants and spoke quietly to her in their native tongue. She bowed and quickly disappeared into the kitchen below, returning presently with a small steaming chalice of pale brown liquid. Its sweet scent was like that of cinnamon and cider, but was at the same time unfamiliar. She placed the chalice before Jovanna with a flourish, smiled and moved on to tend the other guests.

"We call it *halaet,* which means healing. It nourishes the body while the mind and heart struggle to find themselves again. It has been among our people for ages, helping those whose battle is not physical keep up their strength when such a natural and simple thing as eating becomes a chore. It is not a cure, only an aid in the journey to wellness. My own sorrow does not compare to yours, but it is sorrow nonetheless." Phaelen's kind eyes held hers only a moment, but in that instant Jovanna knew compassion as that of a doting uncle or grandfather.

The chieftain turned his attention to the man at his right, Dhresden son of Dhane. The two leaned close and spoke together in the musical tongue of the Kelvren for several moments, seemingly oblivious to their companions seated about them. It appeared to the others as though Phaelen were trying to persuade the younger man of something, but to no avail. Finally, the aged man sat back heavily with a sigh. He gestured towards the stem of the great tree that supported the hall of *hTeme Elua'.*

"You are as solid in your resolve as one of these ancient trees once your mind has been set. 'The branch of a willow that is broken and falls to the ground will root and sprout in the shadow of the tree that bore it, unless the wind or river or man or beast bear it away to another place. There, amidst its new surroundings it will root and flourish and when it has grown, it will stand, a willow still.'"

Dhresden nodded, considering the parable of the old Kelvren. The others said nothing; each consumed by their own thoughts. It was Phaelen who broke the silence. "The time has come," he announced as he rose to his feet. "If you will walk with me, Dhresden will be our guide. You shall rejoin us afterwards, Wyeth."

They stood to their feet and followed Dhresden out of the great hall of *hTeme Elua'*. He led them out a door different from that through which they had entered and onto a series of interconnecting walkways high above the ground, running the length and breadth of the village. As Dhresden escorted his companions and Phaelen toward their destination, his eyes, as well as the others', took in the sights of Kelvar. There were two tiers to the community: the lower level housed trade establishments, stables, and garden plots as well as some residences. Even among the Kelvren, there were those who preferred to reside upon the ground, unless business, pleasure, or necessity took them to the upper level known as the Attic. The Attic consisted of the legal halls, such as *hTeme Elua'*, the chieftain's quarters, two or three taverns and the rest of the citizens' homes. There also were strategically placed watch houses facing outward, affording the sentries clear views of the surrounding wood.

Nearing the northeastern corner of the village, the group followed Dhresden onto another wide lift, which lowered them smoothly to the ground.

"Ahead lies *Rebeq* and the burial chamber of the Kelvren." As Dhresden spoke, the melody of Kelvren songs of mourning came to their ears from up ahead. Those who sang remained hidden somewhere above, offering their sympathy in song but allowing Dhresden and his companions privacy in their sorrow. Lost in the bittersweet symphony of voices, Dhresden's companions were somewhat surprised when he halted. They stood before the largest tree that they had yet seen within the Forgotten Wood. The great, wizened trunk spanned so greatly that twenty men combined could not reach their arms around it. Its limbs, themselves as thick as whole trees, reached high and far. The lowest branches arched out and down to the ground, then curved upward and outward again. The leaves were large and heart-shaped, and in the morning sun shimmered a bright blood red. Large, hinged double doors stood open upon the trunk of the olden tree and upon either side of the doors were hung blazing torches. The group stood there before the stone stairs leading up to the doors, a deep sense of wonder and solemn dignity enveloping them. Time passed unnoticed while the visitors' eyes feasted upon the magnificence of the old tree.

"Behold," Phaelen's voice boomed, "*Rebeq,* the entrance to the catacombs where for centuries we have laid our people to rest. Under the ground beneath this tree lie the remains of many, from the muck-raker to the merchant to the monarch; all are placed at the same level: equal in death as we are in life. This tree is the oldest in all the Forgotten Wood; it was a vast tree many generations ago when our forefathers settled this land. It was then that this tree became the resting place of our people. Half a generation passed before the leaves changed to the color and shape you now see. The fruit we gather from the memorial tree is used to concoct *halaet,* the elixir of which you partook, dear lady. It is uncommon for one of outlander blood to even look upon our hallowed place, but this day is unique as we lay to rest among our brethren an outlander."

As Phaelen finished speaking, four young Kelvren, ceremoniously garbed, bore the memorial case into view. They followed Phaelen up the stairs and to the doorway. The old man took a torch from the wall to guide the footsteps of himself and the pallbearers, while Dhresden took the other torch to assist his company. Into the tree and down many steps they filed until they came to several tunnels that branched off from the main cavern. The chieftain led the way down one of the tunnels, which after a ways opened upon a secondary cavern. The walls of the cavern were shelved, some of which lay empty while upon others were burial cases, many cloaked in dust. Phaelen led them to an empty shelf, where the bearers gently, almost lovingly, lay the body of Dhane to rest. Taking the torch from their chieftain, the four departed, leaving the mourners in the light of Dhresden's torch. In the stillness of the tomb the songs of the Kelvren could still be faintly heard, lamenting the mourners' loss but also rejoicing in the peace and rest of the departed. Handing the torch to Orrick, Dhresden went and knelt with head bowed before the bed of Dhane. Soon Lady Jovanna and Mallory stood at his sides, each with a hand upon his shoulders.

The old man Phaelen spoke yet again, "Long years have passed since Dhane, son of Telfor, Lord of Havenstone, graced my parlor. He has long been a friend to my people, aiding us against the onslaught of the Watendi Swarm and many other perils. Always have I admired his bravery and his voluntary enslavement to honor. It was his commitment to honor that propelled him back to his homeland, though I am confident that his love for Ciana was genuine. It was, as you know lady, the series of events through which we passed that drew them together, rather than unfaithfulness to you. He knew that I would watch over my daughter vigilantly, as well as the child she carried. Though brokenhearted for my daughter and grandson, I was all the more impressed with this outlander. Now this day, as we bid him farewell, I honor him not as his elder, but as a friend to whom he taught many things."

Phaelen fell silent, lost in thought, as were the six beside him. Those to whom his eulogy had revealed unknown truths wondered what other surprises the day held. They had not long to wait.

"In keeping with the common laws of the land," began the chieftain, "and having been appointed chancellor of his kingdom by the deceased, I, Phaelen, student and counselor of the elder ways, do hereby decree and proclaim that the authority and lordship of Dhane, son of Telfor, shall pass to his son Dhresden, heir also to the throne of Kelvar. Stand, Grandson, Lord of Havenstone, and be acknowledged."

The son of Dhane rose nobly to his feet, embraced his grandfather and turned to face his peers. He discovered them all kneeling with heads bowed, pledging loyalty to the new ruler of Havenstone.

"Arise, brethren," Dhresden pleaded, "your places are by my side, not at my feet. We have much ahead of us that will require all of our strength and cunning, for there are foes abroad and their emissaries whom we must yet encounter and overcome. Some of these adversaries I inherit from my father, others will rise in opposition to myself alone. But first, let us walk in the clear light of the day, and breath the fresh air, and strengthen ourselves with feasting."

CHAPTER 3

Once again there was feasting within the great hall of Kelvar. On this occasion, however, the whole of the village was in attendance, celebrating the coronation of Dhresden, the halfblooded Kelvren, as Lord of Havenstone. Phaelen once more shared his table with the young lord's company. They were also joined by Wyeth, who quickly appointed himself historian and grand storyteller of the royal table, quite to the liking of the outlanders. To his credit, his manner in telling stories was quite different from his conveyance of true history, allowing the listener the opportunity of knowing whether they were being educated or entertained. Much food and drink had been consumed when Phaelen Chieftain turned the conversation to that of his guests.

"Tell me, Lady Jovanna," he began, "how does your daughter take to the refinement of royalty? It seems that the last time I saw her she had purposed in her mind that hers was to be that of an explorer or adventurer, and caused you many a fright clambering around upon our walkways and in the boughs of our trees." The old man's eyes twinkled at the memory of young Mallory, barely a child at that time, terrorizing her mother with her daring antics.

"I am pleased to remember with you Mallory's youthful ambitions, but fear that if aught were to happen to me, she would break free from the vestiges of refinement that she has submitted to and depart to conquer and discover new lands." Though the young woman's face reddened mildly, her smile could not be concealed. Her mother continued. "While she has taken on several responsibilities of administration, she also busies herself with the tactics of war and battle. She is quite adept with a sword, is she not, Orrick?"

It was now Orrick's turn to redden, which highlighted the pale scar above his left temple. "True, lady, but in my defense, it must be known that it was I who took your windmill of a daughter under my wing and educated her in the tactics of my land. Rather than blindly and madly flinging a blade about, she now quite purposely directs her sword. It is fortunate for me that Maid Mallory's blade is not as keen as her beauty; but what is one more scar to the likes of me." The big man seemed ignorant of the compliment he had just paid the young lady and went back to his dining, but others at the table, including Mallory, shared quiet smiles.

"These others I have long known, or long known of," began Phaelen, directing his gaze toward the two similarly garbed men sitting opposite him, "but what have two of the Makani to do so far from home, and with a half blood, no less? Long has it been since any of the host of the desert ventured into green lands, or kept company with blade-wielders."

The twins looked upon the face of the wise old chieftain, then into each other's eyes. Presently Khalid spoke. "I would not have expected such a question from a student of the elder ways, but perhaps the trees block your view of the forest. I do not speak in insult, but rather I fear that now may not be a prudent time to reveal our purpose. Perhaps when the chief of the Kelvren and the lord of Havenstone deem fit, we will all retire to a location more suited for secrecy." Khalid had spoken respectfully but with resolve, and it was clear that he would speak no more publicly.

The old man smiled at the shrewdness of Khalid's response, and presently bid them all rise and accompany him to his counsel chamber, located high above the banquet hall in the very top of the ancient oak tree. The staircase they ascended spiraled upward, well out of earshot of any below. Within the chamber they were seated around another circular table, different from the banquet tables in that the center of the table was intact. Its purpose was that of conference rather than dining. The walls of the chamber bore no windows but were instead lined with bookshelves, all of which were filled with volumes upon volumes of bound manuscripts and scrolls. In one corner, a hearth roared, keeping the fingers of the cold, crisp, autumn evening at bay.

"Now then, Khalid of the Makani, what is your purpose in all this," Phaelen's tone was pleasant, but his face was somber.

"There is a debt, which has yet to be paid. It was incurred upon the Makani by Telfor, father of Dhane, long ago. How it came to be is not now for the telling, but for that debt to remain unpaid beyond the third generation of Telfor would be shameful. The honor of the Makani is at stake. We two have been dispatched to the company of Dhresden, born to Dhane, son of Telfor until the balance be vindicated. The future of the young Lord Havenstone is not known, but we will accompany him to whatever end, though our lives may be forfeit."

"And what," Phaelen wondered aloud, "does the future hold for you, grandson? What would you endeavor to do with this newfound authority?"

Dhresden sighed. "My answer is a simple one. I shall return to Havenstone and continue to reign justly, as did my father. I fear that some will resist my claim to the throne, as I have been known openly only as the protector of the Lady Jovanna. At this juncture, only the citizens of Kelvar are aware of grandfather's pronouncement of me as Lord Havenstone. I am confident that all will be made well in time, once the public support and approval of the Lady herself, as well as the Kelvren Chieftain, are made known amongst the whole of the lands."

"Not only will Phaelen and I openly support you," Jovanna put in, "but I have, hidden in my chamber, an edict, signed by your father, naming you as his heir."

Dhresden smiled wryly, nodding. "I always considered him a man of foresight, though this bit of news is quite unexpected and welcomed. My greatest foe may be that of Treyherne, longtime advisor to my father. It may be that he expects to assume the throne now that Dhane has passed, leaving no apparent male heir."

"Then we must tarry no longer," Jovanna declared.

"True, dear lady," Phaelan agreed. "You shall leave at dawn; Wyeth shall accompany you as my spokesman. When I receive word that your throne has been established officially, I shall also dispatch three of our Kelvren to publish throughout the lands the news of your coronation. Rest well this night, your horses and stores shall greet your awakening. Goodnight."

He bid all rise, and Wyeth led the companions of Dhresden down the stairs and back to their guesthouse, but Phaelen remained behind in the council chamber with his grandson several moments longer before retiring.

~ ~ ~

The sky was slowly lightening in the east as the sun made its lazy ascent above the horizon of the Forgotten Wood. The inhabitants of Kelvar began to awaken and busy themselves about their day, unaware that their guests of the past two nights had already departed. The group, now numbering seven, made its way south and west for Havenstone. Dhresden again led his friends along unseen paths through the Wood, remembering how quiet their inward trek had been. Only days before, their hearts had been heavy with sorrow, now there was mirth as they marched along listening to Wyeth's endless narratives and occasional song. Though Dhresden enjoyed the smaller man's tales, he looked forward to the silence that would envelope their passage once they departed from the Wood. Then, he knew, Wyeth would take the role of an attentive traveler, reserving his storytelling for meals and firesides.

Reaching the small, now familiar clearing, they rested and ate beside a modest fire Wyeth had kindled. Before long they were under way again, intending to pass the boundaries of the Forgotten Wood well before sunset and set up camp a few miles beyond in a stand of pines which would offer these pilgrims cover but also allow them to easily keep watch.

Hours passed; the sun was deepening in the west as the group bound for Havenstone emerged from the Wood. Wyeth had quieted a mile prior, suspecting that beyond the shade of the Wood, in the shadows of lands bordering, danger may lurk. Now in stealth, the five men and two women quickly covered the remaining distance in the dark, soon finding themselves standing before an inviting grove of young pines.

"Many feet approach from downwind, Dhresden. They come quickly and quietly, but they bring malice with them." As he spoke, Orrick drew his battle axe from its sheath and held it in his left hand, his spear already in his right.

Dhresden placed himself beside Orrick between the women and the approaching party, the twins flanking his position. To his right, Wyeth nocked an arrow to his bow and prepared to fire. Orrick's companions could now hear the hurried footfalls approaching through the darkness. Presently, they stopped. Though only a stone's throw away, their number remained invisible in the night.

"State your business, or be gone!" Dhresden commanded the blackness before him. His every sense bent toward this likely foe, seeking any movement, any clue as to their intent.

There was a rush, a flurry of movement, as those before him surged towards his company, weapons now glimmering in the night. Dhresden bid those with him to brace for the charge. Only Orrick advanced; with a shout and bestial roar he flung his spear into the midst of the attackers. As he then launched himself among these foes, axe swinging like a reaper, an answering roar reverberated down from the pines. A large form bounded out of the grove and to Orrick's side as the big man cleaved his way into his assailants. From within the dark melee came now the clang of metal and the cries of men in fear and pain; accompanied with the snarls and growls which came not only from his shadowy companion, but from Orrick himself. In moments, the skirmish had ended. The last of the would-be assailants silenced by his blade, Orrick returned bloody but unscathed to Dhresden's side. At his heels padded a great feline of the mountains, gray as wetted stone.

"Fifteen fallen, none escaping, sire," said Orrick, breathing heavily and patting the large cat about the shoulders and back.

"Wyeth, twins, take the ladies to the trees for safety. Blaze a fire and bring me light that we may examine the vanquished and perhaps learn what they were about." Turning back to the victors, Dhresden smiled wryly. "Well done, my friend. And you, Asha, how surprised

I am to see you here." He knelt and looked the beast full in the face, then hugged her about the neck. From somewhere deep within, Asha emitted a quiet purring sound. Released from Dhresden's embrace, she nuzzled the hand of Orrick, who lovingly stroked her head, and produced some dried meat from his own rations to further reward her.

"I suspected that she would not heed my command in this. My concern was that she would pursue us into the very midst of Kelvar, scaring those she encountered to death. Mayhap she sensed the strangeness of the Wood, and chose to await us here. It feels good to again have her at my side, and perhaps this night I shall enjoy again the slumber of my youth." Orrick continued to stroke the big cat's head and back, a proud grin upon his face.

The younger twin, Khaldun, returned carrying a makeshift torch. Taking the torch from him, Dhresden asked how the women faired.

"They fair well, though Miss Mallory seems a bit indignant. I cannot say whether it is due to not being allowed to draw her blade in the skirmish, or that Orrick so readily placed himself, alone, in harm's way. Either way, one or both of you will have some answering to do." Khaldun was the less talkative of the two Makani, not that Khalid was one to wax eloquent, but the few words he ever shared were well worth attention. He returned to the camp to help set up the women's tent while the other two, with Asha in tow, advanced to investigate the slain. The dead lay strewn about. Here and there could be seen an ownerless head, arm or leg, hewn by Orrick's axe, as well as those bodies mangled and torn by Asha. Dhresden and Orrick knelt to examine several of the bodies. They were arrayed as bandits, but appeared well fed and were well armed as bandits rarely are. Hefting one of the swords of the fallen and looking closely at it in the torchlight, Dhresden's countenance darkened.

"These swords," he announced to Orrick, "are swords of Havenstone. The etching upon the hilt and blade identifies them as swords of the Oxmen, the royal watch of Dhane. Father once told me that Treyherne was very particular about the men under his command, insisting that he himself recruit these Oxmen. Dhane allowed it, as Treyherne had proven quite reliable over the years."

"Why would these bandits be armed with such blades, if indeed they were bandits at all?" Orrick was not quick to accuse, but knew it was a question gnawing at the mind of both.

"Either these swords were successfully stolen unbeknownst to Treyherne, or there is treachery afoot for which Treyherne must answer."

The three returned to camp, leaving the vanquished to the care of scavengers. They found their companions about the fire, listening to another of Wyeth's tales as they awaited Dhresden's return. After a brief supper during which Dhresden divulged his findings to the others, the company sought to retire. Orrick found himself forcefully drawn away from the firelight by a spirited Mallory. Soon it was clear that the fire burning behind her gray-green eyes would not be easily extinguished despite Orrick's attempts to calm her.

"What exactly did you imagine that you were doing over there?"

"Protecting Dhresden Lord and his company, maiden." Orrick knew by her tone that his answer would not suffice.

"Protecting? Do you really believe that your carelessness with your life will always end so happily? One of the greatest blows against Dhresden would be the loss of you at his side, and your brashness in battle could undermine not only his confidence, but also his success!" Mallory had become so incensed that she paced before Orrick, breathing heavily.

"I did not act foolishly, miss," said Orrick, struggling to remain calm. "I had scented Asha in the Wood, and knew that she would aid me in battle. It was a strategic move, not one of bravado."

"Why do you abase yourself to him? What oath has he placed upon you, that you should so serve him? I shall speak with him and implore him that he release you."

"He did not enslave me; I have bound myself to him. He does not ask anything of me, even treats me as his equal; but I have taken a vow unto myself, and I will not neglect it."

Mallory stopped pacing and looked up somberly into his blue eyes. "Though your life may be taken from you in fulfilling this oath?"

"Yes."

"But what of those who also look to you for strength? To whom will they look if not to Orrick, the Black Wanderer?" Her voice quavered and she began to weep, "And whom shall I look for each morn, if your life has passed?"

Orrick stood stunned. The few times that he had allowed his mind to wonder what could be had seemed to himself as a transgression of the friendship they shared. He had not imagined that Mallory could entertain an interest in him beyond that of swordsmanship. He had been captivated by her at once, so lovely and strong, so noble and earthy. It was because of her love for the blade that Dhresden had encouraged her tutelage under Orrick, yet another debt to him by Orrick's reckoning. He had put away such thoughts of happiness, especially with one such as Mallory, and now he was as a man awaking to a dream realized.

Mallory mistook his silence and fled in tears to her tent. Orrick, still unsure of the words he would speak, watched helplessly as she disappeared. The elation that had coursed into his very bones now turned his limbs heavy with despair. Slowly he lowered himself to the ground as a warrior overcome though no blade had been swung or arrow loosed. Orrick lay upon the ground staring at the moonless sky, lost in thought. An hour had passed when he heard Asha padding toward him, though when she had left his side he did not recall.

"Alas, Asha," he called quietly, "my skill with blades is far superior to my command of words. I was presented an opportunity to express my affection for Mallory, but my tongue failed me. Perhaps I should have just taken her in my arms and held her close until my words did come. I fear I have broken her heart, and am powerless to mend it."

"It would take more than your lull of muteness to break my heart, Orrick."

Startled, he sprang quickly to his feet to find Mallory standing a few feet away beside Asha. Momentarily stunned again, he asked simply, "Are you—all right?"

"Perhaps my heart was a bit battered, but hearing now your private musings I see it was no fault but my own."

"I am not skilled in speech, as is Wyeth; often I find words cumbersome. There is much, however, that I would share with you, though the telling of it may take some time."

"I would willingly give you my time, were you willing to give me yours, Orrick of the Wanderlands."

As a smile slowly stretched across Mallory's face, Orrick strode forward and lifted her to himself, aware of the delight reflected in her embrace. They spoke together quietly beside the dying fire, their companions asleep either in tents or nearby upon the ground. With reluctance they bid each other goodnight. Mallory briefly pressed her lips against Orrick's cheek and withdrew to her tent. Several moments passed before Orrick drifted into a deep, peaceful slumber, his back resting against Asha's side.

CHAPTER 4

The pilgrims bound for Havenstone awoke to the sound of birds in the dim light of predawn. Amongst the boughs of the pines about them, the small company heard many flitting about and calling to one another. Faintly in the distance could be heard the not-so-musical cawing of the carrion feeders, already busy about their harvest of flesh. The women tried to ignore the noise of the ravens and vultures as they shared a cold breakfast of fruit and dried meat with the others. Khalid and Khaldun packed up their belongings and disappeared to the east edge of the grove. They went to perform mandara, a ritual of the Makani, which heightened the senses but calmed the mind. Mandara involved varying levels of empty-handed combat while blindfolded. The goal was never to conquer, but rather to successfully protect oneself while relying upon senses other than the eyes. The reason for this ritual had been forgotten by all but the Makani, but they avoided discussing it, especially with those they called "blade-wielders."

The sun had crested the horizon when Dhresden led his companions from the shelter of the pines opposite the site of the previous night's skirmish. They traveled in their accustomed order: Dhresden led, followed by the twins; Wyeth hovered about the middle of the column where the women rode, Asha and Orrick bringing up the rear. The journey from Kelvar to Havenstone proper would take three and a half days, but as Dhresden surveyed the northwest sky he feared that a cold autumn rain would impede their progress by the next morning. The weather, however, remained the least of his concerns. Wind and rain were defended against easily enough, but this threat of treachery from within his newly appointed domain troubled his thoughts more.

On they walked, the great forms of the ancient trees of the Forgotten Wood diminishing and finally disappearing from view behind them. The land they now traveled through was lightly wooded, the grass that sprung up beneath the scrubby trees was coarse and dry. Hours passed before their path joined up with the main thoroughfare, a rather wide graveled road upon which many merchants and tradesman were sure to be encountered. Here the going was easier, the footing less cumbersome than the woodland floor as the ground sloped gently downward in the direction they walked. After a couple more hours of brisk walking, they left the road to rest. They removed themselves a stone's throw or two off the edge of the road and set about heating a small, though nourishing meal. Dhresden moved about the group, asking how each fared. Few spoke, though Orrick and Mallory sat close upon the ground, occasionally sharing soft words. Wyeth, not quite accustomed to such travel, was too winded for storytelling, but could be heard occasionally humming a Kelvren tune. The Lady Jovanna sat alone, deep in thought. Dhresden sat down beside her, unsure at first whether she was aware of his presence.

"I am troubled for you, Dhresden. The attempt upon our party last night does not bode well for your ascension to the throne of Havenstone. Though your father entrusted Treyherne with many responsibilities, there was an unexplainable thread of distrust woven into Dhane's assessment of his advisor. Truly Treyherne is a shrewd man, mindful of the mechanics of many things; but it seems now as though he has had a hidden desire for the throne. It appears that he knows you are the heir and thus his barrier to the throne; though how, I cannot fathom. My hope is that I was the target, and that you are not perceived as a threat to his schemes." Jovanna lapsed into silence again, her eyes focused upon some distant reflection.

"Thank you for your concern, my lady, but I am not ready to condemn Treyherne for supposed treachery or treason. There will be time enough for trials after we arrive home. For now, let us be content with the simplicity of these brief days. I fear that complexity shall soon enough overtake us and stand in our way as much as it is able or allowed." As Dhresden finished speaking, he heard a warning signal from Orrick. He took his leave and joined the big man who was intently looking down the road in the direction they had traveled from.

"A rider approaches quickly. It is likely that we shall be spotted as he rides by." Orrick's tone remained even, but his eyes conveyed his concern.

To the others, Dhresden called out, "A rider comes! We know not his aim, ready yourselves!"

Shortly, the horseman rode into view. A reddish mount cantered crisply along the road while the rider busied himself shifting his gaze first here, then there, then back behind. As he drew opposite the group resting in the thicket, he discovered them as Orrick had guessed he would. He then reigned in his mount and stared for a moment at the sorted group. Presently, he offered a friendly, though cautious, "Good day!"

"And many returns," Dhresden replied. The two regarded each other silently, each intent upon determining the character of the other. This newcomer was garbed in deep purple with bright yellow accents and his face, though darkened by age, was brightened by the curiosity of his unblinking blue eyes. Dhresden concluded that this man was no threat, though his curiosity could prove troublesome.

When Dhresden finally spoke, the rider relaxed noticeably. "Please introduce yourself and your business. It may be that we are headed in similar directions."

"And," Orrick boomed, "tell us whether those hauling the wagon are with you."

The man's eyes grew wide at this statement and even wider when he spotted Asha at the big man's side. "J—J—Jairus Hardwin," he stammered, "I'm an innkeeper, and those coming behind me are my employees hauling supplies, though how you were aware of them I fear to ask, for they lag far behind."

Again Dhresden spoke. "We are journeying into the Pasturelands and are seeking good speed, though I fear the weather is going to turn against us. Tell me; how far is it to your inn, Mr. Hardwin?"

Calming, but keeping a wary eye upon the large cat, the inn-keeper replied, "Not terribly far now, sir. It is located north of the highway upon a side road. We shall arrive at the Lonely Reed before nightfall, and most folks just call me Hardy."

As Hardy finished speaking, the first creaks of the lagging wagon could be heard. Soon, a mule-drawn cart came into view, driven by a heavyset man who seemed almost to take no notice of the innkeeper or the group now joining him in the roadway. Before it reached him, Hardy called out, "It's all right! These shall board with us tonight."

The portly man nodded, and from behind his large frame rose two women, each replacing an arrow into a quiver upon her back as they sat down beside him.

"One cannot be too careful: a handful of bandits passed through some days ago. From the coin they spent they seemed to be successful bandits, so I made sure to bring Shika and Tala along; they are excel-lent marks with the bow."

Hardy turned his mount and headed down the highway with Dhresden at his side. The twins, the women, and Wyeth fell into step before and beside the innkeeper's wagon, while Orrick and Asha again took up the rear guard. Dhresden and Hardy bantered about trivialities, but the rest walked in silence until Wyeth spoke up.

"Please forgive me my curiosity, ladies, but where did you acquire those bows? I ask only because they appear to be of Kelvren design and it is rare to see such in the hand of outlanders. Please, where did you get them?"

"Your eyes are keen, little man," Shika said with a smile. "Uncle gave them to us when we were very young, but I remember he said that they had been given to one of our line generations ago. More than that I cannot say."

"Uncle did say that the bows were given directly from the Kelvren to honor a deed of some sort, but what I do not know or cannot recall." Though Tala did not smile as easily as her sister did, she was in no way unfriendly. She cast a watchful eye here and there as they made their slow way.

"This is most curious," Wyeth remarked with increased interest. "Did your uncle mention this person's name?"

Shika laughed musically. "I did not say he was our uncle. 'Uncle' is all anyone knows him as."

"Please, pardon my presumption. Do you recall the name of your ancestor?"

The two bow women gazed off into the distance as though they had not heard the smaller man's question. Wyeth was about to inquire again, but the heavyset man driving the wagon answered for them.

"I did not give them a name, for the owner was known by her title. Her name shall remain unknown, but since you are inclined to know, her title was Nokoma."

"These are the famed Bows of Paynmar? And you then are of the womb of Nokoma! Indeed it is an honor to have made your acquaintance. The legends of Kelvar record much about Nokoma: her skill with the bow as well as her beauty; you both carry those traits. But tell me; does her love of honor and truth flow in your veins as well? Or have you fallen prey to the mundane complacency found in a tavern?"

The eyes of all three flashed angrily at the small man, though for a moment none spoke. Finally, Uncle whispered angrily, "The integrity of these ladies is not to be questioned, even by one of the Forgotten Wood. Temper your words, Kelvren, or speak privately with me."

Wyeth regarded the bigger man with such confidence that Uncle began to doubt whether he really desired a private encounter with this small Kelvren.

"I hope to enjoy further discussion with you after we have refreshed ourselves at the inn. Until then, good speed." With that, Wyeth increased his pace until he was traveling beside Jovanna and Mallory.

Little else of matter passed among the travelers the remainder of the journey to the Lonely Reed. The varied convoy left the highway and traveled northwest upon a well-ridden trail several miles to Hardy's inn. Nearing the inn, there was little 'lonely' about it: the light of many a torch greeted them upon their approach along its cobblestone walkway, while from inside the merrymaking of several could be heard. For its setting, the Lonely Reed was well named: it sat back from the beaten path at the edge of a wide gorge. The gorge acted much like a funnel into which water drained from the surrounding land. It was not a desirable land, that through which this water lazily flowed. It was known as the Bog; a swampy land most avoided, or never returned from.

"I would not have thought," Dhresden began, "that the edge of the Bog would be a desirable location for an inn, Mr. Hardwin, especially with the reputation of its inhabitants."

"True, true, my lord, but I have discovered that which the critters of the swamp, mosquitoes and the like, despair to encounter. The torches you see all about you are not for our benefit of sight. An old hermit who lives in the swamp came to my inn many years ago when I first established it. Business was terrible, what with all the insects buzzing around and feeding off of any guests that came, eventually driving them away. I myself was sick most of the time and unable to keep any help around. So this wiry old man shows up at the bar and asks for a drink. I can't help but notice that none of the swamp varmints are bothering him, so I asked him about it. He told me about a weed that grows plentifully within the Bog that when crushed, emits an odor that keeps the insects away. We place its oils in the torches and it keeps my customers safe from the biting pests. The old man comes in once or twice a month to drink in the gossip and his share of ale. He drinks for free except for the bushel basket he brings me of what he calls 'analgis'. That is the key to my success at the Lonely Reed."

"And what of the other inhabitants of the Bog?"

Hardy, though obviously uncomfortable with that topic, did not avoid the question. "I have not had any trouble with them, except for the occasional fool who drinks too much and staggers off into the swamp to 'prove his valor', never to return. Sometimes I glimpse them, watching, but to what end I do not know. I believe, though, that they are somewhat peaceable, or at least not interested in leaving the comforts of the Bog. Fear not, sir, you and your company will be safe here at the Lonely Reed." With that, Hardy made arrangements for the women's horses at the stable and for the rest at the inn. With a start, he remembered the great cat at Orrick's side and stammered, "W—w—what would you have m—me do with—with—your—cat, sir?"

"Asha belongs to no man, Mr. Hardy," Orrick corrected, "but she will agree to stay with our horses to insure that no one attempts to relieve us of them. Do not worry, I shall rejoin her later."

The horses were moved to a pen off to one side of the stable apart from the other borders' horses. Orrick knelt beside Asha and whispered briefly to her. The beast nuzzled his face and then turned and leapt up into the hayloft, a jump of about twenty feet. She disappeared into the shadows to watch and rest, a sentry even in slumber.

Orrick, Dhresden, and the others made their way to their rooms, bathed, and then met in the dining room. They sat at a long table apart from the rest, content to be left alone while they ate. Shika and Tala made their way about the room, waiting tables. They were watched often by the patrons, though none dared any brazenness, fearing the beautiful sisters' reputation as fighters, as well as the watchful bartender known as Uncle. The meal passed without incident, and the members of Dhresden's group departed to their tasks. Jovanna and Mallory retired to their room for the evening, and the twins, at Dhresden's direction, took up residence in a room beside the ladies. Orrick entered the kitchen and, with five raw steaks in tow, headed for the stable. Dhresden and Wyeth seated themselves at the bar and spoke with Uncle, Shika, and Tala late into the night before retiring. No one had noticed the trio of men seated in the corner as they watched the young ruler and his companions into the evening, or their departure out the door and into the night. The rain had arrived, steady and cold, but it would not delay these ruffians' progress as they hoped it would their quarry's. Dhresden and the others rested well, resigned to the knowledge that their residence at the Lonely Reed would be prolonged by the inclement weather.

CHAPTER 5

The rain continued to fall as the night wore on. Orrick and Asha lay in the loft of the stables where they could remain out of sight but still keep vigil. Orrick had been asleep one or two hours when he awoke to the creaking of the stable door. He lay there listening, hearing two or three hushed voices and a stall door being opened. Asha remained in the shadows while the giant man crept silently to the edge of the loft to see what these men were about. They were a few stalls down from the ladies' horses, readying their own mounts. As they finished and sat atop their horses, they began to speak just loudly enough that Orrick could catch their words.

"Ride hard all night until ya get there. Don't stop for anything or yer gonna miss 'em. Ya get a move on while we figure our paths; maybe we can double our profits."

He chuckled quietly as the other man galloped off, then turned to the third man. "Ya go to the camp watching the north trail from the Wood; I'll head back east down the main way to the sentries posted there. They won't be pleased to hear that they missed 'em, but they'll be sure to reward us when we tell 'em where they are." As they were leaving the stable, he added, "I don't know how they avoided that roving band at the edge of the Wood, but those Kelvren are wily, and he's got their blood in his veins."

It was then that Orrick realized their mischief was aimed at Dhresden. Asha and he leapt down to the stable floor and through the door. The riders had covered a good distance already, but knowing they must catch them, Orrick sprinted after the leader and sent Asha bounding northward after the other man. His legs pumping, trying to maintain good speed and good footing in the rain, Orrick began to gain on the horseman. Closer and closer he drew, ready to drag the man from his saddle and demand answers from him. In his haste, one misstep splashed loudly, startling the horse. The rider turned, and seeing his pursuer, goaded his mount faster, leaving Orrick behind. *I'll head back east down the main way* As the words echoed in his head, Orrick veered left off the trail and into the trees. He ran as quickly as he could in the dark; leaping over fallen logs, racing through brambles, and weaving between trees in his attempt to reach the highway ahead of the rider. The path the horseman followed was not as direct as the path Orrick now took, though his own pace began to slacken as the terrain and weather took their toll. He had been bounding through the brush more than an hour before he reached the highway. Breathing heavily, Orrick fell on all fours in the gravel, afraid he was too late. Finding no spoor to indicate recent passage, Orrick moved to the edge of the road, waiting in the darkness. It was not long before he heard the soft crunching of wet gravel approaching. Wishing he had taken the time to grab his spear and axe from the loft, Orrick gripped the handle of his chain flail and readied his attack. The rider came at a swift trot, hunched slightly forward over the neck of his mount. Hidden by the rain and the night, Orrick stepped forward and swung the long flail in a wide arch toward the neck of the horse. The long chain wrapped twice fully around the horse's neck and rider, the iron ball upon the end coming to rest with a smack against the horseman's back. Gripping the handle in both hands, Orrick heaved upon the flail. The horse spun around and fell stunned upon its side, the rider pinned in place not only by the horse upon his leg, but also the chain wrapped around he and the beast. He writhed in pain as he tried to free himself, hurling curses in Orrick's direction. Orrick drew both of his daggers, strode over to where his quarry lay and stooping down, thrust one a few inches into the man's shoulder. There was a shriek of pain and more cursing. Orrick uttered one word quietly to the man, "Speak." The man's resolve crumbled in the face of this giant's demeanor and he told Orrick that he had heard that someone wanted Dhresden dead and was willing to pay for information about him and those that traveled with him.

"Tell me more." Even in the dark, the ferocity behind Orrick's eyes compelled the man to speak as effectively as a dagger in the arm.

"I don't really know any more—wait! Somethin' about the half-blood wantin' to take over the rule of the Pasturelands! Says he killed Dhane and is holding the Lady Jovanna prisoner. Says he's travelin' with a crew of outcasts from the bordering lands, come here to join forces with those what live in the Bog. There, now, that's all I know, so go ahead an' slay me, you traitorous, foul beast!"

Orrick looked upon this man with pity. Clearly, he was nothing more than a well-intended commoner, deceived by lies and the promise of wealth. The big man proceeded to remove his flail from about the man and horse. Both man and beast quickly got to their feet, the man scrambling to what he believed a safe distance from Orrick. There he stood, short sword drawn to protect against the attack he believed was to come.

"Your patriotism is ill-aimed, I am afraid. There is but one heir to the throne of Havenstone, and you are not well informed as to his identity. For that I will spare you, but I shall relieve you of your horse. Abide in the forest tonight, when you return to the Lonely Reed, you shall find your mount."

With that, Orrick turned to mount the man's horse. The horse nickered and tried to run, evidently spooked by this stranger who sought to ride it. As Orrick focused his attention upon the horse, the man lunged towards him, ready to strike him down. From the trees to his right the brush rustled, and an instant later what had actually spooked the horse sprang into view.

～～～

The sun rose almost unnoticed that morning as the rain continued to fall. Uncle and the girls arose with it and busied themselves in the kitchen preparing breakfast and tending to the horses in the stable. They found the horses of Dhresden's company already tended, though the Wanderlander and Asha were nowhere to be seen.

The boarders at the Lonely Reed trickled down from their rooms much like the rain trickling down the panes of the windows. Soon, Dhresden's table was full, save for the empty chair heralding

Orrick's absence. Dhresden felt Mallory's questioning, almost accusing, eyes upon him.

Dhresden smiled gently at his half-sister. "I know not where your giant has gone, though I am sure he will make his way here soon. He and Asha are not ones to long endure the confines of any four walls without scouting the surrounding wilderness. Fear not, Orrick's devotion lies with us. He will join us shortly. What news he brings, no one may say. We would do well, though, to have our belongings packed and ready for departure."

"Well, I certainly hope he stays out of the Bog," Wyeth piped in. "Some of the stories that bartender told us last night about those that live in the swamp still send shivers up my back. Why, what he said about that creature knocking down trees wider than I can reach as if they were grass, there's no one who could withstand—"

"Some tales," interrupted Dhresden somewhat sternly, "are told to encourage the listener to drink more ale. Your red eyes tell me you may have fallen victim to this ploy. Do not let Uncle's stories and ale cloud your judgment of the Black Wanderer. We shall see him soon."

There was silence at the table the rest of the meal, though Mallory ate little. She herself had overheard fragments of the local tales, tales told in hushed tones even in the safety of the flickering light of the hearth. She had concluded that such fear and awe could not be the result of empty fantasy, and in Orrick's absence the unknown reality of these stories brought dismay.

As breakfast came to a close, the guests dispersed; some to their rooms while others sought a diversion from the weather. Khalid and Khaldun squared off against one another in a game of calculus, a table game of strategy whereby one seeks to capture the other's commander. Wyeth returned to the bar and Uncle's stories while Dhresden seated himself at a table off to a corner where he could monitor the stairs, bar, and two entrances. Orrick's absence did not sit well with him any more than it did with Mallory. The Lady Jovanna trailed her daughter out onto the porch. Mallory sat hunched upon a bench as she gazed out into the rain, hoping at any moment to see Orrick approaching. Jovanna sat down beside her, placing a loving arm about her slender shoulders. For a while, neither spoke. Mallory quietly broke the silence. "Where could he be, Mother?"

Jovanna sighed. "He could be many places, my dear. For every detail that is known of him, there are two that remain hidden. However well you or Dhresden come to know him in the future, for now he is mysterious. His devotion to Dhresden and his love for you is evident enough, and I do not doubt his return. I do not believe ill has befallen him, though it may have befallen others."

The two sat wordlessly, deep in thought. The rain continued to fall steadily, the air cool and damp. All around, the forest was gray and wet, silent but for the rain. Time passed without detection until the creak of the door interrupted their reverie.

"Lunch is served, my ladies," Dhresden announced, "stew to warm the soul. I have taken the liberty of setting your place near the fire, as I am sure you are both chilled."

He stepped aside, and as they rose and reentered the inn, they realized that they had indeed grown cold upon the porch. Their thoughts, with the cadence of the rain, had so enveloped them that they had been unaware of the chill air. Now they could feel the warmth of the fire chasing the dampness away as from their very bones, though Mallory's heart still ached for Orrick's return. The stew proved to be delicious, a hearty blend of vegetables, meat, and spices. Both Mallory and Jovanna were consuming a second helping of the soup when the back door of the inn burst open. The wind had picked up outside, and through the open door it carried the sound of the rain and the quiet rumbling of a wild beast. All within earshot whirled toward the door, some drawing weapons in fear as they realized that the door had been flung open by a large cougar that now stood just inside the doorway, eyes darting about. Only Dhresden and his companions were relieved to see Asha, and stooping to enter the inn behind her came Orrick. He threw back the hood of his heavy black cloak, looked to Dhresden and nodded.

"Get your things, we are leaving," was all Dhresden said to his companions.

They quickly disappeared upstairs, only Mallory hesitating long enough to briefly embrace Orrick. "I am glad you are safe," she whispered, then fled up the stairs.

Dhresden turned toward the bartender. "This should cover our expenses, Uncle. Please convey our thanks to Mr. Hardwin." He tossed a satchel of coin on the bar and turned to go. His eyes fell upon Shika and Tala to whom he called, "The horses we leave to you. I do not doubt we shall meet again." Dhresden gave them a slight bow, and walked out the door with Orrick, the others following close behind.

The rain was falling in heavy sheets, driven by a chill wind. With little discussion, Dhresden fell in behind Orrick and Asha. The twins now formed the rear guard of the column, the women with Wyeth were situated between them and Dhresden. They followed Orrick away from the Lonely Reed and the road down to the very edge of the gorge. Far below in the gloom lay the floor, a swamp-bottomed valley most that wished to live avoided. The wall of the precipice was quite steep, made even more treacherous by the rain. Orrick had already tied one end of a rope around the trunk of a tree to assist their descent. Without pausing to give instructions, the big man scooped up Mallory with one massive arm and, taking the rope in the other hand, led the way down into the valley. Dhresden followed, aiding Jovanna who proved to be more nimble than most would have guessed. Khalid and Khaldun descended with ease and in silence, while a grumbling Wyeth slipped his way down behind them. About halfway to the valley floor, the others caught up with Orrick, Mallory, and Asha. Orrick led them under an outcropping of rock off to the right of where he had stood waiting. There under the shelter of the ledge they discovered an opening to a cave.

"This is where we will stay the night. I have brought dry wood for a fire, but we must wait a couple hours until it is dark so there is no risk of anyone at the inn seeing the smoke. By first light we will head into the swamp. There is more to tell, but I must go back up and remove the rope so no one can easily follow us." With that, he disappeared into the rain.

The rest set about getting as comfortable as they could. It seemed colder in the cave than it had been out in the rain, and though the climb down had warmed them through, it would not last. Orrick returned to find his companions anxiously awaiting his arrival and the news he had yet to share. Kneeling down close to Mallory, Orrick told his tale.

"I awoke in the stable to hear three men scheming to report to someone about our location. I understood their intent to be ill for us, so Asha and I set out to detain them. One escaped entirely and the other two passed without answering many questions. I scouted out this cave to lodge in until our departure, and then came to fetch you."

Orrick the Black Wanderer was not a storyteller; neither was he a braggart. His lack of detail and bravado in relating the events of the past few hours was largely due to his simplicity, but perhaps the chief cause of his modesty at this time was his desire not to upset Mallory.

Only to Dhresden did Orrick reveal more of his adventure, and even to him it remained an unimpassioned narrative.

Dhresden's brow furrowed with this new information. "Truly there is treachery afoot, whether Treyherne's or another's. How deeply the deception runs, and whose it is we would do well to discover."

Dusk had fallen, turning black the gray that had permeated the land. Wyeth busied himself kindling a fire at the back wall of the cave and soon had a small, warming fire blazing. The cave had been well chosen: the ceiling of the cave sloped gently upward toward the entrance, allowing the smoke a clear path to the outside. The floor of their temporary den angled almost imperceptibly down toward the opening, providing fairly level footing while keeping the rainwater at bay. It was quite cozy now within the cave. The twins were busy preparing the evening meal while Wyeth pretended to help. Mostly, the old Kelvren told his stories, with surprisingly few repetitions. Mallory and Orrick sat close upon the giant's great cloak, listening to his tales. They shared whispered thoughts at every opportunity, producing pleasant smiles and not a few laughs from each other. Lady Jovanna and Dhresden sat upon their own padding, drinking in the enjoyment of the moment. Were it not for the cold reality of their situation, it would have seemed that the seven friends were on holiday, camping out in a cave while they waited for the rain to cease.

Asha had appointed herself sentry, seeming to like the crackle of the fire less than her human companions. She crouched near the cave entrance, ever vigilant. At the occasional crack of thunder she would raise her head towards the opening, smelling and listening more than actually looking. Evidently unconcerned with whatever she sensed, she would lower her head once again to rest upon her forepaws. Subtly, Orrick took note of Asha's movements. He doubted any would seek them in this hidden refuge, but even a chance discovery could prove costly.

By the end of the meal, everyone had warmed through and most of their belongings had dried out. One by one, they succumbed to the warmth of the cave and the now gentle lullaby of the rain. Sleep came surprisingly easily for all but Orrick. Mallory had fallen asleep leaning upon his chest. He gently, lovingly lowered her upon his cloak. After brushing her hair from her face, he joined Asha near the cave entrance. While the great cat required less rest than the people she protected, Orrick knew that even she needed the opportunity to recover her strength. He handed her the last of the raw steaks he had taken from the inn and rubbed his hand over her head and ears. Finishing her food, Asha curled up beside Orrick and was soon asleep. She would awake instantly was there a need, but with Orrick at her side, Asha would be able to rest until the need arose. For his part, the Black Wanderer sat with his back against the wall of the cave. For a time, he gazed upon Mallory's sleeping face at the back of their den. He thought of the turn their relationship had taken so recently, and of the future they could have together. As his mind began to drift to memories of his youth in the mountains, Orrick shook himself from his reverie and turned his gaze out into the black wet night.

Some things are better left forgotten, Orrick thought to himself, searching the dark for a distraction from his musings. Something akin to a shiver began to twitch at the back of Orrick's mind. With every fiber of his being he gazed into the night, listening intently, searching for a smell, something—anything—to explain the edge he felt. An hour passed without incident, and Orrick began to be at ease again. Not one subject to needless concern, he concluded that his mind had manufactured the incident to escape his thoughts. About five hours before daybreak, Orrick was almost startled by Dhresden as he sat down beside the big man.

"I do not believe that I will get used to you sneaking up on me, my Lord Dhresden."

"Forgive me, old friend, but I am come to relieve you of your post." Dhresden smiled wryly at Orrick, clearly amused.

Orrick began to object. "I am not tired, and besides, it is more important that you rest."

"I am tired of resting. Go, recline beside my sister; she will be happy to see you when she wakes."

Giving in to Dhresden's sensible proposal, Orrick joined a sleeping Mallory near the fire and was soon fast asleep himself. Dhresden absently stroked Asha as his own thoughts rolled over him. While his father lived, Dhresden had been pleased with the services that Treyherne had provided. His advice had been key in the peace which Dhane had orchestrated during his reign. Now in light of recent developments, Dhresden wondered if he had been naive to evidences of Treyherne's treachery. The young ruler was hesitant to pass judgment on Treyherne without further information; the counselor's apparent faithfulness to his father Dhane afforded him that privilege.

Dhresden cared not for himself; were he enslaved or banished, even slain, he would meet that end gloriously. What he feared was the fate of the women, his stepmother and half-sister, were his days ill-fated. In the shadows of this concern was the hatred of the possibility that his father's memory be dishonored.

With these issues and others, the young Lord Havenstone wrestled the remainder of his watch.

CHAPTER 6

Though roused from slumber shortly before dawn, the group awoke refreshed and ready for travel. Eating a hurried breakfast and readying their packs, they left the shelter of the cave. Morning dawned gray and the rain had begun to fall harder, thunder threatening distantly in the east. Orrick once again produced the rope that had assisted them in their prior descent and secured one end to a stout sapling that had taken root in a crevice upon the face of the cliff.

"I shall lead the descent into the gorge. Once we have all reached the bottom, I shall return and recover the rope; it may be of use to us yet again," Orrick suggested, addressing the group but looking to Dhresden for consent. Before the new ruler of Havenstone could respond, the younger Makani spoke up.

"If it pleases my lord, I would stay and bring the rope down with me after our companions have safely descended."

Others may have interpreted Khaldun's offer an act of cowardice: allowing his companions to descend into unknown danger while he lagged behind, but Dhresden knew well the bravery of the Makani, and he did not doubt Khaldun's character. He regarded the young man only briefly before granting his request.

Their descent proved slower and more treacherous than it had the night prior. The rain now rushed down the incline they descended, seeking to sweep their feet from under them. Orrick led the way, one hand upon the rope, the other gently but securely gripping Mallory by the arm to insure her safety. Dhresden followed lending assistance to Jovanna, as she required it. Wyeth practically slid down the rope, finding it almost impossible to maintain his footing. Khalid followed the old Kelvren almost effortlessly, ready to aid him should his pride allow.

Several moments passed as they made their way down to the swampy floor of the valley. As each reached the base of the cliff, they took up vigil against the unknown. The companions stood in a semicircle, peering into the gloom of the Bog. By now all had heard enough of the legendary inhabitants of the Bog to recognize the need for caution. They all stood motionless, even Asha, watching for danger and waiting for Khaldun to descend. Presently the young Makani arrived, the rope slung in a sack over his shoulder. He too took up watch with the others while Dhresden and Orrick whispered one to another.

"Shall I lead on, my lord?" Orrick offered.

"I know not, my friend. There is a strange sense about this place. Never before have I set foot within the Bog, but there is an air of familiarity here that I cannot quite grasp. This terrain is new to both of us, but I will take the lead."

Orrick nodded assent. Dhresden regarded the swamp before him. The place where they now stood remained firm, but looking about it was clear that many directions would take them into at least waist high mud and water. What other dangers they may encounter could prove deadly were they forced to defend themselves from such a position. The gloom and falling rain made it difficult to distinguish land from water. Without a clear path chosen, Dhresden walked forward and began to weave his way along the narrow bands of solid ground.

"Try to follow my steps precisely, but be careful," he cautioned, "the way is treacherous."

Mallory, with Orrick close behind, followed along carefully. They had gone only a short distance when a low keening reached their ears. All eyes went to Asha, then all but Orrick cast their eyes all about them, seeking the danger she had sensed.

"It is not peril she warns us of," Orrick said, his brow furrowed. "I fear Asha cannot traverse this path we take, and she fears it as well. Accompanying us will require that she pass through the waters. What creatures dwell here in the Bog, no one really knows, but I am sure the water harbors peril we all must avoid."

"She is in danger here, my friend," Dhresden called softly to Orrick. "I am pleased to have her with us, but…"

Orrick stood silent, his eyes upon Asha. The giant cougar was his oldest friend and companion. Together they had seen much blood and battled many a foe. Few besides Dhresden understood that Asha did not belong to Orrick; rather, she saw Orrick as her cub.

The blond giant walked back to where Asha stood and knelt before her. He rubbed his hand over her head, speaking quietly to her in the ancient tongue of the Wanderlands. It was a guttural language that had been thought dead for more than an age. The only word understood by the others was spoken last, "Asha." The cat nuzzled her face against Orrick's shoulder, then turned and disappeared up the side of the valley, lost from view in the rain and mist.

Dhresden and his companions continued their trek through the Bog, managing to keep to solid ground with less difficulty than expected. Their spirits were dampened as thoroughly by Asha's departure as by the rain, but still they pressed on. Midday came without incident or stop, each contenting themselves with a meal of jerked meat and fresh water as they walked. The vegetation through which they passed grew thick and lush, restricting their visibility but also their vision. The Bog was an eerily quiet land; no bird or animal calls were heard, only the patter of rain. Little was seen of animal life, and what the pilgrims did discern was limited to lizards, frogs and snakes.

"Well, at least the rain keeps those awful bugs at bay," grumbled Wyeth.

No one voiced a response, but each of them silently agreed, remembering the stories told by Hardy and Uncle back at the Lonely Reed. On the heels of this thought came the tales of the giant creatures of the Bog. In turns the travelers began to imagine the trunks of trees to be the legs of some beast, that some malicious lizard trailed them in the bush, or that something drifted just beneath the surface of the water, watching, waiting. Plagued by these thoughts and others, they continued on for a time before Orrick halted them.

"Something does not smell right," the mountain man warned Dhresden. "I cannot fully identify it, but it is oddly like—like a salamander."

"Ha!" Wyeth mocked. "Big lad like you worried about a little lizard? Really! This swamp is certainly depressing, but—"

"To produce as much spoor as I am sensing would require either droves piled together, or—"

"Or what?" Dhresden asked.

"Or one of enormous proportions. I do not think we are alone."

Dhresden's brow furrowed as he contemplated this new development. "We cannot go back. Others may be searching for us in the vicinity of the inn. Let us press on and hope that we are only watched. Nevertheless, ready yourselves."

Moments later, Dhresden and his companions found themselves at the edge of the stream that is the center of the valley. The recent rain had swollen it to a width of fifty feet at least, the depth of which was impossible to tell. Scanning the muddy river, no ford could be seen. The travel worn group gathered at its edge, discussing their options.

"We cannot return the route we have just traveled; it takes us first in the wrong direction, and second too close to discovery." Dhresden's tone conveyed his determination. "Trying to parallel the river will lose us too much time. We must cross to the other side, but how I know not."

"We could swim," suggested Orrick, "if we could reasonably expect to survive the passing."

At the mention of swimming, Wyeth blanched. "We do not know what creatures dwell in that murk and I do not think that the seven of us could swim that expanse unnoticed."

"Seven? No. One could do it."

Each turned his eyes to Orrick, all but Mallory eager to hear his plan. "I can swim carrying one end of the rope with me. Once across, we can string the rope from the base of that tree across the way up into this tree here. If we stretch it tight, we can one by one slide the length of the rope to the other side."

None could expose a flaw in his scheme; only Khaldun would speak anything contrary to it.

"It would honor me to swim the distance in your stead, Sir Orrick," he said solemnly, "and I thank you for this allowance." The young Makani bowed slightly, then turned and approached the bank.

"I did not grant it." Orrick said evenly. This was the second occasion on which Khaldun had suggested revision regarding a plan of the Black Wanderer, and the giant wondered at his reasons.

Khaldun stood unmoving a moment, then turned his face toward Orrick. No trace of emotion showed in his eyes; he simply stood as if waiting. Orrick stared placidly back at the smaller man, curious at the outcome of this exchange. He doubted it would come to blows, but out of habit had already measured the distance between them and how quickly the ground could be covered. The others had placed themselves out of the way, unsure whether to intercede.

Finally, Dhresden broke the silence. "We three and Khalid will discuss this further when we lodge for the night. As for now, we must cross the river. Khaldun, you have carried the rope, carry it now to the other side."

Khaldun quickly set about the task, tying one end about his waist and leaving the other, as well as his quarterstaff, for Khalid to tend as the younger man waded into the murky waters. With strong strokes, he propelled himself towards the opposite shore.

Quietly to Orrick, Dhresden whispered, "It is said that the Makani are quite skilled in battle, but I would rather you by my side."

Orrick nodded his assent, but cast a wary eye in Khaldun's direction. In an instant, the giant had bounded to the edge of the water and was feverishly hauling on the rope tethered to Khaldun's midriff. The smaller man practically skipped out of the water, as with each heave, the mountain man pulled him closer to the shore. His face a mask of terror, Khaldun could only hold fast to the rope, trying to ease the pressure to his midsection. All had gathered about Orrick, wondering at his antics. Though none moved to stop him, Khalid looked sternly up at the giant beside him.

"There will be a reckoning, if your pride causes harm to the boy." Khalid then turned his eyes upon the younger Makani as he reached the shallows. Orrick dropped the rope. Pulling his axe from its sheath, the big man launched himself toward Khaldun, roaring bestially. The young Makani staggered and fell, but Orrick's leap took him past the exhausted man. Orrick now stood in thigh deep water, his axe arcing down toward the water. To the amazement of his companions, Orrick brought the weapon down squarely upon the head of some creature, its maw full of teeth as it broke the surface. Driven by Orrick's sinews, the blade bit deep into its skull, immediately stopping its attack. The beast thrashed about in the water briefly, then was still. Its death dance complete, the lizard-like creature sank from view. Orrick returned to shore, where Khaldun lay panting.

"How is he?" Orrick asked Khalid, who had knelt to examine the younger man.

"It would seem, Black Wanderer, that the beast never touched him. His worst injuries will be some bruising around his waist. Although," he added with a rare smile, "those bruises saved his life. For that, thank you."

Orrick nodded. "To serve Lord Havenstone, we must serve each other. I had forgotten that, but neither I, nor any of you, must make that mistake again. We will need to reconsider the crossing."

"Indeed," Dhresden mused. "Rest, everyone, but share what thoughts may be of use. I would rather cross today, and leave yet another obstacle between us and any pursuers."

The travelers rested several moments, hunched under their cloaks as the rain finally began to slacken. Far to the north the clouds had started to break, the promise of sunshine dancing in the minds of the rain-weary group. Unable to discern a method of crossing the river, most had fallen silent. Orrick and Mallory, as had become their custom, huddled close in quiet conversation. Dhresden stood apart from the group, gazing out across the water, his mind a whirl of activity. He feared that his succession of his father's throne was doomed by this treachery. Dhane's impact upon the kingdom of Havenstone and the bordering lands was, as declared by Dhane himself, only the beginning of peace and freedom; Dhresden's reign was intended as the fulfillment of his father's dreams, and his father before him. What was to become of them, and what sacrifices would be required to achieve victory? Dhresden's reverie was interrupted by Mallory's panicked voice.

"Dhresden! Something is wrong with Orrick!"

Quick strides took Dhresden to his sister's side where she leaned over a sweating, feverish Orrick.

"What happened?" Dhresden asked.

"We were talking, and he just fell over without warning!" Mallory was clearly shaken. Orrick lay quite still, his breathing barely perceptible. Dhresden looked into his unblinking blue eyes, searching for a clue as to his condition.

"The serratia he slew must have struck him."

A flurry of weapons flew from sheaths as Dhresden and the others whirled in the direction of this new voice. Not twenty feet from them stood what appeared to be a man, though his skin had the look of a reptile. Behind him stood a reptilian beast much like a long-necked salamander, but whose dimensions well exceeded that of three oxen.

"Do not be alarmed," the newcomer spoke slowly, almost awkwardly. He stood with his arms at his sides and carried no weapons. "We have been watching your passage, and have wondered at the big man's condition. It is rare indeed for anyone to come so close to one of the serratia without injury. The tip of a serratia tail is venomous; it must have lashed him across the hand or some other exposed area as he slew it. I am a healer among my people. May I help?"

Dhresden regarded this stranger silently, unsure as to his purpose but well aware of Orrick's worsening condition. "If you had meant us ill, it seems that you would have already done so. You may treat him; only know that always there are eyes upon you."

As he approached Orrick, Dhresden and the others were better able to scrutinize this healer. His long black hair flowed loosely about his face, his skin the color of sun-yellowed parchment. Where it had appeared as the skin of a reptile, the man was clothed in snakeskin. It covered his entire body, save his head, hands, and feet, and clung tightly to the curves of his muscular frame. About his waist he wore a belt from which hung a small pack and a modest apron covering his front and back just below the waist. He walked without fear into the midst of the travelers.

"My name is Tiblak," he announced as he knelt beside Orrick. He quickly examined each of Orrick's hands in turn, finding a very minor appearing scratch upon his left wrist. "Here is where the poison entered. I must make a cut deeper in the wound, and then apply a medicine within to counter the effects." Tiblak's tone was even, but his eyes told Dhresden that time was escaping. Sensing the urgency, Mallory dropped to her knees opposite Tiblak. Looking over her love's body at the healer and up at Dhresden, she drew a slender dagger from her sleeve.

"Please," she whispered, "Let not a stranger shed his blood, rather one who loves him."

The healer regarded her solemnly, clearly assessing her ability. Taking a deep breath, Mallory steadied her hand and readied her mind. At Tiblak's direction, she made a shallow incision in Orrick's wrist, following the existing wound. Spreading the flesh wide, the healer sprinkled fine black powder into the fresh wound and then bandaged his wrist.

"He will recover in a day or two, but should be allowed to rest. I offer you the comfort and protection of my home while he heals. Long has it been that one from outside the vale lodged among us."

"We accept your offer, Tiblak," Dhresden replied, "but are eager to hear more of your people and their history."

"Yes, of course. But first let us shelter at my home. It will be dark soon, and a hot meal I am sure will do you all good. Saric will bear us along the river to my very doorstep."

At Tiblak's command, the beast he called Saric entered the water and lay down upon the riverbed. This allowed Tiblak and his guests to climb atop his broad back for the jaunt up river. Dhresden and the grateful Khaldun bore a less feverish Orrick onto Saric's back as Mallory looked on. Tiblak, seated at the base of the beast's neck, spoke quietly to the large lizard and it glided gently out into the deeper water of the river.

"What of the serratia, will they not be drawn to your beast?" It was an uneasy Wyeth who voiced the question upon the minds of the travelers.

"They will keep their distance from Saric. His kind has thick skin which is impervious to their venom, though the teeth of the largest serratia could severely wound him."

"That is not a comforting bit of information," Wyeth said, casting about at the murky water around them.

"Oh, do not fear, my Kelvren friend; we slay the large serratia when they are nearing an unmanageable size. Only Saric and his kind do we allow free rein. The behemoth mature slowly, and do not produce offspring often." The healer talked on about behemoths and serratia and other creatures within the Bog as they coasted along the river. Soon Saric came to a stop close to the opposite bank.

"Come, my new friends. Your dinner awaits."

"Is your house much further?" Though Orrick's condition already showed marked improvement, Mallory was anxious for a place for him to rest.

Tiblak chuckled, clearly amused. "Dear lady, my 'house', as you call it, lies but twenty paces away." He gestured to their right at the empty bank. Seeing no structure amidst the trees and vegetation, Wyeth asked, "Do you live underground, in the tradition of the dwarves of bygone days?"

"Though your inquiry hints at mockery, I shall accommodate you. The Elaleu of the Bog do actually reside below ground, though to enter my modest dwelling we must pass under the water as well."

Neither Mallory nor Wyeth was pleased to hear this news, though for different reasons. While Wyeth grumbled unintelligibly, Mallory spoke clearly and plainly. "This man," she placed a hand tenderly upon Orrick's chest, "cannot now swim, neither can we ferry him under the water. It seems to me that much of our time has been waste—"

"No time has been lost." Dhresden interjected. "We are indebted to you for treating our friend, and for taking us across the river; but we have no way of safely transporting Orrick below."

"You all are my guests; it is not for you to concern yourselves with such details. All you need be concerned with is holding tightly to Saric. At my command, he will submerge and take us to my home. It will only take a moment, so do not fear. Use your rope to lash the big man between you, and we will be ready."

It took only a moment to prepare, and at Tiblak's word, the great beast and its passengers sank quickly from view. Above, the sky had begun to darken as the sun set, but below the surface of the water it was already black. Though unable to see, it was evident that they traveled at a speed greater than the swiftest horse any of them had ever ridden. Sooner than expected, Saric and his cargo broke the surface of the water in the midst of a large subterranean chamber. The cave was dimly lit, though it afforded enough light for Dhresden to inspect his party. The twins and women remained impassive, except for Mallory's concern for Orrick. He lingered somewhere between sleep and consciousness, but seemed no worse for the swim, while Wyeth sputtered and cursed quietly in Kelvren. Saric ferried them to an outcropping of rock where they dismounted. Tiblak ran his hands along the beast's great neck, patting him upon the head when he stooped to nuzzle his master.

"I see you brought them, just as you said." All turned to see a woman clad in the same tight snakeskin that Tiblak wore, though she also wore a modest tunic that reached to the top of her knee.

"This is Zhanda, my wife," introduced Tiblak.

"Welcome. Please, bring yourselves near the fire. The children and I will serve you."

Tiblak led the wearied group close to the fire. Its flames rolled and flickered within the confines of an earthen hearth. Heat from the hearth radiated out amongst the travelers, slowly dispersing the cold and wet upon them.

"I am curious, Tiblak," stated the elder Makani, "since we are underground, to where does the smoke from the fire vent?"

"It is different from burrow to burrow," he answered, "but our hearth vents its smoke near a hot spring. The constant steam from the spring conceals the smoke and thus protects the location of our home. That spring also affords me and my family hot water for bathing. The father of Zhanda's grandfather built this burrow and designed all the comforts it provides. He was somewhat of an inventor."

The conversation was interrupted somewhat when Zhanda and the children approached with trays of hot food. Tiblak informed his guests that once ingested, the seasonings of the food acted as an insect repellant, which would be necessary above ground after the clouds broke. Dhresden nodded as he recalled Hardy's story about *analgis*.

As was the custom of Tiblak and his people, Dhresden and the others sat upon blankets around the fire. Zhanda placed her tray upon the ground before her husband and then proceeded to take a tray from each child and place it before one of her guests. When all had been served, Zhanda sat beside Tiblak, who shared his tray with her, while their children, numbering six, returned to the cooking area for their meals. It was then that Mallory realized that only one tray sat before her and Orrick. While the others began eating the hot vegetable stew, Mallory glanced quizzically at their hosts. Zhanda sat watching her, a pleasant smile upon her face.

"Though he seems unable, the medicine will have worked enough that he will eat if you place food in his mouth; it will speed his recovery."

"Oh," Mallory replied, "I am sure that there is more food here than Orrick should consume at this time."

"Among our people," Zhanda explained, "man and wife share a plate at mealtime. It symbolizes the unity of their marriage. It is beautiful, is it not?"

"Yes, it is," Mallory stammered, "but Orrick and I are not yet married—"

"Not yet? What have you been planning?"

Mallory looked quickly at Orrick, who she had thought asleep. He sat looking at her, a wide grin spread across his face, though his eyes betrayed his weakened condition. Too relieved to be embarrassed, Mallory threw her arms around the big man, happy to hear his voice again.

"Welcome back, my good friend," Dhresden exclaimed, chuckling. "You have worried us. This is the home of Tiblak, a healer."

"For your goodness, I am grateful, and indebted."

Tiblak greeted Orrick's thanks with a deep nod. "You have progressed more quickly than I have ever before witnessed, but should still rest another day. You may leave as early as two mornings from now, if you are in haste."

"Two mornings will be soon enough," answered Dhresden. "Though, we must in some way repay you for your hospitality. How may we best express our gratitude to you and your family, Tiblak?"

A shadow passed over the face of the healer as his mind thought over Dhresden's words. "Gold and silver have no use in the Bog. Here all a man has is himself and his family. All other things fade into nothingness when family is threatened." Tiblak paused and glanced at his wife. Zhanda sat with her eyes upon the fire, tears glistening upon her cheeks. Placing an arm about her shoulders, Tiblak went on. "Not all the inhabitants of the Bog are peaceable. Eight nights ago, I was late returning home when a band of Aikon happened upon our home."

"What are Aikon?" asked Orrick.

"Aikon are those who live in the northernmost of the Bog. They are raiders—heartless and ruthless. They come downstream in small groups hoping to stumble upon a burrow and take what they can. I will not cumber you with the details, but they took my two oldest daughters, and killed my son who fought to protect them in my absence. Zhanda also slew one before the other four left with their captives." Tiblak stopped to tend to his wife, who now sobbed openly.

"What will happen to your daughters?" Jovanna's question came gently.

"The Aikon will treat them well, for they are to become wives among them. Often female captives are given to the sons of the raiders to wed when they are of age. Uita and Cle are both too young to wed, and even an Aikon would not risk injury to them by taking them to wife before their bodies are ready. I greatly desire to reclaim my daughters, and avenge my son if possible, but no one will assist me; no one but Phyrus, himself barely a man. He was to marry Uita, and would charge to her aid if I let him."

Dhresden's response came easily. "We would be honored, Tiblak, if you would allow us to return your daughters to you."

A long silence passed as Tiblak regarded the young man before him. No hint of his thoughts showed in his countenance, though clearly he recognized Dhresden's sincerity. "There is much to be learned of you, Dhresden of the Pasturelands. I hope that you will come to trust me as I now trust you to recover my daughters."

"I am sure that time will come, good healer. Now, have you a plan?"

Indeed, Tiblak had concocted several schemes as he sought to rally others to assist him in a rescue. Most he admitted were only the foolhardy daydreams of a distressed father, but he shared with his guests the one plan that, try as he may, he could not find the flaw in. It involved a night raid, hiding their upstream approach from any watching eyes. That any sentries would be posted was doubtful, but early detection was an unnecessary risk. "Their arrogance will be to our advantage. The Aikon do not dwell below ground within burrows, their dwellings consist of grass roofed huts. The primitive city is divided into five sections. The agriculture and livestock area is to the northwest, the craft and trade sector south and east from there, with a section for the rulers at the center of the settlement. Below these three sections is the Barracks, the quarters of the raiders and enforcers. It will be difficult to locate where the girls are being held, but I am confident we will find them somewhere within the Barracks."

"What is the fifth section?"

"It is an area reserved for the sick and the dead. It is set a little apart from the other sections in an effort to isolate any contagious diseases."

"How is it that you know so much about the Aikon and their settlement?" Dhresden asked.

Tiblak cast a wary eye toward his children. Clearly relieved that they were out of earshot, he glanced back at Dhresden and then into the fire. "I was born an Aikon. I had a proficiency for healing and battle, though my heart was not at ease with raiding. I have chosen a different path than that which I was born to, and my life is better for it here among the Elaleu. But my memory of the village of the Aikon is clear enough and will serve us well."

"Very well, then." Dhresden mused. "Will tomorrow evening suit you?"

"A day ago would not have been soon enough, but tomorrow's dusk will allow me to prepare you and the men of your company who are fit to travel."

"Men of the company?!"

"Fit to travel?!"

It was apparent that neither Mallory nor Orrick would be deterred from involvement in rescuing Tiblak's daughters. Sleep came easily around the fire, the travelers surprisingly at ease in the warm burrow.

CHAPTER 7

Jovanna stood close behind Dhresden, both of them shrouded in darkness. Time seemed to have passed so quickly that she could not recall how it had come to this. While the rescuers were slipping into the Aikon village, someone had been detected. They had scattered, and Jovanna and Dhresden had ended up hiding in the shadow of a nearby hut. All around them she could hear the Aikon searching for, and occasionally finding, her companions. It was only a matter of time before they too were all found and put to death by the Aikon. Jovanna looked at Dhresden, afraid that his rule would be ended before it had even begun. Reasoning within herself that Dhresden would pursue her in order to protect her, Jovanna broke from the shadows, running toward safety. A glance over her shoulder showed Dhresden following after her, shouting. She ran harder, spurred on by her love for the young lord, by his need to live. Jovanna ran tirelessly, Dhresden still pursuing, still calling. But why was he yelling? That would only alert the enemy to their location. Again she glanced over her shoulder at him, trying to understand his words. Too late she discerned Dhresden's shouted warning, "My lady, not that way! It is not safe!" Jovanna now found herself in the clutches of the Aikon, their grip firm and their faces grim. She watched as Dhresden launched himself at the enemy, intent upon her rescue. Slowly, Dhresden was losing this battle. Where he slew one, three rose to take his place. By sheer numbers, he was overcome and disarmed. Forced to kneel, Dhresden looked at her in despair. Overcome with grief and guilt, Jovanna hid her face with her hands as one of the Aikon swung a long handled blade at Dhresden's neck, beheading him.

Jovanna sat up quickly in the dim light of Tiblak's burrow, her breathing quick, her heart racing. From the cooking area came the clatter of earthen dishes as Zhanda and her children prepared breakfast. Seeing her guest awake, Zhanda bid her good morning. Jovanna gathered her wits quickly, inquiring as to the whereabouts of the others.

"Tiblak has taken Dhresden to meet with Phyrus, but they will return shortly. The others of your party are in the far cavern, preparing for tonight." Zhanda's eyes focused a moment upon some distant thought. Coming to herself, she offered Jovanna breakfast. As she nibbled at the food, Jovanna considered her dream. Seers had once been common in the land, but though visions had passed from use many years before, the vividness of this dream haunted her. She wrestled with the decision of whether she should stay behind and thus nullify the possibility that the dream come to fruition. With fierce resolve she pushed the ill-bidding dream from her mind, rose from her meal, ready to be reunited with the others. Approaching the far cavern, the sound of iron sharpening iron greeted her ears, as did the grumbling of the old Kelvren.

"...now, do not misunderstand me: I am willing to repay this healer's kindness to the utmost, I just wish it did not entail traveling through murky waters infested with—with who knows what."

Mallory and Orrick sat beside each other, grinning as they listened to Wyeth's rambling. They did not sit idly listening though: they both were busy honing their blades, pausing occasionally to give audience to the Twins engaged in mock battle.

"How long have they been at it?" Jovanna asked.

Orrick stood and bowed respectfully as Mallory replied, "Half an hour. This is the first I have witnessed their ritual, but I know that it usually lasts half this long. Astoundingly, neither has gotten the upper hand, both scoring only one hit."

"Imagine what they could accomplish with a blade in their hands," Wyeth commented.

The twins stopped abruptly, both breathing heavily. As they removed their blindfolds, Khalid eyed Wyeth a moment before speaking. "It is the absence of blades that sets the Makani apart from all other peoples, friend Wyeth. Our people once possessed a love for the edge of steel, but that affinity nearly destroyed us. The ruling council of that age ordered the use of iron weapons in pursuit of lands rich in iron ore. It was easy to detach oneself from the slaughter that followed when iron delivered the death blow. Almost too late the council realized its folly, exiling our people to the sandy coast and banishing blades from our midst. The council deemed barehanded combat the only acceptable method of battle. The truth is, people exhibit more restraint when the only weapon available is their hands; it declares the stark reality of what one is considering when direct touch is required. Many lives have passed, and finally our children have no intimate knowledge of blades, only their history. We exist only because our hands are empty, and we will never forget that."

For a time, no one responded, but then Wyeth spoke up. "I meant no affront, Khalid. Had I known better the history of the Makani, I would not have been so insensitive. Please forgive me."

"Truly there is nothing to forgive, my friend. Ours is a sordid past, extending beyond the origin of the Kelvren. We tend to isolate ourselves, so very few, if any, of your books would contain that history."

"How do the Makani preserve their history? Is it purely word of mouth?" Wyeth's interest as a historian was clearly piqued.

"Our histories are written upon scrolls stored in earthen jars, but my father was the one who educated me of these things. My grandfather was one of the council when my father was a young man."

"But Khalid," said Mallory, "that would make him very old, since the Kelvren claim an almost ancient birth."

Khalid smiled wryly. "True, my young lady. My father died one hundred forty years ago, after the passing of over sixty generations of men."

"Sixty?!" Wyeth exclaimed, "But if the measure of a generation is eighty years, that would have made him…"

"Almost five thousand," Khalid said, finishing his thought for him.

"But how can this be," asked Orrick. "Even the long-lived of the Wanderlands do not pass one hundred fifty."

"And the Kelvren seldom outlive six hundred these days, though it once was one thousand," Wyeth added.

"Before the birth of the Kelvren, your fathers, the elves, lived much longer, some surviving to their ten thousandth birthday before succumbing to old age, or the blade in some cases. The blood of the Montsho with whom the elves spawned Kelvren was purely man-blood. This combination has shortened the average life span considerably, though there are exceptions." The others wondered at this usually subdued man now standing before them, sharing a history few beyond the western Dunes had ever heard. Another silence passed, each lost in thought.

"What then, I wonder, is the number of your days?" Jovanna's inquiry was directed at both Khalid and Khaldun.

Again Khalid's eyes twinkled as he spoke. "I have lived a meager three thousand, four hundred and seventy-eight years."

"And I," Khaldun added, "am only five hundred and two."

Further discussion was forgotten for the time as Dhresden and Tiblak entered the cavern, followed by Phyrus. The young man resembled Tiblak in his appearance, though he stood a little taller and was more heavily muscled. He too wore a loin cloth over his snake skin covering, though where Tiblak's hair was long, Phyrus' hair was closely shaved. Tiblak had shared with his guests the tradition that the young men were considered ready for marriage when they successfully hunted down and slew one of the large constrictors that lived in the Bog. It was not a task so dangerous as one would expect, for the fact that ten men armed with sleeping darts would accompany the would-be victor. These men were restricted to rescuing the young man should he prove unable to vanquish the serpent with his knife. It was this skin that Phyrus now wore as he prepared to rescue his betrothed.

After introductions, Tiblak laid out his simple plan. They were to leave at the setting of the sun, divided into two groups. Half would accompany Tiblak upon Saric while the others joined Phyrus upon his behemoth. The targeted area, known as the Barracks, was divided by a finger of the river into two sections. Each group would infiltrate one of the sections to locate and rescue the captives. They would leave as they had come, unseen and unheard.

"We must go ashore well away from the Barracks to avoid detection, but the night will hide our approach. We will find no mercy among the Aikon, so give none." Tiblak's eyes flashed fiercely, as only a father's could.

"For now," Dhresden added, "finish preparing your weapons and then rest. We leave at dusk with a long night ahead of us."

Hours passed slowly, each anxious to at least be underway. Mallory and Orrick spent much of their time talking or just sitting quietly together. The Twins sat, eyes closed, as if in some meditation. Jovanna and Dhresden spent their time talking with Tiblak and Zhanda as if old friends, Phyrus listening in. Wyeth dazzled the children with countless tales and ballads, much to their delight.

Finally, the time had come to disembark. Zhanda and the children bid them all farewell, lavishing both Tiblak and Phyrus with hugs and kisses. Tiblak and his group, Orrick, Mallory, and the twins, mounted Saric; Phyrus and the others, Dhresden, Jovanna, and Wyeth, climbed aboard Xadu, Phyrus' beast. The two groups entered the water in the dimness of Tiblak's burrow and emerged to the setting of the sun. It was the first time in several days that the travelers had glimpsed its brightness, and it was a welcome sight. Again, with effort, Jovanna pushed from her mind the fear that it would be their last sunset.

The sun's rays diminished quickly in the Bog, and though Saric and Xadu ferried their riders with great speed, it was long dark when Tiblak and Phyrus guided their mounts in close.

"The Aikon village lies close at hand," Tiblak whispered. "Keep silent and hidden. Open battle is not our desire. The group that finds my daughters will return to their behemoth and retreat downstream a safe distance. The other group will cease searching after two hours and rejoin the others."

"What if none of us find them?" Though Wyeth's question was unwelcome, it evidenced genuine concern for Uita and Cle.

"That," Tiblak answered, "is not a problem I wish to have to solve. Safety and success to each of us."

With that, the two groups headed for differing shores, anxious to begin the search. Though Tiblak had assigned leadership of this group to Dhresden, it was clear that Phyrus was hard pressed for patience. Though the dim lights from within the Aikon village were barely perceptible, the young man leapt from Xadu's back to the shore, weapons drawn. Dhresden, Jovanna, and Wyeth followed quickly, though with more stealth and arms sheathed. The three eased up beside Phyrus so quietly that it reminded him of Tiblak's caution. With a nod, he stepped to a flanking position to allow Dhresden the lead. The four rescuers meandered silently from cover to cover, drawing ever closer to their goal. Soon they came to the edge of the west side of the Barracks. Several moments passed as each of them surveyed the Aikon sleeping quarters. Seeing no roaming sentries, they hurried to the shadow of a hut. Tiblak had instructed them to locate a hut in front of which men probably sat around a fire talking and laughing. As casual as it would seem, these men would actually be guarding captives. How Dhresden was to acquire them was a matter of improvisation. Finding the guards proved quite easy, Dhresden simply followed the sound of intoxicated laughter. Six men squatted about a watch fire, seeking to outdo each other with various tales. The next challenge for Dhresden was determining exactly which hut they were guarding. From where they sat, the men could easily monitor any of five huts. Again, a careful vigil rewarded them. As they watched, one of the younger men fetched a brand from the fire and approached one of the huts. He leaned his head and the torch into the hut only a moment before returning to the fire, but in that instant, Phyrus caught sight of Uita and her sister. His first impulse was to bolt to their aid, but the others prevailed against his haste; success hinged upon stealth. To Dhresden's best estimation, an hour had passed, leaving them with but one hour to rescue the women and escape, preferably unseen. Not only would detection jeopardize the mission, both rescue parties would be endangered. Though time was limited, Dhresden and the others agreed that the longer they waited, the fewer guards would be awake, as they continued to fill themselves with ale. Already, one of their number had slumped upon his side, unmoving, much to the amusement of his companions.

As the minutes dragged by, two of the other would-be sentries willingly laid themselves upon the ground to sleep, while another fell over drunk. The young man who had unwittingly revealed the location of their captives to the rescuers still squatted before the fire, facing the girls' hut. No doubt he had been promised one of them to wed, accounting for his vigilance and sobriety. A couple of arm lengths away, a rather paunch man squatted upon his haunches, head sunk to his chest. Soon Dhresden became convinced that the heavy man had also passed out, though amazingly keeping his balance. With time dwindling, the rescuers positioned themselves behind the sole sentry. Leaving the others in the shadows, Dhresden drew his sword and crept closer and closer to his young quarry. His footsteps fell as quietly as the dew, his prey unaware of even the hilt of Dhresden's sword as it rendered him unconscious. Phyrus rushed quickly but quietly to the hut, cautioning the girls to silence in spite of their joy. As they and Dhresden began to make their way toward the others, a scream erupted from the watch fire. The fat man evidently had pitched forward into the fire, and though his companions that awoke directed their immediate attention to their wounded comrade, it took only a moment for them to spy the two men stealing into the shadows with their bounty. One of the Aikon guards produced a small horn from a pouch at his belt and blew. A shrill trumping filled the air, eliciting shouts throughout the village as the Aikon burst from their huts.

"Girls," Dhresden instructed, "you follow Phyrus. Wyeth and I will bring up the rear. Stick to the shadows as best you can. Remember: defend, dodge, disappear. We must succeed. Xadu awaits."

Phyrus led the group, now numbering six, back through the shadows, drawing ever closer to escape. Twice they encountered an Aikon, though on both occasions either Dhresden or Phyrus were able to silence them quickly. Almost free of the village, Jovanna caught her foot upon something in the dark, falling to the ground. Dhresden knelt to assist her while Wyeth sprang past to aid Phyrus. They had unwittingly crossed paths with several of the Aikon. With deadly accuracy, Wyeth fired off several arrows in quick succession, while Phyrus launched himself upon the others, his war staff swinging madly.

Though the Aikon fell neither easily nor quickly, they did indeed fall. These few had slowed Dhresden and the others long enough to allow more of their comrades to arrive, equipped with torches as well as weapons. As the reinforcements trickled in, Jovanna trembled not at the enemy, but at the recollection of her dream.

"Phyrus!" Dhresden yelled. "Take the women and go! I will not let this be a total loss, now go!"

Phyrus, though reluctant to leave anyone behind, led Uita and Cle toward the river and the waiting behemoth. Dispatching one of the enemies, Dhresden glanced toward Jovanna. She danced about, her own light sword holding the enemy at bay.

"Wyeth! Get her out of here!" was all Dhresden could manage before another Aikon was upon him. In quick obedience to the young ruler, Wyeth launched an arrow into Jovanna's opponent and with startling ease, swept her into his arms and bore her into the shadows in pursuit of Phyrus.

Relieved of concern for the lady, Dhresden poured himself into the task at hand: survival. In each hand he gripped a Kelvren broadsword, light and strong; their sharp edges long since turned crimson. About him lay many fallen Aikon, some never to rise, others unable to further threaten him. Aside from a glancing blow across his forehead, he had either parried each lunge, or been saved by his chain mail. Though his strength was dwindling, the bodies strewn about him had slowed the attack. Not only did the carnage about him begin to fill the Aikon with dread, it also provided unsure footing for his attackers. Nevertheless, Dhresden was fading. Sensing his fatigue, two more of the raiders came at him together. Among the flurry of steel came a cry of pain, and then another, as the two Aikon fell motionless. A panting Dhresden sheathed one sword and gripped the other in both hands, drawing on the last of his energy for the rush he knew was inevitable. Standing there, surrounded by enraged raiders intent upon his death, Dhresden was pleased that at least that Tiblak's daughters were safe, and that neither Jovanna or Mallory were there to witness his death.

A man approaching brought Dhresden out of his reverie. Looking up, he saw his newest adversary: the young man Dhresden had rendered unconscious at the watch fire. Vengeance gleamed in his eyes as he drew nearer.

"My name is Gnaro," he snarled. "A man should know who it is that is about to take his head."

With that, his war staff feinted towards Dhresden. Already moving to bar his thrust, Dhresden was forced to fall to the ground to dodge the younger man's actual blow. Coming again to his feet, Dhresden chided himself for his mistake. Gnaro again came at him, trying to overcome his enemy with shear force. Little by little, Dhresden's strength was failing. Finally, Gnaro solidly struck Dhresden in the chest with the heavy butt of his staff. Dhresden staggered several feet backwards before falling. Drawing on the last of his strength, he rose quickly, launching his sword from his hands. The Kelvren blade sailed through the air at the unsuspecting Gnaro, spearing him through the neck. The two adversaries fell simultaneously, one dead, the other panting and exhausted, awaiting death at the hands of the remaining Aikon.

The crowd surrounding Dhresden stood stunned, unsure whether it was safe to approach this warrior, an outsider who, like a whirlwind, left destruction all around. Though unable to hear much beyond his own ragged breathing, Dhresden could see three or four of the elder Aikon urgently whispering to one another. Finally agreeing, they ordered him bound. Two raiders moved to secure the exhausted warrior, but before either had taken a full step, they both fell, unmoving, to the ground. An arrow protruded from the chest of each of them, but from where the missiles had come, none could tell. Several moments passed without incident, and the order was again given to bind Dhresden. Once again, arrows sped to prevent the order's fulfillment. This time, four Aikon fell dead. Leaving their intended prisoner, the Aikon fled to the shadows, hoping to determine the location of this new foe. After another passage of quiet, Dhresden heard someone approaching. With great effort, he turned his head in the direction of the footfalls. He could see a large dark shape drawing nearer. It moved neither slowly nor quickly, apparently content with an unhurried pace. At the edge of the torchlight, the form of a man could be discerned, though, even in the shadows, it was evident that he bore no weapons. Stepping into the light, he was immediately recognized by Dhresden. The man known only as Uncle walked first to the body of Gnaro and pulled the Kelvren blade from his throat. The big man wiped the blade upon the clothes of the fallen man, seemingly oblivious to the Aikon lurking in the shadows. Turning to Dhresden, he sheathed his sword for him and deftly hoisted the smaller man across his shoulders. As he turned to go the way he had come, a dozen or more Aikon rushed from the shadows to strike the bigger man to the ground. Again, arrows flew with deadly accuracy, stopping the rush and sending the raiders again fleeing to the shadows.

Once in the shadows, Uncle's pace quickened. Though the Aikon had been held at bay, they were numerous. Escape was now the only way to victory. As he was borne away, Dhresden kept his eyes to the rear, watchful for the pursuit he knew was certain. Uncle had gone several strides when two smaller forms fell in behind him. Dhresden found himself looking upon the familiar beautiful faces of Shika and Tala. Except for a brief smile of reassurance, the sisters' faces were masked in determination; they too knew the odds were against success. Uncle led them toward the river, winding his way through trees and other brush to hide their passage. Soon they came to the edge of the river. Uncle lowered Dhresden to the ground and, with the ladies, searched the black waters for some sign of help. Far along the shore to the right, torchlight began to spring up, and then also to the left. It seemed as if the Aikon had fanned out behind their quarry and were now seeking to corral them. Time dragged on as the torchlight drew closer, now dimly visible to the rear. Still no one came. Dhresden, as rested as he could be, struggled to his feet.

"It would appear as if you have forfeited your lives for naught," Dhresden commented. "Though for your valor, I thank you."

Tala smiled a rare smile. "Nothing is for naught when it is done for the good of another. That is why we are here. That is why you are here, Dhresden of Havenstone." Dhresden's surprise was obvious. "Yes," Tala continued with another smile, "we know who you are, and what you are about. As lord of Havenstone, you have rights to whatever you wish within these lands, and yet you paid Hardy for your room and board, in excess, I might add. And now, here you are, laying down your life that others might live. You are a ruler like few others, and you must ascend your throne."

Somewhat taken aback by her brief speech, Dhresden took a moment to respond. "How did you know where to find me?" he asked.

"One of the locals probably told them," came a familiar voice. The four squinted at the water, finally discerning Saric and Xadu coasting to shore. "Come aboard, friends!" Tiblak called. The Aikon were now dangerously close. Dhresden and Tala scrambled atop Xadu, while Shika and Uncle boarded Saric. As the rescuers passed safely and silently down river, the Aikon resigned themselves to the reality that their quarry had escaped.

CHAPTER 8

The two behemoth bore their silent cargo swiftly along, aided by the current. Fatigue and relief muzzled the joy each felt at the success of their mission. Tiblak sat with his younger daughter, his arms gently about her as she dozed. Phyrus sat aboard Xadu in much the same posture, his bride-to-be asleep in his arms. Jovanna sat quietly, rejoicing that her dream had been just that: a dream. She looked at her stepson before her, and the young lady that had saved him. Just what the future held for Dhresden, Lord of Havenstone, none could tell, but his allies were growing in number.

The return trip to Tiblak's burrow proved to take considerably less time than the journey to the Aikon village. As they drew close to Tiblak's home, the sun, whose setting rays had bid them fare-well, now greeted their safe return with a glorious sunrise. Breaking the surface with shouts of triumph, Phyrus, Tiblak and his daughters leaped to the waiting arms of Zhanda and the other children. Laughter mingled with tears several moments. Dhresden and the others dismounted quietly, wishing to allow their hosts their special time of reunion. Zhanda, who had been listening intently to Phyrus, came quickly to Dhresden and embraced him.

"Phyrus tells me that you placed my daughters' safety above your own. Thank you. This family is forever indebted to you."

"This family," Dhresden responded gently, "owes me nothing. Your kindness has been reward enough."

"Not so," Tiblak interjected. "Long have those of the Bog watched the lords of Havenstone, fearing that the mantle would be passed to one of questionable character. It is clear, young lord, that you follow closely in the wisdom and uprightness of your father

Dhane and your grandfather Telfor. We here pledge ourselves to you; we place ourselves at your service."

At this, Phyrus, Tiblak, and all of the healer's family knelt before a stunned Dhresden.

"With as much as is within me," Tiblak continued, "I will rally the Elaleu and any of the inhabitants of the Bog that I can to your aid."

Gathering his wits, Dhresden bid them rise. "For your allegiance, I thank you. But how can you speak for the whole of your people when they would not unite with you to retrieve your daughters?"

"The Elaleu have an interesting mindset about the happenings within the Bog," Tiblak responded. "Most are concerned only about their own families, while some extend their responsibilities to include their nearest neighbors. The Aikon are considered our brothers, in that they should not be obliterated in battle. Neither should they be denied new blood into their lines. No one wants their children taken by Aikon, but few there are that are willing to retrieve those abducted."

"But," Orrick asked, "if that is the mindset, how can you expect to unite them?"

"As I said, that is the mindset about the events within the Bog. We are not, however, blind to the happenings beyond our borders. With the passing of your father Dhane, we first feared that his successor would lack integrity. That fear put to rest, we now fear the opposition you may face—that you must be facing, to choose to pass through the Bog. To preserve all we know, the Elaleu, and even the Aikon if the need is great enough, would come willingly to your aid."

"It may be," Dhresden said, "that I will require the aid of the Elaleu, but that is not yet known. For now, all I require of you is rest and guidance out of the Bog. We leave tomorrow morning."

With that, Dhresden and his companions, now including Shika, Tala, and Uncle, retired. Though the sun had scarcely risen, the rescue team was well worn from the night's excursion. Tiblak and the others shared a small breakfast and the details of their adventures with Zhanda and the children for a short while before themselves retiring. Hours passed while the wearied ones slept; Zhanda and the younger children quietly busied themselves with the usual chores of the day, as well as the preparations for a feast that evening to celebrate the successful return of Uita and Cle.

Towards dusk, the travelers bound for Havenstone awoke to the tantalizing aroma of Zhanda's cooking and a quiet, happy melody. Stretching and looking about, Dhresden spied Tiblak strumming a harp-like instrument, as well as Phyrus playing a small drum. As he noticed that his guests were awake, Tiblak smiled a wide grin. His gentle strumming evolved into a lively plucking, and as Phyrus changed his cadence to match it, some of the children began dancing about. Some exhibited leaps and twirls, while others contented themselves with simple rhythmic swaying. On they danced a while, and then one by one they went to their guests, starting with Dhresden, and led them to a seat near the fire. As the music and dancing continued, the meal, for which their mouths had begun watering, was brought out. Leafy greens were a staple among the Elaleu, but it was the plates of smoked meat that had pulled them from slumber. Each plate was laden with bite sized cubes of meat: various fishes, goose and some snake.

After most had finished eating, the dancing resumed, this time Tiblak's children were not contented to be the only ones dancing. Cle came and took Dhresden's hand, and though he was reserved in his movements, he and the young woman waltzed gracefully about. One by one, the children charmed their guests into a dance. Orrick proved to be the most reluctant, giving in only when Mallory helped win him over.

Taking a respite from dancing, Dhresden looked about at his friends. How tempting it was to remain in this burrow, with these companions: hidden, safe, loved. A twinge of sadness edged into his mind. What victories, what defeats, lay ahead for these people? The future was anything but sure, only that hardship could be expected. Throughout his reverie, he found himself often with his eyes upon Tala. Her red-haired sister was clearly the more outspoken, laughing loudly and twirling about with the others who were dancing. Tala herself had even traipsed about with the children; and while she was not unfriendly, she was often quiet and thoughtful, content to watch. Dhresden also knew the legend of Nokoma and the bows of Paynmar, and while both of the sisters were lovely, his eyes were drawn to Tala.

"She is captivating," Jovanna commented. She had sat down unnoticed beside Dhresden, who smiled sheepishly and took a drink. "And clearly she is impressed with the new lord of Havenstone."

Dhresden's smile faded as he spoke. "I am not concerned so much with her assessment of me as a ruler, my lady, as I am with her approval of me as a man. The people will cheer the king while the sun and rain harmonize with their crops, but should the sun burn too hotly, or the rain wash their harvest away, eventually the ruler is the one they blame. You know this as well as I, for it was a burden father carried. But you saw through all the circumstances of the day, the floods and droughts, you gazed upon the man who bore all he could, as well as some things too great for him. True, Dhane was a great ruler, but it was not his crown that made him the man that he was; it was his integrity, his resolve, his compassion for the people, and his hunger for truth. 'No man stands so tall as he who stands for truth, or he who stoops to aid the oppressed.' How many times did he tell me that? Dhane ruled to serve, but it was the heart of the man that guided the crown of the king. If I cannot stand for truth, if I cannot aid the oppressed, if the king the people see is not the man who walks the dim corridors of the citadel, then I have no business even considering Tala, or of being lord of Havenstone."

Dhresden lapsed into silence. Not even to himself had he been so forthcoming as he had just shared with Jovanna. As the moments dragged by, Dhresden feared that Jovanna had interpreted his openness as a rebuttal rather than an expression in confidence.

"We both understand the necessity of uprightness, Dhresden," she said softly, "that public opinion is worthless if your heart is corrupt. But it seems to me that this dark-haired daughter of Nokoma has already glimpsed your character and even grasped your heart, the heart and character of a noble man."

Again silence passed between the two as the revelers rejoiced in dance and song. Finally, Dhresden turned his eyes to Jovanna.

"I did not intend to burden you with these thoughts, but I thank you for your wise counsel. I am blessed indeed to have you as a confidant." He placed an arm about her as the two leaned close, Dhresden placing a kiss atop her head. "And now, if you will excuse me..."

Dhresden rose as he spoke, a smile spreading across his face. He dodged and wove his way through the bounding children until he stood before Tala. She sat looking up at him, a grin teasing the corners of her mouth as she wondered at his approach.

Bowing low but keeping his eyes locked with hers, Dhresden held out his hand. "Join me?" he asked simply.

Tala rose wordlessly, though her full smile conveyed her delight. Their dance was a lively one: an expression of joy, an appreciation of life and loved ones.

The celebration continued a while longer, until all reluctantly agreed that they should retire for tomorrow's journey out of the Bog. Once again, Tiblak and his family expressed their thanks to Dhresden and the others and bid them goodnight. Sleep quickly overcame the still weary rescuers, and with it joyful dreams of dancing and loved ones, though at the fringe of some dreams of those bound for Havenstone, an unknown terror watched, waiting.

~ ~ ~

The sun rose quietly over the Bog, unseen by those below ground. Nevertheless, Dhresden and his companions had already risen and prepared what provisions they had. They now sat one last time about Tiblak's fire, eating a light breakfast Zhanda had prepared with an eye toward their journey; though small in portion, it filled their bellies.

"Do you head now for the Pasturelands and Havenstone?" Tiblak asked.

"Yes," Dhresden answered. "It is urgent that I return. If we travel south and east from here we should arrive in two and a half days."

"Phyrus went scouting a bit while you slept." The tone of Tiblak's voice brought all eyes expectantly to Phyrus.

"It seems that the edge of the Bog is being patrolled by bands of soldiers," he announced. "I spied several groups, numbering at least eighty. They are garbed in blue and yellow and appear well armed."

"Oxmen!" Orrick spat out the word with obvious distaste, while Dhresden's brow furrowed.

"It is doubtful," Jovanna cautioned, "that Treyherne dispatched so many to provide you safe passage."

"If you wish, Phyrus and I will ferry you half a day down river. It may be that the troops are less concentrated to the south."

"Your hospitality knows no bounds, does it, my friend," Dhresden smiled. "However, I fear that the Oxmen will be patrolling the whole of the border. We would only be delaying an encounter, not avoiding one. No, we will head directly for Havenstone. We may find ourselves traveling mostly at night, but we shall observe the attitude of these Oxmen secretly in daylight, and then choose our course. Regrettably, we must depart."

Amidst embraces and words of comfort, the travelers bid their hosts farewell and mounted Saric and Xadu for passage to the surface. Tiblak and Phyrus accompanied them, the older man handing Dhresden a small gift as he and the others dismounted. Tiblak's gift was a small earthen vial.

"This is the nectar of a rare Bog plant once named *ferial* by the Elves. It was initially used as a healing agent to accelerate a patient's recovery, whether from injury or illness. As with all good things, its use became twisted. Eventually, the nectar of *ferial* was used by warriors to gain advantage in battle. For a time, *ferial* gave ferocity and energy to its partakers such as could not be overcome. One of the side effects was blinding rage, a bloodlust such as would diminish the capacity for reasonable thought. Though the initial effects faded, it was discovered that repeated use of the nectar eventually drove its benefactors permanently insane. I give it to you as a healing agent. There is enough here for four healing doses, though I hope this vial sits upon your mantle to the end of this age. If used as other than medicine, it could prove more of a curse than a blessing; I beg you to employ its use only in the face of certain death."

"Thank you, my friend," Dhresden said. "I hope to never uncork this bottle, even for medicinal use, but am grateful for your concern. Farewell; I bid you blessings."

With that, Dhresden led his troupe from Tiblak's sight, towards the next leg of their adventure.

CHAPTER 9

Almost two hours passed as Dhresden guided his diverse group through the thick vegetation of the Bog, carefully avoiding the soft sinking pits that seemed almost to creep into their path. Twice Uncle almost stepped to jeopardy, while Wyeth was fortunate to have Orrick near when the old Kelvren plunged from sight. The Black Wanderer leaped to his aid, thrusting his great arm in after him and heaving the sputtering man to safety.

At the head of the column, Dhresden paused often, glancing back at his friends, he told himself, to be sure they were not overtaxed. In truth, he knew, he longed to again be close to Tala. She had taken up position near the end of the column with the other archers, namely her sister and Wyeth. Dhresden thought again of the dance they had shared, of her eyes as they sparkled in the firelight, her smile glowing in the half light, of how her hand fit his own as if it had been sculpted to match his.

The young ruler was shaken from his thoughts by Orrick's whispered warning, "My lord, the spoor on the wind indicates that we are not far from the edge of the Pasturelands, and the Oxmen."

Dhresden turned to his friend and smiled. "Shall we traipse into view and allow them to escort us to the Outcropping?"

Orrick snorted his disdain. As his smile faded, Dhresden gave Orrick a slight nod, and the nimble giant disappeared amidst the underbrush. Here the vegetation transitioned from the lush greenery of the Bog to the hardwoods native to the Pasturelands. The climatic difference in the Bog was astounding. While the other lands experienced marked seasons, the Bog seemed to remain in a season of perpetual spring. Some attributed this to heat generated by decaying humus, while others proposed a more superstitious cause. Whatever the reason, the Bog was a veritable greenhouse of vegetation. Entering the Pasturelands, the foliage was undergoing the changes of autumn.

The others remained watchful as they awaited Orrick's return, while Dhresden considered their choices. The terrain of the Pasturelands was easy going, but sparse for cover. It was aptly named for its rolling fields, and though there were thick groves of trees in which to take refuge, the distance between them almost guaranteed discovery. Ground could be covered more quickly on horseback if they had mounts, but the roving Oxmen patrols were sure to discover them on foot. A smaller group of one, two, or even three could perhaps pass unnoticed but not a group of ten. Hearing a slight rustling, Dhresden turned to see Orrick returning. The big man's report harbored no solutions.

"The Oxmen are patrolling in loose groups of three," he said. "If they maintain their spacing, we will be spotted as soon as we break cover. Those patrolling the edge of the Pasturelands are steer mounted: slower than horses, but fast enough to apprehend us. Beyond this first patrol, it appears as if there are roaming groups of horsemen, also in threes."

Silence ensued as each considered his words and weighed their options, knowing the decision would be Dhresden's alone.

They did not have long to wait. "It is more or less as I expected," Dhresden announced. "Our only opportunity will be under cover of night. The darkness will hinder our progress considerably. We will set our course by the groves within the Pasturelands. In each grove, we will regroup and, if too near dawn, set up camp. Once we reach the orchards around the Outcropping, we will scout out our entrance into Havenstone and then the Citadel. Until sundown, rest; tonight's trek will be paced as quickly and quietly as we can."

The group had prepared thoroughly before leaving Tiblak's burrow, now there was little else to do while awaiting nightfall. Hunger was sated with dried fruit and meats, while conversation was limited to occasional hushed whispers. Here and there some dozed, though most sat or stood, looking about or staring at nothing.

"Worried about Asha?" Mallory whispered. She had observed the big man searching the brush with his eyes, and occasionally sniffing at the wind.

"I expect her to join us at any time," Orrick answered, "but prefer she arrive either now or after we reach the orchards. If the horses or steer catch her scent, they may be spooked and alert the Oxmen to our presence."

"Should we be worried about them catching our scent?"

"No," Orrick almost chuckled, "most beasts bearing men's burdens become like their masters when it comes to detecting spoor: weak. But if they smell a creature of the wild like Asha, fear will seize them; the Oxmen will no doubt investigate."

The two lapsed into silence with the others, resigned to waiting. As the sun continued its journey across the autumn sky, its beams shone down through the canopy of colored leaves dancing about in the light and the breeze. Little of the beauty around them succeeded in keeping their minds from the task ahead of them, and the sacrifices that may be required.

In due time, the sun began its descent behind the mountains of Orrick's birth. Dhresden and Orrick crept to the edge of the trees and decided upon a copse large enough in which they could all take cover from the eyes of the Oxmen when the sun again rose. Returning to the others, Dhresden addressed his companions.

"I stand here before you," he began, "in mourning and grief; for I fear that we will at least taste of pain, though some may see death. It has been my honor to have led you this far, but now I beg you, my friends, go and live out your lives in peace. I release each of you from any debt you may feel you owe me or my fathers. Please, go now and be at peace." With that, the young ruler turned his face toward the Outcropping and began his twilight journey. As one, the others fell into step behind him, shadows following a shadow.

Again at the edge of the Pasturelands, Dhresden and Orrick stood looking out over the blackness. The wind favored them, as it blew from the direction of their destination, allowing Orrick's nose to sense what lay ahead. The Wanderer set a quick pace and set out across the open field. The cool of autumn had silenced the buzz of insects that was common during the summer months; the only sound now was the rustle of the waist-high grasses as they swayed gently in the breeze. The sky was cloudless, allowing a clear view of the stars as they winked at the pilgrims' progress. Their race was not against the dawn alone, but also the brightness of the moon's beams once it rose. It was nearing full, and though it would help to light their path, it could also reveal their presence to the Oxmen. Not once did Orrick stop as they made their way along, and as the moon crested the horizon a couple of hours before sunrise, the ten travelers entered the shelter of the small copse of trees, just large enough and thick enough to hide their presence. Winded and wearied from their jaunt, they rolled themselves into their cloaks and slept, allowing Uncle and Wyeth the first watch. The sun had risen when Orrick was awakened roughly. Something large and strong rammed forcefully into his shoulder, shoving him sideways from where he slept with his back to a small tree. Rolling to one knee, daggers drawn, he found himself face to face with Asha. Uncle and Wyeth, who had been close to completing their watch, hurried toward the ruckus, expecting to find Oxmen among them. Both men stopped short when they saw the large gray cougar, now nuzzling the giant's chest.

"But—how—she—" they both stammered.

Orrick chuckled his delight. "Do not dismay, my friends. I myself was not aware of her coming until she battered into me. She must have followed my scent, facing the wind, preventing me from scenting her." Slowly Orrick's brow creased with concern.

"What is it?" Mallory asked.

"Maybe nothing, but I hope Asha came to us unnoticed by the Oxmen. I would not desire a standoff in this sparse cluster of trees."

At his comment, they all took up positions at the edges of the cops, gazing out at the rolling meadows to inspect the activity of the patrolling Oxmen. After several moments without cause for concern, the ten travelers, and Asha, rejoined one another in the center of their hideout.

"I believe that the best plan for the daylight hours," Dhresden announced, "is to place five groups of two around the perimeter.

Take the watch in turns: we cannot afford not to rest. Talk only in signs and whispers, and rouse us all if anything appears suspect."

They quickly separated and took up posts—the twins together, Wyeth with Jovanna, Uncle and Shika, Mallory with Orrick and Asha. Dhresden's heart thrilled to find himself sitting at the edge of cover, with the woman who had occupied his thoughts so much of late. Though Tala intended to watch so Dhresden might rest, he knew that sleep would evade him for the beating of his heart. Instead, the two sat each with their backs to a maple sapling, content with the silence as they looked out over the meadow. Hours had passed when Tala offered him some dried fruit. Realizing that he had not yet eaten, Dhresden accepted her gift with a nod and a smile. A short time later, Tala insisted that Dhresden rest. Amused by her resolve, he consented. Leaning his head back against the small tree, Dhresden gazed at her through almost closed eyes. He enjoyed watching her without her knowing, her face serene as she looked about. It struck him as somewhat curious that one so lovely could send her arrows upon the enemy with such deadly accuracy. Dhresden wondered about her childhood, her dreams for the future, and about her mind towards him. He wondered how long he had been asleep when he was awakened by her hand upon his shoulder.

With a smile, Tala set him at ease. "All is well," she whispered. "I was hoping to take a rest also, if you are refreshed."

Dhresden answered her by offering his cloak for a pillow. Tala reclined in the grass, her head upon the folded cloak. It seemed to Dhresden that she went to sleep as soon as she lay down, her breathing even and quiet. With effort, Dhresden looked out over the meadow, wishing he could sit and gaze upon this dark-haired woman who so captivated him.

An hour before sunset, Dhresden roused Tala. She awoke well-rested but hungry. Leaving her to nibble at her fare, Dhresden and Orrick consulted about the next leg of their journey.

"The moon will rise almost an hour later tonight," Dhresden noted. "We should be able to cover more ground than last night."

"Indeed," the bigger man agreed, "but unless the wind favors us again tonight, we may stumble upon some of the Oxmen in the dark.

It is likely that even if dispatched quietly, their absence would alert the others to our presence."

Dhresden nodded, thinking. He had already provided opportunity for his companions to leave the expedition, but despite their resolve, he wished to spare each of them from loss.

"Head for cover at the edge of the Merchant route. If there is time, we will cross that thoroughfare tonight."

Again they were off, the shadows of night about them, the stars overhead the only witness of their passage. The days shortened as autumn crept toward winter, providing a longer night for their surreptitious journey. As Orrick had feared, the wind was not cooperating. Heading due west, the breeze blew gently from the north; a cool air bringing the scents of man and beast alike to his nostrils. Unfortunately, this only revealed to Orrick what lay directly to the north, while ahead of their cautious footsteps lay the unknown. On they walked in silence, peering about intently at every shadow, at every clump of grass or brush that may hide or actually be an enemy. At once, Orrick's nose was assaulted by the pungent scent of Oxmen steer. Stopping quickly, the hair at the nape of his neck prickled as Asha emitted a low rumbling growl. Suddenly, three dark forms rose from the cover of the tall grass, swords sliding from sheaths.

"In the name of Lord Treyherne, who seeks passage!?" demanded the leader of the trio.

"The true lord of Havenstone," Orrick boomed. "Put away your weapons and give passage to your rightful ruler!"

Hushed whispers, indistinct, floated briefly upon the gentle wind, and then, "Orrick?" The voice was strong, yet uncertain. Unsure of what was to come, Dhresden signaled the archers to one side for clear shots while he and the others gripped the hilts of their weapons in readiness. The three Oxmen made no advance, though more unintelligible whispering drifted to Orrick's ears. Finally, the man spoke again.

"I am glad you have returned, Orrick," he said. "I had feared that one of Treyherne's lackeys had disposed of you. Not that it would have been easily accomplished," he added with a chuckle.

As the man spoke, Orrick and Dhresden both recognized the voice of Jzengei, an Oxmen captain. They had encountered the man often in the Citadel, both in military capacity as well as casually. Though Jzengei had always been friendly, there was also an air about him that did not set well with the two friends. Orrick cast a sideways glance at Dhresden before he responded.

"Who do you have with you, Jzengei?"

"Just Akhin and Stafford, but we are ready to escort you safely to the Outcropping in the morning."

Tension mounted in the darkness while Dhresden and Orrick whispered almost imperceptibly. The only sound reaching the ears of the three Oxmen was the soft rustle of the grasses in the autumn breeze.

"There is no reason for you to abandon your post and endanger yourself, Jzengei," Orrick finally replied to the darkness. "The two of us will continue alone."

"Two of you? It was rumored that there were more in your group," Jzengei sounded more confused than suspicious, but that did not allay Dhresden's doubts.

"You should have learned by now not to trust to rumors," Orrick paused. "We take our leave of you now, Jzengei."

"And we take our leave of you, mountain man." Jzengei's tone turned to a sneer as he and his attendants lunged forward through the grass, shouting to any Oxmen within earshot. Their attack was cut short by the whoosh of arrows as Wyeth and the sisters fired their missiles. Though they had been quickly silenced, Oxmen could be heard rallying all about them.

"Follow Orrick, as quick as you can!" Dhresden ordered.

Silence had become secondary as they raced forward, hoping to elude the now alert Oxmen, though unsure what refuge they might find in the sparse cover as dawn also approached.

On they rushed, Orrick leading the way through the graying darkness, the sounds of pursuit flanking them. Dhresden's mind raced as he ran. *The Oxmen will pursue in a zigzag pattern, hoping to discover us. If we have not gained a lead by sunup, they will easily locate and overtake us,* he reasoned. As a plan formed in his mind, he left his rearward position to join Orrick at the front. Quickly the young ruler conveyed his strategy to the giant. Though reluctant to comply, Orrick recognized not only the wisdom of the plan but also the necessity of it. Dropping behind Orrick, Dhresden began to notify the others. They were to split up into three groups, thus more easily avoiding discovery. Each group was to cross the merchant route by dawn if possible, find cover and camp until dark. Dhresden took Tala, Uncle, and Khalid, heading north across the merchant route. Though loathe to part, Orrick and Mallory led separate groups, their familiarity with the area necessitating their roles as guides. Mallory, Wyeth, and Khaldun continued almost due west; Orrick, Jovanna, Shika and Asha angled to the south before taking a westerly course toward another section of the merchant route. Theirs being the most indirect path, they were certain to be the last to rejoin the others.

Mallory raced along, Wyeth and Khaldun in tow, intent on crossing the merchant route before daylight. As she ran, she found herself almost smiling. She was pleased to see Dhresden taking the lead so well; seeing the need and quickly meeting it, even skillfully placing an archer in each group. Focusing upon the task at hand, her smile faded. Though the sounds of the Oxmen dogging after them had become less distinct, the sun's rays had begun to crest the horizon behind them. Pressing forward yet more swiftly, Mallory slowed only when she realized that the road lay just ahead. Fighting to keep their now ragged breathing hushed, the three crept quietly to the sparse cover at the road's edge. Peering cautiously about, they inspected each shadow, bush and tree bole for signs of the Oxmen. Finally satisfied, Mallory, Wyeth, and Khaldun scurried across the merchant route and into the shadow of a few scrub trees and brush, collapsing to the ground as the sun's beams streamed across the Pasturelands.

CHAPTER 10

Orrick thundered silently along, surprised at how well the two women kept up with him. He had not expected them to keep pace so well, but could tell by their breathing that they would not be able to maintain such a rigorous stride for long. He slowed slightly, preferring a slower pace over stopping altogether. Asha loped along effortlessly beside him, content to travel with the Black Wanderer at whatever speed he chose. Looking back again at Jovanna and Shika, Orrick saw the sun rising relentlessly behind them. It had been doubtful that they would cross the road before darkness dissipated, but that had still been their hope. Now Orrick turned his attention to finding cover for them all. The trees around them offered too little concealment and he had begun to despair when he practically fell into their hideout. Leaping over some larger stones rising up out of the grasses, Orrick landed lower than he had anticipated. A natural depression behind the rocks became their resting place, its grasses reaching up to easily conceal them from the eyes of the Oxmen soldiers, while the rocks at the edges of the depression offered enough troublesome footing to keep the Oxmen mounts from treading too closely. Jovanna and Shika slid down the rocks into the shade of the grasses, relieved to cease running. After slaking their thirsts from the waterskins they carried, all four—the two women, the giant, and the cougar—allowed themselves to drift to sleep, content that even in slumber Orrick and Asha would be alert to any danger.

The danger arrived sooner than expected. Sleep had wrapped its arms around them quickly, holding them close in its embrace less than an hour when both Asha and Orrick were ripped from sleep's

grasp by the brutish breathing of several Oxmen mounts. Though
Orrick had earlier feared that the steer would catch Asha's scent
and discover their location, the still air now about them gave him
hope that her spoor would not be carried to their dull nostrils. Not
wanting the ladies to startle awake, Orrick decided to let them continue in slumber. Again closing his eyes, Orrick sought not sleep,
but knowledge of the enemy. Though the still air benefited him, it
also prevented him from numbering the Oxmen by scent. Instead,
he examined every whisper of cloth, every murmur of man and beast
that came to his ears. After a while, Orrick concluded that they had
narrowly escaped the dogged pursuit of at least a dozen Oxmen. The
Oxmen had clearly lost the trail of their quarry and were weaving
through the Pasturelands hoping to stumble upon their trail or even
the fugitives themselves. Another hour passed before Orrick could no
longer detect their presence. Relieved that the enemy had departed,
Orrick refreshed himself from his waterskin and gave himself once
more to sleep's embrace.

~ ~ ~

Well to their north, Dhresden and his detachment had made
good time to the merchant route, crossing unseen in dawn's last
shades of gray. Khalid volunteered to keep first watch. Dhresden and
Tala nestled down close to each other while Uncle reclined against
the bole of a small tree. It seemed that they had left their pursuers well behind, leaving their rendezvous with their comrades easily
before them. Dhresden and Tala longed to savor their time together,
but, resigned to their circumstances, kept quiet and were soon asleep.
The sun was reaching its zenith when Khalid gently roused Dhresden
awake. The young ruler was signaled to silence by the older Makani,
who then motioned for him to follow. As he fell in step behind
Khalid, Dhresden glanced back at Tala. He was struck by how beautiful she was even in slumber. He noticed that Uncle was nowhere in
sight, but it seemed that whatever he and Khalid were about was not
worth waking Tala.

"What have you two been up to?" Dhresden whispered once
they were out of earshot.

"I have come up with a plan to get you and myself into the Citadel," Khalid answered. "Uncle and I discussed it and he finally agreed, but I did not think it necessary to involve Tala."

Dhresden slowed. "We already have a plan, Khalid," he said. "We have no cause to alter our course. Please explain your reasoning."

"Yes, of course," Khalid assured him, still leading him away from camp. "As we have traveled together, our number has grown. This has made it increasingly difficult to pass undetected through the Pasturelands, and though we have come quite far, I am loathe to see any more of our group come to harm, or worse."

The Makani stopped walking and stood looking down into a patch of low scrub brush. Stepping up beside him, Dhresden peered into the bushes. There lay Uncle, blood trickled from his mouth and nose, as well as from an ugly gash over his left eye. Quickly Dhresden knelt to his side, relieved to find him alive.

"What happened here!?" he demanded.

"As I said," Khalid answered, "I have a plan to enter the Citadel, and Uncle took some convincing to agree to it."

Dhresden whirled to his feet, his swords flying from their sheaths. Both rage and sorrow gripped his heart as he realized that this once trusted man had forsaken his oath, and thereby disgraced the Makani.

"May I remind you," Khalid whispered as twenty Oxmen rose from the sparse cover about them, their weapons at the ready, "I did not think it necessary to involve Tala."

~ ~ ~

Tala awoke with a start. Sitting up quickly and looking around, she realized that something was very wrong. The sun was now setting; dusk settling itself about her, but no one had rallied her to prepare for their nighttime trek. Readying her bow, she made a quick examination of the camp, gradually widening her search until she stumbled upon Uncle, still unconscious. The only evidence of Dhresden she found was his weapons lying nearby Uncle's motionless body. Sprinkling water from her canteen upon his face, Tala was relieved to see Uncle's eyelids flutter and then open. Focusing his bleary eyes on her concerned face, Uncle bolted to his feet, only to sink slowly to his hands and knees.

Tala's prior relief vanished. She had seen Uncle battle many men at once, and even some creatures of legend, but had never seen him so weakened and disoriented.

"What happened?"

"Khalid—so fast—no time—" Uncle's eyes closed and his voice trailed off. His head sagged toward earth and Tala feared he would again lose consciousness. Suddenly his head snapped up, his eyes finally free of the haze from his beating. "Dhresden! Where is he?" He scrambled to his feet, steadily this time, looking about for the young lord.

"I do not know, Uncle. I awoke a short time ago, wondering where you all were." Unable to contain herself, Tala reached up and took his head in her hands, turning him to face her directly. Startled, Uncle finally gave her his full attention. "What happened, where is Dhresden?"

"Darkness has now claimed the Pasturelands," Uncle declared. He turned and gathered up Dhresden's arsenal as he spoke. "I will tell you all that has passed, but now let us depart and seek Orrick."

~~~

Khalid had crept quietly into the makeshift camp, pleased to see Dhresden and Tala sleeping soundly. Silently he woke Uncle, motioning that the bigger man follow him. Finally far enough from camp, Khalid turned to face Uncle.

"We have a problem," he said, eyeing Uncle as several Oxmen rose up from the surrounding brush.

Stunned, Uncle looked about at the enemy, then back at an unconcerned Khalid. His confusion fading, Uncle's fists clenched and he leapt toward the smaller man. "Traitor!" he snarled.

Uncle saw a strange, cold smile spread across Khalid's face. As the bigger man closed the gap between them, Khalid met him with a blur of movement such as Uncle had never before encountered. The Makani rained down blow upon blow, rendering Uncle unconscious in but a moment.

~ ~ ~

Uncle and Tala hurried through the darkness, relieved to encounter no Oxmen, but also afraid that with Dhresden's capture all the patrols had been recalled to the Outcropping. Tala had no doubt that Orrick and the others would join them in rescuing Dhresden, a feat made more difficult if the Oxmen were in force within the Outcropping. The hours passed slowly for Tala, her entire being tortured at the unknown dangers her beloved half-blood now faced. Her fears increased when they crossed the access road that stretched from the Outcropping to the Merchant Route without Oxmen interference. Finally, after what seemed many days, they entered the groves south of the Outcropping. Sunlight was creeping over the eastern horizon, promising to reveal their presence if they did not find cover soon. Risking discovery in the hopes of quickly locating the others, Tala and Uncle scurried among the various trees and waning shadows. In the increasing light and mounting frustration, the two seekers crawled under the concealment of the tangled limbs of an apple tree. Sorrow gripped Tala as she leaned against Uncle, his large form powerless to comfort her.

"What has happened?" demanded Orrick, his concerned whisper booming in their ears.

Peering through the tree limbs, they spotted the giant approaching as if he had tracked them, which in truth he had. Orrick's group was supposed to have been the last to arrive. When he found Dhresden and the others were missing, he had begun patrolling the edge of the groves in anticipation of their arrival. Missing them, but finding the spoor of their passing, the Wanderlander set to pursuing them.

Tala and Uncle climbed from beneath the tree, Tala's words spilling from her with a flood of tears. Guiding the two along towards the others, Orrick filtered her deluge through his mind, quickly realizing the seriousness of the situation. They entered a section of the grove where the trees grew taller, littering the ground with various nuts, but allowing their group to reunite in comfort as well as concealment. Seeing only the three of them approach, Jovanna, Mallory and Shika rushed to comfort Tala, her distress evident. After allowing the women a moment of hugs, whispers, and weeping, Orrick addressed the entire group.

"Khalid has joined with Treyherne in his treachery," he began, his eyes resting upon the younger Makani, whose posture stiffened as he prepared to protest. "He beat Uncle senseless," he continued, "but not before Uncle saw the Oxmen that Khalid had gathered to himself." Khaldun's spirit withered visibly, to be quickly revived by his outrage.

"We must rescue Lord Havenstone at once," he declared.

"Yes, young friend," Orrick said, calming him, "but Khalid knew our plan to access the Outcropping from the orchards. It may be that fifty Oxmen are now marching upon us. If so, we cannot delay. We must move in the light of day, accepting the risk, to avoid almost certain demise."

"But how can we enter the Citadel in daylight without discovery?" Wyeth demanded, his Kelvren brow furrowed.

"I had planned to scale the face of the Outcropping from the lakeside, but we would be unable to defend ourselves as we ascended in daylight. Now I am reluctant to concede, that I know no recourse other than to hide until nightfall and then attempt the climb."

"No!" Mallory exclaimed. "There is another way. When we were young and Dhresden would come to visit, we explored most every inch of the Outcropping, even the sewers. That is how we will enter."

"My lady," Orrick solemnly replied, "each of the sewer drains is sealed with thick bars; Dhresden and I saw to that ourselves."

In spite of his reply, Mallory smiled sweetly at him. "Not every hiding place I found was one I shared; I needed one or two places to hide that Dhresden did not know about."

CHAPTER 11

M allory led the group through the groves to the edge of the lake, known as Loch Norde. It was fed by a river that began in the mountains and, being fed by the always snowcapped spires of Orrick's birth, Loch Norde was quite cold. The Outcropping towered ominously above the rescuers as they followed Mallory into the chilly water at the rock's foundation. She led them along a submerged ledge at the base of the Outcropping, the water sometimes at knee height, sometimes as high as the chest. Though Orrick desired otherwise, Asha accompanied them into the water, keeping easy pace even though forced to swim much of the distance. Wyeth kept his peace, though his face betrayed his disdain for the cold water. He, too, was forced to swim the deeper spots. Here and there scrub bushes had taken root in a crack or crevice. Mallory came to a stop beside one of the larger woody plants that jutted out from the rock beside them.

"I discovered this, as I said, when Dhresden and I were exploring in our youth. I carved my name into this little tree," Mallory reminisced, pointing at its dwarfed, scarred trunk, "and now it shows us our entrance into the Citadel."

She looked up, pointing at a spot just above them. The others looked up, searching with their eyes but finding nothing but stone.

"I do not see it," Orrick admitted, "but if it is there, lead us through it."

Mallory smiled, then began scaling the face of the Outcropping, using any vegetation and cracks in the stone for hand and footholds. Ascending less than twenty feet to a shadowed area, she disappeared from sight.

"Mallory!" Orrick exclaimed in as hushed a voice as his heart would allow.

Her head reappeared from the shadows, smiling. "Come along, Orrick, do not fear." With that she again vanished.

Rolling his eyes at Mallory's jesting, Orrick reached to help Jovanna only to find she had already begun her ascent. Once again, the Black Wanderer was impressed with this lady, her elegance and earthiness evident in any situation. Orrick and Asha remained below while the others climbed to the hidden entrance. The giant man wondered if the passage would accommodate the great cat at his side; after all, how large of an opening could be hidden in almost plain sight? When he scaled to the entrance, he was relieved to find that, though it may prove a snug passage, both he and Asha should pass unencumbered. Turning, he gave Asha a low growl. Instantly, the large cougar sprang upward, almost to Orrick's side upon the ledge, her sharp talons pulling her the rest of the distance into the passage. Orrick and Asha crept along the dark tunnel, trailing the scent of the rest of their group. After a time, their spoor grew stronger as man and beast closed the distance between them. Soon Orrick discovered that the floor of the passage dropped off sharply, but in the darkness was unsure of how far. Turning about in the tunnel, the big man pushed himself backwards towards the ledge. Gradually, he lowered his feet toward the unknown, prepared to drag himself back to the safety of the ledge if the drop proved to be too far. The Wanderer almost laughed out loud at himself when he discovered the drop to be not more than three feet. His amusement faded as he discovered naught but sheer stone now before him. Feeling about, it seemed as if the passage had come to a dead end, but his nose told him otherwise. Again trusting to the spoor of his companions, Orrick discovered that the tunnel actually cut back under itself. This section, unlike the last, was narrower and angled down. Soon Orrick was forced to crawl, his wide shoulders and sheathed battle axe barely allowing him passage. He was relieved when he saw dim light ahead. He and Asha emerged from the confines of the stone tunnel, finding themselves in a modestly furnished room, their friends all about them.

"The siege room of the royal family," Orrick said, looking again upon Mallory's grinning face. "I had thought the only entrance to this room to be the one door; it seems my ignorance in this matter is fortunate."

"Absolutely," Mallory agreed, "if you had known, you would have barred the tunnel at both ends in the interest of security, but father believed it prudent to reserve an escape in the event of an invasion. When I showed him my discovery, he told me that the first lord of Havenstone had evidently had it constructed in secrecy, and so its existence passed from knowledge. He asked me to not share its location with anyone unless hard circumstances required it. I agreed, pleased that he trusted me; it also gave me the upper hand in hiding games when Dhresden came to visit." At the memory of her half-brother, Mallory's countenance fell, as did the others'.

"What do we do to get Dhresden back?" It was Tala that broke the silence, her words more of a declaration of resolve than a question.

"First," Orrick announced, "we must discover where they are holding him and what Treyherne plans to do with him. I will take Mallory, Shika, and Khaldun with me. We will return not more than two hours hence. You others rest easy. Asha will alert you if someone other than myself approaches, though I find it unlikely that anyone else would be traipsing about the sewers."

With that, he led the way out of the room into the damp tunnels that made up the drainage system beneath Havenstone. The others resolved themselves to waiting. Tala and Jovanna sat beside each other, neither wanting to sleep, but both unable to escape the fatigue that beset them both physically and emotionally. Soon, the two sat slumped against the wall, fast asleep. Uncle and Wyeth contented themselves with a light meal while they waited. As for their sentry, Asha placed herself near the closed door and lay with her legs tucked under her body, head erect. Though her eyes were closed, the tip of her tail twitched back and forth, attesting to her watchfulness.

～～～

As quickly as he could, Orrick found locations at drainage grates for himself and the others to eavesdrop. In the interest of speed, each was given his own post with instructions to listen and keep out of sight until Orrick returned to collect them at the appropriate time. Unable to see much through the grate besides the sky and the eaves of a couple buildings, Shika could hear and smell the Oxmen stables nearby. Orrick hoped that she may overhear some of the guards gossiping about their prize. Khaldun's vantage point near the main entrance to the Citadel offered a limited view of the Citadel steps if he stood in the right place. The young Makani paced back and forth, able to see from one location but able only to distinguish people's words from practically beneath the grate. Orrick left Mallory beside another entrance to the Citadel while he himself hurried to a drain under the banquet room within the stronghold. Though not as glamorous as storming the Citadel, stealth remained their necessary ally.

Mallory sat in the shadows, her back against the wall of the sewer, eager to hear something—anything—about Dhresden. Few passed this way; lone couriers mostly, on some errand beneath whomever had sent them. The few who traveled together seldom spoke, and then only in hushed whispers. The time seemed to pass so slowly that Mallory began to fear that Orrick had been discovered. It was with great relief that she was startled by his voice in her ear.

"I know where he is, or rather, where he will be," Orrick whispered, "but we must hurry!"

Hand in hand they raced through the gloom to reunite with the others, Khaldun and Shika falling into step as they passed. Soon the four burst into the royal siege room, startling all the occupants to their feet, except Asha.

"If I were any more on edge," Wyeth complained, "each of you would have an arrow stuck in you!" He lowered his bow and replaced an arrow in its quiver.

"We go now," Orrick announced. While each readied for the next aspect of their adventure, the Wanderer shared his newfound knowledge. "I overheard two of the cooks as they prepared Treyherne's evening meal. Treyherne has apparently found Dhresden to be guilty of poisoning Dhane and murdering the rest of us in the Forgotten Wood, of course with the help of Phaelen and the Kelvren."

"So he expects to kill us all," Jovanna said. "Why else would he announce our deaths?"

"Not to mention the hatred for my people he will breed," Wyeth added, "possibly to the point of war."

"What else, Orrick?" Shika spoke quietly, but her concern carried her words to the ears of all. "What will they do with him?"

His face set as stone, only his eyes conveyed his unease. "Treyherne has declared...Firebane." The room became as quiet as death's shadow, none willing to give in to despair.

"It is to be carried out tonight at sunset," Orrick continued. "We have some time to prepare, but must not dally."

"Orrick," Jovanna spoke up, "if we are to do more than prevent Dhresden's death, I will need to retrieve the edict, signed by Dhane, naming Dhresden as his heir."

Orrick shook his head, "We cannot delay, the edict must wait."

"Then I shall go alone, and none shall stop me short of being bound and gagged!"

Before the giant could protest, another spoke up. "No, not alone, my lady." All eyes turned to Khaldun. "I shall accompany you."

His eyes studying the two, Orrick nodded once. "Quick as you can, and meet us back here." As one, they turned to reenter the sewers. "Young Makani," Orrick called, stopping them. "leave me your rope."

~~~

Firebane, a punishment begun in the early days of the Pasturelands, days best forgotten. The first monarch of the Pasturelands was a corrupt warmonger who cared not for his subjects or the laws of the land that the people had established prior to his reign. His name was Claxton. Several times the peoples of the land rose up to dethrone the scoundrel only to be beaten back. To quell these uprisings, Claxton had key leaders of the rebellion seized and publicly executed them. He had ordered a catapult erected atop the Outcropping, and would place a bound "malefactor" in the catapult. Claxton then had the poor soul doused in oil and set fire. After a few agonizing moments, he would order the catapult released, launching the burning, screaming man, or woman, far out into the waters of Loch Norde. Twenty-three men and four women had suffered the rigors of Firebane. This horrific punishment kept the subjects compliant for many years, until a successful coup, led by the only man ever to survive Firebane, abolished its practice and the rule of Claxton.

It was the resurrection of this sordid history of Havenstone that spurred Dhresden's seven remaining companions quickly along their way: Jovanna and Khaldun to retrieve Dhane's declaration, Orrick and the others to save their friend from his fiery doom by force.

It had been long years since Jovanna had traversed the sewers beneath Havenstone, but the matriarch led her companion through the gloom with a resolve and confidence of direction that would have convinced an onlooker that she had passed this way only the day before. So it was that in long moments that seemed hours they came to a stop beneath a trapdoor leading to the bedchamber Jovanna had shared with the king Dhane in his life. She and Khaldun stood there listening, eager to proceed, but unwilling to endanger their self-appointed mission. After several painful moments of caution, Khaldun lifted his quarterstaff and slowly, quietly raised the trap door up and back to where it stayed open. A rug lay over the door, preventing the young Makani from seeing into the room, though it appeared to be dark and quiet within.

"Is it safe?" Jovanna whispered.

"All seems well," Khaldun responded, "but I shall ensure that it is so."

"No!" Jovanna argued. "There is not time. Treyhernne believes the Citadel impenetrable from below, and since they have Dhresden already, it is doubtful that anyone would be lying in wait for us. Now, help me into the room."

Reluctantly Khaldun lifted Jovanna toward the ceiling. She gripped the edges of the opening firmly and heaved herself into the room. She found herself ensnared in the rug for a moment, but as she came free of it she found the room dark and silent, except for the whisper of Khaldun entering the chamber. Again the two of them listened carefully for the slightest hint of danger, their ears finding only the low sound of their own breathing. Quickly, Jovanna moved to the wall at the head of the bed and disappeared behind a hanging tapestry. Khaldun made his way to the door, his quarterstaff at the ready. In moments, Jovanna stepped into view, relief and urgency mingled upon her face.

"Let us join the others," she whispered as she approached the trapdoor.

Khaldun quickly crossed the room and dropped down through the open hatch. Quickly he looked about; seeing no danger, he turned his attention to assisting Jovanna. The matriarch, however, needed no aid in descending. She had slid feet first over the edge and lowered herself to arm's length, then dropped nimbly beside the stunned Makani.

Jovanna looked about, just as Khaldun had, and then, sensing his eyes upon her, returned his gaze.

Coming to himself, Khaldun looked away. "Forgive me, my lady, but a woman of your status is not expected to be so skilled in such issues. You constantly surprise me with your adaptability."

Jovanna smiled pleasantly. "You are not so versed in the histories of Dhane and myself, though the Makani know well the years prior to our reign. When this is over, we shall sit in the new Lord Havenstone's dining hall and I shall share that history with you."

The two smiled at the proposition, but the mentioning of Dhresden brought them back to the task at hand. They turned and sped down the tunnel, eager to unite themselves with Orrick and the others.

CHAPTER 12

O rrick led his group through the sewers until they came to a drain housed in the ceiling overhead. He briefly explained that there were several of these shafts throughout the drainage system and that they allowed water to flow directly into the sewers from the top of the Outcropping, the very site of Dhresden's scheduled sentence.

"I am almost certain that this shaft will allow us the closest access to the platform where lies the catapult," Orrick said. "Treyherne is sure to have the bulk of the Oxmen present to insure his plan's success. He doubts we would be able to thwart his plot, but I am not convinced that the peoples of the Pasturelands are completely hoodwinked. Otherwise, we salvage only Dhresden's life, not his reign." Orrick paused to allow his words to be absorbed.

He looked at each of them in turn, reading many things in their faces. He saw fear, not for themselves, but for their lord should they fail. Also, there was the readiness to give their own lives to succeed in saving Dhresden's. To varying levels, Orrick detected a smoldering rage that Khalid had betrayed them all. But also there was fatigue. They had traveled quickly upon leaving the Bog, but the pace they had kept since Dhresden's abduction had been fevered.

"Not a one of us would ask or even desire it, but we must all eat something. It has been several hours since last we did, and the nourishment will only strengthen our grip upon our swords, and the aim of our arrow's flight. Eat. Eat for the deliverance of Dhresden, Lord Havenstone."

None could argue the validity of the giant's words, though Tala was loathe to dine on even the dried meats and fruits she carried while her love sat bound in the company of wicked men.

As he ate, Orrick spoke quietly to Mallory. "Asha will need to wait here below until the fighting begins. She will ascend much faster and more noisily upon the stone than any of us and could possibly alert the Oxmen. Do not fear, though, Asha will be by our side in a blink when the time comes."

Though comforted by Orrick's confidence, Mallory still harbored uncertainties. "Did you not say that Tiblak had given Dhresden some healing potion? Some sap or nectar that would heal any wound?"

"Indeed, though I know not what has become of it. Tala carries Dhresden's weapons. They were left behind when Khalid betrayed him, though I have not seen nor has Tala mentioned the vial. It may be that Dhresden still has it, though it is more likely that it was taken from him by his captors. Regardless, we will rescue your brother. Take heart, my love." Orrick clasped Mallory's hand in his a moment before rising to his feet. "It is time," he announced.

The shaft fortunately was built using hewn stone, the gaps between the blocks providing sufficient handholds and footholds for the rescuers to climb. The greater problem was how the majority of them were to enter the overhead drain. While Orrick was capable of hefting each of them by turns into the opening and then entering the shaft by himself, the diameter of the drain would prevent him from climbing past the others to where he needed to be to lead them to Dhresden's aid. The only other person strong enough to assist the others into the shaft was Uncle, but he lacked the ability to enter the drain on his own. The remedy was Khaldun's rope.

After Orrick had explained his plan to the others, he tied a fixed loop in one end of the rope and then passed it over his shoulder. Then, he effortlessly leaped upward, grabbing the sides of the drain and pulling himself from view. He quickly ascended the shaft, trailing the rope behind him. Below, Uncle began assisting the others. Though in no way slow, Mallory and the others were not as quick to ascend the shaft as Orrick, but before long Uncle found himself alone in the sewers except for the suggestion of Asha pacing in the shadows. Following Orrick's instructions, he gripped the rope firmly with both hands, gave three gentle tugs, and waited. Before long, Uncle found himself rising easily from the floor of the tunnel and into the shaft. He was able to orient himself quickly, finding holds for his feet and hands as he released the rope. Well above, Orrick continued to climb, the rope still secured about his waist.

The light that filtered into the sewers through the various grates had begun to fade from gray to black when Orrick reached the drain cover in the floor of the Outcropping. From the blackness of the sewer, the giant placed his face close to the grate and closed his eyes, knowing his view would be limited and thus untrustworthy. Instead he trusted to his nostrils and ears to search out the crowd above them. The evening air carried to Orrick the stench of a sweaty man who had drunk too much ale and near him a woman who periodically called the man names of an unflattering nature. Another man who smelled not of ale and sweat but of wine and pipe smoke stood in a group of five or six people jabbering along as though a man were not about to die. Here and there among the audience, though, Orrick heard pieces of conversation indicating that Treyherne's tale of treachery had not been accepted by all who heard it. The strongest smell was that of the oil vats and burning torches, a foreboding stench that sought to hide danger from the Wanderer. But there, amidst the tumult of scents, he smelled the Oxmen. Not the soldiers, so much as the spoor of their mounts that clung to them and warned Orrick of their approximate positions.

Leaning downward, Orrick whispered to Mallory his findings and his recommended course of action. As the information was passed down the shaft in turn, Orrick removed the rope from his waist and secretly secured it through the grate covering the tunnel. With all in readiness, one detail remained: Dhresden. Orrick had purposed to surge from hiding when he determined that his friend was being led toward the catapult. Each second of waiting seemed endless, each breath lending to urgency as they braced to deliver their ruler and friend, or to die trying.

It was the murmur of the crowd and the sudden scent of blood that announced to Orrick Dhresden's arrival. Grasping the drain cover with one hand, Orrick pushed the grate aside as he rose from the darkness of the sewers to the torch lit pavilion. The people about him staggered back, some gasping, some cursing, some silent and openmouthed. Orrick paid them no mind. His attention was focused on the five Oxmen several paces before him. They too were stunned by the giant's arrival, but two of them were recovering and fumbling with their swords. Grasping the grate with both hands, Orrick hurled it into their midst; then he and Mallory were upon them, their own weapons drawn. Wyeth, Tala, and Shika scrambled from the drain, each firing well-placed arrows in the directions Orrick had instructed. In seconds, the small group had strewn the immediate area with over a dozen dead or wounded Oxmen. While the citizens fled from the skirmish, more Oxmen poured out of the stairwells. Those Oxmen nearest Dhresden grabbed the beaten, half-naked "criminal" and, thrusting him into the catapult, began to douse him with oil.

Uncle emerged from the drain and placed himself near the sisters, Shika and Tala, ever protective of them. He acquired a habergeon from the slack grip of a fallen Oxmen and began to sweep the enemy swordsmen aside, clearing a path toward the raised dais that would allow the archers to offer support to Orrick and Mallory.

Aware that the Oxmen would continue to swarm them and that it would be but moments before their own archers arrived to strike them from afar, Orrick loosed a roar so fierce that many among the enemy paused in their onslaught. As they recovered their nerve and pressed forward, Asha burst into sight and, without hesitation, began to rend the Oxmen anew. Even Asha's savage brain seemed to understand the danger Dhresden faced, and the great gray cougar tore her way towards the catapult. The rift she created in the troops quickly filled behind her, slowing Orrick and Mallory as they fought to pursue her, but the great cat steadily drew near Dhresden's location. In desperation, clay pots were hurled at Asha's head. They shattered, against her hard skull, but only succeeded in wetting her face with oil. But then, two Oxmen brandishing torches rushed toward the cat.

Though Asha dispatched her attackers, the oil that had been splattered upon both her and Dhresden was ignited.

Mallory screamed in despair and redoubled her efforts to reach her brother. Orrick's fury drove him deep into the midst of the enemy, burying himself in danger as he tried to save his friends. Asha had slowed in her attack, blinded as she was by the flames engulfing her head and shoulders. Orrick now neared the cougar, yearning to aid his longtime companion but aware that his first act must be to deliver Dhresden. Passing by Asha, Orrick was within a few feet of his half-blood friend when the catapult was released, hurling Dhresden out over the black waters of Lock Norde. Not wasting an instant, Orrick turned and leaped upon Asha's head, trying to smother the flames against his chest and stomach.

Disoriented, the cougar fought to free herself from the grasp of this new assailant. The nearest Oxmen, confused by what was happening, nevertheless rushed in to strike the entangled pair and fell victims to the deadly aim of Wyeth and the sisters. So far unable to escape, Asha had become more determined to free herself from Orrick's iron grasp. She rolled herself to one side and brought her hind legs forward to rake this dogged attacker from his perch. As her head was pulled from his grasp, Asha buried her fangs in Orrick's shoulder, causing the giant to cry out in pain, but hearing the unmistakable voice of her beastlike friend, Asha released him.

No longer aflame, a charred cougar fought beside a bloodied and singed Orrick, battling back toward the sewers that had provided admittance for them. Mallory fell in with them, mourning Dhresden's passing but unwilling to lose another of her companions. Her sword slashing, Mallory advanced half a step ahead of her two wounded friends; all of her grief, anger and love empowering each swing of her sword with a strength and skill beyond her own ability.

As the three neared the drain, Uncle and the archers began their retreat as well. Wyeth and the sisters shouldered their bows and with their swords began slicing and stabbing their way through the Oxmen, with Uncle forming their rear guard. The seven reunited before the sewer entrance, Orrick sending Asha down the opening first, partly to secure the tunnel below, and partly to remove his wounded friend from further danger above. Orrick sheathed his axe and pulled forth his flail from its pouch. Its chain, weighted at the end, swung out over the crouched forms of his companions, maiming any Oxmen who sought to approach within striking distance. While Uncle held the rope at the edge of the drain, the women and then Wyeth slid quickly down into the sewers. Uncle then began to pull the grate to himself. As Orrick brought the flail to a stop, he and Uncle prepared to enter the sewers but were showered with a barrage of arrows from the Oxmen' archers. Cloaked as he was in chain mail, Orrick's injuries remained minor though Uncle fared far worse. The big man had taken the bulk of his wounding to his left side, paralyzing his arm and piercing through into his chest. His eyes met Orrick's, and both men knew that his was a mortal wound.

"Leave me the flail," he wheezed, "and use the rope to secure the grate. Get clear of the citadel as quickly as you can, and then do Tala's bidding."

Unsure of his meaning concerning Tala, Orrick nevertheless handed his dying friend the flail and dropped down the drain. Uncle drew himself to his full height, swinging the flail around at the resurging enemy. As the archers set loose another volley, Uncle released the flail, allowing it to bounce wildly through the crowd. Bending to the grate, he muscled it back into place, and then fell motionless atop it, several more arrows having found their mark.

Warily, the Oxmen approached Uncle's body, not certain that this foe had truly been vanquished. Prodding him tentatively with a sword without result, one of their number then ran him through. Three Oxmen hurriedly sheathed their swords and bent to the task of rolling the heavyset man off the sewer grate. The same three then fell to trying to lift the grate from its place. Unable to lift it, they shuffled their positions to accommodate another Oxmen but were still not able to displace the cover. None had noticed the slender rope that had been tied around one of the bars of the grate, the same rope which Orrick had secured around some piping below. He had tied it so that the drain was held fast, preventing the lifting of the drain cover. Shortly though, one of the Oxmen spied the rope and cut it, allowing the four to lift the drain, but also sent the rope and their means of easy descent to the sewer floor.

A courier brought word from Treyherne with orders to send fifty Oxmen into the sewers after the rebels.

"Fifty!?" one of the Oxmen exclaimed, "there's fifty of our comrades lying dead and wounded around us! How does he expect—"

"Enough!" their commander barked, "I may not agree with all Treyherne does, but I will not stand by and allow Dhane's killers to escape! You, fetch a rope. You others, into the sewers."

CHAPTER 13

Realizing the implication of Khalid's betrayal, and the danger that he and the Oxmen with him posed to Tala, Dhresden dropped his weapons to the ground. Not wanting Tiblak's gift of healing potion to benefit the enemy, Dhresden hid it among his weapons. He was confident that Tala would discover his weapons and the vial of nectar, and that she would use it to aid Uncle if necessary. He then walked into the midst of them, allowing them to bind his arms behind him. A rope was then placed about his neck and he was led like a beast of burden toward the Citadel.

The trek proved uneventful. While the Oxmen appeared to pay Dhresden little attention, their inattention to him seemed forced. It soon became evident that the prisoner, though bound, clearly intimidated his captors. Any communication between the Oxmen was hushed and whispered and those few who met his gaze quickly looked away. Dhresden and Orrick had directly trained most of the officers, and engineered the general training for the Oxmen recruits. He was not some unknown criminal but if they had believed Treyherne's lies, he was a detestable traitor who was worthy of harsh treatment. Still, the Oxmen kept their distance from him; Dhresden almost felt sorry for the one leading him along. Khalid also walked in silence and similar solitude, his quarterstaff resting in the crook of one arm. Dhresden found himself calculating and recalculating the steps between himself and this traitor, and wishing his hands were free, or at least not bound behind his back.

Entering the fringes of the Outcropping, Dhresden's captors escorted their charge along the road, passing villagers busy about their day, whether at work or play, relaxing or scurrying off to some responsibility. Though few knew Dhresden, most had heard of him. His skill as a trainer of the Oxmen had been declared at numerous dinner tables, whispered by many a should-be sleeping lad, and slurred and shouted in various taverns.

These people should know by my reputation alone that I am innocent," Dhresden thought. *By some wicked and charming snake speak Treyherne has beguiled the subjects and even the Oxmen with whom Orrick and I so closely worked. But how am I to counteract this deception? Force alone will only fortify his lies, but Treyherne has shown that he will not be reasoned with. He has gone to great lengths to usurp the throne of Havenstone, and to my shame I did not detect his scheming.*

Turning a corner, Dhresden was brought within sight of the main entrance of the Citadel, and despite his foreboding situation, the vision again filled him with awe. Generations prior, the ruling council of the Pasturelands had foreseen the need of a fortified city and had taken advantage of a natural outcropping of stone that protruded up out of the center of that region. It bore little resemblance to the distant snowcapped spires of the Wanderlands, but was clearly out of place in its pastured setting. The Outcropping rose majestically up from the pastures, its top a grassy plateau, jutting a rock point out towards Loch Norde. It had taken years to complete, but now it stood, walls of fortified stone blocks to protect those citizens who resided atop the plateau, as well as the rulers dwelling within the Citadel. The main entrance itself could be defended from atop the wall, as well as from within the wall itself. Thick wooden doors could be swung closed and barred to prevent access, or, in the event of a siege, a great slab of solid black stone could be released to cut off the common area from the enemy. Resetting the barrier required such effort that it was utilized only in dire need, and hence had been activated only four times. Most of those who could remember the last siege of the Outcropping had long since slept the sleep of their fathers, though a handful remained to tell the tale around a flickering fire to many a bright-eyed child. Treyherne had been there, the seemingly sound advisor, and the Lady Jovanna. At the thought of his stepmother, Dhresden's heart grew heavy. He had felt closer to her since his father's death, had hoped to confide in her and listen to her wisdom as he sought to rule half as well as his father Dhane had. Jovanna and Mallory were to be his family, though adopted, no stronger bond would have existed except for the bond he had hoped to forge with Tala. If Dhresden's heart had been heavy before, it was now rending itself. His hopes and plans for Havenstone would die at the hand of the traitor Treyherne; his friends and loved ones scattered or killed.

"A man knows true defeat when he fails to rise after he falls." The words of his father came back to him from some forgotten corner of a memory, urging him to strength, to take heart and take hope. "You may fall more times than you can count, but victory is closer each time you rise." It had been one of those happy times of childhood when Dhane had come to Kelvar to see his son. Dhresden was eight and a half, and had come to adore his father, though distance fought to keep them strangers. The lord of the Pasturelands rarely came alone, and this time he had brought two pupils with him. The lads, nearing twenty, were studying military tactics and warfare in preparation for the newly formed Oxmen. Dhane had deemed them among the best in the class, and was anxious to employ them in educating his eager son.

Thad and Horace were instructed to spar with Dhresden one at a time, alternating to prevent the boy from getting used to either's fighting style. The weapons they fought with were padded, but this did not prevent the blows from stinging. Dhresden showed great skill for his age, and even managed to catch his opponents off guard a few times, but more often found himself upon the ground from a blow to the head or midsection, or a sweep to the leg. Thad proved quick and skillful, his sword feinting and jabbing, forcing Dhresden to attack and defend quickly. Dhresden enjoyed sparring with Thad: the young man clearly enjoyed seeing Dhresden adapting and excelling in his swordplay. Training with Horace proved less than enjoyable. Though he seemed to mask it well in front of Dhane, Horace clearly detested putting himself at the disposal of a child. He had underestimated Dhresden early on and had received a jab to the stomach, followed by a firm hit to the side of his head. Enraged and embarrassed, Horace fought without honor in an attempt to regain his dignity. He resorted to brute force to defeat the child, pounding at him with all his might, seeking to knock him down as many times as possible. Once Dhresden fell, Horace would retreat, his glaring eyes daring him to get back up, all the while he spoke amiable words in a pleasant tone to hide his true agenda from Dhane. After hours a day for three days of this mixture of training and abuse, Dhresden found himself again on the floor, this time with blood running freely from his nose. Blinking the tears from his eyes, he looked up at the sneering Horace, whose back was placed strategically towards Dhane. Dhresden's tormenter glared at him with evident disgust, not bothering this time to offer any flowery words. Dhresden cast a furtive glance at Thad, who seemed oblivious to the situation, and then his father, whose curious gaze the boy interpreted as disappointment. Dhresden dropped his eyes toward the floor, watching the blood pool before him. It was then that he heard Dhane speak the words that would return to him at his darkest of times.

"There is no shame in falling to the ground, nor is a fall tantamount to defeat. A man knows true defeat when he fails to rise after he falls, when the struggle that was once priceless loses its value, when his own pain outweighs the virtue for which he labored. Remember: you may fall more times than you can count, but victory is closer each time you rise."

Dhresden's eyes flew back to his father's face, seeing now the hope and confidence that his tears and pain had once hidden. Unashamedly wiping both tears and blood upon his sleeve, Dhresden again rose and approached Horace. Again Horace thundered the boy to the ground, but found his young adversary quickly erect before him once more. His rage building at the idea of this whelp thinking he could best him, Horace attacked again, seeking with all his strength to land a blow against Dhresden's head. Reading his intent, Dhresden pulled his head down a bit and cocked his sword at an angle to his left, not to block Horace's weapon but to deflect it. Horace's practice sword glanced harmlessly off of Dhresden's, his own momentum spinning him about, leaving his back exposed. Before his tormentor could recover, Dhresden countered. A blow to the back forced Horace further off balance, and when he placed all of his weight upon one foot, Dhresden's practice sword was there, putting the older boy on the ground by striking the back of Horace's knee. The enraged and humiliated Horace scrambled to his feet, intent on vengeance. He stepped towards Dhresden, whose face was set without fear, only to find Thad barring his way. Taken aback, Horace moved to push past the other young man, but was halted by a voice behind him.

"Thank you for your time, Horace, you may retire," Dhane said. His voice was calm and even, though it whispered a warning that knifed through Horace's blinding anger. Turning to face his lord, Horace bowed and departed, bested in skill and honor by a boy of eight.

Dhane had then escorted his son to dinner, not one of regalia, but of family. The weary but delighted boy sat between his mother and father while his grandfather looked on. Dhresden devoured his meal with all the etiquette he could muster as Dhane masterfully wove the tale of his battles with Thad and the sinister Horace. Dhane and Phaelen took turns telling tales of days gone by, of other noble warriors and the skills with which they fought and lived.

"For all true warriors know that life requires that a man answer for his choices both on the field of battle, and in the secret chambers of his house," Dhane had declared. "And whether he be the king or a pauper he should conduct himself nobly."

It had been late when they all retired, and as exhausted as he was, Dhresden had collapsed atop his bed—no blankets, his clothes and shoes intact. He had fallen asleep immediately, but awoke when a rough hand clamped over his mouth. Horace stood silently over him, his eyes filled with hatred, a knife blade glinting up from his other hand.

Knowing his intent to be malignant, Dhresden drew his knees towards his own chin and thrust his feet against Horace's chest. The young man grunted and gasped, and fell back away from his intended prey, landing on the floor and lying still in the shadows. Dhresden had raced from his room and burst into his mother's, wresting her from sleep with a barrage of hurried words. Once she had calmed him enough to make sense of his chatter, Ciana retrieved a short sword from behind a tapestry and, with her son close behind, approached her bedchamber door. Finding the corridor clear, Ciana sent Dhresden to wake his father. Dhane, his own sword in hand and Dhresden in tow, soon hurried to Ciana's side, the sounds of others' footsteps growing louder somewhere behind. Leaving Dhresden in the hall, his parents approached the unmoving Horace, prepared and even hoping to face resistance. Reaching the young man's side, Dhane prodded him with the tip of his blade without response. With a glance at Ciana, Dhane reached down and grabbed Horace by the shoulder and rolled him over onto his back. The would-be assassin's dead eyes stared at the ceiling, his own knife imbedded in his chest.

CHAPTER 14

"Thought to take over the throne, did you, criminal?" Dhresden found himself standing in the royal hall of the Citadel, ripped from his memory by Treyherne's accusation. Dhresden looked up at the usurper, finding him cloaked in cobalt, a silver crown upon his head. The crown was not that of Lord Havenstone, but of a prince regent; one who rules because the monarch is unable to govern due to age, illness or duties which cause him to be absent. Treyherne glared down upon him from beside the throne, his face hard, though Dhresden saw or sensed the twitch of a smirk. Most would consider Treyherne a handsome man: his now white hair was groomed short, framing a mildly weathered face that boasted strength, his blue eyes seemed to convey an interest in whomever he encountered. Dhresden saw now only a snake.

"What right do you have wearing that crown, villain? Though Dhane has passed, the Lady Jovanna and Miss Mallory by law may reign in his stead. And there is the issue of Dhane's son—"

"Enough!!" Treyherne shouted, "I have no interest in your diversions. What I am interested in is your confession."

"Confession? What—"

"Your confession," Treyherne interrupted, "as to the murder of Lord Dhane, by poisoning, and the murder of Lady Jovanna and Miss Mallory."

Treyherne's tone and accusation boiled Dhresden's blood, but he kept his voice calm. "You are misinformed, serpent, or did you delude yourself?"

Treyherne's smile looked to Dhresden like a viper about to strike. "We have discovered the poison you used, and your former companion will attest to your villainy regarding those poor women. Truly, you are a disappointment."

Dhresden cast a glance at Khalid. The Makani were a people known for their honor; how had this one departed so from his own culture?

"With such overwhelming evidence, why bother to question me?" Dhresden asked.

"Because your victims deserve your confession, and the people demand it. I will have no choice but to have the confession drawn from you. Take him away, to the discussion chamber."

Discussion chamber. A would-be tyrant's diplomatic title for a place of torture. It had been at the least a century since the discussion chamber had been used; Dhresden remembered sitting in the abandoned, dusty room with Mallory when they were young, trying to frighten her with scary stories whispered in the dim candlelight. As he was ushered into the chamber, Dhresden was struck by how much smaller it was than he remembered, and then he was struck by Khalid's quarterstaff. Dhresden, hands bound behind him, fell forward onto the still dusty floor. Dazed though he was by the blow to the back of his head, he managed to twist and land the bulk of his weight on his side rather than smacking his face upon the stone floor.

"Get him up," he heard Khalid say, "and lock him in the collar."

The Oxmen quickly obeyed, lifting Dhresden to his feet and securing him in the collar. The collar was a hinged loop of steel suspended by an iron frame mounted to the stone wall. It featured short fat spikes on the inside of the loop which, when the collar was fastened shut, pressed sharply against the neck of the victim enough to draw blood and inflict pain but not enough to be fatal. Another of the collar's features was that the height was adjustable; it could be raised or lowered to aggravate each candidate's pain and discomfort. The Oxmen had lowered the collar to easily enclose Dhresden in its grasp and had left it adjusted at a comfortable height, though the spikes themselves were inflicting a mild pain that promised to worsen. His hands were left bound behind him and his feet were quickly bound together. Khalid spoke quietly but authoritatively to the Oxmen and they exited the room, leaving the would-be ruler and the traitorous Makani alone. Khalid slouched upon a short stone bench occupying the wall across from Dhresden.

Moments passed while neither spoke, each gazing at nothing, content to let the silence envelop them. It was Khalid that broke the silence, his voice cordial, as if addressing an old friend over tea.

"I hope the others realize the futility of an attempt at rescuing you," he remarked. "It would be a pity if Treyherne got hold of them."

Dhresden looked at Khalid, not bothering to hide his disgust. "You have forfeited your right to worry yourself about them. Were it only I that you had betrayed, I could forgive you but your treatment of Uncle and the way you threatened Tala—no. Your villainy is so deeply rooted that you have deceived yourself."

The Makani seemed unaffected by Dhresden's diatribe and continued his charade of conversation. "I realize that you will never confess to murdering your father, or Jovanna and Mallory," Khalid said, "but I do not believe that Treyherne is actually interested in a confession. I think he quite simply wants to punish you for living, for being who you are and hindering his attainment of the throne."

"And what of you, traitor?" Dhresden asked. "What is your gain in all this? How is it that you justify your treachery?"

At this, Khalid met the young man's gaze; in his eyes Dhresden saw a mixture of rage, cunning, and regret. "It began as a daydream," he confided. "It was in the form of repayment of the debt owed to Dhane's family. I imagined that Khaldun and I would be able to return blessing to the ruler of Havenstone and free our people from the shadow of indebtedness in which we have dwelt for so long. We would leave here as heroes and return home honored warriors. As the days lengthened into years, I schemed in innocence about ways to bring this glorious moment to pass. But my plans began to be less focused on rescuing Dhane and more on rescuing myself from this strange land. I miss the western Dunes, and so I plotted ways to return myself to them." Khalid stopped talking, his eyes seeing not the walls of the torture chamber, but his precious homeland.

Dhresden watched him, his hatred gone, replaced by pity. "What do you miss the most?"

Khalid stayed quiet long enough that Dhresden began to wonder if he had heard the question. The Makani sat unmoving, his breathing slow. "Ceydra. After many years, we were finally granted permission to wed, but before our wedding came to pass, the need for emissaries to the Pasturelands was decreed. Her father, one of the council, asked me to volunteer, perhaps to his political credit, but perhaps some other cause."

Dhresden could tell that Khalid was actually confiding in him, mirroring his own sorrow and longing to be with Tala. "What other cause?" Dhresden asked.

"As I said, Ceydra's father is very politically-minded. I fear that Ceydra is coveted by another man, one whose father is also on the council, and that I am not supposed to return."

"Have you been blinded, Khalid? What will await you when you return, having failed to fulfill the debt that your people decreed must be repaid?"

The Makani's smile was grim, as was his answer. "Blindness has not taken me, though I have not seen clearly all that would pass. Now the situation has progressed to a point from which I fear there is no rescue." The two lapsed into silence, each occupied with his own thoughts and concerns. Into this stillness burst several of the Oxmen. They spread into the room, assessed Dhresden's bonds, and then departed. Treyherne then entered, his silver crown gone and his blue robes replaced now with a simple crimson tunic. He sneered at his captive then spoke to Khalid.

"I have a few questions for our guest," Treyherne said as he pulled on a pair of stiff leather gloves. "You may withdraw to the hall."

The Makani remained seated, his narrowed eyes regarding each of the men before him. "I think I shall remain."

Treyherne seemed unaffected by this statement, but firmly fixed his blue eyes a moment upon Khalid. "Do not interfere," he warned.

Treyherne walked close to his prisoner. Dhresden's demeanor remained impassive, his gaze upon the floor. He refused to provide this usurper the satisfaction he had come seeking.

"It is a shame that no one will ever know that you are Dhane's son and legitimate heir to the throne of Havenstone. You will die with less honor than you lived, known only as the treacherous, fatherless half-blood that poisoned our great ruler in an attempt to steal his throne." Treyherne virtually panted these words, his anger smoldering slowly toward a self-righteous rage, fueled further by Dhresden's lack of response. "It was easy enough to poison the fool," he continued. "Dhane was simply too trusting. I can still remember his look of shock as I stood there watching him breathe his last breath."

Treyherne paused, inspecting his prey for some sign that Dhresden's resolve was weakening. Finding none, Treyherne struck harder with his words. "Yes, I was there. I sneaked into his chamber in the dark of night, knowing that his body would by this time be experiencing severe paralysis. I found Dhane and Jovanna asleep, the lady completely unaware of my presence or of her husband's plight. Quietly I woke him, the night not so dark as to prevent my eyes from feasting upon what I found. His breathing was shallow and quiet, and all Dhane could move was his eyes. I kept my smiling face close to his, wanting my face to be the last thing he saw in this life, wanting him to know that with no sword in hand I had vanquished him."

Still no flicker of response from the younger man. Treyherne was sure his words were inflicting pain upon his captive, but he wanted to see it with his own eyes. "I do hope that no ill befalls Jovanna or your sweet sister Mallory," Treyherne hissed, leaning closer to Dhresden. "I should like to welcome them to my chamber, before relinquishing them to the Oxmen for sport. Some of those men, well they are animals—"

Treyherne found himself crumpled upon the floor at Khalid's feet. The Makani was no more sure of what had happened than Treyherne was. Treyherne lay gasping, clutching at his chest; fear, rage and pain showing on his face. Khalid looked from the false ruler to Dhresden, whose neck was seeping blood into his shirt. It was then that Khalid understood. Dhresden had walled off his anger against

Treyherne's verbal onslaught until Jovanna's and Mallory's honor had been threatened. This last insult had shattered his stoic resolve for pacifism. Dhresden had lifted his feet from the floor, allowing his weight to be held by the collar, which drove its spikes into his neck. Drawing his knees almost to his chest, as he had many years before when Horace had sought his life, Dhresden thrust both his feet against Treyherne's upper body, sending the older man crashing against the opposite wall and then collapsing upon the floor.

"Do you require assistance?" Khalid asked, though he doubted his question would be well received.

"Assistance?!" Treyherne wheezed and grunted as he gathered his feet beneath himself and struggled to rise. "I require—" with another grunt, Treyherne stood erect, "I require your staff!" The enraged older man stood panting, his eyes glaring at the seemingly impassive Dhresden.

Khalid stood unmoving, his quarterstaff at his side. A scant moment passed before Treyherne's venomous gaze was directed at him.

"Do you have sand in your ears, or have you had a sudden attack of conscience?" he hissed.

"I mean no offense," Khalid began, "but a Makani battle staff is a precious thing."

Treyherne continued to glare at him, but something about Khalid's demeanor caught his interest. "Go on," he offered.

"Our battle staffs are made from the red banyai, a tree that grows quite fat and tall. It was superstition that first fostered the practice of cutting down these beautiful specimens and using the middle portion of heartwood solely for the production of staffs. We were not wasteful, the other portions of the tree were also put to use, but the center heartwood was reserved for battle staffs alone. This section of the tree proved to be so strong and durable that after the first generation of staff-wielders were equipped, no more staffs needed made. Either a warrior would fall in battle, or reach an age of rest and pass his staff on to a male in his line, or it would pass to an unwed daughter until she provided an heir to receive the heirloom. In the past few thousand years this staff has passed through many hands, all of them Makani." Khalid met Treyherne's gaze squarely. "It is an honorable weapon, not intended for the task for which you would enlist it."

"Still holding on to your self-righteousness, I see," Treyherne chuckled. "It is of no concern. I realize now that your staff would not draw quite as much blood as I should like to see trickling out of the half-blood. You may retire to the hall."

With a brief look at Dhresden, Khalid turned and left the room, leaving Dhresden and the usurper alone. It was then that Treyherne produced from within his crimson tunic a short horse whip, the tip of which was imbedded with bits of glass and sharp metal. For over an hour's time, Khalid listened to the sound of the whip as it struck Dhresden wherever Treyherne aimed it, and the resulting muffled cries of the young ruler. The whipping was not constant, Khalid could also hear when Treyherne would take leave of the whip and would employ the use of his own gloved hands. There were also moments when all Khalid could hear was the muffled sound of Treyherne's voice taunting and laughter mocking the helpless man. At one point, it sounded as if a body had fallen to the floor, and Khalid almost rushed into the room, expecting to find Dhresden miraculously escaped and Treyherne lying stunned or dead upon the floor. But then the torture and mocking continued, and Khalid found himself bordering on disappointment that Dhresden had not escaped. Finally, Treyherne emerged from the discussion chamber, his crimson tunic glimmering wet where Dhresden's blood had splattered upon him.

"It seems this day is drawing to a close," Treyherne mused aloud to himself. "I think a hot bath is in order before I retire." He stood there a while, relishing his victory. When he spoke again, his tone had become firm, even harsh. "Place him back in the collar," Treyherne instructed the Makani. "And keep him alive until his execution; I want him to walk to his doom."

Khalid stood in the hall until he was sure Treyherne had departed before reentering the discussion chamber. He found Dhresden lying on the floor, his hands still bound behind him. At first, Khalid thought that Dhresden's blood was pooling on the floor around him, but as he drew closer, he realized that it was not pooling, but rather had been splattered upon the floor, walls and even the ceiling with each lash of the whip. The Makani knelt beside Dhresden, checking his life signs and wounding. He found a strong heartbeat despite his treatment, and discovered that the wounds created by Treyherne's whip were shallow. With vicious cunning Treyherne had inflicted pain and drawn blood from his victim without actually endangering his life. No, he would not deny himself the enjoyment of Dhresden's public execution.

Khalid sent for fresh, cool water and various fruits as well as fresh cloths and warm water. Once the requested supplies arrived, Khalid closed and barred the door while he began to tend the half-blood. First he removed the bindings from Dhresden's wrists, and then, with a small cloth wetted with drinking water he bathed Dhresden's face and lips, hoping to revive him. Finding that unsuccessful, Khalid began to cleanse the wounds on his back with warm water. It was during this that Dhresden awoke, weak and confused. Though his wounds were shallow, the risk of dehydration still existed. Mouth dry, Dhresden was unable to speak clearly, nevertheless, Khalid gave him some fruit and cool water, but cautioned him to ingest it slowly.

After finishing his first ration, Dhresden fixed Khalid with his gaze. "Thank you, Khalid, for your help."

It was not the words so much as the tone that pierced Khalid's heart. His thanks sounded so genuine, so heartfelt; but how could an innocent man speak so kindly to his betrayer? Khalid began to regret his shameful choice anew.

"Do not claim the burden for this situation as all your own," Dhresden said. "Treyherne would have moved for the throne with or without your input. However, if you had remained steadfast, your peoples' vow would have been satisfied. Your impatience may have cursed you in the eyes of your people, and I would not put any stock in the promises of Treyherne."

Dhresden lapsed into a fatigued silence, eyes closed, breathing quietly. Khalid sat beside him, his mind a whirl of thoughts and emotions. He sat in deep thought, unaware of the passage of time, until, suddenly, he realized that he could not hear Dhresden's breathing anymore. His eyes darted to the other's face, and then to his chest, looking for the telltale rise and fall of his breathing.

"I am not dead, Khalid," Dhresden told him with a grim smile. "Not yet, anyway. I believe that is scheduled for tomorrow night. Go, retire. I will be fine."

"I have not finished dressing your wounds," Khalid replied.

"You have done more than many would; all that remains is my chest and face and I can tend to that. Thank you for your kindness, I will see you on the morrow."

Khalid sat looking at the floor, but soon, nodded agreement. He stood, opened the door and called two of the Oxmen to him.

"Convey a message to Treyherne," he told one of them. "Tell him that I have tended the prisoner and he is stable, but that if he loses any more blood he will not be in attendance at his own execution. You," Khalid said to the other, "be sure the prisoner is not disturbed. Treyherne will be most displeased if he is robbed the pleasure of viewing his execution."

"Aye, sir!" they said in unison, turning to fulfill their orders.

Khalid turned back to Dhresden, who had taken the opportunity to attend his remaining wounds. His task completed, he was in the process of donning the change of clothes that Khalid had provided.

"I will need to bind you," Khalid said, his regret evident. "But I will tie your hands before you so you may avail yourself of the fruit and water. No one should bother you, but should they look in on you and find you unbound I fear they would overreact."

"Then it would be for my protection that I be bound," Dhresden chuckled. "Very well, tie my hands and be on your way."

CHAPTER 15

Khalid slept fairly well that night, though getting to sleep had proven to be a difficult task. His guilt had become unavoidable, not that he may have brought shame to himself or the Makani, but that he had contributed to the mistreatment of an innocent and honorable man. It was the knowledge of Dhresden's forgiveness that allowed Khalid to finally drift off to sleep, and what allowed him to awaken refreshed and eager to find ways to ease Dhresden's suffering while he awaited execution. Arriving at the discussion chamber, fresh fruit and water in hand, Khalid was surprised to find the door ajar, and the room empty. Unsettled by this discovery, he quickly freed himself of his wares and set about searching for Dhresden.

Khalid hurried through the streets of the Citadel, and as he passed near the amphitheater he discerned the noise of soldiers, murmuring, and above it all, the sound of pain. He burst through the first entrance he came to, finding himself in the stands among village spectators, most of whom looked on with quiet interest. It was a mixed audience comprised of those few who were reluctant to believe Dhresden to be guilty of his charges, those who had fully succumbed to Treyherne's lies, and those who remained undecided as to what was truth. Pushing his way to the front of the stands, Khalid's anger flared as his eyes took in the scene. Treyherne had ordered what looked at first like gallows to be constructed within easy view of the royal box. The prisoner now stood upon the platform, his arms raised up and bound to the overhead beam while several Oxmen, armed with staffs, took turns striking him as Treyherne looked on gleefully. Neither Treyherne nor the Oxmen were aware of the Makani's presence, even as he leaped over the railing and raced toward Dhresden. His sudden arrival at the prisoner's side was enough to end Dhresden's mistreatment, at least temporarily. The Oxmen fell back, startled not only by Khalid's presence, but also his evident outrage on behalf of the traitor. Upon seeing him, Treyherne's venomous smile faded, and his eyes took on the look of a viper threatened, yet itself a threat.

"I apologize," Treyherne chided, "I was reluctant to begin without you, but now that you are here, by all means, take a turn."

"You charged me with keeping the prisoner alive until his sentencing," Khalid fumed. "Did you not receive my warning that any more loss of blood would render the execution unnecessary?"

"Your directive was delivered and quite understood, sandman," Treyherne hissed, "and be sure that my men have been instructed as such. Look at him; is he bleeding?"

Khalid turned his eyes upon the already weary Dhresden. His flesh where he had been struck so many times was a stinging red accented by hues of purple where bruising had already begun to set in. The man himself still managed to stand, though unsteadily, supported as it were by his bonds. His eyes were closed when Khalid arrived, though now his eyelids fluttered, and his gaze came to rest upon the Makani. Neither spoke, but in that moment, much was said between the two.

"It is time, Makani," Treyherne declared angrily, "to settle where your allegiance lies."

It was at that moment that Dhresden saw a change overtake Khalid. He could see clarity in his eyes as the guilt of his choices melted to the background of his mind. He could see his regret and shame moving aside as a new emotion overshadowed him: it was the burden one feels when injustice has been done, when the innocent are slain without cause.

"Khalid," Dhresden began, but was cut off when the other man leaned toward him and said quietly, "See now, my friend, that Makani means 'wind.'"

Khalid then swept among the Oxmen, his movements a whirlwind of fury. His staff darted here and there, stunning the nearest of the enemy and whirling on, only to return just as his first victims began to recover. At first, many of the Oxmen attempted to face off against Khalid, using the staffs they had wielded upon Dhresden, but after several of the Oxmen fell swiftly to the skill of Khalid's staff, swords were drawn. The lone warrior managed to hold his own quite a while, leaving Oxmen unconscious or moaning broken bones. With sadness, Dhresden watched as one of the Oxmen blades cut Khalid's staff in two. Taking a half firmly in each hand, the Makani battled more fiercely, beating the enemy back until a buffer of wounded lay about him. In that brief moment, Khalid took both halves of his staff in one hand and flung them high and far. The pieces of the broken weapon twirled through the air toward the royal box, forcing Treyherne to the floor to avoid being struck. The Oxmen surrounding Khalid stood unmoving, hoping the now unarmed Makani would surrender and not a little stunned by his audacity towards their commander.

Treyherne clambered to his feet, enraged all the more to find his attacker alive. "Kill him, you fools!" he screamed in less than noble fashion.

The first of the Oxmen to rush forward to fulfill his order found his blade contacting Khalid's forearm. Rather than severing it as he had expected, his sword clanged harmlessly off the Makani's arm, only to find Khalid's other fist striking him in the throat, removing him from the skirmish.

Dhresden was awestruck. He had heard of the legendary swiftness of the Makani from his grandfather, and even of the terephthala greaves they wore, but to actually see it unfolding before his eyes was incredible. He watched as Khalid, weaponless, bested another Oxmen, and then two at once, and was beginning to believe that the wind-fighter would outlast all the Oxmen in the amphitheater, until he heard the *whoosh!* of arrows. Khalid had heard them loosed as well, and had held his arms up before himself, protecting his head and chest from many of the arrows, only to be pierced through by more arrows loosed from behind. The Makani fell gracelessly to the ground, his last breath caressing the sandy floor of the amphitheater.

~ ~ ~

A hush hovered oppressively over the amphitheater. Dhresden sagged weakly against his bonds, his remaining strength driven away by grief and loss. The Oxmen were quietly tending their wounded, stunned as much by Khalid's change of heart as by his fighting. Treyherne issued quick commands in a smoldering tone to his generals and then hurriedly left the building.

Dhresden fought to remain alert, but found himself slipping in and out of consciousness. He stirred a bit when his bonds were cut and he collapsed to the ground, but soon was again in the grip of a sleep that offered no rest. Dhresden next awoke, surrounded by darkness and cold, a heavy weight upon him. Feeling in the shadows he discovered a body lying upon him, arrows protruding. Khalid's lifeless body had been cast with Dhresden into a gloomy, dank cell to add to the half-blood's anguish and torture. Alone with the dead, Dhresden gathered Khalid to himself in a brotherly embrace, weeping freely over the loss of a life that in the end had been surrendered honorably. There he sat for several hours, midday coming and passing without incident, food or water. Dhresden's tears had dried, though his heart and soul remained sorrowful. Slowly, Dhresden began to remove the arrows from Khalid's body. He found that to remove them completely, he must push them through his body, a task not welcomed but accepted. Dhresden found that twenty-three arrows had pierced Khalid, but was unable to remove three without breaking them, and two others had been rendered useless upon impact. This left him with eighteen usable arrows; useful for escape, or at the least to punish the Oxmen a little for taking Khalid's life.

Dhresden dragged his friend over against the cell door and then sat with his back against an adjacent wall, trying to rest but also to listen for approaching footsteps. Time dragged on slowly, Dhresden dozed a bit, but each time he nodded off he would startle awake thinking someone was coming. Finally, he was certain that guards approached. He pressed himself against the wall beside the door, two arrows grasped in each hand. As the cell door swung open, Dhresden heard the Oxmen muttering something about the corpse and the blood that had pooled around it in the doorway. Two of the guards started through the doorway, only to slip and fall in Khalid's blood as Dhresden charged from the shadows and burst past them into the hallway. He faced the remainder of a fifteen-man detachment, all now recovering from the shock of Dhresden's attack and drawing swords. They had expected to find a weakened and despondent prisoner, not an armed warrior eager to win his freedom. Dhresden quickly struck two guards down, stabbing an arrow in both of their chests. The next closest guard reached for his sword only to find an arrow pinning his arm to his midsection. Pulling another arrow from his belt, Dhresden continued to fight into the Oxmen. He managed to spear an arrow into another guard, but the third had grasped his sword and was pulling the blade from its sheath. Dhresden and Orrick had trained the Oxmen to turn the draw of their sword into a striking blow, but this man had drawn his sword and then swung it back in preparation to strike. Dhresden deftly stepped into his circle of reach, driving an arrow up through the man's neck with one hand and taking his sword from his grasp with the other. Though he could feel what little strength he had rallied fading already, Dhresden took heart in having cold steel in his grasp again. His foes were at a disadvantage: they did not wish to die at Dhresden's hand, but to kill him now or allow him to escape would mean certain death at Treyherne's bidding. With little in the way of choices, the nine Oxmen before Dhresden advanced upon him with swords drawn, determined not to be found in dereliction of duty. Dhresden met them with fast waning vigor, doing well holding his own, until he was struck from behind. The two Oxmen he had toppled at the cell door had joined the fight, one of them clubbing Dhresden on the back of the head with the flat of his sword. Dhresden fell to the floor dazed, the Oxmen raining kicks down on him until they were certain he had been subdued. They pulled him roughly to his feet and bound his hands behind him, then half led, half dragged him from the prison. It was dusk; Treyherne and Firebane were awaiting him.

Too soon, Dhresden found himself stumbling through one of the entrances to the Outcropping. At once upon entering, he could see the serpent Treyherne watching from within an enclosed viewing box several paces to the left of the catapult, his countenance wicked and triumphant. Without reason to hope, Dhresden resigned himself to the end that must come, grieving not so much his fiery fate as the fate of the nation under Treyherne's corrupt rule. Coming to a stop before the instrument of his death, Dhresden discerned a change in the tenor of the crowd. Looking to his left, he saw a gap growing in the midst of the spectators and then a familiar, giant shape rising above the crowd, hurling something at several Oxmen. Orrick, and others of their company that he could not clearly see through the crowd, were battling toward him, and though the Oxmen were swarming to intercept them, Dhresden began to hope again for deliverance.

At Treyherne's enraged and urgent command, the Oxmen around Dhresden lifted him into the catapult and prepared to carry out his sentence. Dhresden strained to turn his head to see how the battle progressed while his captors began to pour oil over his head and body. He could not see well, but he heard a beastly roar which could only have come from Orrick, and then an answering roar that he knew to be Asha. Within moments, he could see the great cougar tearing through the Oxmen, drawing ever closer. Suddenly flames erupted about him; Dhresden's pain was immediate and twofold. His body ached from the flames, but he anguished over Asha's suffering and the probable doom of Orrick and whomever had accompanied him. He felt that his torment could not have been worse, and then he saw her. Just above the crowd, he spied Tala, her bow aimed at him. Tears streamed from her eyes, though her aim appeared steady. He judged that she must be acting in mercy, delivering her loved one from the fire's pain, but he was simultaneously saddened that she had given up hope. The harshness of his losses: the throne, his life, his love came upon him in a rush, and as the arrow pierced him through and the catapult was released, the most mournful cry that had ever been heard atop the Outcropping issued forth from Dhresden's lips.

In the darkness and flames and pain, Dhresden had no knowledge of when his outward trajectory became a downward fall. His mind raced with thoughts of the past several days and the heartache he and his loved ones had undergone. Through the burning, his thoughts became more self-focused, self-pity growing until an unexplainable resentment enveloped him. Two things happened just before Dhresden hit the water: the flames burned through his bonds, freeing his arms; and Dhresden began to wonder why he was feeling such hatred for his loved ones. But as he slammed deep into the water and the flames were extinguished, all reason left him. Dhresden surfaced moments later feeling refreshed, but took no notice. His face grim, hatred smoldering deep, the man who should be dead wrenched Tala's arrow from his chest and looked grimly at it while floating in the frigid lake. Then, with the arrow still clutched in his fist, Dhresden began to swim towards the unseen shore, unmindful of his increasing strength or vanishing pain. When he finally reached the shallows and waded ashore, his hair remained singed off but his wounds had disappeared. Dhresden took no notice of this miraculous healing; he seethed with hatred and lusted for revenge. Dressed in tatters and armed with an arrow, he set off to take vengeance upon the ones who had betrayed him. And he would start with the worst transgressor of them all—Tala.

CHAPTER 16

The would-be rescuers fled quickly through the sewers the way that they had come. All bore grim countenance, though Orrick's was most dour. He had been unable to save his lord and friend, unable to repay the man to whom he had sworn indebtedness, and at the present he had no idea where two of his comrades were, but he vowed death before he allowed another of his companions to die.

All remained quiet as they raced from the sewers into the royal siege room and quickly barred the door. Looking around the room at the others, Orrick quickly took charge.

"Two of our number are unaccounted for," the giant began, "and I have no intention of leaving without them."

"Neither have I," Wyeth agreed, "but how can the five of us and a huge cougar not be discovered while we search for the lady and Khaldun?"

"We will not be found because I am the only one who will remain." Orrick's words brought immediate protest from Mallory and Wyeth, while Shika and Tala kept silent, but cast a furtive glance at each other.

"I know all your arguments," Orrick's voice boomed over them, bringing them to silence, "for I have argued them with myself already. I have failed Dhresden, and no fault to the rest of you, but I will allow no harm to come to his mother or sister. I will stay, while the rest of you flee to the mountains; my countrymen there will protect you."

"No disrespect to you or your countrymen," Wyeth spoke up wryly, "but the Wanderlanders are not known for their trust of outsiders. What's to keep them from slaying us as trespassers and liars; they have no reason to believe what we say."

"Asha will accompany you," Orrick responded with a distant look in his eye. "She is known to my countrymen and will act as a token of your honesty."

"Also," Wyeth went on, "despite your talent for sneaking about, I believe that I am the better choice to stay; after all, we Kelvren have been keeping out of man's sight for millennia."

Orrick kept quiet a moment, considering Wyeth's argument. It was then that Tala spoke up.

"We need to find Dhresden," she said simply.

Orrick looked at her as if seeing her for the first time. After a moment he spoke in a gentle tone that few ever heard. "I loved Dhresden as much as you, Tala, but we have no time for a proper burial. The lake will have to suffice."

"No," she said firmly, "we must find Dhresden. He is alive and he will need our help."

Concerned suddenly for Tala's sanity, Orrick was about to speak when Mallory interrupted with a probing question.

"Why do you think Dhresden is alive, Tala?"

Again the two sisters glanced at each other before Shika answered for them both. "Tala used the healing potion given by Tiblak to anoint an arrowhead. She then shot it into Dhresden just as he was launched toward the lake."

All kept silent, unwilling to give in to a hope that could prove false. It was Wyeth who next spoke, and that was quietly and gently to Tala. "How much of the potion would have been absorbed, little one?" he asked. "Would it really have been enough to keep him alive through all that he has endured?"

Tala was quiet while she considered Wyeth's question. She had placed the arrow tip down into the vial, intending that the vial shatter upon impact, while the arrow tip entered his body, drawing the potion with it. "I believe that almost half of the serum could have been absorbed. How much would it have taken?"

Wyeth took a deep breath. "Well that depends on the mixture. With the weakest of the common recipes, that should have been enough to keep him alive." It was Wyeth's turn for silent thought before he spoke again. "Tala is right; Dhresden must be found. I wish you speed in finding him" "The little man then moved to the door and unbarred it. He turned and looked at Orrick, who nodded and then followed Wyeth into the hall. Glancing back into the room to be sure the others were out of earshot, the giant leaned down toward the smaller man.

"What have you not told us?" Orrick whispered.

"It is possible that enough of the potion could have been absorbed to heal him, yes, but if it was one of the more pure mixtures, it could drive him temporarily mad. If that is the case, he will be unreasonable and unnaturally strong. I do not know how long it will last, though you will be the one best suited to deal with him, but be careful. Once you have him, flee as you said to the mountains; I will meet you there."

"Thank you, my friend, and you yourself be careful," the giant said, patting Wyeth on the shoulder with his big hand. The two turned away from each other and set about their separate tasks. Leaving the door unbarred so that Wyeth could use the tunnel later if necessary, Orrick, Asha, Mallory, Shika, and Tala began to crawl out Mallory's secret entrance. One by one, as they reached the ledge, the fugitives leaped to the murky depths of Loch Norde. Asha reached the shore beside the groves first, followed by Orrick, and then the women.

"How shall we find him?" Mallory asked as she surveyed the darkness around them.

Orrick stood still, searching the air with his nostrils for the familiar scent of his friend, but met only disappointment. "The wind is light and shifting, we cannot rely upon it for direction, however, if we skirt around the lake we should find him and also bring ourselves closer to my homeland." The giant paused as he considered his next words carefully. "Keep a watchful eye. Treyherne will likely send troops after us, but be sure to keep vigil for Dhresden. We cannot know how he has been effected by the torture he has endured, or even of any side effects he may experience from the medicine."

Not wishing to cause undue alarm, he trusted that his words would provide enough of a sense of caution. Quickly now, Orrick began to lead the silent search for the friend they now hoped to be alive. In daylight with no need for secrecy, the journey around Loch Norde would take a rested group of travelers slightly more than a day to reach the mouth of the river from which the lake was fed. Traveling only at night, weary and facing unknown opposition possibly from friend as well as foe, Orrick had no way to estimate how long their journey would take. The groves were fairly devoid of underbrush, but the fruit trees had been maintained with low branches to allow for easy fruit harvesting, forcing their path to meander. Following the shoreline would allow them to move more quickly, but would put them on a course predictable to any pursuers. Asha would often forge ahead, silent on her padded feet, to scout the immediate area and then crouch under the concealing branches of some old apple or peach tree while she awaited her companions. They had moved along for almost two hours without break or incident, when the shifting wind brought Orrick a familiar smell so briefly that he almost dismissed it. He called the group to a halt, hoping for another sniff to guide their search.

"Rest a moment," Orrick said quietly, "and take turns filling your waterskins at the lake."

Tala sat as patiently as she could against the trunk of one of the smaller trees. She was anxious to find the man she loved but sensible enough to submit to Orrick's capable leadership. When Mallory returned from the lake, Shika came to Tala's side.

"Come sister," she said, "walk with me to the lake. You will be of no use to your beloved if you become dehydrated."

"You go. I will take my fill when you return." It was evident that Tala wanted to be alone.

"No, I will take *my* fill when *you* return," Shika said with a loving smile, though it was clear that she would not relent.

Tala rose and embraced her sister. They had been through much together and had yet to think of themselves before the other.

"I love you, Shika," Tala whispered.

"I love you too," she sighed, "but you are still going to the lake now."

With a chuckle and a squeeze, Tala released her sister and weaved her way through the trees to the water's edge. She gazed out over the water, its surface reflecting the blanket of stars overhead, while its dark depths called out discouragingly, mocking her hope. It seemed so long since she had gazed into Dhresden's dark eyes and glimpsed his very soul; how she longed to set eyes upon him again. And then, suddenly, Dhresden was there beside her.

~ ~ ~

Khaldun and Jovanna hurried cautiously through the dark tunnels, eager to reunite with the others. Their self-appointed mission had taken longer than either of them had expected, and though Jovanna would easily lead the way back to the royal siege room, neither knew what course they should then take; whether to await the return of Orrick and the others, or to flee as they had come. Furthest from them was the desire to desert any of their company in time of need, but neither did they wish to be sacrificed on the altar of indecision or misinformation.

They continued on, coming to a junction where another larger section of tunnel joined up with the main passage through which they traveled. Both Khaldun and Jovanna stopped abruptly and pressed themselves tightly against the wall of the sewer where the shadows were darkest. The sound had been unmistakable: the thud of a body dropping awkwardly to the floor. Surely it would be none of their company, Jovanna thought, knowing that Khaldun was having the same consideration. The hushed angry whispers and cursing that followed confirmed their suspicions; someone not of their party, possibly the Oxmen, had entered the drainage system.

Jovanna and Khaldun huddled there by the wall, knowing that they needed to continue down the main tunnel to reach their goal, but unsure whether the Oxmen were only in the side passage. Paralyzed by uncertainty, the two remained in place, hoping that the Oxmen that were now entering the main passageway a scant thirty paces to their front would pass by without seeing them. There looked to be nine of them, though it was difficult to be sure. Jovanna's hand moved slowly to the hilt of her sword, ready to strike should the Oxmen discover them. Her knuckles began to whiten as she gripped the handle of her sword too firmly, she was becoming more and more tense as the enemy drew nearer. She forced herself to draw a quiet, deep breath and relaxed her grip a bit. She needed to hold her weapon firmly and yet continue to allow the blood to flow freely through her fingers, and then she found herself wondering if that was something her late husband had taught her or Dhresden. Jovanna's heart ached at the thought of Dhane, but hope flickered as she concluded that the Oxmen must be flooding the sewers in response to the successful rescue of Dhresden.

The Oxmen were almost upon them, and Khaldun and Jovanna readied themselves to fight, but then came the sound of another body thudding on the tunnel floor. The Oxmen stopped in their advance, and turned back toward the side passageway. Someone towards the rear of their group was cursing about an arrow protruding from a fallen soldier, and the rest of the searching party of soldiers turned and charged back down the side tunnel they had just left, certain that their enemy lay in that direction.

Waiting just long enough to be sure they would not be spotted by the departing Oxmen, Khaldun and Jovanna sprinted quietly past the passageway through which the Oxmen had exited. Their quick strides brought them almost face to face with nine more Oxmen who were hurrying back to assist their comrades. Two of their number fell stunned almost immediately, Khaldun's quarterstaff not even a blur in the darkness. Jovanna thrust her blade expertly into the closest opponent, twisting him into the path of another of the Oxmen as he fell. She pulled the blade free and swung it in a wide arc; her sword sparked against the stone wall and sliced into the man who was now tripping over his fallen colleague. He screamed briefly in pain and was silent; the remaining Oxmen halted their advance, searching the darkness as best they could. They were uncertain of their enemy, either of its size or skill, and could not know how many of their eighteen had been slain by this shadowed adversary. Khaldun and Jovanna both knew that they must get past the remaining Oxmen before they became surrounded by the reinforcements that must come. The darkness about them served as both an ally and a foe, as did the obstacle of the slain lying about them; but hesitation would be their greatest enemy, and their undoing.

Somewhere in the darkness a bowstring twanged, and both Khaldun and Jovanna cringed as an arrow swished between them and into one of the Oxmen with a sickening thud. Unsure what was happening, whether an enemy behind them was blindly firing arrows into the darkness hoping to strike them or if some unidentified ally were somehow able to see their foe, the two crouched even lower. Twice more a bowstring twanged, and twice more the thud of an arrow piercing armor and flesh was heard, accompanied by the clatter of arms and armor as two dead Oxmen fell to the stone floor. The hurried footfalls of the last Oxman in that group retreating down the tunnel were silenced by yet another arrow.

Knowing the arrows had landed too accurately to have been coincidental, Khaldun and Jovanna rose and turned, awaiting the arrival of whatever ally had assisted them, but in the darkness they neither saw nor heard anyone approaching.

"We must hurry," came Wyeth's voice from a mere stride away in the darkness. "More Oxmen are coming, and they may have thought to bring torches or lamps. Follow me." And with that he passed quickly between them, his short legs carrying him along more swiftly than one would have thought possible. Khaldun's and Jovanna's minds burned with unasked questions, but since silence and stealth were their ally, their curiosity must wait to be quenched. Moments languished by as they stole along through the sewers, finally nearing the door to the royal siege room. Slowing to a stop, the three of them listened intently, straining to hear anything that would serve as a warning of enemy presence in their path. It was doubtful that any of their foe were within the siege room waiting to ambush them, but very likely that Oxmen were gaining on them while they stood, unmoving, silent and listening. The reality of their peril came in the form of a quiet, small scrape that almost went unheard. Wyeth alone had perceived it: the sound of a boot upon stone as someone shifted his weight from one foot to the other, and it had come from the room that the companions had been about to enter. Wyeth signaled Khaldun and Jovanna to follow him, and the three of them proceeded silently down the tunnel until they had reached a distance at which Wyeth believed they could converse without being discovered.

"So the problem now," he concluded, after he had recounted the details of the last hours, including the failed rescue attempt, "is finding safe passage out of the bowels of Havenstone and into the presence of our remaining company." His eyes came to rest on Jovanna, who alone might know of some alternate escape route. She stood there in the darkness, her mind spinning with all that had occurred in her absence, fighting the dread that Dhresden could be, should be, dead. After several patient moments of silence, Wyeth reached out and gently took her hand in his. The contact roused Jovanna from the abyss of despair, and her hushed voice took on a strength that almost startled the two men with her.

"We will need to walk out the cattle gate when the herds are ushered into the fields at daybreak. We must find our way to the stockyards and clothe ourselves in the garb of the herdsmen."

"Is there no other way?" Wyeth asked, not desiring the exposure that would be required to execute Jovanna's plan.

"Nothing else comes to mind," she replied almost haughtily, "except that staying only ensures discovery."

Wyeth and Khaldun nodded agreement, and with Jovanna in the lead the three of them crept cautiously and quickly through the network of tunnels toward the stockyards. Several times they were forced to alter their route, or to duck into a side passage to avoid groups of Oxmen, some bearing torches while others searched in the darkness hoping to stumble upon or be stumbled upon by the fugitives.

The three of them could smell the cattle stalls several long strides before reaching the drain leading up to the stockyards. In the gray predawn light, Wyeth leaped to the underside of the drain and hung there, listening to be sure that it was safe. Presently he found footholds and with his arms, lifted the drain, slid it to the side, and disappeared through the opening. In a moment, he dropped back through the opening and the two men hefted Jovanna up toward the drain. She grasped the sides and pulled herself easily through the opening, followed quickly by Wyeth and then Khaldun. Wyeth directed them to a sliding door at the back of the barn and closed it behind them. They found themselves in a grain room, its aroma a welcome change from that of the sewers. On the floor before them, Jovanna discerned the form of a man, but before she could inquire, Wyeth answered her question.

"He spotted me as I came up from the sewers, and I him. He was a bit slower than I. Oh, he is not dead, my lady, but we will have fled before he awakens." With that Wyeth knelt and removed the drab brown cloak from the unconscious man and tossed it to Khaldun to wear. He retrieved two more herdsmen's cloaks hanging from a peg on the wall and he and Jovanna shrouded themselves in the tattered garb that was their best and only hope for escape.

Leaving the grain room, Jovanna led them toward the free stall, a large fenced holding area used to house several of the animals tended by the inhabitants of the Outcropping. All of the citizen's cattle were free-range, grazing carelessly in the pasturelands under the watchful eyes of the herdsmen until the Rotation. The Rotation was an appointed time when a randomized group of the herd, usually numbering around one hundred, though seasonally almost as high as two hundred, were shepherded from the pasturelands to the city and kept in the free stall. This expedited the butchering of those animals best suited for meat and also the harvesting of milk, as well as selection of promising young stock that could be trained for use as Oxmen mounts. It was customary for more than half of the animals selected for Rotation to return to the field, and it happened that today the remaining chosen animals were being returned to the range. Though scattered throughout the Pasturelands, the herdsmen were a close-knit group, held together by the ties of their occupation and the mild, though sometimes stinging, disdain of the "city dwellers." It was this familiarity between the herdsmen that now threatened the three fugitives. Though the sun had not yet crested the horizon, the hooded cloaks worn by Jovanna and her two companions threatened to be insufficient to hide them from the keen eyes of the herdsmen. It could be the unfamiliar gait of one of them, or the trace of a scent that did not belong that would arouse suspicion. The three of them entered the free stall, weaving their way amidst the cows, goats, and sheep that were slowly making their way toward the cattle gate. Relieved that the animals seemed to accept them as the herdsmen that they appeared to be, Jovanna, Wyeth, and Khaldun began to distance themselves from each other, hoping now to escape detection by the herdsmen.

The three of them had made good progress to this point, and from their cautiously distanced positions, each could spy the open gate through which the line of cattle was passing and through which they planned to escape. Step after step brought them closer to their goal and the opportunity to seek out Orrick and the others. Again Jovanna hoped within herself against the hard bitter truth that loomed over the horizon of her heart, that somehow Dhresden lived. The sight of a hooded and cloaked herdsman standing at the open gate, assessing the herd as it passed through, startled her from her thoughts. The herdsman evidenced no malice, and yet there he was, soon to be within an arm span of her. Jovanna's mind raced, trying to decide what course of action to take: to continue on her current path at the edge of the herd where she may be spoken to and discovered, or to drift in among the herd and place one or two of the beasts between herself and the herdsman where she may risk spooking the herd if they decided she should not be there. Choosing the uncertainty of the herd over sure discovery by the sentinel herdsman, Jovanna slowly made her way into the river of cattle, positioning herself so that a large steer towered to her right, hiding her from the direct gaze of the herdsman. On she walked, matching pace with the great beast beside her as she neared the cattle gate and the promise of evading capture. Jovanna had lost sight of her two companions, but felt certain that they were proceeding as successfully as she; no alarm had been raised, and no cattle had startled or stampeded because of the three intruders among them.

Distracted by her thoughts, or due to her unfamiliarity with the situation, Jovanna failed to notice the shift in the herd. The animals had been traveling along toward the gate in a fairly loose line, but the opening of the cattle gate proved to be more narrow than the width of the traveling herd. The spacing between the beasts had gradually narrowed until Jovanna found herself trapped on all sides by their large forms. Outweighed many fold, there was no way to hold them away, and trying to scurry under the belly of one of them would surely result in being trampled and discovered. Jovanna knew that she may well be crushed if she did not seek help, yet fear that calling for aid may mean capture and death to not only herself but also her companions kept her silent. She would rather herself die than cause the death of such faithful men as Wyeth and Khaldun. And so it was that Jovanna resigned herself to the less than dignified, though still noble, fate of being crushed and trampled by benign beasts in an effort to protect her friends. With all the beauty and grace that she had ever possessed, she walked along, her breathing labored as she began to be crushed; the pressure forcing air from her lungs and refusing to allow her a new breath. The press now upon her was so great that she no longer walked but was held upright and in place by the sheer mass of the ignorant beasts beside her as the early dawn seemed to fade from her view. Jovanna knew that she was losing consciousness, and that once through the cattle gate, the herd would widen and loosen again, releasing the holding pressure upon her and allowing her unconscious body to slip to the ground, only to have the remaining life trampled from her by the unknowing hooves behind. Yet she refused to call for help, even as she fought to breath, to stay awake, to find some handhold or lock of shaggy fur that she could tangle her fingers in and hopefully be dragged along rather than trampled. Alas, the only success she managed was in not crying out, and that largely due to insufficient air to call for help. Raising her eyes to the sky, Jovanna looked once more upon the pink hued clouds above her, even as the black form of Death himself seemed to lean over her, reaching down to grasp her roughly by her outstretched wrist. Her last thought before the darkness took her completely was that she would soon be in the presence of Dhane again, and possibly Dhresden as well.

CHAPTER 17

For a moment, Tala was uncertain of what to do. Dhresden stood but a short distance from her, and she could be in his arms in an instant, yet something held her back. His dark locks had been burned away, and what remained of his garments hung in wet, charred rags about him, yet Tala knew it to be him. It was not his changed appearance that gave her pause. It was his eyes. His dark eyes burned into her own, not with the joy of being alive and of seeing her again, but with what? Here was her love, miraculously alive and yet Tala could feel every muscle in her body tensing, ready to flee from him.

"Tala," Dhresden whispered, his tone hidden in the breathy mention of her name, "I am alive!" He reached one hand toward her weakly, inviting her to come to him even as he stepped toward her. Tala threw her arms about him and sobbed quietly against his chest and neck, so relieved that she had actually found him and that, yes, the gift from Tiblak had truly worked.

"I am alive," Dhresden whispered again, his hand caressing her back as they stood beside the lake. "I am alive," he said, his voice louder, his hand moving to touch her hair. "I am alive!" Dhresden shouted, grasping a fistful of her dark locks and yanking her head painfully back. Tala looked fearfully up into Dhresden's eyes and saw madness. Tiblak's potion had worked too well, too much had been absorbed by Dhresden's tortured body and now his mind was clouded with an insanity from which he may not recover. "I am alive, though you sought to kill me!" Dhresden screamed, spittle flying from his lips as he raged. "But I am alive," he growled, "and I have a gift for you!" Still gripping Tala by her hair with one hand, Dhresden raised his other hand high. Tala saw that in it he held the very arrow she had used to save his life, but the potion had robbed Dhresden of all reason. She felt him tense as he prepared to plunge the tip deeply into her chest.

"Dhresden, I love you!" she managed, through sobs, which only seemed to infuriate him more. He screamed again, wordlessly, in rage, and then again in pain, releasing Tala and clutching his right forearm. In the darkness, Tala could see one of her sister's arrows protruding from Dhresden's arm.

"Run, Tala!" she heard Shika yell from somewhere. Tala scrambled to get up, aware that Dhresden had already snapped the arrow from his arm and was leaping beastlike toward her. She turned away from the lake and started for the groves, but could see that Dhresden was almost upon her. Suddenly another snarling form leapt past her and collided against Dhresden's, the two of them tumbling into the shallows of Loch Norde. Tala halted her retreat, and turned to see what would come of this battle.

Orrick had finally caught wind of Dhresden's scent enough to know his location, though even the stench of his insanity had been carried to the mountain man's nostrils. Wisely, Orrick had stripped himself of his weapons, fearing injury to his friend and mentor, but also fearing the prospect of Dhresden using his weapons against him. And so it was that the Black Wanderer, weaponless but for his bare hands, threw himself at the one man for whom he would have gladly died, hoping to subdue Dhresden until the effects of the potion could wear off. Yet lingering and gnawing at the pit of his stomach was the smoldering fear that Dhresden's poisoned mind would only be at peace in death.

Intending to choke Dhresden into unconsciousness quickly, Orrick had encircled Dhresden's neck with his left arm as their bodies met. As the two landed in the water, Orrick ensnared Dhresden about the midsection with his legs and used his right arm to reinforce his grip on Dhresden's neck. Dhresden reigned blow after blow against Orrick's ribs with his elbows, seeking to dislodge his attacker. Finding no release from the giant's grasp, Dhresden reached up and behind his own head and grabbed a handful of Orrick's golden locks with one hand and began to claw into his left eye with the other. Orrick had realized his crazed friend's intent too late and was instantly blinded in a flash of light and stab of pain. He tightened his grip upon Dhresden's neck in spite of the injury, turning his head this way and that, trying to evade further harm as he waited for Dhresden's strength to fade. It was the second intrusion into Orrick's left eye that relaxed his grip enough for Dhresden to pry himself free of Orrick's arms. He spun quickly in the grasp of Orrick's legs and, now face-to-face, the two began to exchange and block blows to each other's head, chest, and neck. Blinded in his left eye, Orrick was unable to block many of Dhresden's vicious right handed blows. Weakening, and finding himself underwater again and again, Orrick felt his grip on Dhresden again loosening. Through his pain and grief, the giant fought now to simply hold on, both to his crazed friend and to consciousness.

Tala had realized the tide of the battle was turning and fled from the shore to her sister's side. Shika stood a few paces within the edge of the groves, her bow at the ready. Tala gathered her weapons from her sister as Mallory came hurrying up with Asha in tow. The sisters quickly began to inform her of the current situation, but Mallory quickly interrupted them.

"Orrick told me where he was going," she said. "Judging by the look on your faces, Orrick is likely dead and our only hope of subduing Dhresden is in killing him." Mallory stated these facts in apparent indifference, and yet both Shika and Tala could see the sorrow behind her eyes.

"There must be another way," Tala pleaded. "I do not believe he has any weapons—"

"And yet he was able to overcome Orrick," Mallory broke in. "Tala, if there were another way I would choose it, but the man who is coming for us is no longer Dhresden. Like it or not, Dhresden died at Firebane, and I shall not die here at this stranger's hands."

Resigning herself to Mallory's logic, Tala notched an arrow, as did Shika. The sisters waited, one to the right and one to the left of Mallory, who stood with her sword at the ready. Asha paced in front of them, a low growl that seemed more of a whine deep in her chest, as though she, too, were conflicted regarding their situation.

The moments dragged by as the four of them awaited the attack that they knew was coming. No sound came to the women's ears, save that of the light wind gently plucking the autumn leaves from the trees about them. Abruptly Asha ceased her pacing and stood with her face pointing in the direction from which Tala had fled. She no longer made a sound nor did she move, though the tip of her tail twitched nervously and then stopped. A low growl began, but whether from Asha, or somewhere else, Tala could not discern. The growl continued quietly, growing neither in volume nor intensity, and yet the effect on Tala and the others was unnerving. As tense as they had been, the waiting—the unknown—left them more and more unsettled. And then, in the gloom before them, there was the glimmer of movement. Shika and Tala bent their bows and awaited a clear target, while Mallory tensed visibly, her whitening fingers upon the handle of her sword unseen in the darkness. As the shape and form of a man became more evident, the sisters perfected their aim upon the center of his mass.

It was a brief instant before the release of Shika and Tala's arrows that the growling ceased. Suddenly, Asha crouched and tensed, ready to spring. At that instant, Mallory gasped and cried out, "Orrick!" And it was. The giant loomed before them, staggering and swaying, clearly unsteady on his feet. Mallory sheathed her sword and rushed forward. Shika and Tala lowered their arrows, but were shocked when Asha snarled and leaped into the shadows to their right.

As the great cat crashed into the darkness and underbrush of the Grove, a second voice joined hers in beastly chorus, the harmony of growls and snarls warring just out of sight. As far as Mallory and the others knew, Dhresden was still unarmed, but, even weaponless, was his insane ferocity enough to overcome or at least cripple the gray cougar? The two could be heard thrashing and crashing about, their roaring and rumbling ceaseless. The battle carried on unseen, when to the terrified audience's ears something changed. One voice ceased, but the tone of the other, its fierceness seemed less threatening, with possibly a hint of pain. Then came the sound of a great form crashing quickly away from Orrick and the three women, the noise of ferocity and pain seeming to fade with it into the distance.

Fearing that Dhresden had somehow bested Asha, the four companions, hearts sorrowing for all their losses, prepared for what would become the execution of the Lord of Havenstone.

~ ~ ~

Jovanna could feel the warmth of the sun upon her face as she began to wake. The soft caress of a blanket about her and the gentle sway and roll of movement beneath her told her that she had dozed as she rode along in the royal coach. She could hear Dhane speaking through the window of the carriage to someone, and though his words were hushed in an effort not to wake her, she felt certain that he and Dhresden were discussing something important. She strained to make out the words, but could not. There was an urgency in Dhane's tone that she seldom heard, and as she continued to come awake, Jovanna's waking mind feebly resisted the idea that it was neither Dhane's nor Dhresden's voice she was hearing, but she could not discern why. The warmth and comfort of the royal carriage faded as she opened her eyes, replaced by the lumpiness of sacks of grain beneath her and the weight of a herdsman's cloak upon her. Jovanna found two sets of eyes upon her, one set blue, one green, both sparkling with curiosity. Though she could not recall exactly why or how, Jovanna found herself riding in a wagon with several dozen sacks of grain and two small children. She moved to sit up and felt a sharp pain in her ribs, which stabbed into her memory. The events of the past months flooded her consciousness: the passing of Dhane, the journey to his burial, the naming of Dhresden, his capture and execution. In sorrow she recalled the futile efforts of the little rescue party, and her attempt to escape among the herd, only to be crushed between two great beasts and yet...

"You almost died," the little boy said, accusingly. "It's a good thing father saw that you were in trouble. You should not have been there, even Opal knows to stay out from between th—"

"Enough, Dirk!" his sister scolded. "Father said she is our guest, now speak kindly to her or not at all."

Dirk's face darkened a moment before he spoke. This time his dissatisfaction was aimed at Opal. "Being older does not mean you can boss me around!" He paused, unsure of his next words. Emboldened by the justification in his own mind, he went on, "Father also said to always tell the truth and that is just what I was doing!" Dirk punctuated this statement with a sharp nod and folded arms. Before his well-intentioned sister could retort, Jovanna spoke up.

"I thank you for your hospitality, young ones, and I beg your forgiveness for the intrusion." The startled looks on the faces of the children made Jovanna wonder if they had believed her incapable of speech. "Tell me please; where is your father?"

The children sat quietly, gazing at her. Perplexed, Jovanna looked about, seeing the great herd moving along about the wagon, and beyond, the rolling meadows of the Pasturelands.

"Ah, you are awake I see," came a strong but pleasant voice behind her. Jovanna turned to find that she was being addressed by one of the herdsmen. A slender staff rested in the crook of his arm as he stood shrouded in the brown weathered folds of his cloak. His kind eyes regarded her from amidst chiseled features, framed by a bushy red beard and hair. It seemed to Jovanna that there was something he wished to say, or had planned to say, yet held back. After an awkward silent moment, she thanked him for his aid.

"Think nothing of it, miss," he said, a twinkle in his eyes. "It is always a pleasure to assist a member of the royal family!"

Uncertain, Jovanna chose her words carefully. "Royal family?!" she scoffed, "I doubt quite seriously, sir, that any member of the royal family would submit to such transportation or apparel! Why, I think it highly unl—"

"Please, Lady Jovanna," he interrupted gently. "You have nothing to fear in the care of my people. My name is Faust. Come, I shall show you to your companions."

Faust leaned slightly forward, one hand outstretched to help her. Jovanna took his hand, which gently and firmly gripped hers, and stood. She found herself to be a bit unsteady atop the bagged grain at first, but recovered after a brief moment. All about the wagon milled large beasts, the cattle completely obscuring any glimpse of the ground. How she were to be escorted anywhere she could not fathom. Faust's gentle hand continued to grip hers, and when Jovanna would have let go of his hand, he held hers fast.

"You are under my protection now, my lady, and unless you have cattle-hopped before, I must insist that you hold my hand."

Before she could protest or inquire, Faust leapt from the wagon onto the back of the nearest of the herd, pulling her along with him. Standing atop the back of the beast as it walked, the two looked at each other. Jovanna's surprised eyes looked up into Faust's amused and yet protective gaze. It was clear that she need not fear this man. Jovanna smiled at him as much as to say: "If you can do it so can I! Lead on!" Faust flashed a wide grin back at her and the two proceeded to leap from back to back throughout the herd. Jovanna felt a twinge of disappointment when they came at last to their destination. In another wagon they found Wyeth, Khaldun, and another herdsman seated close together on sacks of grain. The three appeared to have been in deep discussion but respectfully stood to greet her. Khaldun bowed low in the custom of his people, while Wyeth ignored pre-scribed etiquette and lifted the woman from off her feet in a broth-erly embrace, whooping joyfully at the same time.

"I am so relieved to see you in such good health, my lady," he exclaimed as he set her down. "I was certain we had lost you, and we would have had it not been for old Faust here! He is the one who spotted you and pulled you to safety. He and his people have promised their protection to the end of our days in honor of your late husband."

Jovanna turned to face Faust once again, who appeared to be mildly blushing. It was she now who offered a hand, not to assist him but rather to thank him. "My gratitude is extended to you once again, Faust. It seems you are a man of integrity, a character which has grown scarce in these dark times."

Faust took her hand and smiled in response, then, clearing his throat, he spoke. "Jhaun leads us," he said gesturing towards the herdsman who had been seated with Wyeth and Khaldun when they arrived. "Any gratitude you feel should be directed towards him."

Jovanna turned to the other herdsman, a kind-faced older man whose long white hair shown brightly in contrast to his drab cloak. "Thank you, grand herdsman Jhaun," she said, "for your assistance, protection and hospitality. I and my companions are ever in your debt."

"You are most welcome, Lady Jovanna," the old man replied, "but my people were placed in your family's debt long years ago, though you seem to know nothing of the matter. Sacks of grain are all I have to offer, but please, sit and talk with me."

As Jovanna and then the men sat down, Jhaun began to explain. "I shall not bore you with the account in great detail; however, some elements bear repeating. In a time early in Dhane's rule, by way of a census he discovered that of the prisoners at the Citadel a large population appeared to have no basis for their incarceration. He could neither find record of their trespasses in the annals of the Citadel nor could he ascertain any type of verbal recollection among the eldest of the scribes at the Citadel. Dhane's plan to discover the answer to this mystery was an unprecedented visit by the Lord of Havenstone himself into the bowels of the dungeon.

"Dhane ignored the protests from his advisors and took three of the royal guard with him, each armed with a torch and a simple wooden club. Dhane knew for whom he was searching; the census had provided him with that information. I was still very young but I remember my mother and father hiding me under some old clothes and blankets and warning me to be quiet. My father was somewhat of a leader of the prisoners at that time, and since his name was on the census as "unaccounted for," it seemed logical that Dhane speak with him. The prisons of that time were more like a series of caves under the Outcropping into which both man and woman were cast to fend for themselves, except for the occasional wagonload of half-rotten bread and vegetables. My father and many others who had been wrongly imprisoned had banded together for protection from the true criminals and their cutthroat ways. It seems that my father had been overheard speaking against the corruption of an advisor to Dhane's predecessor and had been cast into the dungeon for it. Such was the case for many in our community, and Dhane felt burdened to affect some sort of change on our behalf. While he was not naïve to believe that all in our circle were truly innocent, Dhane trusted my father enough to believe that our community was worth redemption and vowed to set us free. As shrewd as he was, Dhane knew that we would not be well received by the general populace, so his plan was for us to become the Herdsmen. We would be given occupation with payment, and we would have a freedom many of us had never known."

Jhaun's aged voice quavered, but after a deep breath he continued. "Forgive me, my lady. It is just that, I was born in that old prison beneath the Citadel, as were many of my childhood friends. Dhane's kindness in giving us freedom has never been and will never be forgotten. In serving you, we serve him. Thank you for the opportunity to partially repay an old debt."

CHAPTER 18

The encounter between Asha and Dhresden, for all its noise, had consisted of very little contact. While the crazed half-blood had thrown himself repeatedly at the gray cougar, Asha kept just out of his reach, her snarls seeming to taunt Dhresden and infuriate his already enraged mind. Suddenly the great cat clubbed the side of Dhresden's head clawlessly with one large paw, which sent him sprawling to the ground. In that instant Asha pounced on him, grasping his leg at the calf in her great jaw. Her teeth bit painfully into Dhresden's leg, and, with a firm grip, Asha turned and bounded away from Orrick and the others, her primitive mind functioning more keenly than the beast's which she bore along with her.

Asha had grasped Dhresden's leg in such a way that he faced away from her as she speedily dragged him along, similar to a rider whose foot became snagged in the stirrup as his mount continued to run. Even so, he fought furiously to twist to an angle from which he could attack her, and Asha was forced to slam Dhresden against a tree or rock or thorny bush as she ran in order to keep him sub-dued. Her prey's snarls soon ceased, and yet the great cat hurried on. His attempts to attack her also ended, and yet Asha continued along. Several long moments passed without a sound or apparent movement from Dhresden before the grey cougar slowed. The dark of night had begun to gray with the new day. Asha stopped, ready to tighten her tired grip on Dhresden's leg and begin bounding again through the whole of the Pasturelands if necessary should he again begin his wild flailing.

Long minutes she stood there panting, his leg in her mouth until, with a soft mewling, Asha released Dhresden and backed slowly away. She crouched cautiously low to the ground watching Dhresden, but saw no movement nor heard any sound from her human companion. Stoic and watchful, Asha kept vigil as the autumn sun broke over the horizon, but after two hours of daylight without any sign of life from Dhresden, the great cat, emitting a mournful sound, rolled to her side and gave in to her great fatigue.

It was just past midday when Asha awoke. The cougar startled awake, unsure exactly what had roused her from exhausted slumber. Blinking at the bright sunlight now shining down on her, Asha discovered that she was being watched. A short distance away, dark eyes set in a brown face twinkled at her. The two remained motionless, each trying to decipher what the other might do. Neither evidenced any malice in their demeanor; in fact, Asha still lay restfully on her side, though in an instant she could assume a much more menacing posture if necessary.

"Asha." The single word and its tone brought the cougar quickly to her feet.

~ ~ ~

Mallory, Shika, and Tala had, with great effort, convinced Orrick to rest while they kept watch. The four were as yet uncertain what had occurred between the great cat and the crazed half-blood, but after the better half of a silent hour and apparent safety, they prevailed upon the Wanderer to at least recline upon the ground. Mallory had provided what care she could for him, but was resigned to binding rough bandages around his head and against his eye. The bleeding had slowed, but the damage to his eye and eyelid required a covering against contamination and infection. Orrick claimed that the pain was minor, but without strong ale or medicine, his only relief was to chew on the dried bitter root of beggar's weed which Mallory carried in her pack for headaches and minor pains. It was toward the end of his wounds being dressed that Orrick, from fatigue, sorrow and pain, fell asleep.

The three women all stood watch for the following hour. No attempts were made to discuss the most recent mournful events; each kept to her own thoughts as they surveilled against attack. Finally,

Shika broke the silence, suggesting that she continue to stand guard while Tala and Mallory slept; and though reluctant, they agreed.

Not long after sunrise, despite his exhaustion, Orrick awoke. He looked about with his good eye, finding Mallory beside him and Tala a few feet away both asleep. Next he spotted Shika; she crouched near her sister, her questioning, concerned eyes on the wounded giant. His confusion was evident to her, his mind swimming through a thick fog of pain and fatigue as he tried to order his thoughts and memories of the last day's events. Orrick's hand rose slowly to his bandaged eye as if discovering the wound for the first time. Shika was relieved to see his hand come away only faintly crimson. The rags covering his eye had become blood-soaked, but the bleeding had stopped. Orrick sat staring at his hand a long while, long enough that Shika began to wonder if more than his body had been wounded. Orrick shook his head to bring himself out of his thoughts, winced at the pain it caused, and turned and laid his hand gently on Mallory's shoulder. He whispered something to her that Shika could not hear and Mallory stirred and looked worriedly up at his face. Orrick managed a weak smile, but even that faint expression flooded Mallory's face with relief. As the two of them shared a long embrace, Shika rose and moved to her sister's side. Tala woke quickly and gathered her few things together, eager for...what? Dhresden must be dead somewhere, otherwise his madness surely would have driven him to find and attack them again by now. Uncle had died at the Outcropping, should she now flee with her sister back to the inn, to scratch out a living serving drinks and meals to boarders at the Lone Reed? They were of noble blood, meant for such splendid adventures as this, and yet it seemed that defeat had come, and that it had taken many forms.

"We cannot stay here," Orrick said, breaking into her thoughts, his voice stronger than anticipated. All three women looked at him expectantly, wondering what exactly his plan now entailed. "Neither Dhresden nor Asha has returned, and of that, I do not know the meaning." He paused and his gaze fell to the ground before him. He may have lost two of his closest friends, the half-blood and the cougar, in one night but that was an issue best pondered from a safe haven. "The quickest avenue out of the Pasturelands, and away from

Treyherne's clutches is to the mountains and my people. The only drawback is this lake," he gestured toward Loche Norde with a wave of his hand and continued. "I am certain that Treyherne will commission Oxmen patrols to circle the lake in an effort to catch or kill all of us. As we observed during our journey to the Citadel, there are numerous Oxmen patrols in the direction from which we came. I do not trust myself to function as I ought in travel, much less in battle, and so I believe we have no other recourse but to flee to the western Dunes in the hopes of eluding the Oxmen altogether. Once we reach their borders, we will head north to the mountains and my country."

Wordlessly, Mallory and Shika readied their packs as Tala had, while Orrick donned his weapons. The logic of the Wanderlander's plan was sound, and yet a glimmer of doubt tugged gently but briefly at a corner of Tala's mind, and then faded, swallowed up in sorrow. No. Dhresden was dead. His body had experienced enough pain and suffering to cause the death of five men, not to mention the condition his tortured mind would have left him in. No, death had visited Dhresden too often and too long, and his broken spirit must now enter the rest of his fathers. In resignation and loss, Tala fell in step with her companions, their grim, tired faces set towards the west, the baggage of their sorrows heavy upon them.

~~~

The herdsmen had set camp shortly before sunset; their nimble hands, familiar with the task, had their tents set up quickly, and their modest cook fires glowed throughout the plain. The tents were scattered about, seemingly without order, a sea of cattle wandering lazily among them until the sun set. Once darkness settled, the animals ceased their grazing and lay about peacefully in groups, content to rest until sunrise under the herdsmen's watchful eyes. The whole day, Jovanna had traveled in wonder, amazed at the bond shared by the cattle and its keepers. She had observed many Oxmen, both in training as well as the Oxmen Elite, and had never witnessed this camaraderie between those riders and their mounts. As she wandered amongst the herd, making her way to her camp, she was further amazed at the interaction between the herdsmen and the animals. She saw men, women, and children checking hooves, playing with the calves and speaking in low gentle tones. Nearing her hosts' tent, Jovanna realized what set the herdsmen apart from the Oxmen whereas the Oxmen valued their mounts, the herdsmen considered the animals to be as much a part of their family as a beast could be.

Jovanna, Wyeth, and Khaldun found themselves in the hospitality of both Jhaun and Faust, their tents pitched on either side of a fire that their households shared. The grand herdsman's household consisted of his wife, Naobi, and a daughter called Pau'Je. Naobi's small frame, kind smile and eyes contrasted with her calloused strong hands as she busied herself about her home, pleasantly talking with her guests. Pau'Je, with Faust's daughter Opal by her side, also busied herself about the tent, quick to help her mother and tend to the visitors, but she kept quiet, responding with little more than a pleasant smile. The neighboring tent housed Faust, his daughter Opal and his son Dirk, who, despite Dirk's displeased attitude at their first encounter, seemed to be quickly becoming fond of Jovanna. He scurried quickly to her side and began to gently but playfully pull on her hand.

"Come with me," he pleaded, "there is someone I want you to meet!"

"Not so fast," Jovanna laughed, "we must honor Naobi's hard work and hospitality, and how could we do that if we are not present when she tries to serve us?"

Dirk's brow furrowed in deep thought and he ceased tugging on Jovanna's arm, though he still clasped her hand in both of his. He was not upset, because he knew she was right: Naobi should be shown respect; and yet he so badly wished not to wait. It was Naobi herself who ended the boy's pained deliberation.

"You two scurry along," she chuckled. "Supper will be ready when you return."

Jovanna smiled her thanks to Naobi and allowed herself to be pulled along by the excited, whooping little boy. The night had deepened and cooled away from the fire as Dirk led her nimbly amongst the herd, his voice now quiet and soothing as he reassured the cattle. They had not gone far from the light of the fire when Dirk stopped.

He lifted his arm and pointed. "There he is," he whispered proudly. In the darkness, Jovanna was unsure of whom he spoke. The only forms she could distinguish were a few large bulls and cows bedded down for the night. Dirk spoke again, low enough that Jovanna could not understand the words. She was about to inquire of the boy what he had said, when a form rose from amidst the livestock and began to move the remaining few feet towards them. Jovanna could tell that it was a young member of the herd since it stood at about the height of the large mature beasts lying in the grass around them. "His name is Ox. He is now large enough for me to ride, and father has been training us both when he can." The boy stepped forward and hugged the young bull about the neck, then stood there alternately petting his nose and patting his side.

Jovanna too stepped forward to greet this new acquaintance, who neither started nor cowered at the approach of this stranger. Jovanna had learned in her short time among the herdsmen that there was little that the herd feared when one of their shepherds was near, even one as young and small as Dirk. Jovanna pet the young bull's forehead, feeling him push gently against her hand as if there were some persistent itch or tickle in just that spot that he needed help with.

"He is quite impressive," Jovanna said quietly. "I believe he will be a leader in the herd one day, or even a captain's mount in the Oxmen."

Dirk did not respond at first, seemingly content to stand with his hand resting on the back of Ox's neck. After a time, the lad spoke, and as he shared his thoughts, Jovanna began to realize what it was that weighed upon him.

"Before Ox was born," Dirk said solemnly, "his mother, Fern, left the herd. Some say she wandered off, but I do not believe it. I think that Fern left hoping to save her baby." He stopped, and Jovanna could sense his burden, but did not quite understand.

"What do you mean, Dirk? Save her baby from what?"

Dirk sighed, took a deep breath, and began to explain. "An Oxmen dispatch came the morning after Fern had disappeared. The soldiers had come to collect any cattle that met certain requirements for a special detachment of the Oxmen. I think that somehow Fern knew that her baby was going to meet those requirements and that she did not want Ox to be with the Oxmen, so she left."

As he spoke, Jovanna began to realize that the boy was afraid of losing Ox, that as a member of the royal family she would confiscate Dirk's little bull.

"Father and the others were busy trying to reason with the Oxmen dispatch, I admit that I did not yet understand all of what was happening, but things got very heated."

Jovanna, however, understood. Whatever the traits were of the beasts the Oxmen were searching for, removing all such animals from the herd would greatly reduce the likelihood of subsequent generations exhibiting those characteristics, traits that serve to enrich the herd through selective breeding.

"Whatever father and the Oxmen were arguing about, I knew that we needed to find Fern, so I grabbed my rod and went searching for her. It took me a while to find her, and it was through no tracking skill that I did. Fern had hidden far from the camp in a thicket of short thorny trees. Near the center of that thicket was where I found her." Dirk's voice grew grim as he continued. "Fern had laid down and had begun to birth her baby when a small pack of wolves found her and attacked her. She was already dead when I got there, but from my hiding spot I could see Ox's little feet where Fern had begun to freshen. As terrified as I was I held my staff the way father and grandfather had shown me and walked slowly towards Fern. When I came to a wolf, I struck it with my rod. The first one, he never got up to run, but the others jumped up at the noise and began to growl at me. I just kept walking toward Fern, sick at the thought of what those devils had done to her, and if a wolf got too close, then I made him yelp. Most of them ran away, but a couple needed to yelp a few more times before leaving me be. I pulled little Ox clear of his mother's body and cleaned his nose out like I have seen father and the other herdsmen do, but it took a little to get Ox breathing. I finally did and was busy trying to get Ox cleaned up when father found me. I knew he was upset that I had gone off alone, but he told me that he was proud of me and that I could keep Ox."

Jovanna was stunned by the boy's story. It certainly seemed that he was telling the truth, but a part of her hoped that Dirk was lying. At a mere ten years old, the boy had seen and endured more tragedy than many experienced in a lifetime, and yet he lived with the fear that his bull, no, his friend, Ox, would be taken from him.

"Dirk," Jovanna soothed, "I do not wish to take Ox away from you, and if it is within my power, I will not allow anyone else to take him from you." The boy's smile lit the darkness as he threw himself at Jovanna, hugging her tightly.

"Thank you, my lady! Thank you so!" Jovanna held the boy a long moment, feeling his relief flood into her. Patting his back, she held him at arm's length and smiled at him.

"Well! We had best be headed back for dinner before Naobi comes looking for us!" They said their goodbyes to Ox and turned in the direction of the cook fire. As they walked, Jovanna asked, "What kinds of animals were the Oxmen seeking that day, Dirk?"

"Strong ones! Young bulls with strong parents."

"But Dirk," Jovanna protested, "we are surrounded by strong animals."

"Yes," the boy admitted, "but they also had to be Hitomi. The Oxmen took all the other Hitomi and now Ox is the only one we have with blue eyes."

CHAPTER 19

A calm had settled upon the camp as the last clatter of after dinner cleanup ended. Jovanna had insisted that she be allowed to assist in the tidying of the plates, pots and pans that had been dirtied in honor of her and her companions. It had seemed at first that Naobi had begrudgingly agreed, but as the work progressed, Jovanna realized that the older woman was pleased to have the opportunity to fellowship the more with her guest. The two younger women, Opal and Pau'Je, also helped, and even entered into the discussion at times. Once the chores were finished, Jovanna spotted Faust and Jhaun sitting near each other by the campfire, which had been allowed to die down to little more than a pile of smoldering embers. Though only coals, it provided enough light to see who you were talking to, and the heat felt good. As she approached the two herdsmen, Jhaun finished smoking his pipe, tapped its ash into the fire and strained to his feet. He greeted Jovanna with a smile.

"Good night, Lady Jovanna. At my age, I have given up on beauty sleep and will settle for plain old sleep." With a chuckle, he hobbled off to his tent. Jovanna sat by the fire, soaking in its warmth before she spoke.

"That is quite an animal your son has," she said, noticing a change in Faust's eyes as he gazed at the fire. "I do believe that Dirk would fight his way through any number of beasts to protect his little bull."

Faust's eyes moved from the fire to Jovanna, and after a brief silence he spoke. "He told you about the wolves did he? Well, that is a bit of a surprise. He has never really told anyone about what happened. I know only because I found him there, but he does not speak of the events of that day."

"He did share some of the details with me, but he kept back enough that I was not entirely sure that he had not embellished the tale."

Faust did not immediately reply. His eyes, now haunted by the image in his mind, were fixed once again on the fire. "My little boy had killed three of those beasts by the time I arrived. The rest had retreated to where they could watch him, possibly with the intent of attacking him, but slinked away at my approach. I will not dishonor you with the description of how we must remove a calf from a dead cow, but the horrors my son went through that day to save that little bull." His voice quavered and trailed off, but then he went on, "Dirk's mother, my wife, died when Dirk was just a toddler. He has gone without so much that a young boy should have. He fought hard for Ox and I will allow no one to take him from Dirk. Not the wolves, not the Oxmen, not even if Treyherne himself showed up demanding the blue-eyed bull."

Jovanna saw before her a different man from whom she had met less than a day prior. Faust had greeted her with a disarming smile and a quiet wit, and she had seen through the day that he was hard working, a gentleman who treated man and beast with respect. Now she glimpsed his passion, and his ferocious love for his son, and no doubt for the rest of his family as well. It was not an unreasonable and blind devotion to his family that Faust had displayed, but it could be clearly seen that he possessed a hatred for the corrupt ways of man, of men like Treyherne. Jovanna had known of the selection of blue-eyed cattle for use in the Oxmen Elite, but had not realized the extent of Treyherne's sedition. As a citizen of the Pasturelands, and even more as an advisor to the king, Treyherne was obligated to uphold and preserve the resources of the land. This of course meant the plant life, but also the animals, both free and bond. By removing all the Hitomi from the herd, Treyherne was removing the trait of blue eyes from the blood line. Practices such as these were forbidden and wasteful.

"And who is Treyherne," Jovanna declared, "that he should separate such friends as Dirk and Ox!? The man is a snake, and should be treated as such!"

Jovanna realized that Faust's eyes were no longer upon the fire, but were now fixed upon her. What was this new expression? What was it in his eyes that invited her confidence?

"Tell me, my lady, what treachery has Treyherne brought against you?" Faust asked the question certain that Treyherne was responsible for Jovanna fleeing the Citadel in the manner in which he had found her.

~ ~ ~

At daybreak the next morning, Jovanna shared with Wyeth and Khaldun what she had learned from Faust. While Khaldun appeared incredulous, Wyeth's words conveyed his own understanding.

"By removing all of the Hitomi from the herd, Treyherne is violating critical laws of the land; fundamental laws the violation of which are grounds for removal from power and imprisonment, and in some cases even death."

"So," Khaldun spoke up, seeking to clarify the implications, "even though Dhresden is dead, Treyherne could still be removed from power on the basis of his lack of compliance with Pastureland law."

"Yes!" Jovanna said, her mind afire with the possibility of still thwarting Treyherne's evil plans.

"Not to be a naysayer, my lady," Wyeth interjected, "but we are fugitives from the law, regardless of the corruption of those in power. We have no assurance that we would ever be able to present our information in a court of law where it could actually effect change. So other than reinforcing what we already know of the snake…"

"True, but if we could get a letter to the right persons in council, Treyherne could be unseated from power and the Pasturelands would be safe again. There are three—no, four—councilors that we could trust: Eriks, Sachshe, Bromlin, and Tungstein."

"Bromlin," Wyeth replied, "I know him. I will approach him and share with him our findings. Will Faust be willing to testify before the Council of Thirteen? They can be an intimidating bunc——"

"He and any or all of the herdsman are ready and willing to do their part in removing Treyherne from power!" It was Faust who had spoken. He had approached unseen and had stood listening to the three of them discuss the situation. "Are you convinced it is most wise, my lady, that Sir Wyeth undertake this task alone? I have able herdsmen who could accompany him."

Jovanna smiled her thanks at Faust, but turned to the old Kelvren with the question. "Well, Wyeth? Do you wish to proceed alone? The herdsmen are commonly seen entering the gates, so you could blend in easily enough with them."

"Thank you, my lady, and herdsman Faust, for the gracious offer and consideration. I will decline, however; and will depart at midday. If I neither return nor send word in seven days, then you will know that some ill has befallen me. My advice to you in that scenario is to flee. In Kelvar you would be safe, even welcomed. Those of the Wanderlands would give you harbor, though their hospitality is sometimes as cold as the stone and snow amidst which they reside. Tiblak would welcome you, though life in the Bog can become tedious." He smiled, but could not manage to keep it from being more of a grimace.

"We of the western Dunes would be honored to have you, my lady." Khaldun bowed low as he spoke. Though left unspoken, Khaldun felt as though the debt his people owed to the honor of Dhane had not yet been satisfied, and now in the shadow of Khalid's traitorous acts and Dhresden's death, Khaldun considered himself even further indebted to Dhane's widow and daughter.

"Thank you, Khaldun," Jovanna replied, her smile and eyes clearly conveying her appreciation to the young Makani. She turned back to Wyeth, "I do not know what path I will take," she admitted, "but I do know that our chances for success are hopeful. I shall therefore expect the best. Now take your leave of us and ready yourself, and do be careful, my friend."

~ ~ ~

Autumn continued to hold on with feeble hands to the climate of the Pasturelands, slowly changing into winter, but the air around Orrick had grown increasingly drier and warmer each day of their journey. The giant trudged westward, the sweat of his brow trickling occasionally into his eyes, or, his eye and the wound where his eye had been. Orrick spent much of this journey in thought, reliving his battle with Dhresden again and again, amazed not at his friend's ferocity, but at Dhresden's shear animal nature and unchecked rage. Orrick and Dhresden had sparred often, both with weapons and bare handed, and though he and the smaller man always kept their intensity somewhat in check, Orrick had known that both of them were capable of much more than that to which they gave themselves over in their practice sessions. The beast that Orrick had battled was something more—and less—than the man he had once called his friend. Orrick had begun to understand why Tiblak's forebears had almost entirely done away with the production of *ferial,* except for medicinal use. The degradation of human reason, coupled with the addictive nature of the potion would have wiped out the inhabitants of the Bog to the last soul. Orrick wondered anew what may have happened to Asha and Dhresden, but again thrust the thought aside. His current mission was the protection and safe passage of the three women in his charge.

The women traveling with the wounded giant did not consider themselves to be in Orrick's care, but rather that he was in theirs. Shika had taken the lead of the column early on, recognizing Orrick's initial disorientation and ignoring his protests that he was fine. Mallory kept near the man she loved, as watchful of him as she was of possible danger hidden about them. Tala brought up the rear of the party, her mind fighting against sorrow for the memory of Dhresden and of what might have been.

The four companions had lost count of the number of days they had traveled, but were relieved to discover the terrain about them changing. Instead of the thick lush grasses which blanketed the Pasturelands, the plant life was transitioning into scrub brush and twisted, stunted trees growing out of a ground composed of sand and stone. It was expected that it would take at least two days of travel into the western Dunes before they would know how best to reach their intended destination: the Cliffs of Hawa Janbiyah. The women had prevailed against Orrick to forego the journey north to the mountains, arguing that the giant man's health prohibited lengthening their journey. Taking shelter with the Makani was the wisest course of action. As the political and economic hub of the western Dunes, the Cliffs was where the rulers of the region could be found, and though Orrick remained uncertain regarding what course of action should be taken next against Treyherne, he knew that he needed to place his companions under the care of the Makani.

The daylight hours in this new terrain grew even warmer, while the nights seemed to become more frigid. Their first night in the western Dunes, the small group had neglected to start a fire as they settled camp for the night. Though Orrick enjoyed the cold air, he found himself searching around in the dark for enough tinder and twigs to light a small fire around which the three women could huddle and warm themselves.

The second morning in the western Dunes, Orrick and his companions awoke to find themselves surrounded. The men about them did not wear the blue and silver of the Oxmen, but rather they wore the long flowing sand-colored cloaks of the Makani. These sixteen strangers, organized into four loose groups, sat quietly upon the ground as though they were reluctant to rouse these visitors to their land and were simply waiting for them to waken on their own.

Recognizing that the Makani surrounding them could have killed him and his three companions while they slept, and still wearied from the journey and his barely healed wounds, Orrick rose slowly to his feet. The Makani each remained seated, though every head and eye turned and fixed upon this one-eyed giant who now towered above them. Orrick fastened his one blue eye on the group nearest him and held the gaze of each of the four men in turn. Finally, the mountain man broke the silence, his voice low but carrying easily to the ears of all.

"I am Orrick, of the Wanderlands. I serve in the honor and memory of Dhane, Lord Havenstone, and have come to seek the hospitality of the Makani for these three women and for myself." He said nothing more, for nothing more would need to be said on his behalf. Orrick had identified himself and had both invoked the name of the revered Dhane and the Makani custom of hospitality. Only an outlaw or an insane man would disregard these two customs, and Orrick judged that the men before him were neither criminal nor crazy. Silence hung heavy in the air until a man in one of the other groups to Orrick's left spoke.

"I know of you, Black Wanderer." Orrick had to turn his head in order to see the man with his good eye. The speaker still crouched upon the ground, eying Orrick thoughtfully. The giant stood looking back at him, waiting for the customary introduction which should next come. To delay the greeting was considered particularly rude, and could indicate that the reception into the Dunes that Orrick had expected may instead take the form of imprisonment. Could it be that Treyherne's treachery had extended to this coast, could the full-scale corruption of the Makani have already taken place? Knowing the speed and skill of these warriors against blades, Orrick decided that the best weapon choice would be his flail, but as he casually slid his hand into his flail pouch, he remembered with a sigh that he had left it with Uncle. And so, blades and bows it would be, should it come to—

"I am Zabayr, of the Dunes. I serve the Makani and our lord, Hazrat Almadi bin Khuzaymah. You shall be our guests, as you have requested, but please, explain to me your mention of Dhane the Havenstone lord."

Orrick regarded Zabayr a moment, then beckoned Mallory to rise and stand beside him. Orrick's presence comforted her, and yet Mallory was not convinced that all was well. Orrick turned back to the Makani commander and stated simply, "This is Dhane's daughter." Instantly all sixteen of the Makani were standing, heads bowed, right hands extended with palms up as though offering their hand to Mallory.

"Please allow us to escort you to the castle of Hazrat Almadi bin Khuzaymah," Zabayr said. "I can see you are wearied from your journey, so please continue to rest here. I will send Waddah to the north to bring khamelleros for you to ride. You are safe now, be not afraid."

~ ~ ~

It was midday before Waddah returned with four khamelleros in tow. He did not ride any of them, neither did he tether them in order to lead them. Waddah simply bounded along at a quick jog, the four awkward looking beasts keeping pace close behind. The man came directly to Zabayr, while the beasts stopped a stone's throw away and stood calmly, their jaws moving much like a cow. In every other way the khamelleros were nothing like a cow. Rather than hooves, the foot of the khamellero was wide, almost webbed, to allow the animal to step on the surface of the desert sand rather than sinking into it. Though a four-legged animal, the body and neck of the khamellero could be likened to that of a swan, but with fur rather than feathers. Its head was not unlike that of a sheep, and atop the back of the khamellero was mounted an odd saddle.

"As soon as you are ready," Zabayr said, "choose a mount for the journey. Each is capable of carrying great burdens, so whatever khamellero you choose will be sufficient to transport you, Orrick of the Wanderlands. The high-backed saddle and armrests will allow the four of you to sleep without fear of falling, should you choose to slumber. We will walk the khamelleros the first few miles so that you can become familiar with their movements, but we will break into a run to cover greater distance for the remainder of the day. If there are no questions, we will begin once you are astride your mounts."

"I have a question," Tala said. "How do we get up on these things?"

Zabayr broke into a wide smile, realizing that he had neglected a very basic detail. "Which khamellero would you choose?" Tala looked at the four of them, then pointed at one that appeared to be a light tawny gray. "Sapphire!" Zabayr called, and the gray khamellero quickly trotted over and knelt down to the ground. At this height, Tala had no difficulty climbing into the saddle, attaching her pack to the saddle horn before her. "Are you ready?" Zabayr asked, and again spoke to the khamellero, who then stood up rather effortlessly.

Within moments Shika, Mallory, and finally, Orrick sat atop their own khamellero, ready to begin the next leg of the journey. With a lurch, the caravan was under way. The khamelleros walked in single file, no bridle or bit forcing them along. The sixteen Makani had formed a diamond pattern around their mounted guests and walked along at the same rate of speed as the khamelleros. The gait of these strange new mounts was much more graceful than any of Orrick's group had anticipated, and all were soon peacefully sleep. So secure was each rider in his saddle that none of them stirred when the khamelleros, as well as the Makani around them, eased into a fast run. Had Orrick or one of the women roused, they would have been amazed at the swift grace of not just their mounts, but also that of the sixteen men on foot keeping pace with the khamelleros.

It was dusk when the four beasts again knelt to the ground, waking their riders. Looking around, Orrick saw Zabayr and the other Makani readying a cook fire, waving an invitation to join them. Drawn as much by the delicious aroma of whatever was being cooked as by the Makanis' hospitality, Orrick and the ladies seated themselves amidst these new acquaintances around the fire. Conversation was scarce at first, but as strips were cut from the meat that was roasting on the spit and passed around, the newly formed group found themselves engaged in pleasant banter about this and that, nothing of substance, though all were at ease. All, that is, except the four Makani who had slipped quietly from the group and were now patrolling the darkness beyond the reach of the fire's glow.

Such was the way of the Makani; all delegations of warriors were composed of groups of four called Arba'a, a practice begun at a young age once the Makani youth had mastered kharida. Kharida is an old Makani word which means "untouched" and is the first quest that a young Makani, boy or girl, must achieve. The idea of kharida is not that the individual be unaffected by the cares or trials of this world, but rather that in spite of the cares and trials of this world, the Makani will achieve and maintain an appropriate state of awareness. The result of this mindset is summarized in one word: selflessness.

A truly selfless person is less concerned for the well-being of himself than for others, and though he sees to the rudimentary needs of his own body, will deny himself of basic provision for the sake of another. It is this type of selflessness that is sought to be instilled within the youth of the Dunes early in their training. Once this has been achieved, the youth's skills are examined to determine where his strengths and weaknesses, likes and dislikes lie. For those who have achieved kharida there is one of two paths: lawyer or warrior. The lawyer is moved to the Library for continued education, while the warrior is sent to the Barrens. Once there, he is then grouped with three others who complement one another, each having strengths where the other is weak. These four warriors will become their own Arba'a, their own team of four.

At length, however, it was time for the visitors to retire. Many thanks were given to their hosts, and then Orrick and his friends moved to the edge of the light cast by the fire, and each rolled himself into a blanket provided by the Makani. Sleep was creeping swiftly upon them when Shika broke the silence. "That meat was delicious! Orrick, do you know what it was?" she asked softly.

Orrick's big smile went unseen in the darkness as he replied. "Khamellero."

All was silent again, but presently he heard Shika's voice, quieter than before. "At least they taste better than they smell."

Once the stifled laughter subsided, sleep enveloped them.

CHAPTER 20

D awn found the group that had fled the Pasturelands well rested, and, after a quick breakfast of some fruit the Makani provided, ready for the remainder of their journey to the Cliffs. More familiar now with their mounts, Orrick and the others were still amazed at their agility and speed, as well as that of the sixteen Makani who somehow kept pace. The mismatched group stopped but a few times during the day, and as the sun's rays began to transform the landscape with its evening hues, they came within sight of the Cliffs of Hawa Janbiyah. The red and gold beams of sunlight reflected off the chief structures of the Makani, hewn as it were directly into the white stone of what appeared to be the edge of the world.

"It is beautiful!" Mallory breathed, the words scarcely a whisper, yet exactly the shared sentiment of her companions. The khamelleros had slowed to a walk and as the group drew nearer the Cliffs, the khamelleros angled closer and closer to the edge of the precipice. Sensing his guests' uneasiness, Zabayr spoke up. "This is the entrance to the Cliffs. Do you see that line of stone?" he asked, pointing their attention to a now shadowed line of large jagged boulders which seemed to run the entire width of the peninsula upon which the city was built. "There is a method that our forefathers had for changing sand into glass. We still have a similar method today, but several thousand years ago the method was different. What you are looking at is a defensive line of sharp jagged glass that is as hard to break as iron. We call this the Shards. It is impassible, and so we must enter the Cliffs on the only remaining road."

As they continued on, angling still closer to the edge of the cliff, Orrick saw that the Shards stood over twice the height of a man, and were half again that in thickness. He also saw that the road upon which they were now being taken was scarcely more than a scratch along the side of the stone, and yet the khamelleros again proved to be surefooted as they bore their riders along the narrow way.

Finally, they reached the widening of the trail; Orrick and the three women dismounted, and found themselves greeted by a throng of people. Men, women, and children all smiled benevolently at these guests, but quickly moved aside to allow them to pass. Zabayr led them quickly through the network of halls and to the chamber where sat several men, apparently awaiting their arrival. All stood and bowed in greeting as they entered the room, and while the ladies and Orrick were seated at Zabayr's direction, their host began with the introductions.

"My lords, may I present to you Orrick, the Black Wanderer and his companions Shika and Tala, daughters of Nokoma, as well as Mallory, daughter of Dhane Lord Havenstone."

"You are most welcome as our esteemed guests," said one of the men. The others about him smiled their agreement, again bowed to these visitors and were then seated. "I am Hazrat Almadi bin Khuzaymah, grand master of the Makani. Though I am pleased to receive you as guests under my roof, I am puzzled as to the composition of your party. Tell me please, where are the Lady Jovanna and the heir Dhresden, and where are the two Makani that were dispatched to assist you?"

Over the next several minutes, Hazrat Khusaymah was informed of the details of the last weeks. Shika and Tala were content to keep silent while Orrick and Mallory conveyed the specifics of their journeying, battles, and loss. The declaration of Khalid's treachery set the Hazrat's eyes smoldering, while the news of Dhresden's death left the man's eyes glistening with unshed tears. Silence descended as Orrick and Mallory concluded conveying the necessary information to the grand master and his council. Long moments passed without response from Khuzaymah or his advisors, all of whom sat with their heads bowed, some with eyes closed, others staring either blankly or intently at a spot upon the table before them. At great length, the Makani ruler cleared his throat and spoke.

"The four of you are welcome for as long as you like; and should any of you choose to travel to your mountain home, Wanderer, or to another land, a squad of my finest Arba'a shall accompany you. Zabayr, please escort our guests to their quarters."

Despite the cautioning hand that Mallory placed upon his arm, Orrick was not to be restrained. "Grandmaster Khusaymah," he thundered, somehow without raising his voice, "It is without disrespect that I inquire further as to your plans. I know enough of the history of the Makani, and of the debt which lies upon all your shoulders, to be in no small measure surprised at your apparent lack of interest in this matter. I implore you not to retreat into some well-intended neutrality, for whether in weeks or months or even years you will discover a host of Treyherne's forces at your door. What will you now do with this knowledge?"

Khusaymah's steely gaze fixed on Orrick, whose face was unflinchingly set like flint toward the Makani ruler.

"Tell me, Orrick, what is it that you would ask of me?" he inquired. "Would you have me declare war upon the Pasturelands? The very lands that I fought beside Dhane to free? Even you were not yet birthed when that war was fought to liberate the Pasturelands from a tyrannical madman! Though that was many years ago, I shudder to think that I and my people would best honor the memory of the Lords of Havenstone by shedding the blood of their subjects."

The Makani ruler fell silent again, as did Orrick. The giant had mistaken the grandmaster's apparent hesitation as something akin to cowardice; now he clearly saw the issues with which Khuzaymah wrestled.

"Forgive me, Grandmaster," Orrick offered after a pause, "I spoke rashly, without thought to your honor. We gratefully accept your hospitality, and offer ourselves to your service as you see fit."

"Thank you, Wanderer," Khusaymah replied, "but the debt is ours, and it is we who are at your service. Tomorrow we shall discuss this further. It may be that together we will decipher what course we should next take. La'lono."

"La'lono, good day," Orrick replied, he and the three women turning to follow Zabayr out of the room.

"Please, this way," Zabayr said, and led them on in silence. The sun had set sometime during their meeting with Khusaymah and his advisors, and the guests found themselves led through quiet halls and courtyards lit by oil lamps which, though they burned dimly, provided adequate light to admire their surroundings. The white stone that comprised the walls, floor, and ceiling were now wheat colored in the flickering yellow lamplight. Even in their dim glow, the ornately carved stone columns, archways, and even great sections of wall would cause any of the visitors to slacken their step, or even to stop for an instant to gaze upon them. Many were simply patterns or familiar shapes, but several appeared to be renditions of life, some of war or a funeral, two young lovers sitting beneath a tree or an old man holding an infant. The detail was so exquisite in these carvings that Mallory and the others found themselves wanting to know the history of each of these scenes that they passed, but resigned themselves to the fact that if it were to happen it must be another day.

~ ~ ~

In the grey moments before dawn, the widowed Lady Jovanna sat before her host's cook fire, or rather, before the last embers of a fire left untended since the previous night's meal. She sat motionless, her borrowed herdsman cloak hiding her frame, the hood pulled up and shadowing her face and eyes so that Faust could not tell whether she slept or woke. He stood silently in the shadows off to her right, unsure what to do.

"I am sorry I let the fire die down so much," Jovanna said, rising and turning to the woodpile. She placed two pieces of firewood in the crook of one arm and managed another in her opposite hand before returning to place them strategically upon the hot coals. "I should have seen to it," she finished, finding her place and sitting again. Remaining silent, Faust tried to determine whether Jovanna again eyed the fire, or himself.

"How long have you been risen?" he asked finally. He awaited her answer in stillness, concerned that he already knew the answer.

The silence had grown thick without a reply from Jovanna before Faust spoke again. "Your old friend is quite resourceful; give him another day or so."

"Ha!" Jovanna laughed mirthlessly, "I have already allowed him extra days. Wyeth said he would send word in seven days' time or less. This is the dawn of the eleventh day! Surely you do not believe that he is merely delayed!? No, not Wyeth; his loyalty is too strong to be deferred by ought but chains or death."

"My lady, we have been traveling away from the Citadel and towards our winter camp since the dawn of the ninth day," Faust argued gently. "It will take some extra time for the old Kelvren to catch up to us. If you wish, we will stay camped here another night. It may be that Wyeth will arrive before the next dawn." Faust had stepped close to her, wanting to comfort her, to somehow lend strength to this strong and yet fragile woman. She had seen so much of death and suffering, and experienced such loss. Stark were their differences: royalty and herdsman, but it was his respect for her that kept Faust from gathering her into his embrace.

"Yes, wait a day," Jovanna murmured, her voice distant. The coals had ignited the new firewood; the flames, flickering yellow light across Jovanna's face, allowed Faust to see her now; her lovely features seemed aged with despair, her beautiful eyes had taken on a hollow, almost haunted look. She spoke again, so abruptly that Faust started. "Wait a day, wait ten days! Time does not matter when your family has been cursed! And cursed for what? For doing what you believed to be right? For doing what in time was proven to be right?! Wait as long as you wish, Faust, but it will not change the sadness of these days or the sorrow of the days to come!"

Faust thought to rebuff her, to tell her she was being silly, that all would be made right, but was silenced when suddenly Jovanna thrust herself into his arms, sobbing quietly, availing herself of the ready strength that his presence provided. How long the two stood holding each other beside the fire neither could tell; it was the clatter of the cook pots and the murmuring of Naobi to Pau'Je and Opal as they readied the morning meal that brought an end to their embrace. Standing now at arm's length from each other, Faust looked tenderly down at Jovanna, who was looking at the ground and busily wiping tears from her eyes. She quickly regained her composure and looking up, smiled her thanks to Faust. An unlikely bond had formed between these two, but to what end neither could guess. Jovanna was thankful for his companionship and counsel, while she seemed to be filling a void in Faust's life that had existed since his wife's death.

"I shall go and see if Naobi will allow me to help," Jovanna said, reluctant to end their moment together.

"Yes," Faust said, emotion heavy in his own voice. "And I will build the fire some more."

"Good morning, ladies," Jovanna greeted her hostess and her helpers as she drew near to them.

"Well, hello, my lady," Naobi replied, her eyes studying Jovanna's face a moment before peering past her in Faust's direction and then back to Jovanna. When she spoke again, Naobi's voice was quiet, but firm. "What is it, lady? What has my son done to upset you? He may be old and strong, but I raised him to accept his punishment with dignity! If he has been in any way disrespectful I will turn him over my knee directly!"

Jovanna was stunned by this small, sweet, old woman's intensity and her words stammered when she finally began to respond. "N—no, Naobi! Faust has been nothing but encouraging and supportive of me." She paused, the reality of Naobi's words suddenly sinking in. "I did not realize, Naobi, that Faust is your son."

Naobi smiled, a twinkle in her eye. "Yes, Faust is our youngest. His brothers left for distant lands, his sisters married and moved on, but Faust stayed. When my husband wakes no more, Faust will become grand herdsman. I love Jhaun, and I do not desire the death of my husband, but in my son I see the future of the herdsmen taking a path different from what we know, but whether to the right or to the left, I cannot say." With that, the old woman turned her attention back to the business at hand.

Unsure entirely of Naobi's words and their meaning, Jovanna began helping with the breakfast preparations.

CHAPTER 21

At Faust's direction, the herdsmen did not break camp that morning. Jovanna was able to pass the time easily; her release of emotions seemed to have in some way refreshed her. She ambled about the camp, helping where she could, but mostly she found herself admiring these simple people as they went about their day. The simplicity of a herdsman's life, however, did not equate to ease. There were the host of cattle to oversee: food and water, inspection for wounds or sickness and their remedy, inspection and care of their hooves, specific care for the old, the young, the heavy with child, and of course the protection of the herd. The herdsmen were charged with, and embraced, the safeguard of the herd from the elements as well as predators: wolves and other wild dogs, the occasional cougar from the mountains, bandits and wandering brigands, and, in times past, invading bands. There was also much the same responsibility for one's family and the herdsmen at large. The clan was also at the mercy of the weather—storms in any season could endanger man and beast, as well as their supplies and food source. The herdsmen preferred the open range to the confines of the Citadel, and so even the harshest of winters drove them to their winter camps rather than to the outskirts of the Citadel. The shadow of the Outcropping would bring provision of stored hay and grains, but it was an indebtedness that the herdsmen had avoided whenever possible.

Walking into the meadow, Jovanna had happened upon a young heifer lying in the tall grasses a stone's throw from camp. She had started when Jovanna approached, but was calmed again by this woman's soft and gentle voice as she mimicked the manner in which she had observed the herdsmen speaking to their charges.

Drawing nearer, Jovanna realized that this young female was great with calf, and that she would presently freshen. It had been a great while since the widowed lady of Havenstone had witnessed a birth, human or animal, but she recognized the tremor of fear and excitement that passed through herself, and certainly through this young mother-to-be. Near enough now, Jovanna reached out her hand to the forehead of the animal, gently but reassuringly running her hand along her head. Thus the two continued, awaiting the emergence of this young life hidden within its mother. At some point, Jovanna realized that she and the heifer were no longer alone. The three sets of eyes peering out from amongst the grasses had at first startled Jovanna, but recognition quickly calmed her. Dirk, Opal, and Pau'Je had crept up to check on her or the heifer; Jovanna did not know which, but she was pleased to have them along. Dirk's expression was a humorous mixture of boyish excitement mingled with the occasional seriousness of one too aged for his years. The youngest of the three, Opal, looked on with dreamy wonder, a consistent smile twitching the corners of her mouth. It was Pau'Je whose unchanging look stirred a mild unrest within Jovanna. The young woman had always maintained a cautious distance from Jovanna, both in proximity and conversation; not that she had even once been rude, but somehow hinting that Pau'Je harbored some degree of distrust towards this noblewoman.

The midday meal had come, and Naobi could be heard calling for Jovanna and the three other onlookers. Pau'Je turned and placed her mouth close to Opal's ear, whispering. Opal smiled brightly, waved goodbye to Jovanna, then hopped to her feet and headed back to camp to pass on Pau'Je's message to Naobi. The remaining three would stay to observe and assist if needed.

After several moments had passed, Jovanna motioned an invitation to Dirk and Pau'Je to come closer. Both were quick to comply, though Dirk was clearly the more eager of the two.

"Dirk," Jovanna said softly, "what is her name?"

Dirk's grin changed into a huge smile as he whispered back, "Ghorlia, she is a cousin to my bull, Ox." Little else was shared between the three beyond a look, a smile, or an occasional whisper. A full hour dragged by before the mood of the animal and then her three nursemaids changed. Ghorlia tensed anew, her whole body stiffening, and then she began to rock side to side.

"Do not allow her to stand!" Dirk's whisper knifed through the silence. "She could try to run from the pain, or the calf could get hurt falling that distance!"

"What should I—" Jovanna began, but stopped when both Dirk and Pau'Je sprang from the ground and gently but firmly leaned heavily on the heifer, preventing her from rising. Jovanna moved close, placing an arm around the back of Ghorlia's neck while continuing to pet her head and speak to her in calm assuring tones. After a few more attempts, Ghorlia ceased trying to rise, though her labor pains were increasing in frequency and ferocity. The young Dirk relocated to the tail of the animal to monitor the birthing process, a chore he had often participated in.

"One of the front hooves is showing!" he whispered, updating them on the progress. "This one has large feet; probably a bull." Several moments passed as the three awaited nature's course, but glancing back at Dirk, Jovanna saw that something unsettling had crept into the young boy's face.

"What is it, Dirk?" Jovanna asked, her stomach twisting in fearful anticipation of the boy's answer.

Dirk looked up, his pained eyes locking on hers. "The calf, it is breached—trying to come out backwards! We must hurry or we may lose both Ghorlia and her baby!"

Jovanna was unsure of what action they should now take and sat unmoving.

"Go back and help Dirk, I will stay here at her head and keep her from rising," said the usually silent Pau'Je, shaking Jovanna to action with her words.

Scurrying to the boy's side, Jovanna was startled at what she found. Dirk had actually reached inside where the calf was, his arm hidden almost to the shoulder. Glancing at Jovanna, Dirk quickly explained. "There are four things we could do: first, we could wait and see what happens. This rarely turns out well for the mom or baby. Second, we can cut Ghorlia's side open and remove the calf.

This is the fastest and safest for the calf, but the mom could die of infection or never birth again. Third, reach in and turn the calf around so he comes out headfirst. Ghorlia's pains are too advanced now; she is pushing hard, her body will not wait for us or allow us to turn the calf. Our only option is to pull the calf out backwards. We need to find both rear feet and tie them together at the ankles; it will take both of us to help pull. I need you to fetch my staff; I left it over where Pau'Je and I were watching from."

Jovanna rushed to the spot to retrieve the boy's staff, but struggled at first to locate it. The tall grasses and deepening shadows hid it from her eyes for a few moments, and it was actually her hands that happened upon it before her eyes discovered it. In that brief moment of relief, Jovanna realized that the setting sun meant two truths. This poor animal had been in labor since before lunchtime and now it was almost dark, and that the day would end without a message from Wyeth or his own arrival. Returning to Dirk's side, Jovanna was relieved to find that he had located both hind feet of the calf, which now were visible. Dirk had removed his rope belt from about his cloak and had tied one end securely around both of the exposed ankles. Taking his staff from Jovanna, he tied the other end of the belt around the middle of the staff.

"Sit here beside me. You hold this side, and I will hold the other. We will begin by leaning back; as we pull, we are applying slow steady pressure. If we try to go too fast one of them will be injured, so remember: slow steady pressure."

And so it was over the next two hours: the noblewoman and shepherd boy sat beside each other, both grasping a staff and gently pulling. It was a slow process, requiring each of them to rest first one hand and then the other, never ceasing to apply the slow steady pressure that little by little allowed more and more of the calf to be seen.

"Here is the hard part," Dirk whispered. "We are at the shoulder, the widest part of the calf. Ghorlia will likely bellow at the pain, but once those shoulders are out, the rest of the calf will come quickly."

With that, the two renewed their efforts, and within moments Ghorlia was protesting loudly against the pain. Her voice began as a low moan, but gradually rose in timbre and became shrill, sending a shiver down Jovanna's back, despite the fact that she was covered in perspiration and not a bit cold. Ghorlia stopped, took a breath, and bellowed again shrilly; the woman and the boy continued at their task, relieved when the resistance seemed to give way. Jovanna, unprepared for the sudden release, found herself lying full out on her back. She barely noticed the stars above her, but took a deep breath and rolled to her feet. She found Dirk kneeling over the newborn, unmoving calf; the boy was busily wiping moisture and fluids away from the calf's mouth and nose. He plucked a reed from the grasses about them and inserted it into the calf's nostril, wiggling it about; stopping only when the lifeless calf jerked, snorted, and then began to breathe on its own. Beaming at Jovanna, Dirk grabbed the rope at the calf's legs and quickly dragged him around to the front of its mother. The boy then removed the rope and leaned in to speak quietly to Ghorlia. He seated himself beside Jovanna, who pulled him close and sat holding him as they watched the exhausted young mother seem to find new energy and begin to lick clean her newborn baby.

It was then that the grasses about them began to rustle, and as the rustling drew nearer and lamps were ignited, Jovanna realized that several of the herdsman had given audience to this miracle in which she had participated. Many were the smiling and now familiar faces which gathered around the happy scene; Jovanna was surprised and pleased to learn that both Naobi and Jhaun had ventured forth despite their aging maladies. When her eyes discovered Faust watching her, his face suddenly illuminated by the light of a passing lamp, her heart fluttered and her breath caught in her throat in a way she had only experienced under the gaze of Dhane. The thought of her departed husband suddenly quelled the joy she had been feeling, replacing it instead with shame and guilt that she should so soon be reveling in the attentions of a man other than Dhane. Breaking suddenly from Faust's gaze, Jovanna turned to walk swiftly towards her quarters, but for the briefest moment, her eyes locked with those of Pau'Je, whose expression lacked any mirth, was even cold. Jovanna's gait remained dignified as she made her way to her tent;

her thoughts, feelings and fears swirling about her. Her family, for all she knew, was dead, and so must be her long-time friend, Wyeth. She now found herself tortured by a mixture of delight over her developing relationship with Faust and the sense of infidelity it elicited at the thought of her deceased husband. Catching sight of her tent in the darkness, Jovanna cast aside all concern for appearances, and ran sobbing, stumbling, into her tent, and, throwing herself down on her bed clothes, continued to weep in despair. No one heard her sobs, and no one saw the dark figure that crept quickly and quietly from the shadows to the door of her tent.

~ ~ ~

Snow fell again in the Pasturelands, adding yet another layer to the already thick white quilting which, weeks prior, had first signaled an end of autumn. It was not at all unusual to see so many snowfalls early in the season, though it was unexpected to find the snow accumulating to such an extent already. The latter end of winter was often so thick with snow that even the trade routes were untraveled until spring, but here in the first half of winter the snow had already halted most, if not all, of the foot traffic as well as travel by beast of burden.

The very snow that prevented most in the region from safe easy travel provided ideal protection for a lone figure hiking ever closer to the Citadel. Though the snow slowed progress, the figure, cloaked in white linen, advanced completely unseen, coming near enough to the outer walls of the Citadel to be spotted by the watchmen and would have been but for the snow. The number of sentries atop the wall had been decreased, as had their watchfulness, due to the absence of travelers throughout the region. Invisible amidst the snow, the ghost halted, settling down in the snow to retrieve some rations from a pack hidden beneath the linens. Chewing slowly, he studied the walls of the Citadel, awaiting nightfall. He looked about as if seeing it for the first time, though in truth he had visited it several times in his life. He could see the main entrance, the gates closed, probably barred, though they could be quickly opened from the inside if needed. He could not see the gate of the herdsmen at the opposite side of the city, but he could smell the entrance. It was not an unpleasant aroma, simply a distinct, familiar one.

The watcher had entered the capitol of the Pasturelands many times, and in many ways, but tonight he would enter by a familiar yet secret way. Rising, he grabbed a handful of snow and ate it as he circled past the main gate, drawing closer to the waters of Loche Norde. The lake itself proclaimed the winter's harshness; the surface already frozen over, though still thin towards the middle. Reaching the water's edge where it met the foot of the stone outcropping upon which the Citadel was built, the figure walked onto the ice, his hand stretched out beside him in contact with the stone. The side of the steep mountain was layered in thick ice, and would offer no foot-hold, yet he walked along, stopping after he had walked several paces. Looking about warily but seeing no one, a low call, like the sound of a winter bird, escaped his lips and was replaced by a silent smile as one end of a rope tumbled down from above, narrowly missing him. Gripping the rope in his strong hands, he tugged twice and was raised quickly to a small opening few knew existed. Entering the tunnel, he wordlessly greeted the lone cloaked figure that had hoisted him from the frozen surface of Loche Norde. He followed the smaller shadowed figure deep into the belly of the mountain, coming at last to a section of the sewers where a small fire burned, its smoke escaping unnoticed through the sewer vents. In the dim light of the meager fire, the two regarded each other a moment before either spoke.

"Do you remain certain of this plan?" the white clad man asked, pushing back his hood and beginning to loosen the ties that would then allow him to remove his linen outer garment.

The smaller, older man answered without hesitation, "Yes, I am certain of the plan, though I remain guarded." He paused, choosing his words carefully. "Not all of the players in our scheme can be accurately predicted, but the one I am sure can be trusted."

"How long will it take to arrive at the meeting place?" The taller man had removed his snow camouflage and gloves and sat thoughtfully rubbing his hands together near the warmth of the small fire.

"We can be there in less than a half hour," he replied, a wry grin playing at the corners of his mouth and eyes as he went on, "and the meeting is not scheduled for more than twice that time."

"Then we had best go now," he said, rising.

The two made good time, arriving sooner than predicted. They climbed from the network of tunnels through an access hatch close to the floor; the small metal door swung freely and silently out from the wall on well-oiled hinges. Both remained crouched for several moments behind a few well-placed wooden barrels and stacked crates, watching and listening for some sign of sabotage. Emerging from concealment, they walked a short distance down the hallway, seeing no one at this late hour, and entered a small study, lit by a single dim lamp. The two deftly searched the room, looking behind the hanging tapestries, the door, even under the table to discover any ambush or assassin lying in wait. Finding the room safe, both took up position at either side of the entrance, easily concealing themselves behind the tapestries in the dark. An hour passed before they heard several stealthy footfalls approaching. The footsteps paused outside the open door, a flurry of hushed, unintelligible whispers cast about, then four men entered the room. They walked in directly to the table, the first two sitting immediately in a chair, the third stood leaning against the table, while the last began pacing about, whether from nervousness, excitement, or something else altogether, none could say. The moments ticked by in silence, broken only by the muffled sound of boots pacing upon the carpeted floor of the little room.

"Are you eager for a new pair of boots, Eriks?" asked the man standing beside the table. "Or are do you wish me to replace the carpet?"

Eriks stopped pacing and whirled abruptly towards his companion, finding no humor in his friend's question. "We could be executed for this, Bromlin! And you loiter about as if waiting for your wife at the market!"

Bromlin took a step towards Eriks, his face stern. "Make no mistake, my friend; execution may be our end, but it is a welcome alternative to waiting for my wife at market." The two men seated at the table attempted unsuccessfully to stifle their laughter, while Bromlin, now smiling, placed an arm about Eriks' shoulders and moved him towards an empty chair. "Relax, Eriks. What we are doing is right; it is for the good of the kingdom."

"Yes, I know," Eriks sighed, sitting heavily in a chair, "but is the timing right? Doing the right thing at the wrong time could still end in disaster."

"You are cautious in your wisdom, friend; that is why you are here." Bromlin turned towards the two already seated. "Sachshe and Tungstein, though not as cautious, bring wisdom as well."

"Wisdom perhaps, but little patience this night," Sachshe grumbled. "My absence from the gatehouse is excusable for only a short time before arousing suspicion. Your mystery man had best arrive soon. Most of the Oxmen have bought in to the lies and vision of Treyherne, though a handful would follow me anywhere."

The two men who had remained hidden behind the tapestries stepped into view, the smaller of the two quietly closing and barring the door. "And to where would you lead them, Sachshe?" the younger man asked, throwing his hood back in the dim light. "Would you rally them through the crags and valleys of the Badlands, to the very gate of Graeta, and the altar of Chayne, as my father did?!" Stunned, none of the four, not even Bromlin, replied. Silence hung heavily as reality settled upon these four members of the Council of Thirteen.

"Yes," Sachshe finally replied, slipping from his chair and kneeling upon the floor. "They would follow me to that land, to face that evil, as your father did, Dhresden, true Lord of Havenstone." His three companions now knelt beside him, pledging their service to a man they had believed dead. Dhresden eyed them each in turn, then, nodding to Wyeth to remain at the door, bid the four rise. "We have much to discuss, and little time." Gathering close around the table, Dhresden asked many questions of these men who had at one time been advisors to his father, Dhane. Aside from an occasional inquiry, he spoke little and listened much, allowing the older men to speak freely of their concerns and observations of the past months and current days. As Sachshe had stated, the Oxmen, for the most part, would remain loyal to Treyherne in the face of any attempt to overthrow the usurper.

"Treyherne has beguiled them with the elixir of power," Tungstein spat. "They have become drunk with the almost unlimited power that he has given them; it is the people who suffer. The riders take what they want: food, arms, ale, cloth, even some of the women. The people feel helpless; they lack the tools and leadership necessary to overthrow Treyherne."

"What of the Council?" Dhresden asked. "Would the Thirteen not stand against him?"

Bromlin and the three other council members hung their heads collectively. "Half of them are too frightened to do anything, and the rest," Eriks sighed, "the rest are now as bad as the riders."

"But our troubles do not lie within our lands alone," Tungstein offered. "I have heard that Treyherne has made league with Ytero Uganji to the south, and that he also has made alliance with whoever leads the devils in the Badlands. Rumors are whispered that Chayne, by some wicked craft, is still alive."

Dhresden's brow furrowed. He had feared that Treyherne's treachery would reach beyond the Pasturelands, but the reality of the extent of his influence, and apparent allies, exceeded the worst of his expectations.

"We must discover whether these alliances truly exist, and how much strength lies therein," Dhresden said. "From all reports, the people of Havenstone grow weary of Treyherne's corruption and would welcome his replacement. His allies from the north and south, however, could attempt to sweep in during the upheaval of Treyherne's overthrow and establish some wicked union. Our resources will be taxed in a battle against the Oxmen; we may not be able to withstand the Ianzama and Chayne's Tulisan as well."

"We will gather all the information we can, Lord Havenstone," Eriks replied, bowing to honor this young lord who had cheated death. He marveled at how Dhresden had survived, but put the question aside for another day. He and his three fellow councilmen again pledged their loyalty and prepared to leave.

Bromlin paused beside the old Kelvren and smiled at him. "And you, Wyeth? How will you occupy your time?"

Wyeth's eyes twinkled as he answered, "I will be around, though few will see me." The twinkle faded as he went on, "If any of you should be discovered, flee the city immediately, but if you cannot, go to the Cattle Gate; it is all but abandoned this time of year. I will find you there and make arrangements for your safe passage."

"But to where shall we flee?" Tungstein asked, a hint of hopelessness lurking in his tone.

"Your choices are but two," Dhresden answered. "Trek to either the Bog or the Wanderlands. I have allies in both lands, though the men of the mountains are notoriously suspicious of people they do not know. Invoke my name, and the name of Orrick, in either land and you shall find sanctuary."

"Orrick? He lives?!" Bromlin said, finally voicing some of his astonishment. "I thought him—and you—well, all of you to be dead."

Dhresden's smile was grim as he replied, "There was death enough, Bromlin, but those are tales for another time, if ever. Now go, and may safety be your companion."

Wyeth raised the bar and slowly swung the door open, listening briefly before stepping into the hallway. The four council members filed through the doorway and down the hall, disappearing into the night shadows. Dhresden and Wyeth retraced their steps to the sewer hatch and quickly entered the hidden channels that offered them stealthy passage through the city. Neither spoke, but instead focused their attentions on determining whether anything lay ahead, or may begin to pursue behind. Soon they came to the small fire that Wyeth had kindled, now barely embers, but he deftly stoked it to a small flame and the two again settled around the meager but welcome warmth as it slowly entered the two men, fighting back winter's icy fingers from their extremities.

"We must determine the extent of this alliance," Dhresden said again, his eyes distant. Silence returned a moment, then he stood, retrieved his white linens and began to again don the camouflage. "Find out what you can and send word if time is short; otherwise, I will see you at the secret entrance in six days."

Wyeth stood as well, his old face unreadable as he handed a satchel to Dhresden and then spoke. "Keep safe, my lord, and may fortune finally smile upon your reign." He made a slight bow, and then wrapped the younger man in a fatherly embrace. The two stood briefly thus, and then Dhresden turned and disappeared down the tunnel.

CHAPTER 22

Khaldun sat shivering inside a snowdrift that he had dug a hollow into for shelter. He had managed to create a snow cave large enough for two people and had harvested enough dead twigs and branches from the nearby tree line to kindle a small fire inside the shelter, its smoke exiting through a small vent in the ceiling. In order to ensure that the fire did not suffocate him, Khaldun had left the entrance to the shelter uncovered, allowing fresh air to flow in. Despite the bare opening, very little firelight, if any, was visible from the outside even in the dark. Khaldun could feel the heat from the fire, but, sitting in the snow, could not seem to shake winter's chill. The young Makani longed for his hot, sandy homeland, and the smiling sun- and wind-weathered faces of family and friends. He was startled from his reverie by a familiar face filling the opening as Dhresden crawled into the shelter.

"I heard nothing of your approach!" Khaldun remarked, somewhat astonished. "This snow, it muffles everything! Why, at home it would take a sandstorm to hide the approach of even one person towards my camp, and yet here you are!"

Dhresden smiled. He had spent much time in lands unfamiliar to his upbringing, and could well remember that there were challenges specific to each region that could either aid in your endeavor, or prove your undoing.

"Do not be dismayed," he said. "You will become a master of this land, if you remain here long enough. You are well concealed in this burrow and the sentry I posted when I left would not allow a foe within fifty yards of you." Khaldun did not appear to be much encouraged by Dhresden's words, and as the two sat silently, the young Makani began again to shiver. Noticing the tremors, Dhresden reached into the satchel that Wyeth had given him.

"I had forgotten," he admitted, handing a small pot to the other man. "Wyeth sent this along for you. He thought it would warm you better than the jerky we carry. Just scoop some snow in with the other ingredients and heat it on the fire."

Lifting the lid and looking inside the pot, Khaldun discovered some dried vegetables, meat, and spices that reminded him of a meal common to his homeland. The snow would melt and mix with the dried food and spices, resulting in a stew that would warm both his body and his spirit.

"But how did he manage this?" Khaldun wondered aloud while quickly adding a few handfuls of snow and setting the pot by the fire.

Dhresden shrugged. "Wyeth knows many things, though he is selective with whom he shares his knowledge, even more cautious is he with his wisdom."

Khaldun looked quizzically at the half-blood, wondering at the depth of his meaning. "Please forgive me, Dhresden." he said, "but I am confused. You speak of knowledge and wisdom as separate. The Makani have taught for many thousand years of knowledge and wisdom, but when we speak of these things, we use one word: *busarahokmah*. It is one of our highest goals, not as an end, but as a means to a better life for each person and for the whole of the people." He paused, thinking. He did not wish to offend his friend, but since he truly sought answers, a friend should be who is asked. "Why would Wyeth, or anyone, not share his knowledge—wisdom, his *busarahokmah*, with the whole of his people?"

Dhresden had heard something of the Makani teachings, and while certainly no scholar of their ways, knew enough to recognize that the goals of their people closely matched those which had been instilled in him since infancy by both his mother and father, estranged though they were. He found Khaldun's question to be an indication of the man's desire to grow and increase in *busarahokmah*, and was pleased.

"The men of the Pasturelands borrowed the usage of "knowledge" and "wisdom" from the Kelvren. For them, the two are separate and very distinct realities and therefore required their own individual words. Knowledge is the gathering, or collection, of the understanding of a thing, whether it is how to kill, how to heal, how to build, how to destroy. This understanding, this knowledge, did not equate to the usage of these things, but simply increased the information within one's head." Dhresden paused, looking at the other man for some sign of comprehension. Though his brow remained furrowed, Khaldun nodded for Dhresden to continue.

"The Kelvren recognized that even a fool was capable of gaining this degree of understanding, the simple gathering of information. What was, or was meant to be, built upon this knowledge was application. The information was worthless if not properly utilized, if not applied to life and to its problems in the correct or most effective and beneficial manner. Wisdom, then, is the proper application or usage of knowledge. I have seen men and women well educated in theories and facts and remain fools. Likewise, I have seen men who could not read or write their own names that could apply the knowledge that they did possess in such a way that it could only be referred to as wisdom." He stopped again, relieved to see that Khaldun's brow was growing less wrinkled. He waited, curious to hear the Makani's response, and soon it came.

"I understand," he said simply, pausing briefly before continuing. "In my homeland, the focus since before my birth has always been to teach not just knowledge, but also wisdom. *Busarahokmah*, then, implies instruction of the whole man, for the whole of life; knowledge is incomplete without correct and active application: wisdom. In spite of this focus," he smiled, "we have more than enough fools in our midst." Both men laughed for a moment at the Makani's jest, but then Khaldun asked another question.

"Why would Wyeth not share his knowledge and his wisdom? Would not this wealth of *busarahokmah* be only benefit to the hearers? If each within the Pasturelands were trained in all these things, imagine the potential!"

Dhresden nodded, and then replied. "Your words are true, Khaldun; and yet they ring hollow in the hearts and lives of many. Both knowledge and wisdom can be abused, misused, or ignored.

The individual is responsible for how they respond to the teaching; the teacher is to be held accountable for the manner in which they teach, what they teach, to whom and to what end. These are the reasons that the Kelvren, and others, guard both their knowledge and wisdom."

Both lapsed into silence, lost in their own reflections until the sounds of the small pot simmering broke quietly into their thoughts.

"Your stew is ready," Dhresden said, turning himself towards the tunnel. "Eat and rest the remainder of the day. I will return at sunset."

"What task beckons you now, Lord Havenstone?" asked Khaldun.

Dhresden smiled as he answered. "Sleep. The sun is rising, and the past hours have wearied me. We should be free from discovery, but if someone does wander near, we will be aware of them before they are in sight of us." He crawled free of the snow shelter and stood, searching his surroundings for any sign of danger. Finding none, he turned and walked to the tree line and continued into the cover of the woods just far enough to be hidden, but where he could still have a line of sight to Khaldun's shelter and beyond. Facing the still dark forest, Dhresden sent a low, quiet whistle out amidst the trees. He stood there, eyes closed, listening, trying to hear the approach of the sentry he had left to guard Khaldun. She could move so quickly, and yet quietly, that Dhresden continued to sharpen his skills against hers as iron upon iron. He felt he had improved under her tutelage, and yet, Dhresden sighed in defeat as he felt her press against his back.

"I must be too fatigued to remain alert," he said as he opened his eyes and turned around. He was unsure whether it was possible, but he felt as though Asha was smirking at him. The cougar brushed past him, and lay down on the leeward side of a fallen log. Dhresden sat beside the great cat, leaning his back against her, sharing and conserving warmth. Asha's usually ghost-gray coat had taken on a white sheen, allowing her to blend in with the snowy surroundings. Cloaked in white, Dhresden became invisible with her in the snow; both fell quickly asleep, entering a rest peculiar to wild things. A slumber that, while restful, allowed the sleeper to maintain an alertness to their surroundings. No foe, no enemy, would ambush this man or cougar while they slept.

~ ~ ~

The rest of that day passed without incident; Dhresden and Asha returned to Khaldun's den at dusk and the three of them stood vigil for two hours, watching for Wyeth. The time passed with no sign of the old Kelvren, or anyone on his behalf, but contact this early had not been anticipated. Dhresden led his companions into the forest, where they scouted for game trails, set snares, and gathered more firewood for Khaldun. Such were the activities of the three watchers for the next several days. More snow fell on top of the already thick layer, hiding or at least obscuring the tracks that Dhresden and his companions had created and further reducing the likelihood of anyone strolling about in the deep snow and happening upon them. Few sounds from within the walls of the Citadel intruded into the natural serenity surrounding the watchers at the edge of the woods, until one morning both Dhresden and Asha jerked awake at a low noise building in the distance. The great cat stood, tail twitching, looking toward the Citadel, while Dhresden kneeled beside her in the snow, both searching for the source of the sound. The volume seemed to build, individual sounds becoming more distinct: the clang of metal, the shouts of men's voices—the sounds of battle. As they continued to watch, the forms of men appeared atop the city walls; and though Dhresden could not discern who was among the fray, he feared Wyeth or members of the council had been compromised and were now fighting for their lives.

Dhresden and Asha crept from the cover of the trees and met Khaldun as he emerged from his shelter. The young Makani, ignorant of what was transpiring while within the snow cave, quickly took in the meaning of the noise and stood at the ready. As the skirmish atop the wall continued, it became evident that four battled against many. The four fought well, but with each foe that was felled, three more would rise to take their place. The four became three, and then two, and as the enemy surged to quash the remnant, the two turned and leaped from the top of the wall and plummeted to the earth, landing with a muffled thud. There were curses and shouts of disbelief from the troops atop the wall as they peered down at the men who had leapt to their doom.

Dhresden saw no movement, but sprinted with Asha and Khaldun in tow to the base of the wall, mindful of the danger that could rain down on them from above. They found Sachs and a man Dhresden did not recognize lying crumpled and bloody in the snow. A quick examination found one to be dead, while Sachs's shallow, ragged breathing gave Dhresden hope. He and Khaldun each grabbed an arm and began to quickly drag the unconscious man away from the wall toward the forest. The crunch of the snow under their feet and the shouts of the guards atop the wall hid the sound of the archers loosing their arrows from even Dhresden's keen ears. The arrows had been loosed hastily, yet had still managed to find their marks. Both Dhresden and Khaldun pitched forward into the snow; the half-blood with two arrows in his back, the Makani with an arrow also in his back, one through his right thigh, while a third had passed clean through his left calf.

Realizing the severity of their situation, Dhresden called Asha close and spoke quickly to her. The gray cougar turned and seized Khaldun firmly about the wounded calf with her great mouth and ran, dragging him along to safety. Baffled at what they had just seen, the archers failed to send a second volley until they realized that Dhresden had risen to his feet and heaved Sachs over his shoulder as he too began to run for cover. The volley, when it finally came, fell short of the intended target. Dhresden and Asha bore their charges deep into the woods, knowing that pursuit was certain. They ceased their retreat atop a low hill, rimmed with cedars, where they had a good vantage and some cover while they assessed their injuries. Sachs still breathed, but barely, and Dhresden was glad to find that the arrow in Khaldun's back had more or less glanced off his shoulder bone, limiting the extent of the injury. The damage to his legs, however, while not lethal, would prevent him from being able to travel at the necessary speed. Dhresden quickly bandaged Khaldun's wounds, then turned his attention to his own. Looking down at his chest, Dhresden could see the point of each arrow protruding, though little blood flowed from around the shafts. He realized that Khaldun was watching him, his face aghast. Dhresden flashed the Makani a smile.

"Fret not, my friend." he said cheerily. "I will not die this day. I do, however, require your aid. I need you to break off the end of the arrows at my back so that I can pull them through from the front."

Khaldun did as he was bid, amazed at Dhresden's calm demeanor. The half-blood jerked in response to each arrow shaft being snapped off, then grimaced and bared his teeth as he withdrew the remainder of the bolts from his body. He cast the arrows aside and knelt beside Sachs, whose wounds were not readily visible, save a rather superficial cut across his cheek and a deep sword slash across his abdomen. Dhresden pressed a hand against the wound, attempting to staunch the slow flow of blood, and heard Khaldun speaking behind him.

"We will need to bandage your wounds as well, Lord Havenstone."

Dhresden did not respond; all his attention was focused upon the unconscious man before him. With his free hand, Dhresden searched Sachs's pockets, hoping to find some note or other message that would convey to Dhresden the cause of the scuffle atop the wall. He did not know how Wyeth fared, or the rest of the council, or the status of Treyherne's alliances. Dhresden's plans succeeded or failed because of the resources that he and his companions discovered, and the lack of information at this time could ultimately prove to lead to his defeat. Dhresden found nothing to indicate that any message had been sent, or even attempted, but was relieved to see that the pressure he had placed directly on Sachs's stomach wound had stopped the bleeding, or had the man died? Dhresden leaned in close to the councilman's face, listening for a shallow breath—to feel the slightest exhale upon his face, to see the tremor of a heartbeat at his temple or neck, and then the man's eyes flickered and opened. His eyes darted about, as though unable to focus on anything long enough to comprehend what he was seeing, but then he winced and reached for his wounded abdomen. Sachs's hand found Dhresden's already pressed against the pain, and his eyes, no longer foggy, looked with earnest into the eyes of his rightful ruler.

"My lord," he rasped, "you must f—flee!"

"Peace, Sachs, peace," Dhresden half whispered; he needed the man coherent and calm in order to determine the validity of his words. Dhresden did not doubt his honesty, but worried that his report could be tainted by delirium from his injuries. The cut to his stomach was severe, but the damage he incurred when he leaped from the high outer wall would likely prove to be fatal. "Tell me, Sachs, what happened."

The dying man breathed deeply, winced, and then spoke. "Eriks, Bromlin, Tungstein and myself approached those members of the council we thought to be trustworthy one by one, finding each of them as disgusted with Treyherne's rule as we. Together, we set to the task of determining the status of the usurper's designs, and the extent of his treachery. It was Councilman Milton who got us discovered. I had told him that woman would prove his undoing," he paused, coughing, the pain evident in his expression. "His mistress, a beautiful, dimwitted thing, is a close cousin to one of the Oxmen captains. She repeated what she had overheard Milton talking about, and her cousin took the information directly to Treyherne. The entire Council of Thirteen was declared traitors, to be executed on sight. We fought to escape, whether any succeeded I know not."

"And what of Wyeth? Was he discovered? Did he escape?" Dhresden's voice remained quiet, but his concern for the old Kelvren was evident.

"I last saw him three days ago," Sachs replied, "and know nothing of what has befallen him."

They let his answer hang in the silence as they considered the brevity of his words. The entire council scattered and killed, Wyeth on the run or dead.

"What of the alliance?" Dhresden asked. "What of Treyherne's union with Uganji and the Badlands?"

"There is no alliance," Sachs answered, his words not as clear as they had been. "There is only—there is only the Horde."

Dhresden and Khaldun locked eyes briefly, then Dhresden turned back to Sachs. "The Horde? What new terror is this?"

Sachs coughed again, his face now very pale. He had begun to shiver, though Dhresden could clearly see beads of perspiration upon the man's face. "The Horde—is led—by Chayne, who has betrothed herself to Uganji. His dowry to her is to be the conquest of the Pasturelands. Treyherne—is a pawn. Chayne supplied him the resources he needed—to kill your father and take control of the throne, but she intends to slaughter him along with the rest of us. Treyherne, however, mistakenly believes that—that his Oxmen force will repel Chayne and her Horde. They are already on the march; Uganji is said to be leading his Ianzama from the south—while Chayne marches from the Badlands with her brigands—they will grind our land—and our people—as in a pestle and mortar—"

"Peace, Sachs," Dhresden whispered, seeing the man fading from this life. "Some things cannot be ground to dust, even by such forces as they. Go now to your fathers' rest, and we shall meet you there when our time here is finished."

CHAPTER 23

The main gates of the Citadel swung slowly open against the thick snow, allowing forty Oxmen to issue forth in pursuit of the councilman and two mystery men. The mounts struggled four wide through the snow, their pace greatly slowed by its depth. As the distance between them and the city widened, he riders surveyed the tree line, looking for movement. They had been charged with the retrieval of council member Sachs, or at least his corpse, and the capture of the two unknown men for questioning. The consequences for failing these orders would mean prison and possibly death for these soldiers, and depending on the mood of Treyherne, could be extended to their families. Riding beside each other in the third row, the captain and his second in command were well aware of the weight that had been placed upon themselves and their men. Liam had entered the Oxmen ranks three days prior to his fourteenth birthday. His father, a merchant, had pushed his son into the service out of a sense of duty, and to escape his own responsibility. Liam's mother had died from sickness a few years prior, and the burden of his father's business and recreational pursuits left no room for his son. Unsurprised and yet heartbroken by his father's decision, Liam had directed all of his emotion, strength, and will into the pursuit of excellence in his training. He had distanced himself from the other youths in the training program, but had been unable to prevent a friendship from forming between himself and the rowdy ten-year-old who began to shadow him. The youngster had been renamed Flint because of his determination not to back down from any challenge, whether in training or among his peers. Through adversity and skill, the two formed a bond that strengthened them through their training and into adulthood. Their loyalties were to each other and to their families first, and then to the ruler of the Pasturelands second. Since Treyherne's claim to the throne of Havenstone, Liam, and Flint had found themselves in a difficult strait. They had been too young to have any part in the adventures of Dhane, but had reveled in the retelling of his conquest against evil. They had often glimpsed Dhresden about the training compound, and even given audience to his lessons to their former superiors, but knew nothing firsthand of the mysterious half-blood or his royal heritage. Liam and Flint had understood that Dhane ruled justly, and that had been sufficient for their needs. Treyherne, it seemed, knew nothing of justice. He reminded Flint of the many older, bigger youths with which he had been forced to contend; who had bullied and belittled him to their own pleasure. To Liam, Treyherne seemed but a larger, more ornate bolt of the same cloth from which his father had been cut; secure in his own supposed rightness, yet selfishly hungry for greater proofs of his own growing power. Liam had felt uneasy at Dhane's passing, for rumors had begun to be whispered regarding some dark conspiracy brewing in the shadows of the Citadel, but there are countless such rumors conjured baselessly by many a mind with idle hands, although to no end. So he and Flint had remained, reluctance to uproot their wives and families from their contented lives had played no small part in this decision. Now, they both feared that they had tarried too long; that even in evading death, they would undergo events worse than the grave.

The leading riders in the forty-man column had dismounted and ventured into the trees, following the trail of their quarry. They had not gone far before one of them returned to report on their findings.

"Captain," he saluted, "we have found Sachs's body, sir."

"What of the other two?"

"Just tracks, sir. One man headed north, and some other tracks turn south, but—" his voice quieted, then stopped.

Liam said nothing, nor did Flint, but the look the two shot each other communicated volumes between the two friends, and then turned back on the scout spurred his tongue.

"The tracks south, it looks like animal tracks—a cougar, I think—and something being dragged along by it."

"Is there any blood?" Flint asked, his voice low and menacing.

"Yes, sir, but it does not appear to be much—not like a cougar would cause." The man paused, his tongue wetting his lips before he continued. "Do you think there could be more, sir?"

"More what?"

"Cougars, sir."

Again Liam and Flint shared a glance.

"Aye," Flint replied, "there could be more. You had best keep an eye out. Now show us these tracks." He and Liam dismounted and followed the now skittish scout into the woods.

Sachs's body had cooled quickly, no heat could be seen rising from his corpse, his eyes had taken on a frosty glaze and his wounds had ceased oozing blood. The tracks north were clearly a man's, and the tracks south did indeed resemble a cougar's. The dragging marks were a mystery. The two narrow lines dug deep, as though a heavy weight had pushed them down and then dragged them through the snow. There were places where the cougar's tracks had been filled in or obliterated, as though something had come along behind it and filled them in, almost like a sleigh.

"I believe the tracks south are of a cougar pulling a wounded man on a makeshift sled." Liam declared. "Flint, take half the men south. Kill the cougar, capture the man, and return him to Lord Treyherne. The rest of the men and I will overtake the man to the north and meet you at the Citadel. Be careful, old friend," he said, his voice quieter now, "Remember; we serve on behalf of our families and must do what is ultimately best for them."

~ ~ ~

The litter that Dhresden had quickly fashioned for Asha to transport the wounded Khaldun upon was not a thing of comfort. It did, however, prove functional, allowing the cougar to slip her head into the harness in order to haul the Makani along, but quickly out of the harness should the need arise to defend the two of them. The odd pair was covering distance quickly, but was also leaving a trail that would be easy to follow should any pursue. In spite of his distaste for winter in the Pasturelands, Khaldun found himself hoping it would snow again and hide their tracks. He knew that the great cat would not be able to keep this pace indefinitely, and with each step that slowed or rest that was taken, the chance increased for the Oxmen to overtake them and thwart their mission.

"Make for the Dunes," Dhresden had commanded. "Inform your leader of the danger from the Ianzama. Almadi bin Khuzaymah must lead the Makani to intercept Uganji; his forces must never reach the Citadel. Remind him of the debt your people owe my father if he hesitates; I will send reinforcements as soon as I am able."

Along their separate paths they went; the man and cougar quick but easy to track, the lone half-blood slower but better concealed. A day and a half passed without incident for either party, but nearing nightfall, Dhresden heard or thought he heard the crunching of heavy feet in the snow far behind him. Silent and unmoving, he bent all his will towards the direction from which he had come, and heard again, clearly this time, the noise of the Oxmen's mounts breaking through the snow in pursuit. It was no coincidence that Liam had sent Flint and his crew south in pursuit of the man and cougar; Liam was the better tracker and had allowed his friend the easy trail. Dhresden had sought speed over stealth often enough for the Oxmen captain to make good time in trailing him, and now they were close enough for Dhresden to hear them. If he focused now on speed alone, his tracks would be so easy to follow that he would soon be overtaken, but he rightly feared that his pursuers possessed enough skill to follow even his cautious footprints well enough to catch up to him. By his own estimation, considering the terrain, there remained another whole day of travel before he reached his goal. Other men had faced similar circumstances and chosen the path they believed to be best; Dhresden would do the same. Facing back the way from which he had come, the half-blood began to close the gap between himself and his pursuers.

~ ~ ~

Liam was reluctant to stop, but the growing darkness required it. Trudging through the snow in the dark could not only lose the trail, but could also obliterate it. He allowed his men to kindle a handful of small fires that would take the edge off the chill night air, and yet would not readily betray their position. The Oxmen sat close to their mounts; no shelters were erected to pass the night, the men accepting the shared heat of their beasts and the meager fire as merely a part of their duty to their king. Liam leaned heavily against his own mount for warmth, choosing not to kindle a fire for himself. Though he would have welcomed its warmth, the damage the fire would have done to his night vision was not acceptable. He preferred to be able to see beyond the range of the fire, sensing the potential threat his quarry posed to himself and his men, and yet unwilling to believe that he and twenty mounted Oxmen soldiers had anything to fear from one lone footman. Liam looked up at the sky, discovering a moon veiled behind thick snow clouds. Though it had not yet begun to fall, he was certain it would within the hour. His thoughts drifted again to home. Not the Citadel, though that was where his family was; Liam did not consider a place to be home. His home was his wife, and his children; wherever they were became his home. Such dark times had come now, and he feared they would grow darker still. Liam told himself that all he needed to do to keep them safe was to follow his orders and fulfill his tasks, and yet he could not stifle the voice that screamed silently in the back of his mind that he risked losing all he held dear under the reign of Treyherne. He shivered, not of cold, but from the dread of what could be. Liam stiffened, the warmth of his adrenaline coursing suddenly through him as he felt a knife point pressing cold against his neck.

"Make no sound, captain," Dhresden whispered, "or it shall be your last." He allowed the other man to turn his head slightly, enough that Liam's eyes could focus on his face. In his eyes, Dhresden saw a flicker of recognition, but Liam gave no attempt to cry out. The two regarded each other, invisible to the troops resting around them.

"There are rumors about you," Liam said just loud enough for Dhresden to hear him. The half-blood cocked his head slightly, inviting the other to expound. "Even as a boy, I heard tell that you were the son of Dhane, that you might one day sit upon the throne of the Citadel, and rightly so. Treyherne claims that you are responsible for Dhane's death, and so—Firebane." Liam had stood atop the parapet that night, and realized that the man to whom he was speaking should be dead. "There have been whispers that you somehow survived, but few actually believe that to be true though most wish for it." He said no more for a while, wondering at the man before him. Somewhere close by one of the soldiers coughed, but all seemed content in their ignorance of the meeting that was currently taking place between their captain and their quarry.

"What of your men?"

"They are loyal to me, so long as I serve Treyherne. The power he has allowed the Oxmen to possess has made them as drunken men, seeking only their own profit and that of their leader."

"What do you wish for, Liam?" Dhresden asked, surprising the man that he knew his name.

"I wish only for my family to be safe," he replied.

"Then we have much in common, Captain," Dhresden said quietly, sheathing his knife.

~ ~ ~

Just before dawn the clouds broke, allowing a magnificent sunrise to glisten its radiant beams upon the new layer of snow that had fallen during the night. The Oxmen dusted snow from themselves and from their mounts as they doused their fires and ate a meager breakfast of dried rations in readiness for the day. Their preparations were interrupted by their captain, who sat tall atop his mount as he spoke.

"I have scouted ahead already this morning, and as I feared, the snow has completely hidden the trail of our prey. You men have ridden hard with me these two days, and are wearied. Camp here, while I circle wider in search of his tracks; when I find them I will signal you and we will finish this!" Liam turned his mount north and rode from sight, trusting that the men would follow his order at least long enough for he and Dhresden to gain substantial lead time. He found Dhresden at their agreed upon meeting point, and the half-blood leaped atop the beast and rode behind Liam as they trotted north through the woods for a quarter hour. Reigning in his mount, Liam allowed Dhresden to descend to the ground. Here their paths separated, and whether they would meet again was uncertain.

"Ride hard, Liam," Dhresden advised, "you will not fair well if you are to be overtaken by those men, should they choose to pursue you rather than myself."

Liam smiled. "I was not their captain simply because of a quick mind; nevertheless, I do not wish to become embroiled in a skirmish with twenty misdirected Oxmen. I will see you, Dhresden, after a while." The two men clasped hands, then parted company. The Oxmen captain covered ground quickly, but left a clear path that would be easy to follow. He guided his mount due east, his assigned mission at the forefront of his mind; while in the shadows of his thoughts, he feared anew for his family. Had he traded one eventual death sentence for another, sooner one? Miles of snow passed beneath him, as hours of worry passed through his tortured mind. He slowed the pace of his mount, allowing the beast to recover a little from their hasty journey. Ultimately, Liam knew that death would come to the Pasturelands at the hand of Treyherne, but if he had attempted to return to the Citadel and then flee with his family, the death blow would have been hastened. If only he had possessed the foresight to depart when the first whispers of treachery had begun; but then, he could not have possessed any part in the remedy. Liam's spirits lifted a bit as he realized that he had been placed squarely on the path that could lead again to happier times in the Pasturelands. It was then that the low rumble of many hooves reached his ears, signaling that the Oxmen had indeed chosen to pursue their former captain. They would likely execute him on the spot, rather than to be burdened with transporting him back to the Citadel for judgment. Liam found some satisfaction in knowing that the troops had tracked himself, that Dhresden was safe, or at least more safe than he was about to be. Liam's mount had recovered its breath and seemed to sense the need to fight or flee; knowing that both may be necessary, Liam spurred the beast to a fast run.

The forest was quickly growing more sparse as the boundary of the Pasturelands drew closer. Liam was likely to be crossing a wide expanse of open field when his pursuers would catch sight of him. Then they would no longer be tracking him, but would be racing toward him to overtake him. He kept a quick pace, but slowed his ox a little, being careful not to deplete his energy; they may yet be required to fight, and he would need the aid of his mount. They rode past the last of the trees and had almost reached the halfway point of the field when a cry of alarm rang out, followed by angry shouts and curses. Liam did not bother to look back, but took care to maintain a consistent speed. They had passed the midway point when Liam hazarded a look behind. The pursuing Oxmen were running their mounts at breakneck speed, risking depleting the beasts' resources, stumbling or even falling. Cautiously optimistic, Liam realized that his pursuers would reach him about the time he reached the tree line and the boundary of the Pasturelands. The Oxmen would not be slowed by this, but would pursue the traitor deep into the neighboring lands. As he drew nearer the edge of the field he weighed his options. Entering the forest would limit the movements of his mount, but the trees would provide some degree of protection from the archers in the group. Remaining in the field obviously provided an easier archery target, but allowed the man and his mount the room for mobility. The muffled thundering of the cattle's hooves had grown louder, as had the shouts and cursings of their riders. Liam felt something strike the rear of his arm, and realized that some of the Oxmen had loosed arrows, one of which had somehow managed to find its mark. He knew the ability of his men, and while good with a bow, none of them possessed the skill required to be accurate from the saddle at this speed and distance; and yet Liam found himself looking down at the bloodied point of an arrow protruding from his left bicep. Having no choice now but to seek the protection of the trees, Liam looked back at the twenty men that sought to slay him, and realized that less than twenty pursued him. As he rode into the forest, Liam realized that a handful of the Oxmen had split off to pursue Dhresden, and what chance did one man have against such well-trained cavalry?

CHAPTER 24

Dhresden had moved as quickly as he could, without blazing a trail for any pursuers to follow. He had centered himself in the tree line, trusting that as snow fell from the branches of the trees, it would help to hide his tracks and that the trees themselves would keep him hidden at distance. He still wore his white linen cloak, allowing himself to blend into the surrounding snow, but if any pursuers followed his trail close enough he knew that no camouflage would protect him. Dhresden heard the Oxmen hunting him long before he saw them.

They were moving slowly, struggling to pick out his trail from among the other marks in the snow. Dhresden had managed to glimpse his pursuers through the trees and decided that they numbered five. He had no reason to believe that they sought him to his benefit, but he needed to be certain of their intent. The Oxmen had spread themselves wide, the center rider setting the pace as he attempted to follow Dhresden's trail. The others had fanned out from the trail to increase their field of view and were relying on their scout for direction. Their eyes swept the landscape, searching for anything out of the ordinary. It was the rider at the far left who first spotted Dhresden's camouflaged form crouching low beside a fallen log. He signaled to the others, and the rider to his right, an archer, took careful aim and loosed an arrow directly into his target. The riders laughed, congratulating the man on his shot, as they moved toward the crumpled form. Two of the Oxmen dismounted about twenty feet from their quarry, and with drawn sword and readied bow moved in to capture or kill the man lying in the snow. Most of the other riders had reached their comrades' mounts and sat waiting; the last two riders rode lazily toward the group. A low curse was heard, and then a shout rang out.

"Not him! It's not him!" The two riders farthest from the group were further startled by a shadow that fell nimbly from the trees above them, landing astride behind one of the Oxmen. Dhresden's knife plunged into the man's back, slid back out, then flew through the air and sank deep into the other rider's eye. Both men slipped lifelessly from their saddles into the snow; neither had even begun to draw their own weapon. The other Oxmen had recovered from their surprise; those already mounted wheeled their beasts about in pursuit of the now mounted and fleeing Dhresden while the other two hurried to their saddles. Dhresden had misjudged the number of his enemy, finding already two more than he had thought; he did not wish to discover even more Oxmen bearing down upon him from farther back. The beast beneath him seemed healthy enough, responding quickly to his guidance through the remainder of the forest and into the open fields. Dhresden hoped the creature was not a sprinter, but rather that it would hold up for the long run that lay before them. He glanced behind, and saw six Oxmen in pursuit. He had managed to put distance between himself and them while in the woods and desired to maintain and even widen the gap here in the fields.

~~~

The pain in Liam's arm had ebbed to a low aching, until necessity forced the rider to use his left arm to maneuver his mount through this strange new section of forest. He had managed to stay ahead of his pursuers, but was troubled by this new terrain. The snow had faded, and the temperature was rising noticeably; the once frozen ground and naked trees had given way to a succulent and leafy green, dotted with an increasing number of sinkholes. Liam found himself sweating freely, beads of perspiration stinging his eyes and blurring his vision as he sought to guide his mount safely through this unfamiliar wood. Riding deeper, he was further dismayed to discover a haze of mist thickening about him; he blinked and squinted, straining to decipher the barely visible way before him. As if occurring slowly, Liam felt the beast beneath him tip forward slightly as her foot landed in a sinkhole. For an instant he envisioned her recovering deftly from the misstep and bearing him farther on, but then the terrible sound of her heavy leg bone shattering reached his ears, followed by the pain-shrilled bawling of his poor mount. Liam and the ox hurtled forward, landing heavily upon the ground, now in the air, and again to the ground. Liam raised himself to his hands and knees, struggling to collect his wits before attempting to walk. He mentally examined himself, finding no pain in his legs or his right arm, but his left arm throbbed with a fresh pain. Fearing it broken, Liam opened his eyes and shifted his weight back to a sitting position. He inspected his left arm, finding nothing broken. The arrow had somehow been pulled from his bicep during the tumble, sending a new rush of pain through his arm as blood flowed anew from the wound. He rose slowly to his feet, pressing his right hand against the wound as best he could to stem the flow of blood as he stumbled toward his wounded beast. Liam had been assigned to this mount his first year of rider training, and the two had endured many trials as they grew into seasoned warriors together. He had chosen the name Copper for her, influenced greatly by her wiry orange coat. Copper lay panting; her one leg twisted and bloody where the bone had splintered and broken through the skin. Under normal circumstances, a mount's break could be splinted and mended, but Liam could not care for her now without bringing death to them both in the process. If he left her, he feared at the least that she would die at the hands of his pursuers, and given their hatred of him as a traitor, it was likely that she could be mistreated on his behalf. Liam knelt beside her head, stroking the side of her neck with his left hand. He spoke to her in a low, calming tone, hearing her breathing slow as she relaxed under the gentle touch of her master and friend. In the distance Liam could hear the Oxmen drawing closer, yet he continued to pet Copper's neck, calming her. Her eyes closed peacefully, for she knew that Liam would care for her as he always had. In that peaceful moment, the butt of Liam's knife swiftly struck the place on her forehead that rendered her painlessly unconscious, and then with the blade he cut her throat. She bled out quickly as Liam fled from his pursuers, fighting now to find his way through the unusual terrain and unfamiliar tears.

~~~

The blankness of the snow-covered landscape had caused the death of many who had risked travel through the Pasturelands in winter, hiding landmarks, the sun, moon and stars, forcing strangers to the land to wander aimlessly, often dying almost within sight of the desired path or even the intended destination. Dhresden was not such a stranger to the land, and neither were his pursuers. He had managed to maintain the space between himself and them, but the distance was not so great that they would lose sight of him. Even if he rode into a copse of trees to obscure their view of him, the trail his mount would leave in the snow would keep the Oxmen close at his heels. To turn and face them, while not altogether foolhardy, was risky at best. Dhresden had trained many of the Oxmen himself, and had made as certain as he could that they had mastered the skills necessary to protect his father. At his best, the encounter would have been a challenge; he had not forgotten the two arrows that had entered his back and protruded from his chest. The pain had ebbed to an ache and the bleeding had long stopped, thanks to the residual effects of the healing potion that Tiblak the healer had given to him. The concentration had been so high that the healing effects had lingered long after the madness had passed, but with each new day or injury the potency dwindled more, and now it had become of such slight benefit that it should not be relied upon and would soon be forgotten. No, Dhresden alone would not battle these Oxmen, but he knew that they would trail him to his destination at his very heels.

More than an hour had passed when Dhresden spied Murion's Plateau at the northeastern edge of the Pasturelands. Long ago, the natural landform had been utilized as a military base from which the northern and eastern boundaries of the Pasturelands could be watched and defended. Its height and straight sides provided vantage and protection, while the ramp that had been tunneled up through its midst afforded defensible access. A glance behind him revealed that he had reached his destination none too soon; the Oxmen had begun to close the gap, though he remained beyond bowshot. Nearer he rode to the plateau, willing his tiring mount to keep pace, and as the opening of the tunnel became clear to his eyes, he saw two columns of riders issue forth from the entrance. The fresh legs of the new riders bore them quickly towards Dhresden, who found himself now with six riders behind and greater than forty before. He had hesitated, even fled from a skirmish against the six Oxmen, but now he spurred his fading mount ever faster towards the approaching sea of new riders. Closer now, the riders took on definition; armorless, armed here and there with swords but mostly with clubs, axes, pitch-forks and other common tools. The brown-cloaked mass began to separate at the center; as though a wall of water had parted before him, allowing him dry passage, and then they washed past him, clos-ing together behind him upon his pursuers. Dhresden continued to ride toward the plateau, slower now, when another rider separated from the group and kept pace at his side.

"You are bleeding, my lord!" he exclaimed indicating the blood on Dhresden's chest. "Shall I call for the healer?"

"That will not be necessary," Dresden replied. "Much of the blood is not mine, and we have more important needs at hand. Assemble the riders, Faust; we depart in an hour and we have much ground to cover."

~ ~ ~

Jovanna had rushed to the top of the south-facing watchtower when news had reached her of Dhresden's approach and of his pursu-ers. Faust had refused to allow her to leave the sanctuary of Murion's Plateau with him, but had promised to bring her stepson to her as soon as he could. From her vantage, she could see the distance between Dhresden and the pursuing Oxmen shortening, and she feared anew that he would be overtaken and killed. It seemed such a long time had passed since he had undergone Firebane, even lon-ger since she had first dreamed of his death when they had been in the Bog. Her visions of Dhresden's death had ceased when Jovanna had believed him to be departed, and since his return her nights had remained untainted with such nightmares. Her waking hours, however, had again become fretful. Dhresden's surprise arrival at the herdsman camp had been cause for celebration, but the lady was haunted by the endless possibilities that threatened to once again take her stepson from her. Relief washed over her when Faust and his men enveloped Dhresden and surrounded his pursuers. Jovanna lingered a moment, her eyes resting upon the six Oxmen surrounded by so many herdsmen. Had they been so deceived by Treyherne, or was it their own corruption that had caused them to embrace his treachery? It was difficult to discern, but it appeared as though the six were attempting to parlay rather than fight, but when she spied Faust riding beside Dhresden toward the plateau she turned and made her way toward their meeting point.

The lady Jovanna passed easily through the crowds of men that she encountered as they spotted her and made way for her. She had become well known among the herdsmen for any of several reasons, not the least of which was the rumored affection that she and Faust shared for each other. They of course revered her as royalty, and they had witnessed her skill with a blade, but her embrace of their ways is what had won their respect and their friendship for her. For her part, Jovanna was oblivious to much of the preferential treatment given by these men, though she easily recognized their hospitality and kindness.

She reached the map room of the outpost before Faust and Dhresden, and, ignoring the rough table and chairs, paced anxiously as she awaited their arrival. Dhresden had appeared to be in good health, but what information had he been able to gather, and where were Khaldun and Wyeth? After what seemed to be a long wait, Jovanna heard footsteps approaching, and, hopefully, her answers with them.

Faust pushed the door open wide, then stepped back to allow Dhresden to enter. Jovanna could see clearly that much information had been shared between the two of them already, and that little if any of it meant well for their cause. She embraced Dhresden as only a mother could for but a moment, then pushed back and held herself at arm's length as she spoke. "Tell me all, my son, and do not think for an instant to withhold anything; you need not protect me from the truth, no matter how dire."

Dhresden's hinted smile was brief, but he was emboldened by this woman's strength. He quickly but thoroughly began to update her on Treyherne's plan and the threats they now faced from both the north and the south. At some point while Dhresden was speaking, Jovanna's arms slid to her sides, and she slumped into a wooden chair, her face dark. Since finding Dhresden alive, she had allowed herself to become increasingly hopeful for their success, and now her hope still flickered, but dimly. Finished speaking, Dhresden knelt beside her, his hand upon hers. He said nothing, but looked upon this noble woman who had stood by his father's side and shared her thoughts, her wisdom, and her strength. Dresden longed for her to again take the role of a trusted advisor to the lord of Havenstone, but he knew that all the events from the death of his father until now weighed heavily upon her, and he did not wish to ask of her more than she could bear. A long moment passed, and then the half-blood spoke.

"Faust, you will remain here with a detachment of men to maintain our possession of this outpost and to keep watch over the Lady Jovanna."

"As you command, my lord," was all that the herdsman could utter before Jovanna broke in.

"He will do no such thing!" Suddenly her strength had returned, and with it, her resolve to see this matter through to the end, whatever that may be. She stood quickly, steadily, and faced Dhresden. "You have need of Faust and all the swords you can muster—even of mine. No. We shall accompany you to repel the northern horde."

Again Dhresden said nothing as he weighed her words, her wisdom, and his need. "There is wisdom in your words," he said finally. "I am grateful for your counsel, and hope you will continue to be of aid through this ordeal and beyond. It remains important, however, that we retain control of Murion's Plateau; neither have I any intention of allowing you directly into harm's way." Jovanna started to protest, but was silenced by Dhresden's next words. "Mother," he began, his voice hushed, "we have lost much as of late, and many of our loved ones have suffered, even died. I am unsure whether Mallory or Tala still lives, but I must protect the sole loved one that is within my power to do so." He paused, and then, no longer hushed, "Faust, my order stands. Select twenty of your best to remain with you and Jovanna; the rest depart with me one hour from now."

~ ~ ~

Liam slogged through the swampy terrain, hoping to elude his pursuers, silently attempting to convince himself that this would be more easily accomplished now that he was on foot. The pain of Copper's death weighed heavily upon him, but the reality of what would befall his family should he fail spurred him on. Liam could no longer hear the dozen Oxmen in pursuit; his own noise masked theirs now that they had ceased yelling and cursing. He knew they had probably spread themselves out to increase their odds of discovering him or evidence of him and were likely close at hand. He paused, held his ragged breath, and listened for some sort of indication of their whereabouts, and was rewarded by the whisper of an arrow hurtling towards him. Liam dropped flat against the ground, the musty smell of mud and vegetation thick in his nostrils. With a thud an arrow struck the bole of a tree to his right, its fletching telling him from whence it had come, but also that it would have skewered him had he not leaped to the ground. He squirmed through the mud until another tree stood between himself and his attacker, then stood and ran ahead through the unfamiliar terrain. Dhresden had instructed him that his goal was the river; Liam wondered how much farther it lay. Another arrow struck a tree ahead of him, while behind he heard one of the Oxmen call excitedly to another. They had gained on their quarry, and would soon overtake him, either in capture or in death. The last arrow had narrowly missed him; Liam began to run at angles away from his attackers, but always towards the east, and the river. This evasive tactic would decrease the risk that an arrow would find its mark, but also shortened the distance between himself and the Oxmen. Deciding that he had placed enough vegetation between himself and the men in pursuit, and that it served him best to out distance the enemy, Liam resumed his easterly course. Within twenty paces, an arrow skimmed over his shoulder, cutting his cloak but leaving him unscathed. He angled right several steps to exit the line of fire, and was greeted with two more arrows in quick succession. Both arrows had missed, but they had been loosed too quickly to have been from one of the Oxmen; there must be at least two to his right. Choosing the danger of one arrow over two, Liam darted left several steps, and dropped to the ground behind a large fallen tree. He did not remain there, but crawled another five paces, then leaped to his feet and began again to sprint towards the river. He was startled by the feeling of something striking his back, but feeling no pain, decided that if it was an arrow that he must have been protected by the leather vest beneath his cloak. Liam cut sharply left again, then straight, glimpsing finally the river up ahead. He surged forward with renewed energy as yet another arrow flew past him, but as he approached the riverbank, prepared to launch out into the murky waters in order to escape his pursuers, an arrow found its mark in the back of his right leg, a hand-breadth above the knee. His momentum carried him forward as he fell, landing almost within arm's reach of the river's brown waters. A triumphant shout went up behind him, and rolling to his back to look behind, Liam could see the Oxmen closing in upon him. In desperation, Liam drew a deep breath, knowing it may be his last, and shouted at the humid forest about him:

"I serve Dhresden, the son of Dhane, the true lord of Havenstone!"

Mocking and cursing greeted him from the angry men approaching, though their clamoring ceased abruptly as Liam heard something large noisily break the surface of the waters behind him. Two of the men had moved close enough that Liam could clearly see their faces, and each man bore an expression that mixed surprise with fear. Risking a quick glance at the river behind him, Liam found himself looking at what appeared to be four large lizard-like creatures protruding from the water, each with a rider astride its back. The riders were human in form, and yet they seemed to have the skin of a lizard or snake. Each carried a long weapon that resembled a spear at one end and a type of axe at the other. The Oxmen had regrouped within ten paces of their quarry, but sat uneasily atop their own mounts while they eyed these other strange riders. No doubt they were displeased to find these trespassers, but whether they would attack or simply demand that they depart their lands, none could guess. A silence that grew more and more uncomfortable for the Oxmen passed, until the leader of the group found the courage to address these strange men.

"We mean no dishonor to you or your land. We will collect our prisoner and depart." His words rang hollow of boldness, and void of any reply from the lizard-like men. The Oxmen leader motioned to two of his men to collect Liam, but as their mounts stepped forward they were halted by the clear, commanding voice of a man.

"Leave him. Leave now. Leave alive." The voice had come from one of the lizard men, evidently older or senior to the others, but without any features that distinguished him from the rest; likewise, their mounts varied little in appearance. It was the dread of Treyherne, coupled with their perception that the four large creatures facing them would be too slow and sluggish in any type of skirmish that resulted in the Oxmen's next move. Two of the Oxmen lurched forward upon their mounts, eager to claim their quarry; the remainder of the group began to rain arrows upon these four creatures and their riders to prevent them from interfering. The arrows struck their mark but failed to penetrate the beasts' hides; three of the creatures leaped from the murky waters, their heads, tails, and riders making short work of the intruders. The fourth lizard remained in the bog waters, but stretching its great neck out, gently grasped Liam in its teeth and lifted him out of harm's way. The great beast placed the wounded man beside its rider, who quickly examined Liam's injuries.

"I am Tiblak," he said, his dark eyes burning into Liam's. "Why do I find a captain of the Havenstone lord, Dhresden, fleeing from his own guard?"

Liam, wounded and weary, stammered his reply, "T—T—Tiblak? The bog healer Dhresden spoke of? There is much I must tell you, and much we must do." The other behemoth and their riders had returned to the water; the Oxmen, dead or fleeing, were no longer a threat to them.

"We go now to my burrow," Tiblak told him. "I shall attend your wounds, and you shall tell me all you know." It was neither a request, nor did Liam wish to hide anything from this man.

CHAPTER 25

The weary Khaldun bounced along behind Asha as the great cougar bore him closer to his homeland. The pair had been traveling for almost two days, with little rest, water or food, yet the grey cat stoically conveyed him along. By Khaldun's estimation, there remained at least another day to their journey, but his wounds and weariness caused him to doubt his assessments. His life lay in Asha's paws, as it were; and the Makani trusted that her bond with Dhresden would keep him safe. They had managed to keep distance between themselves and the Oxmen that pursued them, but at times Khaldun believed he could hear distant sounds of pursuit, and he was certain that the more keen ears of the cougar had heard much more than he. These winter days were short, forcing them to continue their journey into the night, during the night, or before the sun arose to keep ahead of their pursuers. The Makani silently cursed his injuries and the drag marks the litter left for the Oxmen to follow; he knew that Asha must be so much more fatigued than himself, but he was without recourse. He hoped again for snow to hide their passage, and to veil the night sky and render their pursuers blind in the darkness. Then the two of them, but especially Asha, could rest several hours rather than the brief naps they had endured. Darkness settled again over the south of the Pasturelands, greeting Khaldun with the glitter and sparkle of another clear starry night. Thankfully, the moon would not rise until almost dawn; perhaps they would get in a few hours of sleep tonight. Finally, Asha stopped within a sparse copse of trees; she slowly pulled her head from the harness and curled herself into the snow to rest. Khaldun rolled off the litter and slowly limped to her side, giving the exhausted cougar the last of his dried meat and the water from his waterskin. He refilled the skin with snow and placed it under his cloak so that the heat from his body could melt it, then sat leaning against the great cat, warming them both. Asha must have fallen asleep as quickly as the man had, for when he awoke, he could feel her breathing deeply beside him, evidently asleep. The night sky told him that dawn was still at least two hours away; that he should have awoken and not the alert cougar seemed odd to Khaldun. His eyes and ears searched the darkness about him, expecting nothing, and yet the longer he inspected his surroundings, the more uneasy he became. Their first night on the run, they had encountered wolves, but despite their sly cunning and quiet approach, both he and Asha had heard them and drove them away. This eerie threat was too quiet to be wolves, or any wild animal that the Makani knew of, and despite his growing dread the cougar slept on, as if no threat existed. Khaldun leaned forward, searching the darkness frantically now for the threat he was certain existed. Missing the man's weight and warmth against her side, the cougar stirred and then leaped to her feet instantly awake. In a flash, the great cat had fastened her jaws firmly upon the thick layer of Khaldun's garments and bounded into the darkness, bearing him along much as a mother cat would carry off one of her mewling kittens. Unseen in the darkness behind them, Khaldun heard the rustle of hurried footsteps in the snow, followed by the low muttering and cursing of men as they realized that their prey had escaped. The Makani was amazed that the dismounted Oxmen had been able to approach so closely without the big cat detecting them. The fact that the enemy had done so confirmed his fears that this journey was exacting a severe toll upon Asha, and as she half dragged, half carried the wounded man through the snow, Khaldun racked his mind for some means by which to ease the cougar's burden. He was more than willing to be left behind so that Asha could complete the journey unencumbered; he would have considered it an honor die in the repayment of his peoples' debt. Asha, however, could not convey the details of the southern attack and of Dhresden's defensive plan, parts of which were already underway; neither would the cougar be convinced to leave the man behind.

The sun began to rise behind them; the cougar had maintained speed for the past two hours, though Khaldun had noticed that Asha had begun to drag him more than carry him the last few miles. She finally stopped, released her burden, and turned to face the way they had come. The cougar stood a moment, panting heavily, then lay down to rest, her eyes studying the terrain behind them. Khaldun retrieved his waterskin from beneath his cloak and poured the water into Asha's grateful mouth, but he too examined the barrenness behind them. Presently he saw movement, just darkness against the winter backdrop at first, but then the forms of several mounted Oxmen took shape as they charged down upon the two fugitives. Neither the cougar nor the man rose; Asha was too exhausted and Khaldun's wounds would not allow him to rise. So it would seem that the two would die in service of the young lord of Havenstone without Dhresden having ever sat upon his rightful throne. The man's gaze dropped slowly to the snow covered ground before him, only to realize that it was not simply snow upon which he crouched, but sand as well. His brow furrowed in confused thought. They had reached the outskirts of the Dunes! And while this truth would bring no deliverance with it, it brought comfort to the Makani in knowing that he would die within the boundaries of his homeland. Shaking from the pain and the effort, Khaldun struggled to his feet, determined to meet his end fighting. He glanced down at Asha, surprised to find the cougar had not risen; dismayed, in fact, to find that she had slumped over on her side. The poor creature lay there with her eyes closed, exhausted and indifferent to the fate approaching them. Asha had fought and endured much on his behalf, and Khaldun would repay her sacrifice with that of his own. The Oxmen were almost upon them now, their speed constant, as though they intended to trample the two of them to death. The wounded Khaldun braced himself for the moment when he would unleash his remaining strength upon this foe; he would imprint forever upon the memories of those who survived this battle the inhuman fury of the Makani. He was vaguely aware that he had walled off the pain from his injuries; that he had entered the Makani warrior trance of fire and ice. The opposing elements described the calmness of mind that allowed the warrior to think clearly without distraction from pain or fear, coupled with the rushing flow of blood and adrenaline that would galvanize each dodge, thrust, and blow that this battle would require of him. Despite his injuries, Khaldun leaped through the air, knocking the lead rider senseless to the ground.

~~~

Flint led his band of Oxmen in pursuit of the cougar and injured man with every intent of capturing or neutralizing them for the good of Treyherne's cause, and yet in the silence of his mind he heard again the hushed discussions that he and Liam had shared. The obvious corruption that had so quickly eroded the moral fabric of many of their peers would only lead to the destruction of the whole of the Pasturelands, and of themselves and their families, unless bold measures were taken. They had recalled together the honor of Dhane and of the half-blood rumored to be his son that even the enemies of the throne of Havenstone were apportioned certain mercies. And yet these months since Treyherne had begun to rule had evidenced such degradation in society that Flint and Liam thought to flee to, well, to where they did not yet know, but they now feared for the lives, hearts, and minds of their loved ones as they never had during Dhane's time in power. Flint and his Oxmen trudged along, following for two days the drag marks left by the cougar, then resting the night. The men spoke little, and addressed Flint even more rarely. Their second in command, though smaller in stature than most, was not one for idle talk. The Oxmen contented themselves in groups surrounding small fires when camp was set on the second night of their pursuit; Flint had instructed them to eat well, warm themselves and get a good night's rest. His plan was to ride hard the next day in order to close the gap and overtake their quarry, and well-rested and well-fed troops were better fit for that task. At his direction, camp was broken early and the march began before the sun had begun to break over the horizon. The initial progress was slow, but once full daylight surrounded them and illuminated the path of their prey, they broke into a full gallop. The pace was maintained for almost an hour, and then slowed to a swiftness that could be sustained for long periods of time. Although none of the troops spotted the cougar or the man, Flint believed that they had drawn much closer. As night fell, he instructed the Oxmen to tend to their mounts and rest well, but forbade any fires. Flint left his own mount in the charge of another of the troops and began to very slowly and quietly follow the trail on foot. The clear night sky provided just enough light that he could see the spoor of his prey, and he walked gingerly along, placing each foot slowly and silently in the snow as he went. The progress was tedious and deliberate, but Flint was hoping that his silent passage would bring him within bow range of the cougar and the man by daybreak. In the early light of the new day he planned to bring down the cougar first, then the man could either be killed or captured for questioning. Hours passed slowly; the man found himself sweating at the strain to remain as silent as the night about him. Occasionally, he would stoop to the ground and scoop a bite of snow into his mouth, not willing to risk even the noise his waterskin might make in the ears of the cougar. By his best estimation, Flint determined it to be an hour or two before dawn. Fighting the urge to increase his pace, Flint actually slowed his progress even more, convinced that he must be getting close to his prey. He worried in one breath that he would not reach them in time to level a shot at the cougar, and in the next that he would stumble upon them without realizing it and allow them to escape. Pausing and kneeling yet again to search the terrain ahead of him and to listen for some indication of the man and cougar, Flint again played through a conversation that he and Liam had whispered in secrecy. That Treyherne lacked the morality of his predecessor was evident in his tolerance and even encouragement of the deviant behavior of the Oxmen troops. This was not the level of excellence that the two friends had trained for; they feared for their nation and for their families. The thought nagged at Flint, that in fulfilling his assignment he would be contributing to the erosion of the morality of his people. He had paused longer now than he had previously, and as he rose to his feet again, Flint moved forward with new motivation. If this man with the cougar was intent upon overthrowing Treyherne and reversing the degradation of Havenstone society, then he and Liam could do nothing but aid them. Again he fought to remain silent in his progress, but this decision to make a difference in the direction of his nation and family had energized him. Though his purpose in seeking the man and cougar had changed, the fact that they would perceive him as a threat remained. Flint risked being attacked as he attempted to befriend them, but the man had resolved that this choice was the honorable one. He stopped, certain that he had finally heard some indication of the cougar and the man's presence. Flint tensed, ready for some form of attack, and then groaned in his spirit as he realized that they were hurrying away from him. He rushed forward, shouting after them, but was unable to intercept them. Flint sank to the ground, exhausted from his slow arduous walk and the emotional drain upon him. He knew that he could not now overtake the cougar on foot, and his shouting was sure to draw the attention and presence of the Oxmen behind him. He waited, resting, as the sun crept above the horizon and the sounds of his mounted soldiers drew closer behind him.

"Are you alright, sir?" Flint looked up. The Oxmen sat atop their mounts looking down at their commander. To Flint's cautious eye, many of them appeared to regard him with suspicion rather than curiosity or concern. He rose, took the reins of his mount, and stepped up into the saddle.

"They were here, and I almost had them," he said. "We will continue, we will overtake, but we shall not strike until my order to do so is given." He still held out hope that he would be able in some way to unite with the man and cougar and deliver them from the hand of the Oxmen. As the column galloped along, Flint stole occasional glances at the men about him, searching their faces for some sign of the same struggles he had resolved in the night. Being able to recruit one or two allies from the troops about him would increase his odds of success, but none of the men he observed appeared to doubt their mission or their ruler. Around noon, Flint called a halt and instructed the men to rest.

"I will scout ahead a little, and we will continue shortly." Flint's words brought again the same looks of distrust that he had glimpsed earlier that morning, and as he rode ahead, he was keenly aware of a hush of whispers that rippled through the group. He feared that his control over these Oxmen had grown tenuous at best, and a glance back at them revealed that they had come to certain conclusions. The Oxmen had mounted, and were in pursuit now of him. There was very little distance separating Flint from the Oxmen, and he knew that flight was now his course of action. The decision of whether to attempt to distract the Oxmen from following the cougar and man or seek to ally himself with the Oxmen's quarry was made in an instant, sending Flint and his mount sprinting along the cougar's trail. On he raced, attempting to keep far enough ahead of the Oxmen that he would be able to communicate his intentions to the man with the cougar, but with each glance behind Flint saw his former subordinates closing the gap. Cresting a rise, he spotted his objective, but was dismayed to see that they were no longer fleeing. The cougar lay upon its side, dead or resting Flint could not tell, and the man was struggling to rise. Flint spurred his mount on, demanding greater speed from the already weary animal, certain that the Oxmen behind him were requiring the same from their mounts. Within another few strides Flint would be beside them, but then he realized that the man, though obviously wounded, had somehow managed to launch himself into the air, but Flint was unconscious for what happened next.

~ ~ ~

His impact with the lead rider had sent Khaldun spiraling to the ground, landing awkwardly in a heap in the path of the other Oxmen. He had reopened some of his wounds and could feel his blood oozing, hot against his skin. Glancing behind him, Khaldun could see the man he had struck lying motionless upon the ground, whether dead or alive the Makani did not care; what concerned him was that his companion, the cougar, still lay upon her side, indifferent to the activity and noise of approaching hoof beats. Khaldun lamented that they two would face death with so little resistance, preferring to meet his end fighting. He struggled again to stand, but could only rise to a kneeling position. He sighed, resignation settling upon him, and lifted his eyes to the Oxmen approaching. Would they dismount to execute him? Or would they be content just to trample him under hoof? He preferred a clean death, and took small comfort in seeing the Oxmen begin to slow as they approached, but then Khaldun realized that the riders had turned their attention away from himself and Asha, and that they were focused now upon the sixteen khamelleros and Arba'a riders now racing toward them.

The Oxmen readied their blades, certain that they would slice apart this new enemy with little effort. What chance would these Makani have, outnumbered, armed only with tree branches, and riding such awkward-looking creatures? The ensuing battle was intense, though brief. Sparks flew as the wind-fighters deflected the blades of the Oxmen with their terephthala-clad forearms, each seeking to bring their wooden quarterstaff to bear against the enemy. A few of the Makani were wounded in the skirmish, one mortally. Two of the khamellero had been slain by the desperate Oxmen, all of whom lay strewn about. The Makani had not struck all lethal blows; several Oxmen had received broken bones, or been rendered unconscious, though six of them had been killed immediately by a well-placed blow to the head or neck. The victorious Makani kept careful watch upon the defeated Oxmen, though all taste for battle had left the wounded men, while the Arba'a captain dismounted and approached Khaldun.

"How badly are you wounded?" asked the captain, kneeling and glancing over his wounded countryman. Fighting to remain conscious, Khaldun looked up at the other man, their eyes meeting for the first time. Recognition flickered across the captain's face, and possibly across Khaldun's, but then the wounded Makani collapsed, senseless, to the ground.

The captain rolled Khaldun onto his back and regarded him again. His brow furrowed as he studied the man, one hand placed tenderly upon Khaldun's chest measuring his breathing and heart rate, but also something else. He knelt so for a moment before he was interrupted by three of his men approaching.

"We are ready, Andalhyn," one of the three said, addressing his captain by name. "The slain khamelleros have been quartered and packed, and the wounded that cannot walk have mounted as well. What of the enemy wounded sir?"

"Leave them," Andalhyn said, his words and tone simple. "They cannot harm us. Let them limp back like the dogs they have become to their master."

"We have beasts available for this wounded man and yourself, but what of the cougar?"

Andalhyn looked now upon the great beast which had, to this point, lain indifferently upon the ground a mere stone's throw away. As the man turned his gaze upon her, he found her regarding him intently. Andalhyn stood slowly, looking back into the eyes of an intelligent creature rather than that of a dumb beast. He pondered what should be done, then spoke, not to his men, but to Asha.

"I would rather you walk along with us, if you are able."

The cougar blinked at him, then rolled to her feet and rose, her tail twitching, her eyes expectantly upon Andalhyn. The captain and his men stood dumbfounded a moment, glancing first at one another, and then back at the cat. Finally, Andalhyn found his voice and his composure.

"Load this one onto my mount; I shall walk with the cougar."

"Yes, sir!" the men replied, though they looked quizzically at one another, and cautiously at the cougar as they stooped to lift Khaldun. There had never been cause for these men to doubt or question their captain, and they would do neither at this time. Momentarily they had secured Khaldun atop the captain's khamellero and formed up, some mounted, some on foot, for the trek to their home within the Cliffs of Hawa Janbiyah. At full strength, the Arba'a could have managed the distance by nightfall, but encumbered and wounded as they were they would likely not arrive until the middle of the following day if they were required to stop for the night. Andalhyn led, setting a brisk pace, with the cougar beside him, yet she remained at a cautious distance. Behind him rode four of his most fit Arba'a, followed by the mounted wounded and those who had given up their mounts to travel on foot, while the remainder of healthy riders brought up the rear. Andalhyn glanced occasionally to his flank, inspecting and measuring the condition of the wounded and the soldiers on foot; he was unwilling to further tax his men, but hoped to reach the Cliffs late in the evening. His usually stoic face hinted at his haste, but was held in check by his concern for his men. The captain's mind would drift to thoughts, scenes, and memories of happier times for many of his quick paces, until he shook them temporarily from his mind. He would inventory his men and his two guests, then return to surveying the landscape ahead until his mind drifted again. The pattern continued until several miles had been trampled underfoot and the sun was somewhere between zenith and the horizon. Again shaking himself from his daydreams, Andalhyn checked his companions. He found the cougar off to his left keeping stride easily, but could see that the soldiers on foot were struggling to maintain the pace. With difficulty, Andalhyn halted the march and ordered that the men and animals take food and water. He provided water and some dried meat for the cougar, leaving it for her to consume, while he approached the still unconscious Khaldun. The captain's khamellero laid down at his command, allowing Andalhyn to inspect the man's condition. He gently poured water into the man's mouth, pausing as he swallowed involuntarily. Khaldun's condition appeared to be stable, but Andalhyn still wanted him in the hands of the healers at the Cliffs as soon as was possible. Sensing someone's approach, Andalhyn stood, turning to face his second in command.

"Have you surveyed the men?" Andalhyn asked, already knowing the answer.

"Yes, sir," he replied. "The men are well, and are ready to return to marching."

The captain regarded this soldier, a friend in many rights. "Night is falling, Mikhal. A third of our men are wounded; all are wearied. Why on earth would they be volunteering to travel through the night?" There was an edge to his tone, as if hinting at some insubordination on Mikhal's part.

"If I may," Andalhyn nodded his assent, and the other man continued, "the men believe that this man and cougar are somehow connected to the giant mountain man and his companions who have taken shelter among our people. They believe it is best to reunite them sooner rather than later. Each of us is aware of our people's debt to the line of Dhane, and we wish to do our part in its fulfillment."

Andalhyn considered the man's words a while, his own eyes upon the ground, but seeing. "What else, Mikhal?" the captain asked, his eyes now burning into the other man's. Mikhal had served with him for several lives of men, and the bond that he and Andalhyn had formed hinted to something more than his second in command had already shared.

"A handful of the men, suspect to know who it is that we are taking—returning—to the Cliffs," he answered.

"And what of it!?" his voice remained low, but there was a fire in Andalhyn's tone that startled Mikhal.

"Sir, none of the men are opposed to our mission, or to your command. You have kept certain details hidden from us, and we trust you in this. I ask on behalf of your men that you allow us to march with you through the night."

The fire faded from Andalhyn's eyes as Mikhal's words sank in. He had not anticipated such loyalty in this endeavor, and the willingness of his men to almost blindly support him was humbling. "Thank you, Mikhal," he said finally. "Please forgive my anger; it was misplaced. If the men are able, let us press on."

"Yes, sir. I shall give the order to prepare to march. We should reach the Cliffs early tomorrow," Mikhal bowed and turned to go, but paused. "It is good to see him, Andalhyn. I too had feared the worst," he said, and was gone.

CHAPTER 26

D hresden, accompanied by almost three hundred herdsmen, rode north away from Murion's Plateau. Jovanna and Faust remained at the outpost, in the company of twenty of Faust's most trusted and most skilled herdsmen, their mission two-fold: to maintain control of the fort, and to protect the one known survivor of Dhresden's family. As he headed now to intercept Chayne and her mob of brigands at the edge of the Badlands, his mind wandered to Khaldun and Asha, and to Liam the Oxmen commander. Had they accomplished their missions, or would the southern border of his beloved land be left unguarded and the Pasturelands be razed by Uganji and his ruthless Ianzama? He thought of his companions that he knew to be dead, and of those whom he feared dead; he stoically mourned the unknown fate of old friends, family, and those whom he had longed to know better. He had not begun this journey with naive expectations, but the sequence of events, and their cost, had been grossly underestimated. He now marched to face an unknown and quite possibly overwhelming number of bloodthirsty invaders, led by a madwoman. Minutes turned to hours before the boundary of the Pasturelands came into view, a border landmarked by a maze of canyons that twisted and turned, filled with cutbacks and dead ends, the canyon walls themselves brittle, offering no footholds or handholds. It was a wonderful natural defense, funneling the enemy through the passageways and onto the edge of the defenders' waiting sword, yet Dhresden had lost too much to remain overly optimistic. He and the herdsmen rode to within a stone's throw of the entrance to the canyons, the only true entrance from the side of the Pasturelands.

Three or four false entrances were also visible, each winding into the maze of passageways various distances, all leading only to dead ends.

No sight or sound could be discerned of the advancing horde that Sachsman in dying had voiced to the young lord, a matter that further troubled Dhresden. His brow furrowed as he considered the situation. No other means of ingress existed from the Badlands, at least not without riding into the Wanderlands to the west or the Forgotten Woods to the east; but even as deranged as Chayne had proven to be, she would not risk interference from the mountain men or the Kelvren at this stage of her invasion. No, this passage was the only means by which she could hope to initiate her conquest of the Pasturelands. It was doubtful that Chayne's forces would consist of much more than foot soldiers, but it could be expected that she and several of her band would be mounted, likely upon vorshtig. These wild and vicious horses were so fierce and seemed to have such a penchant for violence upon both man and beast that the locals had given them the name vorshtig, or literally "demon-horse." There seemed to be no taming of them, but somehow Chayne's horde had managed to utilize the beasts as warhorses, fierce mounts that would ruthlessly kick and bite at their riders' enemies, tearing, rending, and trampling both man and beast underfoot. It had been recorded in the histories of Havenstone that bands of Oxmen who had encountered even a single vorshtig had suffered the loss of at least one of their larger mounts, as well as a handful of men. Dhresden had seen the ferocity of the vorshtig only through the stories told to him by his father and grandfather; the awe and horror that both had described to him did not cheer his mood as he awaited the return of the two scouts he had dispatched into the canyons. Distracted by his musings, Dhresden was unsure how long the scouts had been gone, but the two emerged from the maze of passageways after what seemed like almost two hours.

"My lord," the two herdsmen remained astride their mounts, but both bowed their heads respectfully as they awaited Dhresden's response. Dhresden had selected a father and his grown son as scouts, a selection Faust had suggested before they left Murion's Plateau. Dhresden had kept the two close to himself during the trek to the border, observing them, measuring them. He had found them to be confident and capable riders, but also cautious observers of their surroundings. Most of the herdsmen riding with him were naturally watchful of their environment, having been trained at a young age to be on the lookout for predators that could threaten the herd, but this father and son seemed to be more guarded in their demeanor than the other herdsmen. Dhresden had been pleased to enlist the duo for the scouting expedition.

"What have you found?" Dhresden asked. "Is there any sign of them?"

"Yes, my lord," the father replied. Both raised their eyes to meet Dhresden's as they reported their findings. "We rode quietly for the better part of an hour before we were close enough that our mounts could smell their camp. At that point we left our oxen and went on foot, keeping to the shadows until we could see them. They have set up camp, tents and small cook fires, but seem to be content where they are. It could be that they are awaiting more of their forces to join them before they advance, but they are not breaking camp, nor does there appear to be any other preparations occurring."

"How many could you discern? Were you able to number them?"

"It is difficult to say for sure," the father replied, "we could see two hundred, though there may have been more that remained inside the tents. We did see at least fifty of the vorshtig wandering through the camp, though we could not be certain of the exact number."

Dhresden nodded his thanks as he considered his next steps. He and the herdsmen could set up camp here in the Pasturelands with an alternating battalion of men guarding the mouth of the canyons. This would force the enemy to attack with scarce numbers at a time and allow Dhresden and his men to repel them with just a few of their force as well, rotating to fresh troops as needed. The second option was to ride in and attack Chayne's encamped forces before any of her reinforcements arrived. This would hasten battle and bloodshed, but could dishearten her army and end this part of the war early. Dhresden's bloodlust had faded with the effects of the *ferial* that Tiblak had entrusted to him, and yet he wished to hasten peace for his homeland.

"Set watches for the night," the Havenstone Lord instructed. "We attack at dawn."

～～～

Dhresden's sleep proved restless that night, his attempts at slumber ending shortly after midnight. He sat with his back against his mount, as did the sleeping herdsmen about him, but his eyes looked up at the moon's brightness above him. Gazing at it, he saw a few snowflakes fluttering serenely towards earth; the simple beauty of that scene ended after a few moments as the snow began to fall steadily, blanketing him and the herdsmen, their mounts, and the path they would walk in a few short hours. The snow itself would have no effect upon the sure feet of the oxen, but would prove to disadvantage Chayne's footmen. Dhresden took some satisfaction in this development, but sleep still eluded him; as justified and necessary as the bloodshed at dawn would be, he would take no joy in it.

More than an hour before daybreak, he and the herdsmen shook the inches of new snow from themselves and dusted clean their mounts, ready now to follow the son of Dhane into battle. At their request, Dhresden had allowed his two scouts to take up positions at the head of the column, while he fell into step a few paces behind them. The defenders of the Pasturelands rode swiftly but quietly into the maze of canyons, the predawn darkness hiding them from sight, the snow muffling their footsteps. They had ridden more than half an hour when both father and son turned and nodded to Dhresden. Knowing that Chayne's army was encamped just around the next turn, all readied their armaments. Swords slipped from sheaths; axes, spears, clubs, pitchforks and other makeshift weapons were lifted from their resting places; the ragtag but determined army rushed into the enemy's camp as first light crested the upper edge of the canyons. They encountered no one at the first three rows of tents, but at the far edge of the camp Dhresden spied a host of mounted cavalry and footmen; ready, watching, waiting, as if...

The men before him dropped quickly from view, their mounts bellowing in pain. Dhresden's mount lurched forward as well, the sickening crack of bones being broken filling his ears as Dhresden realized that Chayne had anticipated such an attack. She had ordered a series of holes dug at the edge of the camp, small but deep enough to accept an ox leg, as well as a web of ropes and snares hidden just beneath the snow level. The poor creatures at the front of the assault had not been able to avoid the snow-hidden traps, and their momentum had pushed them forward, shattering their ensnared legs. Some riders had been crushed or trapped beneath the bawling, writhing creatures, but a few had managed to free themselves from the chaos and were attempting to ready their makeshift weapons against the Horde's expected counterattack. Dhresden finally pulled free from his fallen mount, found his sword, and surveyed the situation. Due to the narrowness of the canyon, the chaos of wounded men and animals prevented the uninjured herdsmen from continuing to advance. A few had dismounted and were attempting to pick their way through the carnage to support the handful that now stood alone at the forward edge of what had once been a surprise attack. Seeing the Horde cavalry charging towards them, Dhresden called for his troops to fall back into the protection of the passage through which they had just come, but as the command was given, Dhresden realized that his rear guard was also under attack. Countless Horde footmen had somehow swarmed from the rear, many crushed by the herdsmen mounts, but despite their losses, their number gave them the advantage. As Dhresden turned his eyes back toward the enemy cavalry, his eyes met those of the young scout. He was kneeling in the snow, his hands cradling his father's bloodied head, whose blank eyes stared lifelessly at nothing. There was no condemnation in the son's countenance, and yet Dhresden silently cursed himself. Had it been for naught? Had the pain, the bloodshed and the loss of life been all for nothing? The young scout gently lowered his father's head to the ground and, taking the slain man's sword in his hand, stood to his feet. Gesturing for Dhresden to flee, he turned and rushed to face the vorshtig onslaught. The demon-horses swept over him and the handful of men with him, trampling them to the ground. As they reached the mass of still writhing oxen, the vor-shtig, unable to traverse past them, attacked the helpless creatures that they could reach. Temporarily safe in the midst of the carnage of thrashing wounded men and animals, Dhresden spied Chayne atop one of the mad horses. Freeing a pitchfork from the slaughter about him, Dhresden flung the makeshift weapon at her, hoping to salvage some semblance of victory. The madwoman, however, had spotted the half-blood, and anticipated some sort of attack. She deftly batted the missile aside with her sword, hurling a maniacal laugh back at Dhresden. She and Dhresden both understood that the tide of this battle, and likely that of the war, flowed in the favor of Chayne and her horde; but then, something in her expression changed. The laugh and taunting smile faded, replaced suddenly with rage. She screamed wordlessly, and quickly commanded her cavalry to retreat. As she and her forces fled, Dhresden turned to discover that at the rear of his column, Chayne's foot soldiers were being vanquished; the herdsmen had finally been bolstered by reinforcements from the Wanderlands. Several of the giant men from Orrick's region had rushed in behind the enemy, their iron sinews rending limb and life with grand axes, hammers, and long swords, while their animal companions, wolves, cougars, and bear, tore flesh alongside them. Dhresden had taken a risk with the life of one of Faust's herdsmen, and though he had volunteered after Dhresden had made the risks of the task quite clear, the young lord had been haunted by the possibility that he had sent the cattleman to his doom. He had been dispatched by Dhresden as an emissary to the mountain men of the Wanderlands to request aid, but even if none of Treyherne's treachery had reached within their boundaries, the response was difficult to predict. The Wanderlanders were distrustful even of one another, being a nation of disjointed tribes who could not agree on how to select a ruler, much less on who that ruler should be. They had managed to maintain a loose alliance through the formation of the Llögruta, a body comprised of twen-ty-one elders of the Wanderlands, all respected despite the inherent distrust harbored between the tribes. The Llogruta had been initially instituted with the intent of selecting a national leader, but for many years had been diminished to a law council with moderate authority.

As the last of Chayne's Tulisan retreated and the herdsmen began to tend to their wounded men and beasts, Dhresden made his way toward the mountain men, anxious to greet them and to discover their number.

Nearing the Wanderlanders, Dhresden was somewhat taken aback at their number. First, he was stunned to discover less than thirty men, but then he was amazed to realize that the addition of these twenty-three men had turned the tide of their battle against the Horde. The addition of their beast companions was a strategic boon in and of itself, but the prowess and force of the men themselves was not to be overlooked. The Wanderlanders were a people bred for war, though not to their own destruction. Before their twelfth year, all Wanderland youth, male and female, had undergone their ordeal. Briefly, the ordeal required the young individual to survive two weeks of solitude in the wilderness; all food, shelter, and protection were the responsibility of the lone youth. There was also the requirement of obtaining a beast companion, whether by procurement of an infant animal, or through other means. Harsh was the task, and few there were who had not successfully endured this rite of passage.

"Hail, Konaird!" Dhresden called, recognizing the leader's face among the group. The commander cast a steely, piercing look in Dhresden's direction; seeing the half-blood lord, a smile broadened behind his braided mustache and beard, and he strode forward to greet him. Like Orrick, Konaird's large frame was heavily muscled, though the man before Dhresden bore wild red curls upon his head, fiery green eyes and a stomach that boasted his love of ale. He laid a hand heavily upon Dhresden's shoulder in familiar greeting. Konaird both liked and respected the smaller man, and had been one of the loudest to voice that support be sent to Dhresden's aid.

"Glad to see you, Dhresden. It would seem that we arrived none too soon!" Konaird's broad smile remained, but the seriousness in his eyes betrayed his concern for the young ruler. There were claims made by most of the families in the Wanderlands to the mountain throne, but Konaird's tribe was one of a handful that had produced some evidence to the fact. Orrick and Dhresden both had been hopeful that Konaird would have been selected as leader, but were dismayed to hear that the deliberations had come to naught.

"Please accept my deep gratitude to you, Konaird, and to your men, for coming to our assistance." As they continued to speak, Dhresden knelt to greet the creature at Konaird's side, a smoky-brown wolf with gleaming teeth and black eyes. "I am uncertain how Chayne's forces were able to attack our rear guard. It may be that they came through the pass prior to our arrival and remained hidden until we had entered."

"We found where they had come over the walls of the canyons," Konaird said. "They used ladders, and the spoor indicates that they came over only after you and your men passed by."

"That would explain why her camp seemed to be somewhat vacant, but I am concerned that she will have reinforcements arriving. There is also the likelihood that more of the Tulisan will traverse the canyon walls in an attempt to surround us or even to bypass us on their march to the Citadel."

"Prior to your messenger reaching us, our lands had gotten word that Chayne was on the move," Konaird's voice dropped in volume as he went on. "There are even rumors that she has obtained Ianzama support, and has recruited Ikshton's JabalKriger to her cause."

Both lapsed into silence for a moment. "Good to see you again, Loki," Dhresden murmured, as he gave the wolf a last pat upon its shoulders, then rose slowly to his feet. He moved slightly closer to Konaird, speaking more quietly than he had before.

"Indeed she has united with Ytero Uganji, his forces invade from the south, but I had not yet heard of the possibility of aid to her from Vlad Ikshton. What would propel him to such an end?"

"The JabalKing has always been unpredictable, Lord Havenstone," Konaird replied, "and likely has grown weary of his surroundings. The evils of the former days, the days your father brought to an end, were harsh for all but were more severe for some. Vlad lost many things, his humanity not the least among them. Long ago I was surprised when he first hired himself out, but now he is little more than a mercenary, covetous and cruel."

"How many strong has he become?"

Konaird took a breath, calculating. "Last I knew, his fighting men numbered two hundred, and the swine totaled five hundred. I thought he was mad all those years ago when he began with that first hog, but he has developed a fighting force to be reckoned with."

"Is he likely to listen to reason?" Dhresden asked.

"Possibly, from an old friend,"

~ ~ ~

JabalKriger. This was the name that Vlad had given his band of hogwarriors, though he considered the men to be his warriors and the pigs to be his children. The man had suffered great loss during a time that many had forgotten, but the memory remained painfully vivid to this man. Following the war, Vlad had isolated himself in the wilderness of the lands beyond his mountain home, finally settling north and east of the Badlands. He had befriended a wild boar, which had allowed the man to dwell with its drove. Years Ikshton dwelt as a wild man, keeping the company of only this family of pigs, until loss again found him. Merciless hunters had found the drove, and had targeted everything within sight; many of the young ones had been slaughtered as well. The great boar hurried to the protection of his family with Ikshton in tow, though the man fell behind. His lungs burned as he sought to overtake his companion, and renewed his efforts as he heard the cries of men up ahead mingled with the screams of a raging boar. The sight of a half-naked wild man leaping into their presence immobilized the hunters, never once expecting that this man was allied with the hogs. The great boar lay upon his side, his breathing labored; he had been pierced through by many arrows and edged weapons, and in his eyes Vlad saw death creeping into his body. He also saw an expectation, not of vengeance, but of responsibility to the drove. The sorrow and rage of this moment united with the lifetime of loss he had endured, and Vlad embraced the familiar pain. And so it was that six of band of nine hunters met their doom at the hands of a sobbing, enraged wild man. The three who survived did so only by fleeing, and few who heard their tale ventured into what became Ikshton's land.

CHAPTER 27

Night hung thick and dark over the palace city of Hazrat Almadi bin Khuzaymah, while the ocean tidewaters beat rhythmically against the base of the Cliffs of Hawa Janbiyah at the edge of the desert region known as the Dunes. The Black Wanderer slept peacefully in this refuge city now, having become familiar with its sights, sounds, and smells. The wet winter air of this desert region was held at bay by the smoldering fire near the sleeping mat upon which he slumbered, but a sound out of place drew him from rest. He lay motionless in the dim light from the embers of the fire, hearing slow cautious feet creeping into his chamber. Unrecognizable in the darkness, the form leaned towards Orrick, reaching for him—in an instant the giant had grabbed the intruder, hefting him off the ground and forcefully against the wall. A familiar voice cried out wordlessly, but it was enough.

"Please forgive me, Zabayr," Orrick said, gently setting the other man to the ground. "I awoke with a start. What brings you here to me at this hour?"

The Makani bowed low in the custom of his people as he spoke. "Please forgive my intrusion, friend Orrick, but the grand master summons you."

Orrick's brow furrowed more at the other man's words. "What ill news has come to us that he would ask for me in the still of the night? Speak Zabayr: what do you know?"

"Friend Orrick, I know little of the news, only that it was brought to us in the company of a creature of the mountains."

Suddenly Orrick was moving towards the door. "Where?" The single word demanded not simply an answer, but quick action.

"Please, follow me." Zabayr ran the necessary steps to place himself ahead of the giant, and the two sped quietly through the dark halls. Within moments they had reached the infirmary, which was comprised of a large well-lit chamber where treatment and surgeries occurred, and several smaller attached compartments used for recovery, birthing, and often departure to a life beyond this one. Zabayr remained in the hall, while Orrick burst through the door to the main room. He found Khuzaymah in hushed discussion with four other men, while a man who appeared to be a healer stood by. They ceased talking upon Orrick's arrival, and though he recognized none of the four, Orrick could tell from their garb that they had been patrolling the desert, likely a captain and his three chief officers. Orrick bowed a respectful greeting to the group of men, though his expression clearly conveyed his unspoken and urgent inquiry.

"Orrick," Khuzaymah welcomed the giant, "this is Andalhyn and three of his men. They fought a band of Oxmen at the edge of our land and rescued a wounded Makani, as well as a grey cougar." A smile broadened upon the face of the grand master as he saw relief wash over the other man. Khuzaymah directed the giant to a side chamber, in which Orrick found Khaldun and Asha. The man was bandaged and unconscious, but his breathing and color were good. The great cougar padded quietly to Orrick's ready embrace. Asha had been burned badly when they had fought to rescue Dhresden atop the Outcropping, and his last visions of her had been when she dragged Dhresden, healed and deranged from the potion *ferial*, into the wilderness. She had saved Orrick and the women with him, but he had long feared that this beloved friend had been killed in the process. Her wounds had healed nicely, though the fur in the burned areas had grown back a lighter grey than the rest. Orrick hugged the purring cougar, mumbling words in his native tongue that only Asha could understand. No one else spoke, not wishing to interrupt their reunion, but after a time Khuzaymah cleared his throat.

"The healer examined the cougar as best as he could, it seems that she was dehydrated and exhausted from dragging Khaldun upon a litter; they had been pursued a great distance by a number of Oxmen. Khaldun is still weak from several old injuries, as well as a brief battle with the enemy. He has not maintained consciousness for long, but when he is, he blusters along about the lord of Havenstone, and enemies from the south. I have not deciphered it all, but we are readying our troops in preparation for, well, anything."

Orrick stood, turning his attention to the men before him, but kept one hand gently upon Asha's shoulder. The release of emotion that he had allowed himself had passed, and his handsome face took on a setting of stone with his next words. "Khaldun is no fool. Though his fevered condition does not allow us to know exactly what evil is coming, be certain that it is real. Healer! How long before Khaldun is well enough to speak sense?"

The Makani physician blanched and shrank visibly before the intensity of the mountain man, but his answer came in a steady, sure tone. "There is no way to be sure, though a familiar voice would comfort him while his body fights the fever and infection caused by his wounds."

The healer left the other men to their plans, eager to return to the comfort of his quarters. Orrick and the others were quiet, each lost in thought, until Khuzaymah's voice interrupted their musings.

"We will leave you alone with him, Andalhyn, and return to you again on the morrow," He turned to the three travel-weary Makani before him, "You men rest well in your homes; thank you for your service, though I may again require it when we are certain of this new threat. Friend Orrick, it seems that there is little else for us to attend to this night. I hope you are able to return to your slumber easily."

"Yes, grand master, thank you." Orrick nodded respectfully. "May I walk a ways with you?"

"Of course," Khuzaymah replied. He turned and led the other man from the infirmary, Asha in tow. Neither spoke until they were more than a stone's throw from the infirmary. "Well, Black Wanderer? Ask your question."

"This Andalhyn, clearly you trust him, but how does he know Khaldun? Did they serve together?"

The Makani Lord chuckled quietly before answering. "Yes," he said finally. "He and Khaldun know each other well. In fact, it was Andalhyn who suggested Khaldun as one of our emissaries to assist

Dhresden, and thus fulfill the debt owed by our people. It is a hard thing for a father to watch his son depart on such an undertaking; a mission that could likely end in death."

Orrick was surprised by these new details. "So Andalhyn is Khaldun's father? A hard thing indeed to see your son in such condition after you had recommended him for that service."

"Indeed," Khuzaymah agreed. "Without the participation of Andalhyn's brother, he may not have allowed Khaldun to embark upon such a mission, but that too has not ended as the poor captain, nor I, would have expected."

Orrick stopped walking as he looked full into the face of the grand master. "Are you saying that Andalhyn and Khalid were brothers? That would mean that Dhresden was betrayed—"

"By Khaldun's uncle," Khuzaymah said, finishing Orrick's thought. "The tale of Andalhyn's kin is long and riddled with heartache, but I am confident in him and his son. I hope that the morrow will bring us answers. Goodnight, friend Orrick; I do hope that you rest well."

The giant bowed farewell, his eyes upon the Grand Master as he walked from sight. His mind raced with the information it newly possessed, and with the possibilities that it lacked. He and Asha walked slowly back to his chamber, but he found no solace in slumber.

~ ~ ~

Several shadowy forms made their way through the darkness of the Badlands, weaving a path out of the glow of the cook fires of Tulisan. Neither the outlaws nor their wild horse companions were aware of the motley group that passed through their midst, nor would they have believed that a Kelvren half-blood, two giant mountain men, a wolf, and a bear had traversed their camp undetected. Thankful for the long winter night, Dhresden and his companions passed out of bowshot of Chayne's camp by the time that the eastern sky had begun to lighten. The burly Konaird led the way, his wolf beside him, while Dhresden followed. Behind the young lord, a mountain man named Thorne walked with his animal companion: a large reddish-brown bear. Thorne was a wiry, clean-shaven man with long flowing hair reaching halfway down his back. At first glance, one would have thought the two to be mismatched, but the lean man and the lumbering bear were inseparable companions.

The group had made good time in the darkness, but as the sun crested the horizon, they set their steps to cover the several miles to the plantation of Vlad Ikshton, father of the JabalKriger. Contact with any of Chayne's brigands was not anticipated, but even a chance encounter could doom the small group, and if Ikshton had joined forces with Chayne, the eventual interaction with the JabalKriger could prove fatal. The urgency of their situation, however, did not allow for travel solely at night, and so they pressed on, ever vigilant for danger in the growing light of this new day. Close to noon, Konaird halted the group, his eyes cautiously scanning the land before them.

"We have reached the edge of Ikshton's land," he said. "I do not expect a warm welcome, but if he will give us audience, perchance then we can turn an enemy again into an ally."

Their path took them along a winding brook; the land to the right and left sloped gently upward, both hiding their own passage and concealing the approach of others. They had traveled deep into Vlad's country, but had not yet caught sight of man or beast save for the occasional sighting of a crow, pigeon, or snowbird. Konaird had said little of the history between himself and Ikshton, but in what had not been said it was clear to Dhresden that the two had once shared much happier times. As with most of the peoples of their day, age was an irrelevant measurement; most measured their time in this life by what was gained in wisdom and shared in justice. Though the half-blood would-be ruler was unsure of the age of either Konaird or Vlad, he was certain that they had been not more than young men during the reign of his father, though it seemed that their friendship predated Dhane's ascension to the throne of Havenstone.

The private musings of the small group were interrupted by the succulent aroma of roasting meat. The fragrant bouquet awoke the pangs of hunger that man and beast alike had suppressed for the sake of their mission, but for Konaird it aroused not simply craving but also curiosity.

"That smells like pork," he whispered to his companions. "Vlad forbids the slaughter of any of his stock for food, except in the most dire of circumstances. That means that whoever is on the other side of this rise is likely not any of his JabalKriger. Thorne," he said, eyeing the lithe younger man, "creep yonder and tell what you see."

Thorne turned to his animal companion and, placing one hand on the beast's head, spoke quiet words briefly to the bear. He then made his way up towards the crest of the hill, keeping low and finally coming to a crawl nearing the summit. He lay there a short while, taking in the scene before him; he then crawled backwards slowly, finally turning and hurrying back to report his findings.

"There are five brigands and two of the vorshtig about an acre breadth beyond the crest of the hill. It appears as if the demon horses may have attacked and killed a few of Ikshton's swine; the brigands are roasting one of the poor things, but have allowed the vorshtig to sport with the other carcasses."

Konaird nodded thanks to the other man, his brow knit in thought as he considered this new information. After a moment, he looked expectantly at Dhresden.

"If you believe that slaying these miscreants will indebt Ikshton to us, then let us proceed." Dhresden offered, placing his hand upon the hilt of his sword as he spoke.

The red-haired mountain man hesitated, weighing their prospects for attack. The silence became uncomfortable until finally he spoke. "I believe that this is our best opportunity to gain favorable audience with the JabalKing, but an acre breadth is quite a distance to cover, especially when two of our enemy are vorshtig. We can cover the distance quickly, but we will not take them by surprise; they will have time to ready themselves for our attack. We must neutralize the demon horses first, but do not dismiss the Tulisan; they will pick us off if our attention is too focused upon the vorshtig. Thorne, did any of the men have bows?"

"At least two, but possibly the others as well," he replied.

"Then we must keep watch for loosed arrows. We would do well to keep the vorshtig between the brigands and ourselves, but it is likely that the demon horses will not cooperate. Thorne, you and Torsten focus on the vorshtig; Dhresden will aid you. Loki and I will neutralize the Tulisan." Konaird's eyes fastened upon the half-blood.

"If we fall, save yourself. Send word to the mountain of our end; I expect you will receive an army to your aid." He smiled grimly as he spoke his next words, "It may be that I will unite the tribes of the Wanderlands in my death."

~ ~ ~

Dhresden had witnessed the speed of Konaird and his wolf companion, Loki, in battle prior to this moment, but was amazed again by their speed and agility. Thorne and Torsten kept pace easily with the other two as they breached the crest of the hill and charged down upon the unsuspecting enemy. Man and beast kept silent as they rushed to close the gap and strike down the vorshtig and men. The demon horses were so intent upon their desecration of their victims that they were not aware of any threat until more than half the distance between them had been covered by Dhresden and his companions. The two vorshtig wheeled immediately towards their attackers, each emitting abysmal screams, typical of their breed. The five men accompanying the horses had begun feasting on the pig they had been roasting, and were quick to drop the warm greasy meat from their hands and take up arms. Konaird had watched the men from the crest of the hill and had chosen this moment to attack; they would need any advantage they could manage.

No longer was surprise on the side of Dhresden and his companions; this battle would now be won by whichever force could withstand the onslaught of enemy man and beast. Konaird and the wolf, Loki, led the charge, but brushed past the two vorshtig, intent upon the men farther down the hill. To Dhresden's dismay, he saw three of the brigands bringing bows to bear upon Konaird while the other two rushed forward with sword in hand. The archers seemed to be struggling with their bows, but whether from greasy fingers, the cold or some other cause Konaird could not tell. Behind him, Torsten had closed with the first demon horse, the bear had charged ahead and attacked the underbelly of the vorshtig as it lunged forward, its forelegs striking down on the back of the bear. Torsten's momentum propelled his enemy backwards to the ground, his great bear teeth ripping into the soft midsection of the horse. The demon creature would not die easily though, it raked at Torsten with its hind legs, much like a cat would, and though the act caused injury to its attacker, the bear would be the victor. Meanwhile, Thorne and Dhresden met the onslaught of the second vorshtig. Thorne had engaged the creature with his spear, planting the butt of the weapon against the ground in an attempt to skewer the beast as it charged. The vorshtig batted at the weapon with its forelegs, snapping the spearhead from its wooden shaft. Thorne managed to strike the underside of his attacker with the remainder of his weapon, but the splintered shaft barely penetrated the beast's hide. Dhresden had rushed to the side of the vorshtig, a sword in each hand. As he moved close to drive a weapon home, the horse, occupied as it were by Thorne, struck out with a hind leg, narrowly missing its mark. Dhresden countered, hacking at the horse's leg with one sword, spinning close and thrusting the other deep into the creature's side. The vorshtig shrieked, circling away from Dhresden's blade while kicking fiercely at the halfblood. Wrenching his sword from the shrieking beast, Dhresden was certain he had struck a mortal blow, but the demon horse continued to attack with its full strength. Thorne had abandoned his ruined spear, and had produced a spike axe from a sheath upon his back. This weapon, though still characteristic of the mountain men, differed from the double bit battle axe that Dhresden had become used to seeing in Orrick's hands. Thorne's weapon was composed of the traditional axe blade, but protruding from the back was a sharp spike over two handbreadths in length. The spike axe had proven to be very effective for the younger Wanderlander, but against his foe this day it almost cost him his life. Thorne had swung his weapon at the vorshtig, missed, and found the beast suddenly before him, its front legs flailing at him, its teeth fiercely snapping the air before his face. Thorne swung the spike axe again; in his rush to defend himself he failed to rotate the weapon in his grasp, and struck his attacker in the shoulder, the spike burying deep in muscle and bone. Enraged again, the horse pivoted away, but the weapon would not pull free. Holding fast as he attempted to free the spike axe, Thorne first found himself beside, then beneath the unearthly beast. He released the handle of his weapon, but not before feeling the fury of the vorshtig's hooves.

Thorne covered his head and rolled in the direction he believe safety lay; hearing the demon horse thundering closer, but suddenly the air became still. Cautiously lifting his head, Thorne saw Torsten standing before him, the vorshtig hanging limply by its neck from the great bear's maw. The wounded mountain man smiled, uttering something only Torsten could understand. The beast released the now dead enemy and moved quickly to Thorne's side; the man felt sore all over, and feared that his shin bone at least had been broken. "How do you fair, Thorne?"

He looked up, finding Dhresden leaning over the slain vorshtig. As he watched, the young Lord of Havenstone pulled first one, and then the other of his swords from the creature's body. It would seem that Thorne owed his life to both his animal companion and this half-blood king.

"I shall live," the injured man replied, "but I shall not run for a while." He laughed as he struggled to his feet, and then stopped. "Where is Konaird?"

Dhresden turned, and the two of them spied the fierce, red-haired man sitting beside the fire the Tulisan had occupied moments before. They found him eating some of the pork that had been roasted, as if his life had not just weighed in the balance, but as they drew nearer they could see that he too had sustained injuries during the skirmish. How many arrows the brigands had managed to loose was unclear, but one had narrowly missed Konaird's head, actually piercing him through the ear, while another remained lodged in his right bicep. The mountain man's chest was protected by chain mail, his arms by layered leather. While the leather had been punctured by the arrow, it had slowed it down, preventing the bone from being shattered. Konaird smiled grimly as his companions approached, gesturing towards the roasted pig.

"Help yourselves; it is actually quite good," he said, wincing as he brought a morsel to his mouth with his wounded arm. Dhresden and Thorne stood eying him; their concern about the arrow imbedded in Konaird's arm was evident. "Eat!" he demanded, "you can help me with this afterwards."

First Thorne, then Dhresden, knelt and took a slice from the hog, though neither had eaten much before the small band realized that another party was approaching from the northeast. Konaird spoke to Loki first, then the others.

"Keep your places, do not allow Torsten to move," he said, his voice low. "Be wary, but let us see how this plays out."

Konaird continued to feast upon the meat with his wounded arm, keeping his good arm free to take up the war hammer at his side. The approaching party was comprised of eleven men and seven hogs; they neither rushed forward nor crept along, but their path was direct. Ten of the men walked along with the hogs, while one pig was ridden by a man of commanding presence. His grim face was badly scarred, whether by flame or blade was difficult to discern, and if one looked closely enough, his legs hung limply astride his mount. The injuries he had suffered did not negate his threat as an adversary, and it was he that Konaird intended first to strike down should the need arise. The mounted JabalKriger led his company within twenty feet of Dhresden's and stopped, surveying the scene a moment before fastening his eyes upon Konaird.

"You have looked better, Konaird," he said, his voice steady, almost indifferent.

"As have you, Aksel," the Wanderlander replied. "Is that still Honae you ride? She must be getting on in years."

Aksel nodded, "She is nigh to thirty years, but still strong and able. Loki looks young to me still." Both men almost smiled, but the moment passed and silence hung in the air as they regarded each other. Finally, the JabalKriger spoke again. "Should I attempt to slay you and this half-blood outlaw, or is there a viable reason I should escort you the rest of the way to Ikshton's palace?"

Konaird rose slowly to his feet at this unveiled threat before he spoke, his left hand firmly gripping his war hammer. "I came to speak to our old friend regarding his new alliances, and found those allies of Ikshton's disparaging his own property. We have executed judgment upon them on his behalf and desire an audience with him."

Aksel remained silent as he weighed Konaird's words. Dhresden had kept his surprise at the two men's knowledge of each other veiled;

their familiarity causing the young ruler to consider that perhaps they would be successful in their endeavor to turn Ikshton from the path he was on. Within minutes Dhresden and the mountain men had agreed to surrender their weapons and were keeping stride with Aksel and the JabalKriger as they were attended the remainder of their journey. Neither group spoke, content to dwell upon their own thoughts, both of the past and what was to occur. Dhresden had spent little to no time in this region, and he took care to note the characteristics of the land. The forest here was comprised mostly of evergreens, though the skeletal structure of several leafless trees dotted the wood, biding their time until spring would allow them to replenish their glory. The snow and ice hid many of the features of the land, such as the rocks and boulders that sprang up from the mossy forest floor, and the succulent broadleaf grasses that blanketed the more sunny areas beneath and between the wide-reaching tree branches overhead. The half-blood's eyes failed to spy much in the way of wildlife besides swine, save for the occasional rabbit, deer, or predator tracks. There seemed to be an air of barrenness upon the land, caused by something more oppressive than the characteristic bleakness of winter. Dhresden glanced at his two human companions, wondering if the sensation was peculiar to him alone, or if they too sensed the foreboding as of desolation. Neither Konaird nor Thorne gave any evidence of concern for their surroundings, though they did keep note of the location of their escorts, especially of Aksel and the hogs. Though magic and sorcery had fallen out of common use during the early years of his father Dhane's reign, Dhresden had been made aware of the dangers of such enchantments as a youngster through his study of politics and history. The half-blood found himself hoping that the oppression that he sensed was due only to the gray winter season and the grim events of the day, and not to any unnatural cause.

Were it not for the cheerlessness they shared, the night would have detested winter for weakening its darkness. The sun had disappeared behind the horizon, but the snow blanketing the area reflected the light of the moon and stars, thwarting the night's attempt at total darkness. On the mixed group trudged, no torch or lantern necessary, until finally the glow of the lamps of Ikshton's palace loomed ahead.

CHAPTER 28

Orrick was awake, sitting upon a low stool near a corner of his apartment when Zabayr rapped upon the chamber door shortly after dawn.

"Good day, mountain friend," the Makani greeted him. He studied the man towering over him a moment before speaking again. Orrick's visage was firmly set, not in anger, but with clear determination. Even so, there was something else Zabayr saw, and it concerned him. "Did you sleep at all," he asked, "and have you eaten?"

Orrick was silent, but then, "Has Khaldun awakened? And is he talking sensibly yet?"

"He is awake, yes," Zabayr answered, "But he has refused to explain himself even to the Grandmaster Khuzaymah unless you are present."

This information boded ill for them all; surely Khaldun would not risk dishonoring his chieftain without great cause. Orrick nodded to Zabayr, and he and Asha followed along behind the Makani as he led them again to the infirmary. Entering the main chamber, Orrick greeted Andalhyn's three officers, as well as a few other Makani that he did not recognize. Zabayr directed Orrick to the side compartment in which Khaldun had been placed for recovery, but remained in the central chamber with the others. Orrick bid Asha wait outside the door, and as the giant mountain man stooped to pass through the doorway, he found his host Khuzaymah and Andalhyn standing beside Khaldun's bed. The wounded man was sitting upright upon the bed, his color good, his eyes clear and focused. Upon seeing Orrick, he swung his legs off the bed and stood, surprisingly steadily, to greet the mountain man. Orrick stepped close enough to grip Khaldun's shoulders, and found himself wrapped in a brotherly embrace by the smaller man.

Surprised at first, Orrick returned the hold. "Good to see you, my friend," Orrick said, softly. "I am relieved that you are well."

The two pulled back from one another, standing now an arm's length away. They regarded each other, noting the visible changes and wondering at the unseen scars that they each knew the other bore.

"Your eye," Khaldun began, "he said that he had injured you."

Orrick's eye burned into Khaldun's at these words. "He? Of whom do you speak?"

"Dhresden, of course," he replied. "He told me of your battle, of his attempt to kill Tala as if he were relaying the details of a nightmare that had remained all too vivid after waking."

Orrick's brow furrowed as he puzzled through the news. When he had seen Asha, he had concluded that she had been forced to kill Dhresden in his mad condition. He had not allowed himself to hope for such a miracle that they had both survived, and yet here was Khaldun, advising him of that very thing.

Unsure of Orrick's thoughts but eager to continue to divulge more of his own information, Khaldun went on. "He expressed deep regret and longs to see you again."

Orrick nodded thoughtfully, and then, "What else? What enemy from the south did he send you to warn us of?"

"Dhresden seeks to thwart the attack of Chayne and her Horde of brigands approaching through the Badlands at the north. He has dispatched me to rally the Makani to neutralize Chayne's allies marching upon Havenstone from the south; through promise of marriage she has secured alliance with Uganji and his Ianzama. They wish to lay waste to the Pasturelands, Treyherne included. Dhresden also said that he was requesting reinforcements to our aid, though when they arrive and from where he did not say."

"The Ianzama are as ruthless as their leader," Khuzaymah said, "not to mention the threat of the Brigade."

"Archers," Orrick stated. "That would keep the Brigade at bay.

"We are the Makani," Khuzaymah replied, as if those few words were sufficient response. It was Andalhyn who spoke next, answering Orrick's brewing question.

"Millennia ago we Makani did away with our edged weapons, including arrows. Most were burned, though there are still some useful tools hidden away in a keep beneath the palace. They were left there as a reminder of the dangers of such weapons and their misuse. We can retrieve them and put them to use at the hands of those who still remember how to loose them; but we will still be required to come into close contact with the invaders."

"Forgive me," Khaldun interjected, "but what is this Brigade and why do you all fear it?" Orrick looked to Khaldun's countrymen for response, surprised that the younger Makani did not already know the answer.

"Son—" Andalhyn began, but was interrupted by the grandmaster.

"It has long been the custom of our people, Khaldun, to restrict the public histories of the Makani. We feared that in thoroughly teaching the failings of our people we would set ourselves upon a course to repeat them." Khaldun's face bore such an expression of disbelief that Khuzaymah was compelled to go on. "Oh the history is not lost; it is carefully recorded and protected within the archives. It is simply not provided to the general populace."

Khaldun was visibly fighting to restrain himself, but his voice took on a tone of skepticism. "How can future generations benefit from the mistakes of the past if they are made to remain ignorant of previous failures? Who is to say what could be prevented with simply the knowledge of how best *not* to proceed?"

"That is another discussion for another time!" Andalhyn's voice remained calm, but it possessed a fierceness that quieted his son.

"The last time our people fought against the Brigade," the Grandmaster went on, "we suffered great losses, both in battle and in the weeks following. This Brigade, the men are all ill; they are plague-ridden with leprosy. I doubt you are very familiar with the disease, but it has multiple, horrible stages; each of them contagious. The poor wretches infected with leprosy lose feeling in their extremities, and eventually all over as their flesh rots away. They are already condemned to death as it were by the disease, and since they often do not feel pain, and guaranteed to die anyway, they have no fear in battle. Uganji and his predecessors have exploited the lives and condition of these people for centuries under the promise of great spoil, and it has been a successful tactic. Many of our men survived the battle against the Lepers Brigade, only to discover later that they were dying. A few killed themselves; others entered self-imposed exile to finish out their lives, only a handful sought the skill of the healers but to no avail. This is the nature of the enemy now marching upon Dhresden's domain, and the Lord of Havenstone would ask that I place my soldiers against the Ianzama and the Lepers Brigade once again." The Makani ruler seemed shrunken now, as if the news and the strain of events to come had drained his energy and shriveled his muscles.

Orrick regarded each of them in turn, unsure of the intent of the Makani on this matter. It could be interpreted that the wind-warriors were considering not uniting in Dhresden's aid.

As if reading his mind, Andalhyn stood at attention and spoke. "Shall I rally our warriors to protect the Pasturelands, as well as the Dunes, from this old enemy? Shall we vanquish this threat and free ourselves once and for all from our indebtedness to Dhane? What is your bidding, grandmaster?" His tone and posture were at the disposal of Khuzaymah's wishes, though it was clear that he wished to proceed as he had mentioned. Silence hung in the air while the men around the old Makani ruler awaited his orders. For Orrick, and likely for the others as well, the moments ticked along slowly, transforming the empty air into a thick, uncomfortable silence.

"I do not relish this war," the Grandmaster said with a sigh. "I fear that even in victory, death beckons us to himself. And while hiding within the Cliffs, behind the protection of the Shards, may lengthen our days, no! We shall hasten to the embrace of death in a day rather than to recline upon the cushions of dishonor for long years!"

The few Makani within the small room, even the wounded and sore Khaldun, flashed to their feet. "Yes, grand master! Our lives for you! Our deaths for you!" they shouted forth the battle oath of their people, eager not for war or death, but for victory and honor.

Andalhyn turned to his men and quickly gave each of them orders. "Take a detachment of Arba'a and ride out on khamelleros; return with word of the enemy's location. Number all available warriors; assign a third of them to police the city, prepare the rest for battle. Send out riders to any bands we have outside the city; instruct them to return and join the protectors that we leave behind. Join me in four hours in the map room."

"Yes, captain!" they barked in unison, and then hurried from the room. Andalhyn turned his attention to Orrick. "I do not suppose it is worthwhile for me to ask you to remain within the safety of the Cliffs while we march against the Ianzama, but you," he turned to Khaldun, "will remain here until you are well enough to be useful to your mother." Khaldun opened his mouth to protest, but his father would allow him no words. "This is not a discussion, son. I shall see you again before we depart." He turned and bowed to Khuzaymah, who nodded his approval of Andalhyn's plan. The Makani captain spun and exited the infirmary with Orrick and Asha in tow.

～～～

Dhresden and his companions, the two mountain men and even the bear and the wolf, were ushered into the great hall of Vlad Ikshton's palace. The fortress itself was of beautiful stone and timber construction, with high arching ceilings and large glass windows to allow sunlight to flood each of the rooms. In the dark of night and the glow of dim torchlight, much of the beauty of the place was lost, replaced instead with a sense of foreboding or sadness. Dhresden's group found themselves in the main hall of the palace surrounded by more than thirty of Ikshton's JabalKriger, though only a handful of actual swine could be seen inside. Before them stood a great throne, chiseled from a large black boulder uncommon to this region; Dhresden mused that it must have been a tedious and exhausting task to ferry the object across the land between here and the mountains. Forward and to either side of the throne were two large fire pits set in the stone floor. The smoke from the blazing logs rolled up towards the ceiling and was funneled into pipes which vented the smoke outside the castle. The firelight flickered upon the face of their host as he slouched upon his throne, peering at each of them in turn. Vlad was a handsome man, clean-shaven unlike the majority of his countrymen, though his hair flowed long and blond to his shoulders like many of the Wanderlanders. A smile played at the corners of the man's mouth, but it was not mirth that gleamed in his eyes. Silence weighed heavily in the air until the JabalKing addressed Dhresden's escort.

"What have you brought before me, Aksel?" he asked. "Something for sport, or another splinter to irritate me?" The man's tone was a mystery, seeming to be a mixture of boredom and irritation, though Dhresden supposed there was veiled interest as well.

"We discovered these men and their beasts near the southeast stream after they slaughtered five of Chayne's brigands and two of the demon-horses," Aksel reported. He paused as if unsure what next to say, then went on. "The Tulisan had killed several of your hogs and were defiling the bodies when this group attacked them."

"And you think that this one act on my behalf entitles you to an audience with me?" the JabalKing inquired, his tone level, even calm, yet menacing. "How fickle do you believe me to be, Konaird Ergtus of the Wanderlands? Your trespass into my lands is no less of an invasion because you presume to act in my stead."

Ikshton glared at the group in silence, his demeanor growing more visibly angered with each passing moment. Dhresden glanced at Konaird, who shook his head almost imperceptibly. The mountain man had warned the half-blood of some of the traditions of the JabalKriger, especially of the parley. The three men stood, silently awaiting the invitation to speak according to the custom of this strange land that Ikshton had settled long years ago. If no opportunity were given to speak, it would indicate the JabalKing's intent to slay the men before him. Having surrendered their arms, Dhresden and his companions' fate would lie in the strength of their empty hands and the tooth and nail of the two beasts with them.

"What did you do with the bodies?" Ikshton asked, his eyes still upon the trespassers.

"The brigands and horses we burned; your hogs we buried," Aksel cleared his throat and went on, "at the insistence of these men."

Again silence enveloped the great room, but the rage that had been building behind the JabalKing's eyes began to fade. He considered the implications of this burial, the work that had been invested in digging into the frozen ground in order to place his children at rest rather than vanquishing them in flames. This was the first compassion shown to Ikshton's people by outsiders in several long years, and the significance of this act did not go unnoticed.

"You may speak, Konaird." The JabalKing's voice had softened; the fury fading. "What have you to do with me?"

The Wanderlander wasted no time in conveying their mission. "I come to ask that you break union with Chayne; that you not take part in the desolation of a land that should be your ally, a land that we bled together to protect in time past."

The hog-master laughed, loud and scoffing, while his face evidenced clear surprise. "I do not rush to the destruction of the Pasturelands, but rather to its salvation!"

"The destruction of the Pasturelands is exactly the intent of Chayne, and of those who align with her!" Dhresden had spoken out of turn, and found two spear points caressing his chest, and two others at his back.

"I did not address you, half-blood," Vlad sneered, rising to his feet. "You are here, and alive, because of the respect that I have for Konaird, and because of the honor he has demonstrated to my children. Your incompetence has led these lands into these hard times, and I will hear nothing further from you at this time."

"Lord Ikshton," Konaird pleaded, "he speaks the truth. We have encountered Chayne and are certain of her intent. I mean to defend the Pasturelands and, if able, to install Dhresden upon the throne of Havenstone, as is his rightful place."

The JabalKing appeared genuinely confused by the mountain man's short speech and did not retort immediately. With a wave, he dismissed the warriors holding Dhresden at spear point, and sat in obvious contemplation of the situation before him.

"Chayne besought my aid months ago," he began, "fearing that Treyherne was constructing a plot to kill Dhane and steal the throne. She even indicated remorse and regret for her part in following her mother's treacherous plans all those years ago. She provided quite a convincing argument for trusting her. She sees Treyherne's usurping of the throne as an opportunity for her to make right the iniquities of the past, both hers and her mother's before her."

Konaird cast a furtive glance at Dhresden. Clearly Ikshton believed the claims made by Chayne, whether because of a convincing performance that she had provided or due to some enchantment that he had been placed under, neither could tell. Konaird chose his next words carefully.

"Vlad," he said quietly, addressing the hog-master in the familiar tone from when they were friends, "we have encountered Chayne and her forces, and I can assure you that her plans for the Pasturelands are less than well-intentioned."

Ikshton sat unmoving upon his throne, his eyes upon Konaird though it was clear that he was seeing something from another time. After a long enough silence that even Aksel had grown uncomfortable, the JabalKing's eyes cleared, and Konaird found himself looking again into the brokenness that he had seen within Vlad Ikshton so many years before.

"Are you certain?" he asked, his voice barely a whisper. Konaird nodded his answer, seeing tears begin to form and then flow down his old friend's face. "Then I have failed her yet again," he mourned. He wept openly now, all pageantry and formality of his position cast aside. Each within the throne room was at a loss as to how to respond; the JabalKriger, even Aksel, stood aloof, unsure how to comfort the man who had always embodied the strength of their people. Finally, Konaird, with a glance at Aksel, stepped to his old friend's assistance. The weeping lord fell into the mountain man's ready embrace, seeking strength, in search of comfort.

"Who is it, Vlad?" Konaird asked several minutes later when he trusted that the man was able to answer. "Who is it that you believe you have failed?"

Amidst fresh sobs, Konaird deciphered his answer: "Aracelis." Konaird was stunned by his one-time friend's confession.

"Vlad," he began, his tone soothing, "your wife has long been gone, and her passing was in no way your responsibility."

The JabalKing renewed his sobbing, and through ragged breathing and tears finally replied. "It was my responsibility to protect her, to keep her safe! She should never have died; should never have endured such treatment!"

Konaird was quiet, feeling the weight of the man's words. He had sorted through much of the same sentiment in dealing with loss in his own life, and though his own recovery had occurred over several years it was clear that Vlad had not reached the same place of acceptance or resignation that Konaird had. "How, Vlad, how is it that you believe that you have done disservice to Aracelis? Please, old friend; I wish to help you and it pains me to see you like this."

Konaird's presence and words seemed to calm the other man, at least enough that he could talk and be understood. The JabalKing stood to his feet, collecting himself as best he could, and invited Konaird to join him in another room off the main hall. He instructed Aksel to see to the refreshment of the rest of Konaird's group, and to afterwards show them to their quarters for the night.

CHAPTER 29

The home of the Makani bustled with activity as Andalhyn directed the soldiers and all able-bodied citizens in their preparations to battle Uganji's Ianzama, especially the Lepers Brigade. Orrick assisted in the preparations, discussing strategies with the Makani captain and his chief officers, but not before he shared the news of Dhresden's survival with Mallory. The young lord's half-sister received the news gladly, throwing her arms about her giant love with an exultant shout. Tears streamed down her face, but finally of joy rather than from the loss with which they had all become too well-acquainted.

"Have you told Tala yet?" she asked, eager for her brother's beloved to rejoice with her at the news.

The giant's brow knit in thought as he answered. "No, I have not. And knowing the danger Dhresden faces in the north, I wonder at the wisdom of telling her he is alive." He stopped short; the rest of his words, though unspoken, did not go unheard. Mallory did not speak at first; her eyes were open wide, her mouth hanging agape in disbelief. She searched her lover's face, unsure of what she sought, and gradually her eyes narrowed and her mouth snapped shut at the command of clenching jaw muscles.

"Orrick!" she hissed. "How could you! How! After all of the obstacles, the pain, the loss that we have endured," she paused, her voice trembling, to compose herself, "to now surrender to doubt? Dhresden lives. And for as long as I draw breath I will bend my every fiber to the task of setting him upon his rightful throne. Of all our allies, you, I had thought, would be aligned with me in this." She ceased speaking, content that she had said her peace, but at the same time concerned that she had gone too far; that she had wounded her giant strongman, and that deeply. Orrick stood before her, his powerful form almost limp as he reeled from Mallory's brief lashing. His mind poured over her words again and again as he labored to decipher his own mindset regarding Dhresden. As he had spoken, he had not felt any misgivings about his half-blood friend's success in the north, but did his words evidence some weakness of character or flawed confidence that he had failed to discover in himself? If this were the case, then it would mean that Orrick had failed in greater ways than he had previously realized. The Wanderer had sufficient cause to be the champion of Dhresden's reign, to herald the new Lord of Havenstone with voice and sword and axe; yet he stood dumbly before Mallory as he fought to comprehend his own state of mind.

"Mallory," he said, his voice low and heavy with emotion, "I would never—your brother—I did not speak faithless words. My words were only for Tala's well-being." He paused, his voice becoming stronger. "If the concern was misplaced, so be it, but do not question my loyalty to Dhresden, to his throne, or to you."

The two regarded each other in silence, Mallory searching Orrick's eye to determine the veracity of his words. The venom of her words had been directed at her own unspoken fears, and Orrick's voiced concerns had exposed her own doubts. Mallory realized in that moment that she had attacked the wrong person; that she should have better evaluated her own mind on the issue of Dhresden's precarious situation. Instead, she had lashed out at the one closest to her, when she should have been confiding in him and seeking his counsel, his comfort.

"Oh, Orrick!" She exclaimed, throwing her arms around the giant's neck, "Please forgive me! It is I who has doubted, and in my shame and guilt I have judged you. I have thought Dhresden dead so many times. Since hearing that he lives, I live in fear that the grave will claim him before we can set things right." She sobbed the words into Orrick's chest, feeling his forgiveness envelope her even as his arms encircled her in a loving embrace. The two stood thus, until Mallory's sobbing ceased; as they withdrew from one another to barely arm's length, Mallory noticed a glistening upon Orrick's cheeks, and was at once convicted anew of her accusations of the Wanderer and encouraged by his brief show of emotion. They laughed quietly at each other, wiping one another's tears away.

"If you think it best that she be made aware," Orrick spoke first, "then you should tell Tala the new information we have heard of Dhresden. I will go with you if you wish."

"You are not like other men, Orrick the Black Wanderer," Mallory beamed at the giant. "I am thankful that you are so tough-skinned that you tolerate me."

Soon the pair was walking to the makeshift training area where the daughters of Nokoma were busily instructing select Makani in the construction and basic mastery of archery weapons. Shika stood at a work table, surrounded by attentive students, demonstrating the correct stringing of bows and honing of shafts and arrow tips. Not far away, Tala called out to her students as she sought to improve their marksmanship; her voice was not loud, but it demanded obedience. Orrick and Mallory drew nearer the elder daughter of Nokoma until she spied their approach. They stopped, inviting Tala to join them. With a word she dismissed her pupils and walked briskly to Mallory's side. She said nothing, but looked at the couple expectantly. Mallory hesitated, suddenly uncertain of her decision.

"Tala," Orrick smiled, "Mallory has some news she wishes to share with you."

"Yes, thank you, Orrick," she stammered. "Tala, we have received word from trusted sources within the Pasturelands of a threat in the North. It has been confirmed that the remnants of Chayne's Tulisan are in league with Uganji's forces, and that they are intent upon the devastation of the whole of the Pasturelands."

"What forces are available in the north?" Tala asked, her demeanor remained calm, but there was an intensity behind her eyes that Mallory knew still burned for Dhresden's sake. "Do we have any trusted soldiers? Can we expect support at all from your kinsman in the mountains?" Her questions were aimed at both Orrick and Mallory, and while she trusted the pair with her life, she felt that there was some bit of information that they possessed but had not yet shared with her.

"We do have some loyal forces to the north," Mallory replied, "and we do anticipate reinforcements from Orrick's countrymen." She hesitated again, took a deep breath, and continued. "We are optimistic regarding success in that region, largely due to the warrior that has risen to command the remnant of forces stationed there. Tala, it is Dhresden. He is alive!" Both Mallory and Orrick smiled expectantly, awaiting a flood of joy, but saw only a guarded interest in Tala's eyes. She looked at both of them in turn, her silence erasing their mirth.

"What is it, Tala?" Orrick asked. "What gives you pause?"

The dark-haired archer's gaze shifted to the ground before her, and stayed there a long moment before she spoke. "I had thought—" she began, "that our love—that the strength of our love could overcome—anything." She was silent again, though not for long. "You were there, Orrick—you stopped him—he was going to kill me. Should not our love have been stronger than—" She stopped suddenly, sobbing, her stoicism gone. Unsure of what to say, Mallory said nothing. Instead, she clasped her gently; lending comfort, even strength to this lady warrior in her time of need.

"To me the message has come," Orrick said quietly after several moments had passed. "Khaldun has brought this news to us; he has eaten and spoken with Dhresden, and brings a message of your lover's remorse. I have spoken with the healers here at Hawa Janbiyah, and based on the histories that are available and their knowledge of the body, mind, and medicine, they all have concurred that the effects of the *ferial* upon Dhresden's body and mind are completely expected. This is no reflection upon his love for you, Tala." The gentleness of this giant's tone spoke to Tala's heart even as his words addressed her mind. She knew that he was right, and was relieved to admit so. Releasing herself from Mallory's embrace with a pat upon the other's back, Tala composed herself, dried her tears and cleared her throat.

"Thank you both," she said, "but if the Lord of Havenstone is to succeed in the north, does he not require archers?"

~ ~ ~

"It has been too long. We should have received word by now."

Faust gazed upon Jovanna at her station, one that had become typical of late; standing atop the watchtower of Murion's Plateau, her eyes searching the northeastern border for signs of her half-blood stepson, or of any of his men. Days had turned into weeks since Dhresden had ridden from their sight, and still no message had been received of the battles that were to be fought against Chayne's Tulisan.

"Little of this adventure has progressed as we had anticipated, my lady," Faust replied after a time. "Shall I send out riders to discover the state of affairs to the north?"

Jovanna kept her gaze towards the horizon, but in her mind's eye she could see Faust's expression: one of patience and compassion, and not a little amused. "Every few days we rehearse this drama, herdsman," she sighed, "and upon each occasion I draw closer to accepting your offer." She turned to face this man, a commoner, yes, but a leader of noble character. He had shown such compassion and dignity in ministering to her over the past months, and their formal association had developed into a private romance of sorts. The most they had shared beyond their hearts and minds was an occasional embrace or clasp of hands, yet the strength of their bond had become evident to the few herdsmen residing with them at the post. "No, Faust, do not send riders. Lord Havenstone directed us to hold this post, and with the few men we have, we will require all of them to accomplish that task in the event of an attack." Jovanna sighed, "I suppose I ought to be accustomed to events being out of my control, but..." Her voice trailed away, her mind occupied again with thoughts of the past months. Faust let her wander for a time, and then brought her back to the present with a word.

"Lady," was all he said, was all he need say. Jovanna shook herself from her reverie, and focused her attention upon the herdsman. Faust did not return her gaze, but stood with his eyes looking beyond Jovanna. The lady turned in the direction of his staring, back to the northeastern border, and there she discovered a lone rider hastening towards the watchtower. He was not clothed in the common garb of the herdsmen, and he rode an animal smaller than that of Faust's people. As he drew nearer, he was discerned to be one of Chayne's

Tulisan; the beast racing beneath him was one of the wild Vorshtig. A shout went up among those occupying the fort, and though little threat would come from a single enemy outside their walls, the herdsmen realized that one of these Tulisan usually indicated that others were in the area; readiness would be the herdsmen's ally. The brigand rode to within thirty paces of the sheer wall of the plateau before stopping, though the demon horse beneath him stomped and snorted and paced in evident rage. The distance separating him from Faust and Jovanna did not prevent them from hearing clearly the message he bore.

"I bring a message from the high queen of the western region, Chayne of the Tulisan! Behold, says she: 'You are all dead men!' The half-blood scourge has failed, and we march upon the Pasturelands to place Chayne upon the throne of the Citadel. Flee from before us, and you may yet find mercy under her boot. Resist and the Tulisan and Ianzama shall together crush you! I return in three days' time, and my brethren ride with me!"

The Tulisan rider spat upon the ground beside him, then wheeled his raging mount and sped away to whence he had come. Faust could see that his men had been shaken by this encounter, but not at the fear of death, rather, the fear of failure. Jovanna, however, felt the loss of Dhresden rending her heart yet again. She swayed, casting a hand upon the top of the wall to steady herself and found herself upheld, not by her own strength, but rather that of Faust. Secure in his grasp, she succumbed to the swoon that had sought to take her, and awoke a short time later in her chamber. Jovanna threw back the heavy blanket that had been placed upon her, and finding herself still fully clothed, boots and all, she rose and headed for the map room, which had become the seat of decisions and planning within the fort atop Muriel's Plateau. As anticipated, there she found Faust and his chief herdsmen in conference.

"It is no idle bluff, Faust," one of the men was saying, his face grim. "We must decide what our part is to be in the process, stay and fight, or flee and live. We are barely twenty! How are we to stand against the assault that is to come!? We must flee that we may live!"

"And how are we to live with ourselves," Faust replied, "when days or years hence our families are slaughtered by the Tulisan? Will it be enough that we endured a moment more of life, only to have it snuffed out at the hands of Chayne's men?" The others went quiet, and Faust let the question hang in the silence as his eyes burned into those of the few who would return his gaze. It was one of the younger men that finally broke the silence.

"Faust is right, father," he said, his voice strong yet respectful. "If we flee, we escape possible execution, but the noose would remain about our necks, ever tightening until we find ourselves conquered." A murmur began to rumble through the herdsmen gathered in the map room, until all were in agreement.

"We will fight beside you, Faust!" A cheer erupted at this proclamation, and as the war cries faded a question was asked. "How shall we proceed?"

At this, the herdsman's face darkened. "Ready all riders, we depart at dawn. We shall take the fight to our enemies." Faust's countenance was grim with determination, but the events of the predawn hours would cause alteration to his plan.

~ ~ ~

Dhresden had left Murion's Plateau in the company of three hundred herdsmen and had lost almost fifty in the first encounter with Chayne's Tulisan. Bolstered by reinforcements from the Wanderlands consisting of twenty-three men and their animal companions, the small army had done well to hold their own against the brigands and their demon horses. Each side sustained injury and even death with each wave of attack by the Tulisan and Vorshtig, but even more threatening than the physical danger was the unspoken fear that sought to weave itself into the minds of these men. Each wondered whether the rumors about the JabalKriger involvement were true, and if so, what chance they really stood against such collective forces. Plagued by these fears the ensemble of herdsman and the handful of Wanderlanders fought on; but at dusk of the seventh day since Dhresden's small band had journeyed covertly to seek audience with the JabalKing, the scouts returned with disheartening news. A column three wide of what appeared to be hogwarriors was approaching the Tulisan-Vorshtig camp. The length of the column was impossible to determine, but it was certainly in excess of four hundred. It was likely that the three forces would seek to overrun the smaller opposing army as early as dawn of the next day. It would seem that the attempt to appeal to the JabalKing to withdraw his support from Chayne had failed, and what had become of the young Havenstone heir none could tell. The watch was doubled for the night, with strict orders to quietly rouse the men at least an hour prior to daylight, though few were those to whom sleep would come.

~ ~ ~

The journey from Vlad Ikshton's great hall had been a forced march—quick and hurried, with little breaks even for food or water. Were it not for his concern for his pigs there would have been no breaks at all, for the JabalKing was in a foul mood. Though the years and events of his life had transformed him into little more than a hermit willing to hire out himself as a mercenary, the man still disliked raising arms against one whom he had once considered a friend.

"No fires!" he barked at his first in command. "And be sure all are at the ready; we attack at moonrise!"

"It shall be as you have said!" Aksel replied, dipping his head low in a bow as he wheeled the beast beneath him around.

"And Aksel," Vlad called, his voice calmer, "see to it that Honae gets plenty of water and food."

"Of course," he answered, and was gone.

The moon would rise, almost full, over halfway through the night, though still well before sunrise. Its brightness would allow his forces to attack the enemy while they were unprepared; it would begin as a slaughter, but resistance was sure to build at the first sounds of battle. The JabalKing sighed heavily, his mind upon the imminent battle, and the lives that would be lost yet again because of the greed and selfishness of mortal man. He wondered if this occurrence would find him aligned with the victors, or if he would taste anew the bitterness of defeat and loss. His loved ones, though not human, would be mourned nonetheless, and the guilt that he had for years fought to be free of would rush upon him again.

Ikshton shook himself from such thoughts, though the shadow of them lingered, just as Aksel reentered his presence.

"The moon rises, my lord," the scarred and partly crippled man announced, surprising the hog master that hours had passed since they last spoke. "The men are silently at the ready; we await only your command, and we will execute your justice upon this enemy."

The JabalKing's countenance grew dark at these words, and his own utterance reflected his distaste for the task at hand. "Justice is the least of my possessions, Aksel. I possess war, and the tools of war, and that is what will be executed upon those who did not need to be my enemy. When this is over, I will certainly possess more than my share of regrets, for my cup has run over already." He lapsed silent again, and those about him held their peace. A long moment passed until the JabalKing again spoke, his voice strong. "Signal the attack, but be as silent as the moon itself."

~ ~ ~

The herdsmen encamped within the maze that led to the bad-lands were ripped from slumber by the sounds of battle. They found the few Wanderland forces that had been sent to their aid and their animal companions standing at the ready between them and the tumult, though no enemy could be discerned even in the light of the waxing moon. The noise of war assaulted them—the clash of weapons, the cries of war animals, and the voices of men raised in anger, fear, and death—and yet the battle seemed to rage beyond their sight, but between whom none could be sure. The herdsmen hurriedly gathered their arms and lighted upon their mounts, still uncertain what their action should be, but convinced that the melee would momentarily envelope them. The makeshift army looked to the hardened Wanderlanders for direction and for strength. The mountain men stood stoically, seemingly at ease, their faces impassive, while their eyes intensely studied the moon-kissed landscape. The herdsmen, emboldened by these men, took heart, loosening their grip upon their weapons and the reins of their mounts. As the white was fading from their knuckles, they discerned the warning cry of one of the Wanderlanders. "The Vorshtig are upon us! Show no mercy! Send them to the grave!" And indeed the demon horses had appeared, their eyes flashing red in the moonlight, their teeth and hooves lashing out at their enemy, all the while screaming fear into the very souls of the herdsmen. At the heels of the beasts came Chayne's footmen, the Tulisan; their faces were fierce, their own weapons eager to taste the blood of their enemies. Beasts and men cried out in pain and rage, and warriors from both sides fell cleaved, bludgeoned and pierced, many never to rise again, as the battle thundered on. None could be certain of how long men and beast fought together to subdue or destroy their adversary, but the sun had fully cleared the horizon when the surviving herdsmen and Wanderlanders perceived that the JabalKing's hogwarriors were now rushing to reinforce those remaining vorshtig and Tulisan. Despair at the sight of the JabalKriger turned to stunned disbelief and then exultant cheers as the swine and soldiers swarmed among Chayne's brigands, not to reinforce them, but to destroy them. The Wanderlanders began to caution the herdsmen, concerned that the hogwarriors had seized an opportunity to take control of the Pasturelands, and that their blades would turn next upon them. And so the tide of emotions turned again to fear and dread, until a cry of jubilation went up from the surviving mountain men. Straining to see the cause of their joy, the herdsmen finally spotted the young lord of Havenstone, accompanied by the two, now wounded, Wanderland warriors they had feared dead. They strode along beside the JabalKing, each taking in the scene before them with grim face; victory had come at great cost of life. Within moments they had reached the remnant of Dhresden's fighters, and once the cheers had subsided enough to be heard, the half-blood Lord of Havenstone addressed the bloodied throng.

"Countrymen and allies, I salute you!" Dhresden paused, allowing the resulting cheers to again subside. "You have held this horde at bay; you have defended your homeland from outside invaders! It is with heavy heart that I now ask you to bleed yet again with me, for Treyherne has wrought folly within our midst, and the head of the serpent must be severed!" Again cheers erupted, and in their wake, Dhresden continued. "You have given much on my behalf, and I cannot ever restore that which you have lost; but in the vision that my father, Dhane, possessed for our land, a vision that I seek to implement with your support, we can together rebuild a home for ourselves. The JabalKing and his troops have rallied to our aid; be at ease and rest this day. Attend your wounds, for tomorrow we march upon the Citadel, to free our home from the treachery of the serpent's grasp!"

As the last of the cheers were fading, Konaird and Thorne, with their animals, reunited with their countrymen; the JabalKriger surrounded the smaller group, establishing a protective perimeter. Hogwarrior healers moved throughout the mixed army, treating herdsmen, Wanderlander and JabalKriger alike for their injuries. Dhresden also moved through the crowd, his face and words encouraging, while his heart dismayed to see the losses these brave men had suffered. He stopped here and there to help bind a wound, pitch a tent, squeeze a hand. Dhresden had passed the breadth of the camp, and had become heavy in spirit.

"Lord Havenstone!" a call came from his left, "Lord Havenstone!" It was one of the herdsmen, who came near and bowed before him.

"Rise and speak freely," Dhresden said, "We have been bled dry of formality here."

"Yes, my lord, I am sorry to bother you, but the other reinforcements, their leaders have requested your presence."

Dhresden's brow furrowed, not comprehending. "Other reinforcements? Of whom do you speak?"

"Begging your pardon, my lord, but I mean the herdsmen that arrived at dawn. They bolstered us at the rear, just as the JabalKriger arrived at the forefront of the battle. I shall lead you to their command tent, if it pleases you."

"Lead on," he commanded. Dhresden followed the other man to the edge of the camp, where he pointed at a tent and joined a few other herdsmen at a cook fire. Dhresden walked cautiously to the door of the tent, raised the flap and peered inside.

CHAPTER 30

T
he hours had passed quickly, but Andalhyn's officers arrived in the war room at the appointed time. The commander and the grandmaster were seated at a large table, upon which lay an unrolled map of their region. Orrick, Mallory, and Shika stood near the wall where they could see and hear the discussion, and provide input whether it was solicited or not.

"What have you to report?" Andalhyn began. "Where is the enemy situated, what is his course, what is his speed?"

"Sir," replied one of his officers, "the Ianzama lie almost two days south of our border, it appears as though they aim to pass west of the bog region and then march upon the Pasturelands. The Ianzama are mostly footmen, though there are about a hundred cavalry."

"Cavalry?" Khuzaymah seemed surprised. "Upon what do they ride?"

"Great gray beasts the likes of which I have never before seen! Their legs seem too short and thick to move at speed, and yet our scouts witnessed bursts of speed that could rival our khamelleros. Protruding from the top of each beasts' snout stands what appears to be a pointed horn of sorts, but whether it is truly to be considered a weapon none can say."

"Oh, it is a weapon, I assure you," Khuzaymah declared, "Though it has been a lifetime since I have seen rhinoceros." He paused, remembering something long ago, then went on. "They are quick, but not for long runs. The horn can be used to ram, flip or throw almost anything. Rhinoceros are fierce and strong, and will continue to fight even if their rider is struck down. Their bones are strong and their hides are thick; even when our weapons were edged we struggled to bring even one of them down. What of the lepers?"

"They are being transported in shrouded wagons, each pulled by one of the rhinoceros; it seems Ytero Uganji wishes to preserve their strength for battle. If we are estimating the number of leper soldiers in each wagon correctly, there are approximately seven hundred."

"What of Uganji, how is he traveling?" it was Orrick who had spoken, though no one in the room seemed surprised. "And if he is stricken down, will his men lose heart? Will they flee?"

"If he is struck down in battle they would likely retreat and assess their wounded, if the losses were great enough they would possibly leave our lands."

"What if we were to send an assassin to claim Uganji?" Orrick was beginning to feel that the odds favored the Ianzama, and he wished to end this battle as soon as possible.

"An assassination of Uganji would enrage the Ianzama and they would attack with or without their king." Khuzaymah's countenance was stern as he spoke, but his eyes twinkled slyly with his next words. "If the Ianzama leader were to die from something less obvious, the superstitions of the people might drive them away in fear."

"If I may, grandmaster," Orrick said, with a step forward, "please allow me the slaying of Uganji." He could sense Mallory stiffen, and draw a breath to protest, but then she said nothing. He knew that she would demand a reckoning when they were alone, but he also realized that if she would hear him out that she would then understand.

Khuzaymah eyed Orrick as if seeing him for the first time. "Ignoring the question of why I would send the largest man I have ever met on a clandestine mission of stealth and secrecy," the Makani leader said, "I am compelled to ask why you would volunteer for such a task."

Orrick stood unmoving, his eye still upon the grandmaster. He did not speak, and after several moments it became clear that he did not intend to answer. His countenance harbored no disrespect or ill will; he simply was choosing not to reply.

"Wanderlander," Andalhyn said, breaking the silence, "Hazrat Almadi bin Khuzaymah has made inquiry, and you are compelled to answer his question." The Makani captain had stood to his feet as he spoke, and though the top of his head barely reached the shoulder of the mountain man he showed no fear.

Orrick smiled and dipped his head slightly in a display of respect before speaking. "An inquiry you have made and an answer you shall have," he replied, "but I would have anticipated an eagerness to quell this battle before it begins, especially without the risk of Makani life."

Andalhyn relaxed a little at his words and returned to his seat. "Please proceed."

"I have pledged my life in the service of Dhresden, lord of Havenstone and heir to the throne of Kelvar; and if he were naught but a half-blood warrior, my allegiance would remain his." Orrick paused, but continued without prompting. "Years ago, when Dhresden was barely a man, he saved my life. I love him as though he was my kin, and I gladly risk death on his behalf."

Silence returned, solemn and reflective. Most had dropped their gaze to the floor, hushed by the wild devotion and unflinching affection and loyalty Orrick had just described.

"Truly, your honor rivals that of the Makani," Khuzaymah complemented him, "and if this alone was the foundation of your request I would be wrong not to grant it. However, you have not told all. There remains yet more information that you must share; a detail dwarfed by your commitment to Dhresden, yet great enough to haunt you still. Fear not, Orrick; but speak."

The giant nodded, resignation flooding his face, then spoke. "As I said, Dhresden saved my life. I had been enslaved for several years before our paths crossed, but despite our vast differences our friendship formed quickly. At great cost, Dhresden secured my freedom and I was finally free of Ytero Uganji." Orrick could hear Mallory quietly weeping beside him, one hand pressed gently against his arm; he had intended to share this with her, alone, without an audience.

"Well, Wanderlander," the Grandmaster began, "I do not begrudge you the desire to take the man's life; both upon the basis of justice as well as on behalf of the Havenstone lord; nevertheless, I must deny your request. It would be a difficult task for you if you were thinking clearly, but with the amount of emotion you bring to the situation, I fear it would be impossible for you. Andalhyn, you will submit an assassination plot to me in two hours; for now, have you a battle strategy for the Ianzama?"

"Yes, Hazrat," the commander affirmed, "we will intercept the Ianzama at the Hourglass, a narrow bit of land between the ocean and the Bog. We should be able to arrive early enough to dig pits that should render the rhinoceros useless. The archers we have will rain down arrows upon the Leper's Brigade; the rest will fall to the wind-warriors. If all goes according to plan, the mysterious reinforcements will not be necessary."

"I could carry in a thimble the number of events that have gone according to plan during this endeavor, commander." Mallory declared. Her voice rang not of defiance, but of realism tinged with regret. "I would caution you to establish several countermeasures should all *not* go according to plan."

~ ~ ~

Dinner began as silently as the rest of the afternoon had gone, and as Mallory and Orrick teased their food, eating very little, Mallory pushed back from her plate and spoke.

"Orrick," she began, but the giant kept his eye upon his meal. "I know that there is much about each other that we are still discovering, and I am not naïve to think that I will be told all of your past, but I had hoped that we would spend the years of the rest of our lives getting better acquainted."

The Black Wanderer finally looked slowly up from his plate to meet Mallory's gaze. "It is as I have hoped as well, Miss Mallory." The couple clasped hands across the table before Mallory went on.

"That is why, Orrick, why I must ask you to release this assassination idea. Ytero Uganji will stand in judgment, either in this life or the next, but your place now is with me. Would it help you to talk about it? About your time in slavery?"

Orrick sat a moment, impressed again with this woman he loved. He smiled, raised her hand to his lips for a tender kiss, then began to recount to her details of his past that few among the living were privy to; and as they spoke, a half squad of Arba'a departed the palace atop the Cliffs of Hawa Janbiyah under cover of darkness. The eight khamellero and their riders passed quietly along the narrow pathway that led past the shards, and after several leagues, turned south. One of their number had agreed to undertake the solitary mission of infiltrating the Ianzama camp and ending Ytero Uganji's life in what must not be determined to be an assassination. In his hands lay the opportunity to end this battle before it ever began, though if he failed, he would be the first of many to die at the hands of the Ianzama. Traveling at more than twice the speed that the Ianzama would have been, by noon the Arba'a passed through the Hourglass, the strait that Andalhyn had referenced in his battle plan. As dusk approached, their pace slowed; they had glimpsed the cook fires of the enemy and needed to proceed more cautiously. In the waning light, the Arba'a sought to spy out the quarters of the Ianzama leader, determining that it must be the well-guarded tent near the center of the camp. Yhendorn bid his companions farewell, and in turn they spoke blessings upon him for safety and success. Leaving his khamellero in their charge, Yhendorn began his approach, a tedious endeavor that required him to keep to the shadows as much as possible. Several times the man was almost discovered; twice one of the Ianzama came within a handbreadth of him, and once his hand was actually stepped upon, yet without being detected. He had glimpsed a few of the rhinoceros in the gloom, and was impressed with the size and evident strength of these beasts; he did not relish a meeting with them upon the field of battle.

It was an hour past midnight when Yhendorn was finally able to slip into a shadowy corner of Uganji's tent. The shelter, larger than the others in the camp, was divided into three sections: a large, main area that imitated a throne room, a bedchamber, and a much smaller storage area. The first chamber was empty except for Uganji's personal attendant, who lay asleep upon a pallet of blankets, ready to be awakened should his master require his service. In the bedchamber, Ytero Uganji snored loudly upon an extravagant arrangement of ornate pillows and blankets. It was into the supply area that Yhendorn had crept, and as he gazed at the food stores and wine about him, he began to finalize the plan that he and Andalhyn had constructed. Kifosha in diluted form had long been used by the Makani to dull pain and even to tranquilize those wounded in battle for surgery. The vial that Yhendorn carried was of such potency that it would kill whomever ingested it, leaving the victim free of any signs or symptoms of foul play. The wares about him would be reserved for the Ianzama leader's use and would not be consumed by any other than himself, unless he were entertaining a guest of royal importance. The plan was now perfect: using the kifosha, Yhendorn would taint the breakfast food already set out for the morning, and Ytero Uganji would be dead within an hour after eating.

The soft sound of Uganji's attendant shifting upon his bed in the antechamber pointed out the flaw in Yhendorn's plot. Would the Ianzama leader have his food tasted prior to eating it himself? And if so, how long would he wait before he would dine? And when both Uganji and his servant fell dead in the same strange manner it would not be perceived as coincidence, but as treachery, and the goal of the assassination would be thwarted. If Yhendorn was to utilize the kifosha to poison Uganji, it would need to be administered to him and to him alone. The assassin crept from the shadows, careful to remain as quiet as the night; he drew slowly closer to his prey, finding him sound asleep. Uganji lay upon his side, mouth agape, which would not do. Using a strip of ragged cloth, Yhendorn tickled the exposed arm of Uganji. He twitched, swiping at his flesh with his other hand, but did not change position. Yhendorn waited several long minutes, then again attempted to manipulate the warlord without waking him. This game continued until finally, more than an hour later, Uganji lay upon his back. A whisper of cloth moving in the antechamber caused the Makani to retreat again to the shadows of the storage area; a brief moment later, Uganji's attendant walked sleepily into the room. The yawning man, a boy really, carried a few sticks of wood in the crook of one arm; he made his way to the master's fire and gently placed each log upon the existing coals. The dry wood crackled and popped, causing Yhendorn's prey to stir. Sitting up, Uganji glanced around the tent, then his eyes fastened upon the boy.

"Can you not perform your simple tasks without waking me!?" he growled, cursing. The boy, now fully awake, fell prostrate upon the floor and lay there trembling. His master was not a reasonable man, and the lad had felt his disfavor on many occasions, as the unhealed stripes upon his body and face attested. "Perhaps another flaying will improve your performance! Bring me the lash!" The boy did not move, but instead lay upon the ground, groaned in fear and began to sob; he pleaded unintelligibly for mercy, but only moved Uganji's heart to rage. He leaped from his bed and kicked the boy in the midsection as he moved to retrieve the short whip. Gasping now, the young slave scrambled to his feet and ran, which to the older, quicker man became a new method of torment upon the boy. Uganji allowed the slave to dart about the tent, but always made sure to stay between his prey and escape. The Ianzama ruler had landed several stripes upon the boy, and though his clothes had provided some protection, his tunic now hung in tatters; old and new wounds bled freely, including one ragged gash upon his left cheek. In desperation, the lad fled to the seeming protection of the storage area, though the refuge that he sought he found to be occupied, and that by an enemy of his lord.

~ ~ ~

Far north and east of the Ianzama camp, another of Dhresden's allies moved cautiously through the darkness; though to refer to her simply as one of the half-blood's allies would have been a disservice to this daughter of Nokoma. Tala marched towards the citadel for the protection of the peoples of the Pasturelands and its peaceful neighbors, but also to the honor and protection of the man whom she loved. She traveled alone, except for the khamellero upon which she rode, Sapphire, the same that had carried her safely and swiftly to the Makani fortress. Carefully Tala surveyed the moonlit landscape, though that did not prevent her thoughts from reflecting upon her departure from the Dunes. Even now, the woman archer could not recall what she had said to prevail upon Orrick, Mallory, Zabayr and even her sister Shika to allow her to travel alone. The discussions over dinner had been heated, even to the point of Shika throwing a plate against the wall. The pottery had shattered, and somehow with it, so had the opposition to Tala's plan; though not without some minor adjustments. Rather than journeying upon horse, which were quite scarce in the Dunes, into and through the snow-laden terrain of the Pasturelands, Tala agreed to ride upon a khamellero. The beast, though not indigenous to the region, would tolerate the cold of the area much the same as the frigidness of the desert night, and the webbed feet of the beast would allow easier passage through the snow than any horse or ox ever could. She also carried extra rations, weapons, clothing, and even wore a light Makani cloak woven of terephthala. And so, with a hug from Mallory and Orrick, a parting Makani blessing from Zabayr, and a lingering embrace from her sister, Tala and Sapphire made for the cold north. The daughters of Nokoma had spent only brief moments separate from each other, and though neither could be certain just how long it would be before they were together again, both knew it would likely be many days. Eager to accomplish her task, Tala left at sunset; astride Sapphire she made good time, passing what she believed was the area where Andalhyn had recovered Khaldun and Asha. The Oxmen had fled, leaving the dead where they lay. The bodies of men and the carcasses of beasts had been ravaged by wolves, vultures and other scavengers; their bones scattered about in disarray. It had been long enough that the bones had been picked clean, and the beasts that had feasted upon the dead should have moved on by now. As they passed into the borders of the Pasturelands, Tala took note of the effect that the changed terrain had upon her mount; snow had replaced the sand and stone of the Dunes, yet Sapphire seemed to take no notice. Her gait did not slow, and the awkward looking creature continued to bear her along effortlessly. Tala wondered casually whether she traveled a route similar to that of Khaldun and the cougar, but with the passage of time there would be no way to know; their tracks would have been hidden beneath weeks of winter snow. The two dim lights she spied up ahead gave her cause to reign in her mount; to expect allegiance to the true Lord of Havenstone from whoever sat around the campfires would be a fool's errand. One of the fires lay almost directly ahead, while the other stood several leagues off to the left; passing too closely to either of them could result in discovery, but circumventing the camp on the left would cause a great loss of time. Tala spurred her mount to the right, an adjustment that kept her close to her desired course yet should allow her to avoid detection. An hour passed, during which Tala cast several cautious glances at the nearest fire, but at the hour mark, she realized that she had come as close as she would to the threat, and that each step now that Sapphire took would carry them farther away. The comfort of this revelation dissipated in an instant when the khamellero snorted; the same moment when Tala realized that she was not alone. The solitary woman reigned in her mount as her eyes search about as far as the moonlight would reveal. She spotted the shadowy form of a man less than ten paces from her, and upon seeing his small frame she almost called out, believing for a moment that it was Wyeth, but even in the moonlight she could see that the man bore the uniform of an Oxmen officer of some rank. It must be an ambush attempt; Tala tensed and was about to spur Sapphire on to seek safety when the man called out.

"Hail, Makani warrior! I see you too have passed east of the watch fires of the Oxmen, Oxmen that condemn themselves in opposing the true Lord of Havenstone!" He paused, as if expecting some form of reply. Tala should flee; she had no basis upon which to place any trust in the man's words and yet she found herself lingering. The woman regarded him cautiously; he stood comfortably still, not shifting his footing or eyes like some street hustler trying to mask a thinly veiled lie. Still, she could not risk her life or her mission on a feeling. In an instant, the man before her found himself down range of the sharp end of an arrow. Tala had produced, drawn and leveled the bow and arrow with such speed and adeptness that the man had no time to react; and while the archer had not released the missile, the stranger recognized that, when fired, it would not miss its mark.

"Though a stranger to you, I am no enemy," he spread his empty hands wide, away from his body as he spoke. "I appear before you as I truly am, an Oxmen commander second; you, however, appear to be Makani, and yet by the weapon in your hands you are not." He said nothing more, and the ensuing silence seemed to ask Tala for answers.

"And who exactly is it that you call the true lord of Havenstone?" Tala finally asked. "Do you mean Treyherne, born of noble blood, advisor to Dhane; or do you refer to the half-blood barbarian who claims to be the son of Dhane?"

"If I have misjudged you, then let your arrow give me rest from the evil into which this land sinks, but I have aligned myself with Dhresden, son of Dhane, the only true lord of Havenstone!" The man dropped his arms to his sides and looked defiantly back at Tala, daring her to execute him for his allegiance.

"Speak freely, ox master," Tala said, returning her weapons to their place. "I have lost too much time with you already; what is it you seek?"

"I seek to make a difference! I have been labeled a traitor by Treyherne's Oxmen and as such have condemned my family to death or worse. I want to live or die in such a way that I know it was not—wasted." His words had been strong and vibrant, even inspiring; yet haunted by the fate of his family and the lack of direction.

Tala sat quietly a moment, considering the man before her; if indeed he were loyal to Dhresden, the skills of an Oxmen second in command would well be put to use. However, if he were false, if he meant harm to Dhresden or herself, he would be put to death.

"Summon your ox, ox master," Tala replied, "or attempt to keep up without one."

He turned his face to the left a little and sent out a low whistle; shortly, a large form approached in the snow and came to stand beside the man. He swung easily up into the saddle and rode the ox closer to Tala. He smiled before he spoke. "Did you steal that khamellero, or are you on good terms with the Makani?"

Tala smiled back, stifling a laugh. "Have you a name, or shall I simply keep calling you ox master?"

"Oh, I do have a name, but most times I answer to Flint. And you?"

"I am Tala and I intend to be northeast of the outcropping by midday. Follow me."

CHAPTER 31

Dhresden had been uncertain who it was that would greet him when he entered what had been referred to as the command tent of the mysterious reinforcements that had arrived; peering into the tent he was surprised at what he discovered. Cloaked figures crouched around a fire of hot coals, and as one they turned to face Dhresden as he entered; even in the dim light each of their three faces was familiar. All rose to their feet, but it was she who came to him and greeted him with a long embrace. She had again feared him to be dead and now rejoiced to see him alive and well.

"It is good to see you, mother," Dhresden said after some time had passed.

"And you, Dhresden," Jovanna smiled, "your journey to intercept Vlad Ikshton's JabalKriger took longer than we had anticipated, and we designed to mobilize the herdsmen to seek you out."

"I am glad to see each of you and to have your support, but I did not wish to leave Murion's Plateau unprotected."

"We did not leave the fort unprotected," Faust replied, "I left the twenty hand-picked men that you allowed me to secure the fort. They were reinforced by part of the detachment that your other friend brought." Faust gestured towards the third member of their party. It was the second embrace that Dhresden would receive this evening; the smaller man lifted the half-blood from the ground as he wrapped him in a brotherly hug.

"I had feared you dead," Dhresden said, almost grunting, as his feet again touched the ground.

"Nay, lad," Wyeth replied, "but the things that I observed within the citadel, especially with the members of the council, made me doubt that we would succeed in our endeavor. So, after the death of Sachs, I ventured to Kelvar to update Phaelen chieftain on the situation and to request warriors to your cause."

"Thank you, Wyeth, my dear old friend," Dhresden gripped the other man's shoulder briefly, his eyes on some distant thought. "You honor me and you reverence her memory."

Wyeth, never short for words, was silent a moment. "Your mother, she would be so proud to see the man that you have become," he said quietly. "No, Dhresden, it is you who honor me; it is you who reverence Ciana's memory."

The moment passed as misty eyes were wiped away, and the warriors turned back to the business at hand. "How many Kelvren did grandfather send with you?" Dhresden asked.

"He sent three hundred," Wyeth answered, surprising the other man at the number. "Though a third of that number are now encamped at Murion's Plateau with the handful of herdsmen you left there."

"Three hundred is more than I had hoped for," Dhresden noted, "but I shall not send any of them back!" The comment brought smiles and grins to the faces of his companions, but they soon faded as the discussion continued. "It would seem that Chayne and her Tulisan have been quelled, thanks largely to the aid of Vlad Ikshton."

"Can we expect him to march against Treyherne with us?" Jovanna asked, her voice expectant and her eyes hopeful.

"No, my lady," Dhresden replied, "The JabalKing allied with us only to neutralize Chayne's forces. His men will be searching the dead for her body, and if Chayne is not found, Ikshton plans to pursue the survivors that he may overtake the woman." His brow wrinkled in thought as he continued, "There is a history that involves the two of them, the hog-king and the witch-princess, that I hope he will put to rest soon. Nevertheless, we march upon the Citadel without the aid of the JabalKriger."

"It is well," Wyeth replied. "The Kelvren warriors and the herdsmen will together place you upon your rightful throne."

"Yes," the Havenstone lord agreed, "and the Wanderlanders that have come will bolster our troops as well. I am told that they now number twenty-six men, plus their beast companions."

"Shall I send out riders to mobilize the men at Murion's Plateau?" Faust asked. "They could meet us on route to the Citadel."

"Yes," Dhresden nodded, "send word at first light; we will rest tomorrow and depart at the following dawn. Deliverance for the oppressed and judgment for the wicked are coming to Havenstone."

~ ~ ~

Ytero Uganji charged after the boy, further enraged by his feeble attempt to escape. As he entered the storage area, he was struck squarely against the forehead, and fell back the way he had come. The man lay unmoving upon the ground, his eyes closed; he had been knocked senseless by the unseen Makani. Upon seeing that the man was unconscious, Yhendorn's attention now turned to the slave boy. The wind-warrior held the battered youth by his ragged clothes with one hand and with the other covered his mouth to ensure that he did not raise the alarm. A long moment passed while they stood thus, the man's eyes burning into the wide eyes of the boy, until the younger slowly raised his hands as if to signify that he surrendered, or that he was not a threat to the assassin. Yhendorn slowly removed his hand from the boy's mouth, and though he did not release him with his other hand he did relax his grip some. Yhendorn's plans must of necessity change, but what path should he take in the face of these recent occurrences?

~ ~ ~

"How do they look, Shika?" Orrick asked. He and Mallory had been watching the Makani practicing with their bows and could tell that the daughter of Nokoma did not approve. She startled, as though she had been unaware of their presence, then, with a shrug of her shoulders and a shake of her head, answered the giant's inquiry.

"They are quick learners," she began, "they have mastered the production of arrows better than the aiming of them, but each shall loose their arrows into the enemy; this is about survival, not competition."

"Truly, yet you seem displeased. If these foundling Makani archers are not the cause, then what is?"

Shika dropped her eyes to the ground but did not answer. "It is Tala, is it not?" Mallory asked, answering for the other woman. "You miss her, and fear for her; both for her safe passage and for what pain she will endure if harm comes to my brother." Shika nodded, fighting to hold back quiet tears. "Oh, Shika," Mallory grieved, wrapping her in a comforting embrace, "these are not your fears alone; both Orrick and I have shared these concerns. No, we cannot be certain of what joys or sorrows await us, but we will pursue what is right and just and good in spite of the danger, despite the risk."

"I know," Shika agreed, "but it is difficult, knowing the pain she has already endured. I am optimistic for their future, and I thank you for sharing this burden with me." She squeezed Mallory a brief moment before releasing her, drawing yet more strength from her.

Suddenly Zabayr was beside them, and though his breath was not labored, it was clear that he had rushed to their side.

"What is it, my friend?" Orrick asked.

"The Arba'a have returned from the Ianzama camp; Khuzaymah and Andalhyn await you in the war room." The two of them turned and quickly made their way to the chamber. Upon entering, Orrick and Zabayr bowed in greeting to the Makani lord. Andalhyn and a few other advisors sat near their king, while another Makani warrior stood before them. Beside him, or rather, shielded beneath his arm, cowered a boy who, though wrapped in a blanket of woven khamell-ero hair, beneath wore the tatters of a beggar or a slave.

"Orrick," Khuzaymah greeted the giant, "I am pleased that you arrived so quickly. I present to you Yhendorn and the assassin of Ytero Uganji." As Orrick's eyes locked with those of the wind warrior before him, a mixture of relief and regret welled up within the Wanderlander. He knew that justice had been served upon the leader of the Ianzama, but for many years had longed for his own hands to be the instruments of the monster's demise.

"I greet you, Yhendorn, slayer of the wicked. Thank you for your service to the lord of Havenstone, and to many others."

"You misunderstand, Orrick," Khuzaymah replied. "Yhendorn was unsuccessful in his attempt to poison Uganji."

A tremble passed through Orrick's confused soul, but his voice remained strong. "Forgive me, friend Khuzaymah, but—is Ytero Uganji, ruler of the Ianzama—is he dead?"

"He is dead," Yhendorn answered, "but it was not I who slew him."

"Who then?" Orrick asked, struggling to contain his frustration. "Who is it that killed that heartless and cruel creature?!"

"I did!" It was the young voice of the boy that had once cowered beneath Yhendorn's protection, though now he stood alone, his eyes daring someone to condemn his actions.

Orrick looked again to Yhendorn, whose own eyes regarded the boy beside him with something akin to pride.

"His name is Korbyn, and it is true," the Makani confirmed. He recounted the events of his infiltration into the Ianzama camp, his attempts to administer the poison to Uganji, and the cruel leader's treatment of the boy. "After I released him, he asked if I had been sent by his people, by his parents, to rescue him. When I told him of my mission, he offered to aid me if I agreed to help him escape. I agreed, and next I knew, the boy had produced a dagger and plunged it into the chest of the unconscious man. When he was finished, I observed that Ytero Uganji was indeed dead."

Orrick was quiet for a long moment. "Zabayr," the mountain man said finally, "see to it that Korbyn gets a hot meal, a bath and fresh clothes. Yhendorn will check on him shortly."

The boy hesitated, but with quiet reassurance from his Makani guardian, Korbyn followed Zabayr from the chamber. No one spoke immediately after the door closed behind the two of them; it was Orrick who broke the silence.

"Will Uganji's death rally the Horde, or will they disperse?" he asked the grandmaster.

"Though it clearly was not an accidental or natural death, it will appear as though the boy acted alone and then fled. I cannot say whether it will result in open war or a retreat." The man lapsed into silence, a distant look having overtaken him.

"Yhendorn, what is there that you have not told us?"

The wind warrior took a heavy breath before answering, but when he did, his tone was apologetic. "I realize that I failed in my mission, and for the missed opportunity to end this war I seek your pardon; however, I am not blind to the danger that likely still threatens our people, and all the people of the region. I do take pleasure in the end of the boy's suffering, though our nation may suffer in his stead. If there is to be any measure of Korbyn's sorrows at the hands of Ytero Uganji, then it is to be in the stripes upon his flesh and the dagger holes in Uganji's chest."

"What do you mean?" Khuzaymah asked. "How many times did the boy run him through?"

"No less than ten, my lord."

The war-hardened veterans in the room again went silent, each contemplating the possible depths of woe Korbyn had endured, until Orrick spoke.

"I assure you," he declared, his voice heavy, "the slaves of the Ianzama endure much worse than you can imagine."

"Yhendorn," Khuzaymah said, "I wish you to escort the boy to his homeland. Find his village, find his family. You leave at dawn. The rest of us prepare for battle. We shall meet the enemy in the field."

~ ~ ~

An army, its composition varied, its numbers united, had set up camp half a day's journey from the Outcropping, the citadel of the Pasturelands. Unexpected allies had gathered to the aid of the true Lord of Havenstone, and soon they would spill blood, both their own and that of the enemy's forces, in order to place Dhresden upon his rightful throne. Heavy was the burden of the cost the young ruler was asking of his allies, heavier still the guilt he would bear if he were to do nothing. He tallied the numbers again in his head: two hundred Kelvren, twenty-six Wanderlanders plus their beast companions, and two hundred and sixty herdsmen. Less than five hundred, almost half of which were not skilled as soldiers, to battle the thousands of well-trained Oxmen under Treyherne's control. More allies were otherwise engaged; they too would shed blood in their own endeavors to see this land made safe and kept safe.

The battle against Treyherne's forces could easily turn into a siege, a development that Dhresden wished to avoid. The fortifications of the city and the stores that had been prepared against the winter season would allow the Oxmen to outlast the half-blood's forces in the event of a siege. Besieging his city would result in his own defeat and the duress of the citizens within; no harm would come to Treyherne. No, the only paths to victory lay in drawing Treyherne's forces out of the protection of the city walls, or in opening the gates from the interior so that Dhresden and his soldiers could attack from within.

The usurped ruler was shaken from his thoughts by the squeak and crunch of feet approaching through the snow. He looked up and saw Faust approaching, a look of mild concern plagued his bearded face.

"What is it, Faust?" Dhresden asked as he rose to his feet.

"Our scouts to the southern perimeter spotted two riders, I have sent out a dozen men to intercept them and bring them here. Further reports state that there has been no trouble, and that they have come willingly."

"Why, then, this consternation upon your face?" Dresden inquired further.

"The reports, sir, they state that one rider is upon an ox, while the other rides something else, something not of the Pasturelands, Kelvar or the mountains."

"I should like to hear some day what you know of Kelvar," Dhresden smiled wryly, "Instruct the men to be wary, but bring them to me." Faust departed quickly. Dhresden liked the man, and he was pleased that this herdsman had been able to provide comfort to his mother—his mother: he had come to think of the lady Jovanna as more than his father's widow or his stepmother, but rather as a beloved matriarch. Pulling his mind back to the issue at hand, Dhresden wondered at the riders that were coming. Did their presence bode well, or would their arrival bestow more evils upon him and his companions?

Deep in thought, Dhresden shook himself from his musings; he was unsure of how much time had passed, though it was clear that more than an hour had lapsed. The half-blood tossed a few sticks and a log on the dying fire before him, and as the flames rekindled he lifted his eyes towards the sound of approaching feet. In the poor lighting, he could spy Faust and three other herdsmen escorting two large forms towards him, though at a spear's throw away, the two large mounts were left hitched at the fringe of the other beasts. Two forms continued with Faust and his men, the smaller almost the right size to be Wyeth, but Dhresden could determine by his movements that it was not. The other individual, though shrouded in a cloak and the darkness, possessed a bearing and carriage whose familiarity stirred great emotion within Dhresden's being. He rose slowly to his feet, at which point the familiar form almost ran towards him. Dhresden, too, ran forward, but stopped short of his mark and fell to his knees in the snow and mud. The other slowed, and closed the gap at a walk; it was Dhresden who spoke first.

"I—am unworthy—of your presence, daughter of Nokoma," he managed, his voice heavy with emotion. "You are most welcome—though if you wish to depart from my company—I will not forbid it; I will understand."

Tala stood less than an arm's length from her beloved, but Dhresden's guilt had paralyzed him; he felt unworthy of her. An awkward moment of silence passed, and then Dhresden found Tala kneeling before him in the snow. Tears flowed from her eyes, mimicking those glistening upon Dhresden's own cheeks.

"Dhresden," she said, "will you forgive me for shooting you with an arrow?" Finally, Dhresden's eyes met those of Tala, and an instant later, the two of them were locked in an embrace; both alternating between crying and laughing. Presently, Dhresden stood and led Tala to the warmth and the glow of the fire, where they huddled close and continued to speak in hushed voices. Faust and his men, as well as Tala's travel companion, fell back to the shadows, content to leave the two lovers at least the semblance of privacy while they recounted to each other the last months' events.

Faust approached the smaller man, and motioned for him to follow. "Let us find a warming fire for you as well, oxman. I should like to hear how it is that you have come to us."

There was no malice or suspicion in his tone, but Flint was certain that it lay just beneath the surface of the herdsman, and rightly so: the Oxmen had been so corrupted by Treyherne that most would readily run the half-blood through. Prudence demanded that he be examined, Flint only hoped that the truth of his words would be evident. He was aware of the continued presence of Faust's three men keeping pace behind him, and thought it best to broach the subject willingly.

"So, herdsman," Flint began, "what will it be? Are you to beat answers from me? It is winter, so perhaps you could tie me to a tree until the cold causes me to talk? Or maybe just some hot coals to burn away the lies?"

Faust chuckled, seeming genuinely amused by the oxman's candor. "That is not the way of things here," he replied, offering Flint a seat before another campfire. "We are common folk, but we try to behave in noble fashion. Please tell me how it is that you are separate from your battalion, and how it is that you are in the company of this daughter of Nokoma. And if your answers to not ring true, we will beat you, freeze you, and then set you ablaze." Both men smiled broadly at the last of Faust's words, and, drawing a deeper breath, Flint began to share his tale.

CHAPTER 32

"The scouts have returned, my lord, and they report that the Ianzama are marching toward our boundary; though it does not appear that they rush forth in vengeance."

"How long before they breach our border?"

"At their present speed, they will arrive within sight of the Hourglass a few short hours after we arrive."

Andalhyn frowned, considering the news. If the scouts' estimations were correct, that would leave not enough time to prepare for the rhinoceros' attack. Without the holes and barriers, how would they withstand the beasts' onslaught? He would need to discuss this with Zabayr, Orrick and his other advisors. "Send word to our Hazrat: we expect contact by day's end tomorrow, and we are formulating contingency plans should our original scheme fail. Also, speed up the march, I want us at the strait awaiting them. Notify my advisors and the giant that I will speak with them at the next rest." The man nodded and was gone. Before a quarter hour passed, the column of Makani soldiers had increased their pace, but whether it would be enough none could ascertain. If he were to order a forced march, a speed that would certainly put their arrival at the hourglass ahead of the Ianzama, Andalhyn feared that his forces would be too fatigued to fight. And so, at the next stop for water, the Makani commander met with the giant man Orrick, Zabayr, and three others to seek counsel and discuss alternative battle plans. After sharing the updates that he had, Andalhyn looked at each of the other men in turn and invited them to speak.

"We agree with you, Andalhyn," said one of the advisors the commander had summoned. Two others stood beside the man, nodding in consensus.

"I concur that a forced march would give our enemy an advantage," began Zabayr, "but not engaging them at the strait puts us at a disadvantage. If the Ianzama are allowed control of that narrow bit of land we will be unable to attack in force, and their numbers are overwhelming enough that facing them on open ground only would delay them in reaching our city, our homes, and our families. I urge that we hasten to the hourglass so that we might make our preparations and better defend our land and our people."

"Perhaps you are all correct," Orrick interjected, his eye was aimed at the ground before him, but his mind saw something else entirely. He lifted his gaze to the men around him, finding their confused attention fixed upon him. "Forfeiting control of the Hourglass is as foolhardy as meeting the Ianzama on open ground, and as reckless as arriving at the strait too fatigued to fight. What if a detachment of warriors sped to the very presence of the enemy?"

"To what end, Wanderlander?" Andalhyn asked, clearly intrigued.

"Harass them; attack, strike, flee—slow their advance. Allow our main force to arrive with energy to entrench and wage war."

"A secondary force could be sent to begin preparations at the Hourglass," Zabayr suggested, eager to be under way should his commander agree to the strategy.

Andalhyn remained silent as he considered the giant's plan. "You two," he said, indicating Orrick and Zabayr, "assemble men and riders to accompany you to the south of the Hourglass. Do not take less than four squads of Arba'a, and be not careless with your lives. You three," he said to his other advisors, "ready thirty men to travel with you to the strait, and get digging! We may yet triumph!"

In less than an hour the warriors from the Dunes were underway again, and the two advance parties had passed out of sight of the main Makani war force. Orrick and Zabayr spurred their Arba'a squad, numbering sixty-four, at an almost reckless pace, leaving the column of diggers behind. Orrick intended to slow upon reaching the Hourglass and allow the men and their mounts to recover their strength for their assault upon the Ianzama, but for now many miles must be covered. The mountain man was glad that he had left Mallory and Asha together at the Cliffs; he could not bear the risk to them had they accompanied him, nor would Mallory have approved of his current mission. His beloved would view his actions as needlessly placing himself in harm's way, while Orrick considered that his involvement in delaying the Ianzama was in protection of Mallory.

Winded and weary, Orrick and Zabayr slowed the pace of their forces as they passed through the Hourglass. They had ridden through the night, but without the moon's light they had been forced to slow in the darkness. At dawn's first light they had returned to their breakneck speed, and were finally able to slow upon reaching the strait near noon. After an hour of recovery at this slower pace, a scout was dispatched ahead to determine how far the enemy lay. When he returned less than an hour later with news of their position, Orrick and Zabayr discussed the options facing them and their troops. The men as well as the khamelleros had given so much already, and now they risked bloodshed to provide time for their countrymen to better prepare for battle. The scout reported that the Ianzama traveled at a slower pace, due to the use of twenty large wagons to transport the brigade, but the rhinoceros not utilized to pull wagons appeared to number eighty. Once at the battle site, the burdened beasts could quickly be uncoupled from the wagons and enter the fray. The enemy's cavalry could be quick, and this was the greatest threat to the small Makani force, and casualties were anticipated. Their mission was to slow the Ianzama, not stop them, to irritate them and distract them much like a mosquito or gnat, and yet even an insect could be squashed if it were not wary in its movements.

Orrick and Zabayr each took command of a third of their forces, entrusting the remaining group to the leadership of the scout. Zabayr would circle his men south and east, keeping hidden from the eyes of the Ianzama, and Orrick and his unit would do the same traveling south and east. Once they were in position, the scout feigned a frontal attack, drawing the attention of the enemy forces, especially their cavalry. As expected, the foot soldiers ceased marching, while the cavalry rallied to the front to meet the Makani attack. At the last, the scout and his men cut sharply west, away from the counter attack of the enemy. The rhinoceros riders pursued, eager to punish the small Makani force for its audacity in coming against such a superior army, and then Zabayr attacked the enemy's flank, wounding and killing several footmen in the initial wave. The Ianzama sounded the alert, and their cavalry broke off pursuit of the scout and wheeled to defend against this new threat. Zabayr's men effected heavy losses before they too diverted away from the cavalry, again leading the rhinoceros charge away from the main force. Now it was Orrick's turn to spill Ianzama blood, both his blades and the quarterstaffs of the Makani did just that. Soon the Wanderlander and his men darted away from the reinforcing cavalry, and the scout's forces returned to torment the enemy. The Ianzama, however, had tired of this game, and had divided their cavalry into units numbering ten. Each unit had begun to take up position around the foot soldiers and brigade wagons, which the scout and his men had failed to discern. These were the first casualties of Orrick's plan, and though the rigors of life had proven the mountain man to be strong, he winced at the loss of life. The khamellero bearing the scout was the first to fall, and then the three nearest beasts. The scout was thrown from his saddle, landed heavily upon the ground and rolled to his feet. He was clearly dazed, but he brandished his quarterstaff with all the confidence of a battalion captain. He called loudly for the remainder of his unit to retreat, most of which readily obeyed. A handful of the foolhardy faithful continued their charge, intent upon whisking their leader away from the enemy, only to collide against a wall of heavily muscled flesh, reinforced with bone and horn. The rhinoceros were content to trample these enemies, but the defiance of the scout would not be so readily undone. He had leapt clear of several attempts against his life, and had even managed to strike two or three riders from their perch, but in an instant he was caught by the horn of the enemy, half gored, half crushed. As the remaining khamelleros and their riders fled this gruesome death, the cavalry relented, and retreated to their place at the edge of the Ianzama forces.

Orrick had heard the sounds of death upon many battlefields, but the cries of Makani and khamellero combined in a symphony of sorrow that attempted to shatter the resolve of the hearer. Neither Orrick nor Zabayr would allow themselves or their men to succumb to the temptation. For the remainder of the day, the Makani forces kept their enemy from advancing, even effecting raids in the waning half-light of dusk. In darkness, Orrick and Zabayr united their forces north of the enemy encampment, both to take assessment of their losses and to plan for the next stage of their mission. Of the sixty-four warriors that had accompanied them, eighteen men and their khamellero lay dead upon the field of battle. The wounded numbered zero, for the rhinoceros did not maim, only kill. While the Makani had inflicted heavy losses upon the foot soldiers and several of the riders, none of the rhinoceros had fallen, and whether they even registered pain none could say. The giant eyed the men about him in the darkness; he saw no evidence of cowardice—fear, yes, but no lack of bravery.

His voice heavy with admiration, Orrick addressed the men. "The wind-warriors have fought well today! Those we have lost, we have lost to honorable death, and we will complement their sacrifice with the blood of Ianzama tonight! Rest a few moments, while Zabayr and I finalize our plan." His words were well received, though out of earshot of the men, Zabayr took issue with Orrick's plan.

"With respect, Orrick, that is not what we will do."

"I do not understand. This is exactly what we had discussed, there is no alternative or reason not to proceed."

"I agree that there is no alternative," Zabayr replied, "but with the alteration of one detail. You are to remain outside the camp."

The Wanderlander's countenance darkened as he considered Zabayr's request. "And why do you believe that is necessary?"

"Out of respect, respect for Mallory. My people, and those who stand with us, may be wiped out by this invading force, but I will not allow you to be taken from her in this camp. Follow my plan, and return to the Hourglass on the morrow. Leave by noon, no matter the outcome of the night."

Orrick stood silent, pondering the words of his companion, and with a heavy sigh, nodded agreement. "It has been an honor to know you, Makani Zabayr, and I expect to see you on the morning."

Zabayr smiled. "The honor has been mine, Black Wanderlander. I also look to see you on the morrow." And then, turning his face towards the men, Zabayr signaled the riders to mount up; the night raid was about to begin.

~ ~ ~

Andalhyn and the bulk of the Makani forces arrived at the Hourglass a full day after Orrick and Zabayr's small tactical force had passed through the narrow bit of land. He was encouraged to find the advance crew hard at work, digging pitfalls, erecting obstacles and barricades, however; aware of the numbers of enemy troops marching toward them, and the power of the Ianzama cavalry, Andalhyn ordered forty more of his men to assist in the preparations. By day's end, enough barricades had been constructed south of the Hourglass to force the cavalry to approach in a single column, and enough holes had been dug to render the majority of the rhinoceros useless. Teams of sentries were sent south beyond the battlements to watch for the enemy, and the remainder of the camp settled down for a well-deserved rest. The night passed without incident, but with no sign of the enemy or contact from Orrick, Andalhyn had begun to doubt their plan. He did not give voice to his concerns, but by midday he was prepared to send out scouts to determine the location of the Ianzama as well as his own unaccounted for men. A commotion at the outskirts of the camp stole his attention, and a glance southward revealed two Makani upon khamelleros entering the camp. They paused briefly to address the first ranking officer they encountered, who turned and pointed in the direction of the Makani commander. The two rode quickly to Andalhyn's tent, dismounted and offered a salute.

"What news?" Andalhyn asked, eager for some reassurance that they had not wasted time, effort or lives.

"Orrick and Zabayr's men are en route, sir!"

"And what of the Ianzama?"

"I am to assure you that detailed report will be provided upon their arrival, sir, but I am afraid that I have no other information."

Andalhyn nodded, his brow wrinkled in thought. "Yes, thank you both. Tend to your mounts, but I may have need of you again soon." This news not only left many of the commander's questions unanswered, it also added inquiries. Orrick and Zabayr's men marched towards him, but of the two leaders, no information had been given. True, they had volunteered and even planned the mission, but the idea of one or both of them becoming a casualty of this war, especially at such an early phase, did not sit well with the commander. It was the better part of an hour before he had the answers he sought.

As the column of khamelleros came into view, Andalhyn was alarmed at the number of beasts that appeared to be riderless. He was further troubled when he realized that some of what he had perceived as riderless carried the form of a man lying across the saddle, though wounded or dead he could not determine. Andalhyn was relieved when he spotted Orrick riding tall in his saddle, and there, next to him, Zabayr rode of his own power, though his countryman was clearly weakened and slouched forward.

"See to these men," he commanded his aide, "and see that hot food is prepared for them while their wounds are tended. Orrick, Zabayr, what has happened? How are you injured?"

"Forgive me, commander, I—"

"He requires a healer, Andalhyn," Orrick interrupted. "His leg was crushed, the swelling is great, and he is feverish. I will tell you all that I know, but he should see a healer now." The giant had dismounted as he spoke, and now he leaned close to the Makani commander and whispered to him alone. "I fear that he will lose the leg regardless, but I am certainly no healer."

"You are no healer indeed, mountain man; I am not deaf, my leg is broken. I realize that it is severe, and I accept whatever the outcome will be."

"Well, his spirits are good," Andalhyn mused, taking little comfort in that fact. He summoned four men to convey Zabayr to the healer's tent, then led Orrick to camp headquarters. He directed the giant to sit, took a breath, then spoke. "I am glad to see you both alive, Wanderlander. Please tell me of our successes and failures in this endeavor."

"Our first contact with the Ianzama came two days ago. We divided into three parties and systematically attacked the enemy, focusing our attention on the foot soldiers. We inflicted significant casualties and managed to keep clear of their cavalry for the first few raids, but by our fourth attack the Ianzama had adapted their tactics and we lost a few men. We withdrew and contented ourselves with feigning attacks, which forced them to remain immobile and maintain a defensive stance. That night, Zabayr and several others raided the camp on foot, intending to kill any riders that they could and possibly even some rhinoceros. They had assassinated at least a dozen men, but when they attempted to kill or incapacitate one of the rhinoceros, the beast uttered some terrible noise, which resulted in the whole of the creatures stampeding through that section of the camp. Zabayr's leg was crushed, several others were wounded to varying degrees and four were killed. Those who could got themselves and others to safety, but we were unable to retrieve all of our dead. We left yesterday morning, but it has been a slow trek. We kept a group at our flank to occasionally attack and slow the enemy, but they may be within reach of the hourglass by nightfall."

Andalhyn sat silent for a moment as he considered the information that Orrick had given him. In one regard, the mission had been a success, but he feared that the cost of that success had been much higher than anticipated. "Do you have an idea of the numbers of casualties, for our men as well as the Ianzama?"

"Of our sixty-four: nine deceased, twenty-two injured severely, and five khamellero were lost. The specifics of the Ianzama are difficult to assess, though we effected at least twenty kills, and as many injuries, but those who were stampeded I cannot quantify."

Andalhyn was stunned. "You mean they trampled their own men? Do you believe it was intentional?"

"From interviewing our men, Zabayr included, I do not believe they targeted their own men, but there was no effort made to protect them either."

"I had hoped," the commander admitted, "that our enemy was not as ruthless as the histories claim. It is clear, however, that they are bent upon the destruction of these lands and any who oppose them. I will send word to the southern guard, in the meantime, let us get you fed."

Standing swiftly to his feet, Orrick protested. "With respect, I should like to see how Zabayr is before I eat."

Andalhyn smiled. "I was certain that you would want to check on him, so I had meals brought to a residence adjacent to the healer's quarters. I expect Zabayr will join you there if he is not already eying your portion."

~ ~ ~

"So tell me, Faust: how is it that the oldest person in this army is awarded the task of reconnaissance?" The two men stood beneath the low limbs of a spruce tree, within the hollow created by the snow that had fallen outside the reach of the tree's branches.

Faust looked down at the smaller man, amused as well as a little annoyed. "Flint, Wyeth is Kelvren," he replied. "No one is better equipped than he, and he did not go alone; three others went with him."

"But still, he's rather old. Do you honestly think I would not be a better choice? I know the city well, and how long has it been since he was there anyway?"

"Less than a week," answered another voice, startling the smaller man. Both men turned to discover that Dhresden had entered the shelter of the spruce tree behind them, how long the usurped ruler had stood thus, listening, neither could guess, though his countenance reflected a general distaste for the conversation he had heard.

"My lord," Flint said, apologetically, "it is not your leadership that causes me to question, it is my lack of knowledge. I wish for this endeavor to succeed, and my limited awareness of details gives me concern."

It was a long, quiet, awkward moment later that the half-blood spoke. "It is your lack of confidence that gives me concern, ox master.

Doubtless you were unaware of several details under the leadership of your commander; did you follow him with the same reserve?"

"No, my lord, I did not."

"Then tell me, from where does this insubordination stem?"

Flint again answered without hesitation, "Liam became my friend long before he was my commander. I have always known and understood that his actions would be in the best interests of our families, our nation, and ourselves when possible. We have both shed blood, and bled it in the pursuit of our duties, and though Liam is none of my kin, he is a closer friend than any my mother could have borne unto me. I am certain you can appreciate my position."

"I do not seek the same kindred spirit that you share with Liam," Dhresden replied, "but I covet your allegiance and your trust. Believe me when I say that it is for your family as much as mine that I seek my rightful throne."

"For my family as much as yours, you say? Those are powerful words, words that you must understand I find difficult to completely accept."

"Yes, Flint, I do understand; but it is important for you to grasp that I am not a man of words alone." The half-blood withdrew a sealed letter from his cloak and handed it to the other man. "Your wife, your sons, and your daughter are well, or at least they were two weeks ago."

CHAPTER 33

Two days later, longer, more restless days than Flint had endured for quite a while, Dhresden allowed the smaller man an audience in the Havenstone lord's council. Standing with Dhresden were the herdsman Faust, Konaird the mountain man, the ladies Jovannah and Tala, and the Kelvren Wyeth. It was the report that the old Kelvren were to give that had so intrigued Flint and troubled his thoughts. He knew the information that Wyeth brought from within the citadel would be used to form the strategy that was intended to result in placing Dhresden upon his rightful throne, and for that Flint was already eager; but the man also hoped for news of his family, and of Liam's.

"Well, old friend?" asked Dhresden, his tone even, "What news do you bring from within the walls?"

"Treyherne believes you to be dead, and expects that winter will cause any remaining whisper of resistance to wither and die. There continue to be rumors murmured among the citizens that you live, but without some sort of confirmation that it is true, that too will fade and die. Given Treyherne's permissive attitude, the Oxmen have become even more corrupt in their boredom. Several townsfolk have been imprisoned, killed, or worse for failing to cowtail to them. The few families I have spoken with directly continue to fare well, but this evil, if left unchecked, will destroy all." Wyeth's eyes locked briefly with Flint's as he spoke, but then he moved on. "The people of Havenstone are ripe for rebellion against the snake, they but lack a leader. An army of reinforcements would strengthen their resolve as well."

"So," Konaird drolled in his mountain accent, "if we gain entrance, the citizens will support us, even join us in putting this usurper down?"

"But how are we to enter?" Faust asked. "Opening the main gate is sure to be detected."

"I am surprised at you, herdsman." It was Jovannah who spoke, a smile upon her lips. "Do you not remember how it is that we became acquainted?"

Faust reddened slightly, but seemed genuinely amused. "So we are to enter through the cattle gate at the stockyards. It is not typical for the herdsmen to reenter the Citadel once winter camp has been established, but neither is it unheard of. In years where the winter had proven to be unseasonably harsh and the supplies necessary to care for the cattle were not expected to be sufficient, it has been necessary to implement a winter Rotation. This slaughtering of a portion of the herd reduces the strain on the remainder of cattle, and also boosts morale within the Citadel with fresh meat."

"We could enter near dusk, herdsmen leading the way, and be upon the Oxmen before they realize their danger," Dhresden announced. "Dusk would put the townsfolk off the streets and into the safety of their homes, whereas any who wish to join our cause may. Tell me, Faust, what steps must be taken?"

"Word must be sent that there is a need for Rotation, and the herd portion usually arrives within four days' time."

"Has a request for winter Rotation ever been denied?" asked Konaird.

"No, never. The appeal of fresh meat at this stage of winter is much too palatable. We are practically guaranteed entrance."

"Well then, Faust," Dhresden said, "send word immediately. Each of you, ready your troops; two days hence at dusk we rid Havenstone of her snake problem."

~ ~ ~

The enemy was on the move before sunup, but not without detection by the Makani scouts. The southern guard withdrew as they had been instructed, placing the entire wind warrior army to the north of the Hourglass. The fortifications that had been built now lay between the two forces, hopefully to the effect of leveling the playing field. If the details came together as anticipated, the Ianzama cavalry would be rendered ineffective, and the Lepers Brigade kept at bay with the newly acquired archery skills taught to the Makani by the daughter of Nokoma. If the Ianzama foot soldiers did not retreat at that point, the battle would progress to man against man, and while the Makani fought with the agility of the wind, the Ianzama were strong and fierce, and would likely fight to the last man rather than to surrender.

Though both Andalhyn and Orrick had protested, Zabayr joined them at the command post to observe the progress of the battle and to advise as necessary. His injuries prevented him the strength to stand on his own, so he sat comfortably atop a khamellero; and though the beast lay with its legs folded underneath itself, it provided an elevated view of the scene before him.

The enemy came into view as the sun crested the southeastern horizon, its radiant beams shining full in the face of the Makani forces; an advantage the Ianzama would have for the next hour or two. Eager to profit from any benefit afforded them, the rhinoceros riders charged towards the narrow bit of land created by the encroachment of the Bog on one side and the sea upon the other. The Hourglass indeed was a natural pinch point against enemy invasion, but in the face of their numbers and their resources, the land feature itself did not ensure victory. The lead rider reached the first barricade and rammed through it without slowing noticeably; he galloped on, somehow avoiding the pits and trenches that had been dug. Coming to another barricade, the beast leaped to clear the obstacle, but landed, a front leg finding a pitfall. The heavy thick bone snapped audibly, sending the beast into a tumble and crushing the rider. Others were meeting similar fates, until a battle horn sounded, recalling the cavalry. Half of the Ianzama mounted force lay or limped upon the battlefield, no longer a threat to the Makani, but instead an obstacle to their masters. Momentarily another horn sounded, signaling the advance of the Lepers Brigade. Their dreaded numbers advanced neither quickly nor slowly, but moved with a steady, measured, and determined pace. Upon reaching the barricades and pitfalls constructed by the Makani, the diseased troops began to use any debris available, wrecked barricades, dead soldiers, and even the wounded, to mark or fill holes so that the remaining cavalry would be able to maneuver the dangerous terrain.

Andalhyn ordered the Makani archers forward, and though the enemy lay at the furthermost of their range, arrows began to rain down upon them. Most arrows found their mark, though few of the enemy actually fell but rather continued their forward march. While the first phase of Andalhyn's plan had been effective, the intent to neutralize the Lepers Brigade with the use of archery was failing. Several marched on with multiple arrows protruding from their bodies, preparing the way for the cavalry and still a force to be reckoned with themselves.

"We will need to meet them where they are," Andalhyn announced to his advisors. "If we delay, the cavalry will be upon us."

"Either way," Orrick offered, "the cavalry will likely advance as far as they can, but better to face that evil sooner rather than later. Doing so now allows us the opportunity of retreating past the remaining obstacles,"

"What if there was a way to turn the lepers to your service, or to at least lose the heart for battle against us?" asked a voice familiar to none but Orrick. Andalhyn, Orrick, and the other advisors turned towards the speaker, finding a slender man dressed in a loincloth, his skin appearing at first as if it were that of a snake.

"Tiblak?!" Orrick exclaimed, not attempting to hide his astonishment. "I am surprised to find you here!"

"And I am surprised that you were not detained by any of our forces," Zabayr commented, his displeasure evident.

"Yes, of course I encountered resistance, but when I declared to them that I had been sent by Dhresden Lord Havenstone, and that I had been instructed to meet up with Orrick the Black Wanderlander, the lady Mallory, the daughters of Nokoma, and even the grey cougar Asha, I am sure you understand and will pardon what appears initially to be a dereliction of their duty."

"I am certain we can discuss the details of how you came to this knowledge later," said Andalhyn, "but if Orrick can attest to you, I will accept your council and assistance. What is it that you bring to our battle?"

Soon the Makani archers, accompanied by Orrick, Tiblak, and four other Bogmen, were found advancing to within shouting distance of the Lepers Brigade. A proposition was to be made, the outcome of which could readily determine the direction of the battle, and the fate of the Pasturelands.

"Hail, mighty and feared men of the Lepers Brigade!" Orrick called to the diseased soldiers. "We desire to speak to your captain!"

No audible response came from the men who continued to march upon the Makani representatives, save some murmured cursing and quiet derisive laughter.

"Your captain!" Orrick repeated, "I would speak with him of your cure!"

Again some quiet laughter, almost lost in the louder angry shouts and cursing emanating from the brigade.

"I do not mock you!" Orrick called, attempting again to reason with the now angry soldiers. "With me stands a healer! He possesses the remedy for your illness!"

Unintelligible shouts erupted from the diseased men, their thundering drowning out any other words the Wanderlander would speak. He turned and nodded to Tiblak, who handed an arrow to one of the Makani archers. He loosed the arrow swiftly, striking one of the lepers of the foremost ranks squarely in the chest. As with the others, he evidenced no sign that he felt any pain, neither did he slow his advance.

"How long?" Orrick asked, eying the enemy's continued approach.

Tiblak sighed heavily before answering. "It does depend heavily upon the extent of the illness," he replied. "We are attempting to use a dose that is potent enough to heal rather quickly, but not so strong as to cause the madness that would afflict their minds. There is no point in healing them, only to then have to fight them off anyway."

It was a full half hour before the effects of the *ferial* began to be noticed. The Brigade ceased their advance, turning their attention to their now fallen comrade. The sensation of pain had returned as his body utilized the medicine to heal not only tissue damage but also nerve degradation; the other lepers, thinking him to have been poisoned, set about removing his garments in order to attend to his wounds. The cursings and cries that had begun to build from quiet murmurs to enraged shouts suddenly ceased, replaced instead by whispers of awe and even tears of disbelief. Momentarily a lone figure emerged from the stunned group of soldiers and walked pointedly toward Orrick and his companions. As he approached, he made a show of dropping his weapons, and then to remove what armor he had, until he stood not ten feet from his enemy, clad only in his tattered cloak and apparel. He spread his arms wide, indicating that he was no threat, before speaking.

"I am Erastos, captain of the Lepers Brigade," he stated, "though it would seem that your healer would endeavor to change our name."

"Yes, Erastos, it is true;" Orrick replied, "we offer you and your men a cure. The only payment we ask of you is to leave this battlefield and return to your homes, to the lives you left behind, or to new lives if you so please."

The diseased captain did not attempt to hide his wonder, but Orrick was himself surprised at the leper's evident displeasure. "You would heal us without requiring our aid against the Ianzama? And to what home, what life, would you have me to return? My wife and children succumbed to a leprous death many years ago, caring for them is how I became ill."

"What then," asked Orrick, "what do you propose?"

The other man was silent for a long moment before he answered. "We will fight for you; defend your land against the Ianzama who have profited from our misfortune for so long. Upon your victory, then you shall heal those of us that survive; it may be that we will then be ready for the new start that you have spoken of."

And so it was, that the seven hundred members of the Lepers Brigade became the first line of defense for the Makani forces against the Ianzama invaders. The warriors who a moment ago had been endeavoring to clear a path of attack for the remaining cavalry now reversed their direction, reviving barricades and reestablishing pitfalls to aid in the defense of the Makani homeland as well as the whole of the Pasturelands. It was then that the remainder of enemy cavalry, accompanied by the Ianzama foot soldiers, advanced hastily upon the smaller force.

~ ~ ~

Confident that their avenue of entrance into the Citadel would prove successful for the herd, Dhresden now turned his attention to the task of how the men, not to mention the mountain beasts, would enter without raising suspicion or alarm. It was not unusual in the instance of a winter Rotation for the dozens of cattle to be driven to the Citadel by only a handful of men, but how to infiltrate the capitol with so many beasts and all his motley troops was the topic of discussion. Dhresden listened to each of his advisors, weighing their ideas against his own, as well as the risks. When the last plot from his companions concluded, Dhresden's eyes again fell to the campfire before them as he formulated his final plan. "Thank you all for your counsel and alliance," he said presently, his eyes now moving through the group. "I know that there have been many sacrifices made in this endeavor already, and that tomorrow may well usher several of us from this life into the next, but for your efforts, for your friendship, I am forever grateful. Now, as to the matter of entrance of our army into the Citadel, Wyeth, I need you and thirty of the other Kelvren within the city walls prior to the Rotation; you will be responsible to neutralize the watchmen upon the wall overlooking the cattle entrance so that they cannot raise the alarm. You will also need to assist the few herdsmen who will be escorting the beasts through the gate. The gate needs to remain open so that the other herdsmen and the Wanderlanders may enter; again, without raising any alarm. The stable will not house all of our forces, so the column will need to take to the streets quickly. Wyeth will divide his three hundred warriors into two teams and will storm the tops of the wall. They will establish control of the parapet, the gates, the various sets of stairs accessing the parapet and the immediate area around the stairs at ground level.

The remainder of the army will converge upon the Outcropping, force entrance if necessary, and remove Treyherne from the throne of my forbears. Any Oxmen resistance that we encounter will be addressed with whatever level of force is necessary; I only hope that the common citizens will remain safe within their homes. Is there anything that I have overlooked?"

None of the advisors, having already spoken their minds, had any cause for doubt of this wise young ruler or his plans.

"If it please you, Lord Havenstone," Wyeth said, breaking the silence, "we Kelvren will depart in one hour, that we may infiltrate the Citadel in darkness."

"Thank you, Wyeth; once the main force breaches the perimeter, I will look for Tala to accompany you upon the wall. Thank you all," Dhresden said, dismissing them. The young ruler's advisors departed, except for one. Tala had remained behind, eager to broach the matter privately; Dhresden was not at all surprised. "Do not be cross with me, Tala," he began, "but my decision stands."

"I wish to be by your side, Dhresden," she argued, "we have been apart much as of late. Fail or succeed, life or death, my place is with you."

"I agree, my love," Dhresden replied, "and once the throne is returned to me, and we are wed, you will sit beside me as the lady of Havenstone; but I cannot claim the throne with my attention focused upon your safety. I need you safe with Wyeth and the Kelvren so that my energies are fixed upon ousting Treyherne; there is also the matter of the huge asset that you provide from the parapet as an archer."

"Well," Tala replied after an awkward silence, "as long as I will still be able to fight on your behalf, then I will agree to your plan. I could not bear the notion that I was squirreled away like some porcelain dish, kept safe for my own sake."

"Oh, goodness no!" Dhresden exclaimed, "I would not risk your wrath in such fashion!" The two laughed aloud and hugged as if a war was not occurring about them. The mirth lingered after the laughter had faded, but soon the raw reality of the morrow took over their thoughts again.

"What of the Lady Jovanna?" Tala asked, not attempting to hide the concern in her voice. "Where will she be during the battle?"

Dhresden smiled in response to the question, but his eyes held a sadness and concern that spoke more clearly than his next words. "That is a matter of discussion that has not yet concluded," he said. "I have requested that she submit to any of several different options, but, intent upon taking the Citadel with us, she has not yet yielded to my alternatives."

"Nor will I," said Jovanna as she reentered the tent. Her beautiful voice was soft as she looked upon the two young lovers, but the strength of her tone assured them that she would not be coddled. "Dhresden, there are things I wish to speak of with you, and I am glad that Tala is here as it concerns her as well. Can we sit now, and reason together of events beyond this battle?"

"Of course, mother," Dhresden replied, gesturing for the two women to be seated before he himself sat. "But I need ask, why must we speak of these things now? May we not discuss such matters once the throne is rightfully settled?"

Jovannah's smile was genuine, though a deep sadness and regret washed over her. "I still hope that it is so, my son; but I may not be available to you at the conclusion of this war."

Both Dhresden and Tala were startled by her words, and while Tala moved to protest, it was Dhresden who spoke first. "What do you mean? Have you had a vision? Why have you not spoken of this to me before now?"

The older woman smiled, touched by her stepson's concern. "They are dreams, Dhresden, not visions. A vision is clear and sure, with nothing that can be done to change it. The dream, however, is open to interpretation, and sometimes able to be altered."

"Then tell me of this dream," he declared, "and I will give you the interpretation!"

Jovannah's smile faded as she replied. "The interpretation is not for you to give, my dear; but the knowledge of what may come to pass has been gifted to me, and I now share that with the two of you."

"And what of Faust? Have you warned him of your possible demise?"

"I have," she replied, "and in greater detail than you shall be told. We can cheat death only occasionally, but Faust is prepared to do his part. As for the two of you," Jovannah lifted her hands up as she prepared to declare the message of her dream to Dhresden and Tala. "Many shall be your children, though the joy of your bloodline will long delay. You shall have peace in the land in which you dwell all the days of your life, though you must prepare for the days of old which are even now awakening. Your successor should beware the return of fabled ancestors, for his intent is not for blessing." Jovannah dropped her hands into her lap and was silent. Dhresden and Tala also were silent, contemplating the words that the Lady had shared with them. Both knew instinctively that Jovannah would be very selective about answers she might give to any questions that they were to ask. Finally, Dhresden spoke.

"So, given the nature of these revelations, limited as they may be, am I to understand that we will win this war?"

"The exact outcome of the next days is veiled from my sight; I can only be certain that you both survive this war," Jovannah corrected.

"You spoke of children," Tala said, "but I do not understand your meaning. What more can you tell me?"

"Only that your heart is bigger than you realize, and that regarding family you should follow where your heart leads; Dhresden will confirm your direction when the time is right."

"How are we to prepare for the days of old? And what ancestor seeks to do my family harm?"

A sad smile darkened Jovannah's beautiful face before she answered. "Once you enter the time of peace, speak with Wyeth of this old woman's dream and of the days of old. He will guide you in preparing for what is to come, that your children may be ready. And as for the dangerous ancestor, teach wisdom and compassion to your children, that they may discern the enemy and know their course of action, yet without shame."

"Is there nothing else you can tell us? Perhaps something that is not a riddle?" Dhresden had hoped that his stepmother's dream would bring direction and answers, but felt like his future possessed more questions than ever before.

"I am afraid not, but I assure you that it will become clear when it needs to be. Now bid me goodnight, we have quite a day tomorrow."

CHAPTER 34

D hresden did not rest well that night, fraught as his dreams
and thoughts were with concern for the lady Jovannah
and her riddles. He rose early, listening to the camp come
alive with the sounds of preparation for war. After a light breakfast,
Dhresden wandered through the camp, finding spirits high, though
everyone seemed to grow more edgy as the day wore on. Dhresden
spent the day with no one in particular, though often he could be
found in the presence of Tala, and he touched base more than once
with Faust, the lady Jovannah, Flint, the remaining Kelvren warriors,
and the Wanderlanders. The young lord stopped often to speak with
nameless men who had pledged themselves to his throne, even aiding
in their preparations, no matter how menial the task seemed. It was
this nobility, taught to him by his father, his grandfather, and his
mothers, as well as by advisors such as Wyeth, that drew faithful fol-
lowers to the half-blood. Early in life, Dhresden had been instructed
that nobility was not a birthright, but rather a responsibility, and that
nobleness could be embraced by a man or woman of any station,
background, or nation. He lived it now, before the eyes of loyal subjects, but he witnessed it in their own deeds as well. Though Jovannah
had assured his and Tala's survival, Dhresden longed for victory for
the sakes of his people; he feared that the cost of Treyherne's continued rule would be more than they could bear.

Finally, an hour before dusk, it was time. The few herdsman and the beasts entering the city under the guise of the winter
Rotation departed, with Dhresden and the remainder of his force
trailing them on foot. They would await the cover of darkness and
the signal from Wyeth to enter by way of the cattle gate. Watching

from the black edge of night, the minutes dragged by, until, well past sunset, the cattle gate opened slowly, allowing a glimpse of a lantern once, twice, and again. Silently, Dhresden and his crew rushed through the darkness and snow to the entrance, finding that Wyeth's force had taken control of the immediate area as planned, and now, reinforced with additional troops, had begun sweeping the parapet, neutralizing Treyherne's Oxmen as they went. The rest of Dhresden's army flooded the streets of Havenstone, finding, as he had hoped, that most of the common people had retired to their places of dwelling. Here on the ground fewer Oxmen were found, and though the majority were dispatched without difficulty, the few who required a greater effort brought Dhresden's infiltration to the attention of the townsfolk, who peered cautiously from their windows as their true king sought to recover his throne. Most of the Oxmen they encountered had resisted Dhresden's advance, though a handful had surrendered their arms and claimed fealty to the half-blood. Undeserving of trust, these had been placed in the charge of certain of the herdsmen, which could hence no longer offer support to the main force of the army. Limited as they already were, Dhresden's mind began to harbor doubt that the remaining company would succeed in breeching the Citadel and deposing Treyherne. As they converged upon the main entryway to the Outcropping, a host of the Oxmen awaited them. Somehow word had spread of Dhresden's attack, and the snake Treyherne had filled the courtyard with his loyal guard. Uncertain of the count of their enemy, it was evident that the ragtag invaders were outnumbered at least three to one. The odds against them, Dhresden and his army threw themselves at the enemy; within moments, the blood of man, Kelvren, ox, and mountain beast was spilled and mingled in the mud and snow. The Oxmen suffered heavy casualties, but it would be only a matter of time before their sheer numbers tipped the battle in their favor. Even as he cut down one of the Oxmen, Dhresden mourned for his enemies and considered retreat in order to save lives on both sides. Though it might preserve life in the short term, Dhresden realized that it would only provide temporary respite for the peoples of the Pasturelands and its neighbors. With renewed determination, he struck down another adversary, saddened that it must be so but with a mixture of deep sorrow and mirth, he realized that a host of the townspeople had flanked the Oxmen. Armed with axes, pitchforks, hammers and other tools, the commoners of Havenstone now fought for their freedom from tyranny.

~ ~ ~

Erastos and the other lepers stood their ground stoically as the Ianzama rhinoceros riders charged towards them. The diseased warriors embraced this battle on behalf of the Pasturelands, not out of the promise of healing, but rather for the opportunity to die in the pursuit of what, finally, was a righteous cause. Out of hopelessness, the lepers had submitted to the rule of the Ianzama, trading their loyalty to a bloodthirsty and ruthless nation for the temporary pleasures of the spoils of conquest. History had begun to record them as a savage mercenary force that cared nought for life; whether or not any of the brigade drew breath after nightfall, this day would change that legacy.

The Makani archers had sent many arrows past the Lepers Brigade, hoping to at least slow the cavalry's advance, and though several riders had been struck down, the beasts hastened on. Though Shika, her aim true, had managed to bring down two of the rhinoceros, she braced for the sickening sight that she was certain would come: the Ianzama cavalry grinding the Lepers Brigade into the earth, like sand before the ocean tide. As the attackers reached the narrowest section of the hourglass, large, lizard-like beasts sprang from the waters of the Bog, crushing the rhinoceros or propelling them into the surf, where they struggled in the shifting sands. The behemoths were swift and deadly in the water, but were much less capable on dry land. With the cavalry neutralized, the Lepers Brigade turned their attention to the enemy infantry, as did the Makani archers. The rest of the wind-warriors surged forward, sweeping past the lepers and darted among the Ianzama, striking deathblows and otherwise dispatching their enemies.

The battle raged on through midday, and though casualties fell of both the Makani and the lepers, it was the Ianzama dead that littered the ground and encumbered movement. Orrick, Andalhyn, and others at the foremost of the battle dripped sweat mingled with blood, fighting the threat of their own weapons slipping from their grasp as much as they battled the enemy. Finally, amidst the clash of weapons and the shouts, screams and moans of warriors, a horn sounded well to the rear of the Ianzama horde. It was the signal for retreat, and it was a sound welcomed by the men of both camps. With at least two hours remaining of usable daylight, Andalhyn commissioned a half arba'a to trail the retreating Ianzama; the eight khamellero riders were ordered not to engage, but rather to surveil the enemy's actions, which should entail departing these lands. The rest of the Makani army, including the Lepers Brigade, set to tending to their wounded. Tiblak and the other Bog healers moved through the host, administering doses of ferial to the seriously wounded, and of course, to the surviving members of the Lepers Brigade. In the midst of the carnage, Tiblak found Orrick, still clutching his battle axe as he sought to help the wounded.

"There is much blood upon you, mountain man," Tiblak commented, "is any of it yours?"

The question brought a slight smile to the giant's weary face. "A little, my friend," he answered, "though not enough to warrant your skills. However, I have been unable to release my axe from my grip, a phenomenon that I have not experienced in a long time."

Tiblak nodded. "You are dehydrated; your body needs water. I doubt you are the only one with this need, but it is a minor concern in comparison to much of the injuries I have seen today. I could alleviate the symptoms with this tonic, but you will still require water for a full recovery."

"Thank you, Tiblak, but water alone will suffice. If after tending to these bloodied allies any of your potion remains, I am certain that Zabayr would welcome a speedy recovery. Also, as I have informed Andalhyn, Shika and I will retrieve Mallory from Hawa Janbiyah palace and then journey to Havenstone to reunite with Dhresden."

The healer nodded in agreement. "I am certain that the oxman Liam would desire to accompany you," he said. "He survived this battle, with few injuries; I encountered him about a half hour ago."

He jerked his head in Liam's general direction as he gripped Orrick's hand in a farewell greeting. "Peace and safety, my friend."

"And to you and your family as well," Orrick replied, and then turned and walked away. As the sky set ablaze with the colors of sunset, Orrick found both Shika and Liam, and the three prepared for the journey to the Dune palace.

~ ~ ~

The Oxmen resistance that did not lay dead about him sat under watchful guard, leaving only a small detachment of soldiers between Dhresden and Treyherne. As proud as the half-blood was of the commoners rising against oppression, too many had been lost, though Dhresden took mild comfort in the truth that they had died free. Dhresden pushed aside the doubt that still lingered at the edge of his mind, and, eager to put to death the misgivings that had begun to gnaw at him, led his army through the Citadel entrance. The great double doors splintered and fell inward under the might of the herdsmen's mounts, allowing the true lord of Havenstone and his soldiers to flood the grand hall opposite the ornate stairway that led up to the Outcropping, throne room, and other royal quarters. Much of the structure's furnishings had been piled and strewn about at the foot of the stairs, as well as upon the lower stairs themselves and the first landing. Treyherne had succeeded in neutralizing the half-blood's cavalry, and from beyond the obstacles flew a shower of arrows. Hugging low to his mount, Dhresden charged forward with Oxmen and mountain men in tow. A woman's cry of pain from behind brought Jovannah's dream rushing to the forefront of his mind again, and with great sorrow and rage Dhresden leaped from his saddle, clearing the obstacles before him and landing amidst the archers who had just stricken down his allies, and his stepmother. These men would find no quarter from the half-blood's fury, or the men and beasts that accompanied him. The archers fell quickly, and as Dhresden's army fought their way up the stairs, they met other Oxmen wielding swords, pikes, axes, and other weapons, and though they were more difficult to dispatch, Treyherne's forces were diminishing. The battle continued on, until the throne room was breached, and Dhresden came, finally, face to face with his father's murderer. It was clear that Treyherne had no intention of surrender; the usurper had held twenty mounted Oxmen in reserve, along with at least eighty foot soldiers, to make his final stand. Wasting no time, the freedom fighters engaged the enemy, utilizing the Wanderlanders and their animal companions against the cavalry and matching their infantry against the enemy's. The beautiful stone floor built by Dhresden's forebears quickly became red and slick with the blood of man and beast, but was not a battle that would soon end. It was almost sunrise when Treyherne finally lay stricken and dying at Dhresden's feet; the Oxmen who had survived to this point quickly threw down their arms in surrender, hoping for mercy and finding it, or at least the opportunity for formal sentencing. Panting and exhausted, Dhresden surveyed the room about him. Such pain, such suffering, such loss, and why? The lust of one man for the power belonging to another. With each war, or battle or death that he witnessed, Dhresden hoped that man would learn the perils of selfishness, and flee the temptation of needless self-promotion. Even in this victory, Dhresden knew that the unnumbered dead would long be remembered in times of sleeplessness and quiet reflection.

"Hail, Lord Havenstone," came a voice near him. Dhresden turned to find a bloodied and panting Flint kneeling before him. "Your throne awaits, my lord."

"No, my friend," Dhresden replied, taking his arm and lifting him to his feet, "we must tend to the wounded, and mourn our dead; but soon we shall see the throne rightfully filled."

Leaving another detachment to oversee the surrendered Oxmen who were allowed to be tending to their own dead and wounded, Dhresden and the remainder of his army retraced their steps, binding their wounded and segregating the dead. In the great hall on the ground level, he found Faust, kneeling upon the floor, cradling Jovannah in his arms. The herdsman rocked her lifeless form gently, his own eyes closed as were hers, seemingly unaware of the two arrows which protruded from his back and shoulder. Blood stained the front of Jovannah's garments, and it was clear that arrows had pierced her through as well.

Fighting back a sob, Dhresden spoke gently. "Faust—" was all he could manage. The herdsman ceased rocking, and turned his face towards Dhresden, his eyes now open. "We congratulate you on your victory, Lord Havenstone!" He said no more, but the smile that spread slowly across his face seemed strangely out of place. It was then that Dhresden realized that the lady Jovannah's eyes were now open, and that she too smiled up at him. The grief that he had fought to hold back now burst forth in tears of relief, which were allowed to flow freely, wetting Dhresden's face as well as Jovannah's as the half-blood knelt over her.

As the three regained composure, Dhresden began to examine his stepmother's injuries. One arrow had lodged in her armor at the shoulder, causing only bruising; another had narrowly missed her head, but had sliced along her scalp, leaving a bloody wound that would be hidden beneath her hair when healed. The third had pierced her chest near her right shoulder, a wound that would be slow to heal but had also missed all vital organs and arteries. Faust's wounds, though not life threatening, would require more time to heal. The arrow that protruded from the herdsman's back should have passed through his heart and lungs and killed him, but it had struck bone and lost momentum, never reaching his vitals, while the missile that had struck his shoulder had passed through, stopping when it hit Jovannah's armor.

"How did it strike both of you?" Dhresden asked.

Jovannah smiled, casting her eyes upon Faust. "I told you, my son, that I had shared the details of my dream more fully with this man than I had with you; and so it was that he threw himself before me, shielding me with his own body. If he had not done so, the two arrows that struck him would have killed me."

Dhresden had grown fond of this herdsman, but now he looked upon Faust with a love and respect that few had ever earned. He embraced the other man as a brother, careful of his wounds. "Thank you, Faust. You have delivered me from yet another grief in this foolish war. Thank you for caring for my mother." Dhresden held him thus, until another voice interrupted.

"You need to come with me, my boy." It was Wyeth, and while he met eyes with Dhresden, his face was downcast.

"What is it, Wyeth," Dhresden asked, "what troubles you?"

"It is Tala; she has been wounded. I will take you to her now." As Wyeth and Dhresden hurried off, Jovannah tried to comfort herself with the memory of the dream that foretold of Tala's survival, but was haunted by her own words to Dhresden the previous day: *The dream, however, is open to interpretation, and sometimes able to be altered.*

Though Wyeth led him to Tala's side in minutes, to Dhresden it seemed as hours before he could kneel beside his beloved. Tala lay upon a makeshift bed of woven tapestries that the Kelvren warriors had pulled from the wall, while a healer bent over her tending the worst of her wounds. Her breathing, though shallow, gave evidence of the life that she clung to, though she remained unconscious as Dhresden gripped her hand and gently kissed her. He looked to the healer, who appeared to be finishing up with some stitching of a wound in Tala's abdomen.

"The wounding is deep, my lord, and I have repaired all that I can. If infection can be prevented, then she will live. How much damage was truly done to her insides will only be known with time."

"Yes, thank you," Dhresden said absently, his eyes fixed upon Tala's face. "Wyeth," he said presently, "prepare a room in the royal quarters, she will need to be comfortable while she heals. And please see to Jovannah and Faust as well."

Wyeth said nothing, but gripped Dhresden's shoulder a moment before departing. He commissioned two healers to accompany him to tend to the lady and the herdsman, then saw to the preparations of quarters for Tala. He selected the suite reserved by Dhresden's forbears as a residence for visiting dignitaries, a large private dwelling filled with lush and comfortable furnishings. He then helped to transport Tala to the room and saw to appointment of healers to be on hand, as well as attendants to provide meals for Dhresden who refused to leave her side. Jovannah and Faust were slowly recovering in nearby rooms, and it fell to Wyeth to oversee the continued cleanup of Havenstone. Being winter, burial of the dead was impossible; the frozen ground seemed impervious to any digging efforts. The residents of Havenstone faced two options: store the dead until winter thaw, at which point they could bury them, or consume them in flame, allowing their ashes to be scattered throughout the Pasturelands in the spring. Though burial was the preferred method of passing for the peoples of the Pasturelands, waiting until winter passed created a macabre setting, drawing out the grieving period and delaying necessary emotional healing. Most yielded to mass burnings of their dead, though a few prevailed to private funerals, desiring to collect the ashes of the individual fallen for a more personal farewell. Among these were the Wanderlanders and the Kelvren, who desired to transport the ashes of their dead to their homelands and their kin. Days grew into weeks as Havenstone slowly recovered from Treyherne's rule, but still the throne remained empty as Dhresden awaited Tala's recovery.

CHAPTER 35

The daylight hours were ever so slightly lengthening as winter's grip upon the Pasturelands began to weaken. Even as spring hinted at its distant arrival, the four beasts trekking from the Dunes passed through a cold, white landscape that was unfamiliar to them. The deep snow did not prohibit their movements, however, as their feet, which were uniquely equipped to walk upon sand, also allowed them ease of passage upon the top of the snowy ground. It had taken most of a day, but the khamelleros had become accustomed to the presence of the large gray cougar that traveled with them. The sun shined brightly, helping to warm the beasts' riders as they neared their destination.

"We should arrive by day's end," the giant said to his companions. He wore his customary black chain mail and weapons, but had recently added an eyepatch to his apparel.

"Yes," Mallory agreed, "I am eager to see home again."

"It was good of Wyeth to send word to us of Dhresden's victory," Shika commented, "though I had hoped that the message would provide more information than simply that. I have felt an uneasiness about the battle for Havenstone, and it has not allayed; I fear for my sister."

"And I for my family, as well as others," added Liam. The Oxmen commander was as anxious to see his family as he was to be free of the beast beneath him. There was nothing wrong with the Khamellero, it was simply very different from the gait of the mount to which he was accustomed.

The day passed slowly, but without incident, and, as anticipated, the silhouette of the Outcropping came into view shortly before dusk. The sight of their journey's end caused them to spur their mounts to a quicker pace, as did the column of smoke that rose from Havenstone, and with it, the putrid odor of singed hair and flesh.

The gates of the city opened, allowing them to enter. They were greeted by smiles from the townsfolk, and by Konaird, commander of the Wanderland detachment that had come to Dhresden's aid. Beside him stood a shorter man, garbed as an Oxmen commander, whose eyes sought those of Liam.

"Ho there, Orrick!" he called, waving his good arm. Though his wounded right arm was healing well, it still pained him to lift it high. Loki, Konaird's wolf companion, trotted forward to meet Asha, the great cougar, as if the two were old friends. Orrick dropped from his perch upon the khamellero, then turned to assist Mallory before greeting his fellow mountain man with a brotherly embrace.

"Please, Konaird," Orrick asked, "tell us the details of this battle, and of the losses, for we fear for our loved ones. Liam," Orrick addressed the other man, who also had dismounted and greeted his companion Flint. "please leave us and tend to your family."

"Thank you, Orrick. I will see you again soon." he replied, then left quickly with Flint to reunite with his family.

"Follow me," Konaird said, after he had assisted Shika to the ground. He led Orrick, Mallory, and Shika through the streets of Havenstone, drawing ever closer to the Citadel in the waning light. He divulged to them the details of the past months—the battle in the Badlands, the JabalKriger, the conquest of Havenstone, and Treyherne's death, as well as the injuries to Jovannah, and to Tala. It was only recently that the daughter of Nokoma had awoken, weak and disoriented from injury, fever, and lack of food. Dhresden had done his best to nourish her, drizzling spoonfuls of broth into her mouth periodically, hoping that the scant provisions would aid in her recovery. He had barely left her side, and himself had become weak from lack of nourishment. Ushered quickly into Tala's room, Orrick and the others found her sitting upright in bed, or at least propped up with pillows, Dhresden sat beside her, while Jovannah, Faust, and Wyeth looked on. Seeing their guests, Dhresden rose to his feet and quickly gripped the giant to himself; the two had not seen each other since the half-blood had almost killed Orrick. Mallory and Jovannah hugged each other, relief flooding through both mother and daughter at finding each other alive and well. Shika took Dhresden's place at Tala's side, neither sister speaking while they embraced each other. Finally, their grip upon each other loosened, and they spoke.

"Do not cry, little sister," Tala said, her voice still weak. "I am much better now, and will be out of this bed soon enough."

"And when you are ready," Dhresden added, "and if you still wish it to be, we shall be wed."

"Of course, my love," Tala answered, her smile brightening the room. "But the invitations must go out soon in order for the guests to attend."

The group of close friends, now more like family, laughed together at Tala's wit and the joys that now lay before them. And so it was that announcements were dispatched to the allies of Havenstone, both near and far, of the coronation of the new lord of Havenstone, and of his betrothal to the daughter of Nokoma. The public ceremony crowning Dhresden as lord Havenstone occurred in mid spring; the Pasturelands were clothed in their finest and freshest flora and fauna, as were the royal family and honored guests. It was the first of many happy times in the reign of Dhresden, the half-blood Lord Havenstone.

A few months passed between the coronation and the wedding, during which Jovannah and Faust were wed. The lady forfeited her residence in the palace, preferring the open plains of the pasturelands to the confines of the Citadel. She aided her husband as he governed the herdsmen, and though the two embraced the nomadic habit of the herd, they were welcome guests and constant advisors to the young Lord of Havenstone.

Tala's marriage to Dhresden was of necessity a spectacular affair. Certain guests traveled from far distant lands, several with an entourage, but the late summer wedding accommodated their arrival. Attendants included friends from the Dunes, the Bog, Kelvar, and the Wanderlands as well as elsewhere. Political emissaries were sent from far away, as were many gifts.

It was a bright beautiful winter day that greeted the union of Mallory and Orrick in matrimony; half the guests in attendance were numbered as beast companions. The giant and his sweet wife introduced twin sons the following spring.

The joy of children eluded Dhresden and Tala; though she had survived it, the injury to Tala's abdomen had rendered it difficult for her to conceive. It would be several years before their son was born, but by then the two had opened their hearts and had adopted eight other children as their own. And so it was that Jovannah's dream and declaration had thus far come to pass:

> "Many shall be your children, though the joy of your bloodline will long delay. You shall have peace in the land in which you dwell all the days of your life, though you must prepare for the days of old which are even now awakening. Your successor should beware the return of fabled ancestors, for his intent is not for blessing."

But with these joys came the reality of the warning of ill times to come, and the burden of preparing his children for those times. Dhresden and Tala took their responsibility seriously, but bore it lightly upon their young ones. The half-blood sought counsel from Wyeth, as Jovannah had advised. The old Kelvren spoke of a warfare that had faded from use in the Pasturelands early in the reign of Dhresden's father, Dhane. Though not in use, the knowledge of it had been preserved by the Kelvren, the stewards of the Elder ways, as well as by some others. Wyeth commissioned certain Kelvren to aid in the training of the royal family, and it became commonplace for some cloaked and hooded stranger to arrive from parts unknown at the Citadel bearing credentials affirming that they too had been commissioned by Wyeth for the further education of Dhresden's children. Each of their nine children was taught these skills, for the lord and lady of Havenstone loved their progeny equally. The training of their children was a joy, and as the couple grew gray together, their young ones matured into adulthood: intelligent, wise, compassionate, and yet just. It would be long years before Dhresden was laid to rest beneath the tree *Rebeq*, within the burial chamber of the Kelvren.

The deeds and adventures of the sons and daughters of Dhresden are recorded elsewhere, and usher in a new age of wonder and adventure, of joys and sorrows, of mercy and justice, of love, and of rage.

ABOUT THE AUTHOR

Besides raising five children, climbing trees, and stacking his own firewood, Matthew Storey is likely to be found at his computer weaving worlds fantastic. Hailing from a small town in upstate New York named for a legendary figure of Roman manliness and civic virtue, Storey is as his name implies: a teller of tales and a forthright constructor of thoughtful meandering. The author could be mistaken for a warrior-historian lost in an era not his own, recalling and retelling times of legend in his mind's eye and providing this current generation with fictional works that hold hostage the reader's attention, while at the same time setting free the imagination.

He is a husband, a father, a teacher, a mentor, and an arborist of the highest order. He is no stranger to the ins, outs, ups, and downs of human nature, forever greeting struggle and tribulation with a clear eye and a knowing grin. For behind that eye hides a vast inner world of kings and serpents, of saviors and men.

Behind the knowing grin, well, Matt supposes you'll need to crack the spine for that answer. While his initial success and related sequels have been in the form of fantasy adventure novels, Matt hopes that his crime and thriller writings will meet with the same success. He, his beautiful wife of twenty-two years and their five children currently reside in the upstate of South Carolina.